SUB ROSA
AMERICA

(and the Fall
of the New Atlantis)

Book I
Gone To Croatan

by

Elana Freeland

ISBN-13:978-1468081220

Cover art by Louis Williams,
"The Guardian of the Innermost," 1991

The *Sub Rosa America* Series
Book I: Gone to Croatan
Book II: The Future Arrives By Stealth
Book III: Indian Country
Book IV: Jundi-Shapur
Book V: From Trinity to Trinity

The entire series is available on Amazon.

Dedicated to the Three Kings

John F. Kennedy
Martin Luther King, Jr.
Robert F. Kennedy

and what might have been, and may still,
far in the future.

Acknowledgements

To researchers and whistleblowers, living and dead, for peering behind the curtain into what Professor Peter Dale Scott calls deep politics.

Sub Rosa America
Major Characters

Seven (Lilya Eliade)   Old when the novel opens in 2019, she flashes back to her early twenties in 1970 when she met Hermano and underwent an initiation in Santa Barbara. Nexus for all characters. Born in 1947.

Hermano   Eastern European Time-traveler known in past ages as the Comte de Saint-Germain and Christian Rosenkreutz. Traveling the Americas with Ghost Bear. Ultimately sets in motion the pilgrimage to Dallas.

Ghost Bear   Lakota Sioux Time-traveler medicine man traveling with Hermano. His son White Bull has been arrested.

Thomas   Seven's true love, scientist and recluse on the run from the elite Gardner New England Gardner family and Dr. Greenbaum. Half of a Mengele twin experiment entailing his "dead" identical twin Didymus, now an intelligence agent being used to track him. Yale graduate, born in 1943.

Didymus   Thomas' twin brother taken at birth and reared under Paperclip (Didy) Nazi MK-ULTRA. Programmed to be a CIA assassin. His unknown Hauser assignment: to locate and kill his twin. Born in 1943.

Simon Iff   Didymus' CIA handler with an FBI cover. Reports to Dr. Greenbaum and keeps a distant tail on the vehicles en route to Dallas. Born in 1927.

Ray Kofi   Black disillusioned Marxist graduate
             student at UCSB and Seven's friend.
Sought as a scapegoat for the April 18, 1970 shooting
of student Kevin Moran. Born in 1944.

Mannie   Brooklyn Jew who arrives in California
             after a long bus ride and ends up going to
Dallas with the pilgrims. Excited to participate in the
Sixties Revolution but instead encounters the chaos
of COINTELPRO. Naïve, Mannie sees into the heart of
people and events. Born in 1948.

Baby Rose   Beautiful blond girl found wandering
             near Ojai who has escaped Jordan Ranch
and is being sought by Dr. Greenbaum as an MK-
ULTRA data bank. Has a variety of "alters" ("Alice")
her new friends are unaware of. Underwent
programming with Didymus under Drs. Greenbaum
and Gottlieb. Born in 1952.

Vicente   Timekeeper grandson of a powerful
Liputzli   Mayan archaeologist Timekeeper. Sent
(Vince)   north to chronicle the demise of *el norte*.
             With his grandfather's *Book of Days* to
guide him, he has been touring Southwest tribes and
is hitchhiking back to White Sands to see where the
worlds were torn apart when the pilgrims pick him.
Born December 7, 1941, Pearl Harbor Day.

Hiram   Thomas' uncle. Raised between Scotland
Gardner   and America by fascist relatives and
             placed in key positions for the sake of the
Enterprise. Ruthlessly dominates Thomas' family;
sacrificed Didymus at birth to MK-ULTRA. Elite
gopher for Dr. Greenbaum. Born 1918, graduated
Yale 1940. Lives in New York.

8

Laurence Gardner Thomas' father, dominated since childhood by his brother Hiram. Born in 1920, graduated Harvard 1942. Lives in Philadelphia.

The Colonel Seven's retired US Air Force neighbor, served in every major 20th century war up to Vietnam. He and his Cadillac join the pilgrimage to Dallas.

Dr. Greenbaum An MK-ULTRA "spychiatrist" under Dr. Sydney Gottlieb, as well as a Paperclip Nazi. Programmed Didymus and oversaw Thomas under the Mengele twin program. Programmed Baby Rose for sex and memory. Member of elite Satanic cult in Mexico. Lives in Washington, DC.

Magician/ Sibelius/ Jaguar Priest Works for Dr. Greenbaum. Occult capabilities. By day, a corporate CEO; by night, a seer of elite Satanic cult in Mexico.

Kabbalist Works for the Magician. Astrological capabilities.

BOOK I

Gone to Croatan

Though this be madness, yet there is method in it.

- *Hamlet*, II, ii, 207

We've unmasked madmen, Watson, wielding scepters, reason run riot, justice howling at the moon.

- Sherlock Holmes in *Murder By Decree*, 1978

In the dark time, the eyes begin to see.

- Theodore Roethke

Book I
Gone to Croatan

Table of Contents

The Story

The story goes that human beings are parasites that have been living off the good graces of Earth (a noble ancient) for millions of years, back to the Tertiary Epoch of Adam, adamah meaning earth and blood. As Time's translation, the human being spins through space, keeping tempo to a Platonic count of 25,920 years, an æonic waltz through the Zodiac wrapped in the arms of Solus Invictus while precariously tilting from his embrace no less than 21.8 degrees and no more than 23.4 degrees lest we burn or freeze or magnetic pole shifts tumble mountains and boulders southward, oceans slosh mightily for days, and ice and rock and volcanic gas belts spend thousands of years raising mountain ranges all over again.

The last Flood 11,600 years ago at the end of the Pleistocene epoch rolled north over the plains of Manchuria, Mongolia, and Siberia to the Arctic Ocean, still pulsating in myths of Atlantis for which 20,000- foot- thick melting ice caps were invented to cover over the grievous electromagnetic errors of mighty but misled predecessors.

By anno domini 1, two hundred million human beings were scurrying about, intent on what they couldn't live without, while war, famine, weather, murder, disease, and the Grim Reaper did what they could to keep the numbers down. That Homo sapiens sapiens live just one Platonic day of 72 years means they must learn one life after another to listen as a child all over again, sifting through the myths and rumors left behind by dusty millennia until finally, behind bewildered eyelids, they see through the ever-changing appearances of wheat that looks like chaff and chaff like wheat, planting and winnowing until

17

*their last breath for the sake of what stirs as a vague
memory or premonition. How in four score years can
a human being hope to resurrect a fragile self-
conception, whatever epoch they awaken in?*

*It is thus that a consideration of sheer numbers
sets the stage for contemplating the tangled skein of
that most human of frailties,* compassion.

1
Winter 2019

Some say the world will end in fire,
Some say in ice.
From what I've tasted of desire
I hold with those who favor fire.
But if it had to perish twice,
I think I know enough of hate
To say that for destruction ice
Is also great
And would suffice.

- Robert Frost, "Fire and Ice"

Old Seven was toiling her way up a narrow switchback along a shoulder of the Park Range in the Colorado Rockies, everything about her pointing to a trek of hard purpose, the brown and green thermal Goretex draped with cedar fronds over the high-tech space blanket cloaking her heavy pack, the fact that it was nigh the dead of winter. A crossbow hung within easy reach, swinging in time to the pace set by her stout walking stick and hiking boots.

It was late fall of the year 2019 and her step was as slow and sure as it was fifty years before. She had walked eleven hundred miles east along the Oregon Trail, threading from one river to the next, a continuous silver cord that had bound east to west for thousands of years, from the rolling Columbia to the Snake, the Sweetwater, and now the Platte. At Independence Rock rising like a beached whale from the prairie sea she had charcoaled *GONE TO CROATAN* on the lip of a fissure that would fill with flowers come spring, after which she had finally left the Trail to cut south along the North Platte.

She stopped to breathe in draughts of piercing air and rest her loaded back against the lichen-covered trail face. Listening to her own breathing in the snow-muffled silence soothed her. Slipping off her mittens, she watched as the blue veins under the thin skin on the tops of her hands shrank and buried themselves deeper into her creature warmth. Absent-mindedly caressing the silver bracelet inlaid with copper that Thomas had crafted for her years before, she removed her Polartechs and squinted through the late afternoon glare toward the southeast, her nut-brown eyes old with the world but still flecked with gold. In the light, her pupils expanded and contracted like a hawk's.

The sound of an engine made her raised the binoculars and click onto day vision to scan the clear blue miles across the valley that formed a V with the Medicine Bow Mountains. A white-hot knot coiled in her stomach when she caught sight of a squadron of seven black helicopters. Apaches? Kiowas? Or surveillance or attack drones? Blackhawks might mean USAF Special Operations Command, SOCOM, seven combat troop assault choppers, eleven to twenty-two men each, floodlights, aerials, pylons, droptanks, in-flight refueling booms, unmanned A160T Hummingbirds with Forester radar and ARGUS-IS multiplex spy eyes. From this distance, the dark red lettering was impossible to read.

America was crawling with UN peacekeepers, foreign troops without a stake out of Fort Logan or Carson, Peterson Air Force Base, Lowry, NORAD cached in Cheyenne Mountain, or Table Mountain just north of Boulder. Satellite Control monitored GPS from both Sunnydale and the Consolidated Space Operations Center at Colorado Springs. The heart of Colorado and the guts of the American air and space war zone were now one and the same. A few nights before, she'd dreamed of a massive gilded *dragon* above the Rockies, its shiny scales rippling electromagnetically as it stared steadily at her. Vince spoke of a dragon known as *Avanyu* among the Pueblo Indians . . .

The whisper-mode approach was a barely audible *whop whop whop* from the mufflers. Yes, it was a patrol in imminent assault mode, their bearings north-northwest, toward Rawlins where she'd noted that the old Wyoming Frontier Prison had been reactivated, platoons in UN blue on maneuvers. Was this patrol headed there? They were gradually descending, maybe for their heat sensors to separate humans from other life forms. If they didn't switch course, they would pass directly over her. She entertained no illusions that they were looking for her but wondered briefly about Thomas and Vince, or militias who'd been preparing for decades for these times. Still, she should take precautions, particularly if they had a technical remote viewer on board.

Lowering the binoculars, she felt for the Takyon amulet around her neck. Closing her eyes, she contemplated *Stone,* only *Stone*, slowing her breath down down down, not sure if the granite behind her was *k'an che*, a stone of light, seat of a supernatural. She hoped so. Like St. Odilia in Alsace in 666, when a lichen-veiled rock had opened and taken her in, Seven concentrated, so that when the choppers *whop whop whopped* over, all she could hear was stone and all she could see was silence.

Closed, automated cyberculture had claimed the land. Those like Seven who had managed to avoid being charged with terrorism had moved off grid to become anachronisms that the very survival of the human soul might, in the end, depend upon. In all the little towns and outposts she came upon, she watched for TLOs, terrorist liaison officers who could be anyone—police, firefighters, utility workers, librarians, ranchers, store clerks—pointing little RFID zappers to read anything that said who you were, then getting on their earpiece or implant to alert the nearest fusion center to send out a drone.

TSA inspections, ITS tracking . . . She'd avoided public transportation for years and carried her own zapper to sniff out electronic devices running SPOT programs (screening passengers by observation) measuring for facial expressions and voice tension. CTS pods (combat zones that see) were everywhere now, disguised as water fountains, trees, mailboxes, utility poles. Attract their attention and she could be digitally strip-searched by a passive millimeter wave imager, then tracked by satellite.

Surveillance was everywhere. Miniaturized CCTV cameras in lamps, clocks, radios, televisions, purses or picture frames remotely directed to pan, tilt, zoom, or focus. Fingerprints, retinal patterns, and hand geometry. All expectation of privacy had long vanished, even in homes. The new generations were accustomed to hidden cameras and endless canting about security. LUCID smart dust communicated what they sensed to receivers finely tuned to the frequencies in clothing, food, furniture, bloodstreams and genes. Smart dust was inside your head talking to brain neurons, listening to thoughts, then transmitting them to other smart dust. *They talk to each other: a world once dumb now speaks.* People were listening to what their toothbrush said about cavities, what the mirror said about their eyes and diabetes and hardening of the arteries, what their toilet discovered by chemically analyzing their bowel movements, what their smart clothes said about their vital signs. HOMERs (holographic medical electronic representations) scanned their bodies and planned the surgery the surgical robot would perform. Even mail no longer traveled anonymously, thanks to the smart stamps introduced first by Executive Order and then by the Mailing Industry Task Force committee formed after 9/11. Nine corporations had been represented on that one committee: Hughes Electronics, subsidiary of General Motors, Perseus investment banking, Canon, Hewlett-Packard, IBM, Lockheed Martin, Pitney Bowes, Symbol Technologies and Stamps.

The world State had collectively spawned an omniscient, hungry Egregore possessing all who professed an orderly, beneficent new world order while quietly culling whole human lineages. Night and day, billions prayed for a cataclysm to topple the cyberstate, like Atlantis half a Great Year before. Thanks to their quantum computers, the nine world State governors knew who was sending these obnoxious prayers against the State and had slated them for nonexistence.

It was a tiresomely repetitive story, except for one unique fact: that the Second Coming was scheduled for completion on February 24, 2040. Vince had explained to her years ago that the Lords of Xibalbá would not easily allow ingress through their Nine Kingdoms. Since 1932, the Etheric Christ had overcome seven of the nine kingdoms, one per Jupiter cycle, and now the Earth Severer and Life Spirit were locked in immortal combat inside human psyches and collapsing civilizations. Biological life was shriveling up, human souls rotting. It was a balls out time, full steam ahead, human dignity be damned. All natural powers of reason and feeling were being twisted into a mechanized hive mind called the Singularity. Free will was falling away with the misguided centuries that had destroyed it.

The totalitarian elite that had served the Egregore they didn't really believe in—pouring their wills, their families, their integrity, their imagination and natural desires into its diabolical maws—did not realize that the creation would devour the creators.

23

Johan Galtung and Robert Jungk and their *Mankind 2000* could exalt neurological surveillance and brain-computer interface all they wanted, but the Egregore would snatch the prize from the divine intent driving what Yogananda called *the cloud-colored Christ* deep into the etheric Earth.

Old Seven stepped out of the granite face and continued her trek as the choppers disappeared into the northwest. Medicine Bow Peak was still visible in the north as she moved along the Michigan fork of the North Platte she'd picked up at Walden while making her way across the Kawuneeche Valley, birthplace of the infant Colorado River she and her friends had crossed so many years before, and into Rocky Mountain National Park.

She paused to listen to the silence, barely a whisper of wind, Nature holding Her breath. The windless silence struck her as odd, given that the valley was open to the cold north. She trekked on, meditating on the Medicine Bow Mountains above and ahead dimly silhouetted in the electromagnetic haze. *Medicine Bow* had come from the Arapahoe, Cheyenne, and Ute who had gathered yew for their bows. Was this why NORAD had chosen this remarkable power spot with its lifeblood rivers? The magnetic Continental Divide snaked through the park, the rain falling into Poudre Lake flowing to the Atlantic, the rain falling in Shadow Mountain Lake flowing to the Pacific.

And the park was where Thomas and Vince had found the ancient Chamber of Dreams not yet discovered by military initiates in quest of it. They had studied the cave's floor, markings, stains, the character of who and what had gone on there, then had traveled to New England to study the stone chambers European colonists had called root cellars, built long before like beehives, their stones laid inward and curving up to a capstone to make a flat roof.

They had marveled at how the massive capstones had been lifted and fitted exactly. Thomas had read in the book *Magie Chaldéenne* that priests of Heliopolis made high winds blow and raised heavy stones by means of low-frequency sound. Vince's grandfather had heard from a Mayan priest who had spent years in Tibet that a vibrating condensed sound field could nullify the power of gravitation. Tibetan priests were masters of sound, like throat singers, and used the harmonic values of matter, gravity, velocity, etc. for building. The priest had watched as a block of stone 1 x 1.5 meters was moved by yak onto a polished stone of great antiquity with a cavity carved into it. Then thirteen big drums and Ragdon trumpets in an arc of 90° at an exact harmonic distance of 63.7079 meters from the slab and block created a terrible din as the stone block slowly began to sway, then took off in a parabolic path for the designated spot on the cliff.

Thomas and Vince had toured Mystery Hill near North Salem, New Hampshire, a 22-walled formation with roof slabs weighing tons, some sunk deep in the earth with high-arching underground vaults, structures said to be at least 4,000 years old. Thomas pondered harmonic unified equations tuned to matter, certain that they were the key to constructing sonically propelled anti-gravitational flying machines. Celtic and Phoenician mariners had established settlements in New England, then moved west into Ohio and Oklahoma. Hebrews had come to Tennessee, Vikings along the North American coast, Welsh led by Prince Madoc at Mobile Bay in Alabama, and there was the seven-year voyage of St. Brendan and his scholarly monks in their 36-foot *curragh*. Old Seven recalled how Thomas had nodded as Vince talked, contemplating with another part of his great mind how he would build high-frequency sonic generators and discs that would lift from the center and resonate at frequencies in sympathy with unified fields.

They had then hiked into rocky uplands in the Appalachians that long ago had been much higher, back when eastern Texas, Arkansas, Kansas, and Oklahoma were still underwater. A great center of commerce and culture had once been in Illinois where the Great Lakes were, but the greatest center had been in the Rocky Mountains. Old Seven looked about: over the past 10,000 years from here to old Mexico, it had been submerged four times.

But it was from a middle-aged Nebraskan named Bill that Thomas had gotten the idea of building an invisible plasma Tesla dome over the cave, like the military's electro-optical Project Chameleo. The three men had shared a lean-to and Coleman stove in the shadow of an east ridge in the autumn hills of New Hampshire, Thomas and Vince hanging on Bill's tales of discovery gleaned from years of wandering. How west of the Colorado River in the Grand Canyon, it had broken up when the mountains were pushed up not millions of years ago but thousands; how his Choctaw grandfather's father found the ruins of a pyramid bigger than the Pyramid of Giza in an overgrown canyon, but when he approached, he felt an invisible *wall* of repelling frequency and was overcome by wooziness. Bill himself had discovered that buffalo wallows near Omaha were actually entries to underground dwellings dating back to the Tertiary period. In Blue Licks Spring, Kentucky, he'd seen the bones of a Pleistocene mastodon and a local archaeology buff had asked if he'd seen the *stone pavement* under the bones.

Then when the night reached the point it always does around a crackling fire away from ordinary affairs, Bill had shared that his boy had been killed in

Vietnam. He'd jabbed at the fire. "It wasn't just that he died, it's that the military version of how he died made no sense." His gaze sank into the flames, reaching down for what he'd lost. "I fought like hell for freedom in Europe and look at what it got us: rich men's lies." He glanced at the two young men, one light and one dark. "My boy was Special Forces. When you're Special Forces, everything's a lie but the brotherhood you share. He was where our troops weren't supposed to be, in Laos." He shook his head to throw off the pain. "Sons of bitches. And for what? Not freedom, not to eradicate Communism. For heroin. For the world drug business, that's what my boy died for. The French weren't quite brutal enough to get it set up, but the Americans were." He looked at Thomas. "A lot of people criticize your generation, saying you're not grateful for all we fought for. But I don't know anymore. I feel like I'm waking up from a nightmare turned into another nightmare."

Why am I thinking about that? Old Seven wondered, jabbing at the shallow snow with her walking stick. *The mind wanders in old age,* she observed, then laughed. She'd visited the Chamber of Dreams a half dozen times, witnessing the slow build-up of the shortwave, thermopowered batteries with nontoxic nanotubes, orgone energy "shooters," oraccu blankets, etc. She'd carried in a small 5-Kilowatt generator powered by permanent magnets that she'd found in a Macy's shopping bag at her front door. Books, obscure vellum manuscripts, clothing, bedding, sealed grains, beans, and teas, tools, gauss meters, laser discs, a GWEN-integrated compact LPI unit with stereo, computer, and telephone capabilities.

When bitter turns sweet
We'll meet
Where three rivers nurse
At one mountain breast

Except for dreams, rumors, packages at her door, and cryptic bits of mail, it had been three years since she'd seen Thomas and nearly fifteen since seeing Vince. *Is Kay dead?* Gerde asked in the fairy tale about the Snow Queen. *No,* the roses answered, *he is not dead.* Once she'd holed up for the winter in northern New Mexico without telling Thomas and still received a package with the Takyon amulet she still wore. Vince's ornate handwriting explained how the amulet created a three-foot protective force field vibrating at 1098 cycles per second to suck up electromagnetic field photons, disorganize the matrix of EM fields, and simulate Seven's bio-field so as to deflect tactical and psyops assault modes. The Takyon transformed her into a chameleon able to blend in with the environment around her, like when the helicopters *whop whopped* over her. Vince's note also cautioned that the amulet was the only way to access the Chamber of Dreams inside the plasma dome.

The Colorado, the North Platte, the Cache la Poudre—yes, she was close now. Gingerly from inside her parka, she lifted a vellum replica of a very old map, older by far than the United States of America. Finely scripted across the top was *Amaruca*, the *A* a flamboyant feathered serpent with a crown on its head. The Peruvian name for Quetzalcoatl had been *Amaru.* The Land of the Plumed Serpent, *Amaruca,* was the Land of Quetzalcoatl. In 987 CE, the Toltec king Topiltzin-Quetzalcoatl was defeated by Tezcatlipoca, the Smoking Mirror commander of the Eagle, Jaguar, and Coyote military orders. After abandoning his city of Tula northwest of Mexico City, Topiltzin-Quetzalcoatl had made his way through the mountains to the port at Coatzacoalcos, the Place of the Serpent on Bahía de Campeche, where he promised his people he would return, then set sail on a *raft of serpents* east for the homeland, Tlapallan, the Red Land. Cortés arrived 532 (66.5 x 8) years later and Madame Blavatsky 356 years after Cortés (44.5 x 8) before sailing to New York to found the Theosophical Society. Together, the two sums of years equal 888.

A refugee in quest of the Chamber of Dreams, Seven felt a particular kinship with the Incan king Tupac Amaru who, in 1533, with 40,000 soldiers, fled the Spaniard Pizarro. Descending into the Socavón del Inca, a vast primeval honeycomb of tunnels and caves weaving beneath Peru into Ecuador, Bolivia, and Chile like an ancient, sacred tapestry, Tupac and his loyal warrior priests traveled the subterranean labyrinth for so many years that they forgot what the Sun looked like. At last, they broke the seal of the Earth's surface and ascended into a pearl of a city cached among the mountains called Gran Paytite, a hoary Lemurian guardian of secrets from a distant human past. Even satellite tomography has been incapable of locating Gran Paytite.

Old Seven stabbed at the snowy trail, recalling the deep earth tremors out on the Great Rift weeks before. A great Earth event was on its way. She had seen an eagle drop a snake and heard birds cry at night, the Earth growling beneath her feet. The spring she stooped to drink from yesterday had been cloudy and smelled of sulfur, and the midday sun had a thick ring around it. Beneath her breath, she chanted, *Circulo en el sol, aguacero o tremblor.* Last night, the stars had burned and wavered like tiny tongues of fire. She passed her glance over the ancient mountains around her, wondering why in a white out people walked clockwise and not counterclockwise.

Pangaea! As a child, she'd yearned to be a mermaid swimming deep into a Mer-Kingdom among the sea's mountains like the Mid-Atlantic Ridge that writhed north-south, a *kundalini* scar of an old Earth wound that from time to time bled, torn open again and again to be washed clean by the salty deep. How the hot plasmic blood must have roared when it broke the surface and thrust the *kundalini* serpent's scaly plates westward, ripping Pangaea like a chicken, tearing South America from the rib of Africa and North America from Europe, the Appalachians from the Alps. And after all this time North America still careened north-northwest at the dizzying velocity of one or two inches a year, away from Europe toward a rendezvous with Asia and Siberia, sailing like the *Pequod*, her prow slicing the waves, heaving up sediment onto the continental plate beneath the eastern slopes of the Canadian Rockies, then onto the old continental plate at the edge of the West Coast, giving birth to Mexico, Nevada, the coastal ranges of California, Oregon, Washington, Idaho, British Columbia, and Alaska. Islands, small continents, submarine mountain ranges, plateaus, the Great Plains—all was being driven down, down into the Mer-Kingdom, Xibalbá, swallowed whole beneath the old sea floor now driven upward to force the North American plate eastward, up into the first Sierra Nevada.

Hunahpú and Ixbalamqué had been playing ball in the ball courts of Xibalbá against its Lords, hitting the ball so hard that it nudged a South Pacific volcanic trench north-northeast as the old continental plate on the West Coast fractured vertically, horizontally, every which way, shaping the snaky mold of the Rockies and the chain of ranges between Alaska and Mexico known as the Great Divide. Up, up they rose from the Earth's crust three miles thick while the cauldron continued to cook fifty miles below.

Colorado reminded Seven of Tibet, another roof of the world like the Lower Forty-Eight with their 50-plus peaks towering more than 14,000 feet above sea level in the Sawatch, San Juan, and Colorado Rockies.

30

As mountains go, the Rockies and Tetons were just babies, a mere five to seven million years old, while Yellowstone a little north was of another epoch entirely, its birth hearkening back thousands of miles beneath the Earth's thin skin. The granite, gneiss, and schist of the Colorado Rockies had been cooked in the belly of the Old Continent, whereas the rock in the Rockies of Montana, Alberta, British Columbia, and Alaska was a tombstone of bodies left behind by seas receding 90 million years ago, transmuting into limestone, sandstone, quartzite, slate, gravel, and clay.

Did the Cordilleran Ice Sheet lie along the Rocky Mountains from southern Alaska through British Columbia, most of Alberta, Washington, Idaho, and Montana 12,000 years ago? Did the Sun rise in the Gulf of Mexico and set toward the Yukon when the broad ice-free corridor connected Asia and Alaska? Argon and potassium dated the oldest Earth rock at 4,100 million years old, and it was still growing along the edges of continental plates sixty miles thick. Were the tremors about the Old Continent breaking up? Would Scylla and Charybdis be breakdancing once again?

In 79 CE, Vesuvius buried Pompeii in the Bay of Naples on the Tyrrhenian Sea in the blink of an eye by Vesuvius. Never once had it been active within human memory. In the midst of their daily rounds, Roman citizens were turned to statues by hot mud and lava. Their homely artifacts testified to the brevity and precariousness of life on Earth: frescoes and mosaics, bowls, spindles, shears, medical instruments all whispered that the dead were just a heartbeat away and would return momentarily to pick up where they left off.

The submarine volcano Krakatau off Java erupted and sank in 416 CE, then slowly crept up again until August 27, 1883, when four blasts unleashed pyroclastic flows and 15-foot tsunamis drowned 36,000 people and dragged Krakatau under once again. A steam ship was catapulted two miles inland. Barographs around the world quivered, and the plumes of volcanic dust caused Tennyson in England to write, *For day by day, thro' many a blood-red eve . . . The wrathful sunset glared . . .*

If such an event was repeated, what would happen to the radioactive materials at Yucca Flats north of Las Vegas? Would they be swept west along fissure lines into Death Valley, south between the Spring Mountains and Spotted Range toward Devil's Hole, into the cauldrons beneath the Mono Lake Bulge? Noxious gases would arise from Lake Elsinore or the Salton Sea . . . Lake Elsinore, where Vince had watched *Hamlet* just before they had met. Neutron beams would penetrate the largest and deepest bunkers and continue to the planet's interior, accelerate the decay of radioactive isotopes, generate more neutrons, more and more heat . . . All the nuclear tests had been followed by increased seismic activity somewhere, accelerating volcanic activity being nuclear.

All of nature said something was coming. She must push on under the aegis of Pike's Peak, called by the Ute *Ta-Va-Ah-Gath*, Sun Mountain. Instinctively, she apologized to the mountain for the war machine grinding in its belly like a bad meal. The world was a mix of violent and beautiful forces. How naive they'd been that night at Wheeler Springs in the slate gorge north of Ojai, when it all began. Little did they know the rabbit hole they were about to fall into, and what it would cost them.

Wheeler, spin!

Treadle out the tale that five

and two in belly jelly within

did under midnight sky and Mars
share a vat of wet sulphuric heat
and wonder at and touch
Barbara's beating drum
beating with someone floating
in Barbara's floating while
we up to the dark miles looked,
floating . . .

2
The Matilija
Spring 1970

Find the cost of freedom
Buried in the ground,
Mother Earth will swallow you,
Lay your body down.

- Crosby, Stills, Nash, and Young, 1974

Like a Botticelli still life standing in the close little
wreck of a cabin at the hot springs in the canyons
north of Ojai on the Matilija River, Barbara was deftly
folding carrots, onion, and cabbage in the *wok*, adding
the *seitan* she had kneaded and rinsed earlier. She
was tall and dark, browned by the California sun,
arms slender but not frail, hands muscular, blunt-
fingered and large, nose straight and perfectly
chiseled like her round, pure brow, her belly
ballooning with yet another child beneath the Indian
madras skirt and its thousand all-seeing Eyes of God
peering out at Seven. Barbara's eyes were blue and
wry over some benign private joke she knew but
never told, secretly laughing at how seriously human
beings around her played their parts. The Celtic poet
Yeats wrote about her, *a woman of so shining*
loveliness That men threshed corn at midnight by a
tress, A little stolen tress . . .

Outside, Chumash ghosts haunted the talkative
waters still bearing messages from the Lords of the
Underworld. California mule train drivers and
pioneers had hiked that valley at the end of the 19th
century, arriving exhausted and yearning to be
rejuvenated by the healing water. Sulphur hissed up
from the Earth's veins in that exquisite slate gorge.

The two remaining cabins had last been refurbished in the early Twenties when a health spa for the rich had mingled with the Chumash and mule train ghosts until fire swept through and a flash flood washed away an era. Some said the Chumash had sent the fire and flood as retribution for the murder of Chief Matilija right there at Wheeler Springs; others swore they had seen Wheeler Blumberg's ghost picking among the charred remains of his great wood and stone hotel, the pipes that had once carried healing sulphurous waters into every room rusted. Still etched in the bones of the adjacent lodge were smoky cellar cardrooms and the mahogany bar once graced by luminaries like Jack Dempsey and the Costello gang drinking their way through Prohibition.

Since Wheeler's dream had washed out to sea, less well-heeled guests had been taking refuge there, squatters and campers like Barbara and her family, oblivious to phantoms but still peering into the darkness and listening to the cataract's roar like old Rip Van Winkle's Catskills bowling ball rolling down an invisible wooden alley to topple invisible pins.

On this particular black velvet night in the spring of 1970, a year and a half after the Summer of Love and its subsequent October funeral in the Haight, a million stars hovered and hummed over the Matilija twisting around stones and over the slate plates that littered the springs. After a tearful call from Barbara, Seven had driven down from Santa Barbara earlier in the afternoon with food and was now leaning against the door jamb of the tiny wreck of a cabin no bigger than a toolshed, watching Barbara make dinner in the soft kerosene light, listening to her latest tale of woe about her husband Aaron. No money, no food stamps left, no doubt due to a dope deal Aaron couldn't pass up, and so this was their makeshift residence: a shanty of boards, a charred table, three dilapidated chairs, a stained double mattress with torn sheets and thin blankets, diapers and clothes, Barbara hauling water from the fresh-water springs above the hot springs belching sulphur. It hurt Seven to see her living like this, even though Rhea excused it, insisting that real hippies should be able to live anywhere.

Seven glanced out at the lantern standing sentinel on the picnic table Aaron had scavenged from the latest flash flood and listened to the symphony of camp life—Barbara talking and knocking the wooden spoon against the *wok*, the stir fry sizzling, the gas spluttering, the distant rush of the water leap-frogging over stone, naked and dirt-layered Ariel and Syd shrieking as they hopped from rock to rock in quest of marshmallow sticks, Aaron calling out as he gathered branches and charred timber on the banks.

Ariel and Syd rushed in and spun around their mother, laughing, poking their marshmallow sticks up to show her. Still stirring, she dutifully murmured, "Far *out,* far *out.*"

Once the children ran back into the darkness, Seven began roasting sesame seeds over the other burner. The two young women laughed and stirred, standing close, content to be cooking and eating like peasants out under the fiery stars at the western edge of fat America, content that children should run free for a season.

When the seeds popped, Seven ground them in the *suribachi,* tossing in a pinch of sea salt from off the coast of France, then carried the *suribachi* and pot of brown rice out to the table in the clearing where the children were already swinging their legs, Ariel shaving the end of her little brother's marshmallow stick with the tiny Swiss Army knife Aaron had taught her to use. Almost six, Ariel relished teaching Syd everything, except during the brief moments of hating him for dogging her wake. Syd had been named for Syd Barrett of Pink Floyd because Aaron had partied with Barrett and Alice Cooper a few years before in Venice, California. Barbara didn't think Syd Barrett was much of a role model, but she liked the name Syd.

While Aaron coaxed a fire from the dry wood he and the children had gathered the women and children sat at the table and spooned brown rice, *seitan,* and vegetables into plastic cottage cheese containers, then liberally sprinkled *gomasio* and *tamari* soy sauce. Surreptitiously, Seven watched how deft Aaron's Taurus body was, despising everything about him. How could Barbara put up with all of his infidelities? He was Ariel's second father and probably good in bed. Women had and kept invisible choices. Seven had read that in Peru men played music and fucked and talked in the shade while their colorfully dressed women hiked up the mountains with children on their backs to the terraces and hoed all day. Was it enough for those women that the men played the music of the gods, fucked all night, and made beautiful babies? Still, there were other ways to love and be free than having sex with every young body you took a fancy to. Seven would have told Aaron to pack up long ago. He could work hard, but mostly he smoked marijuana and conjured his next liaison while Barbara and the children hitchhiked into town for the welfare check. If it weren't for the State of California, where would they be?

Seven remembered early on when Aaron had cast his smoldering Semitic eyes on her and made her blush. Years later, after Barbara was dead, Seven finally found him and children holed up in Oregon in fear of the Mafia. True to form, Aaron was sleeping with a 17-year-old beauty not much older than Ariel. Aaron had gotten drunk so he could weep and cling to Seven about the woman they both had loved, then in the middle of the night had snuck downstairs to try to fuck her. After all those years, he was still a trickle of

37

a man who had had the good fortune to run off for a time into Barbara's pure and mighty mountain lake.

Rhea didn't think much of Aaron, either, but her artist's eye was taken with his raw maleness. She painted him in all of his male glory next to a regal, long-necked goose, both in hot pink and staring defiantly from the canvas. Aaron couldn't understand why she had added the goose and it bothered him that women smiled when they looked at the painting.

The children bolted their food, eager for marshmallows, as the deepening darkness and soft lantern light and fire melted adult differences and disappointments and moved them all toward the dreaming penumbra of day loosing its grip on them and gliding west so tomorrow could walk backwards toward them. Aaron took a third or fourth helping and followed the children to the fire to supervise the art of melting the marshmallows' creamy insides while Barbara and Seven carried the bowls, chopsticks, spoons, and *wok* down to the Matilija to rub them clean with sand in the cool water, much as Chumash women might have, all the while listening to the xylophone of shallow water playing over the stones as the sweet scent of Aaron's sagelike marijuana curled around their nostrils. Giving each other a knowing look, they turned back for the clearing, Barbara whispering that Aaron had looked everywhere for the renowned nine-ton brass tub Jack Dempsey had soaked in and finally had to settle for an old 12x12 redwood tub he'd found half-buried in mudslide rubble. He'd worked all day at digging it out and reconfiguring the corroded pipes so the hot springs would pump in and out, his labor a *pièce de résistance*.

The dishes washed and camp in order, they all shed their clothes in the sheen of the rising half moon. Aaron mixed hot and cold water in a bucket and poured it over the sticky children soaping

38

themselves with Dr. Bronner's Peppermint Soap, laughing and squealing until they were rinsed and could do the same to Aaron. The bucket passed to Seven and Barbara and one by one they all slid into the healing vat just heartbeats before they heard the drone of an engine and saw headlights casting silver cords of light through the darkness.

Naked as a satyr, Aaron leaped from the tub. Telling the children to remain with their mother, he held the lantern aloft and picked his way toward the turnout where their cars were parked. Watching the lantern bob into the thick darkness, Seven mused on an Inuit story she had heard up on Vancouver Island during a Cedar Circle sweat about Raven paddling downriver in a bidarka, his paddle going *swish! slap! swoop!,* his voice singing, *What is this dark village I am coming to?* as a child cried, *Raven! Does he really exist?* and the tiny bidarka went *ping-crunch!* as it scraped up on the riverbank.

The engine went silent, the headlights blinked out. Overhead, the jeweled dome hummed with a million stars as the cataract drone thrummed ceaselessly on the women and children listening intently to slamming car doors, the murmur of voices, the rhythmic crunch of footsteps as the lantern swung back through the black. Unconsciously, Seven swirled the vat water with her fingertips until she'd discerned a sun-browned face with a salt-and-pepper stubble framed with a Druid tonsure. Coarse dark hair cascaded down the back of the man's thick muslin robe bound by a knotted cord around the middle.

"Forgive us for disturbing you," the man's gentle Slavic voice intoned, "but my companions and I lost our way and only need a place to rest and food for a woman with child. I am called Hermano, and my companions are Raven and her father-in-law Ghost Bear."

Emerging from the shadows behind him was a tall Indian of indeterminate age in blue jeans and a plaid Western shirt, his cheekbones high and wide framing sloe eyes, his black braids greying. Beside him, the young woman in buckskins was dark and very pregnant. Her blue-black hair was also braided, her eyes and facial structure different from his. Both faces were closed, perhaps embarrassed by easy *wasichu* nudity, but they nodded in greeting.

"They're heading south to Indio and then east to Four Corners," Aaron announced as he set the lantern down.

The Slavic accent spiraled Seven back to her childhood with her Roumanian grandmother reading tea leaves in a cup in their East Detroit kitchen for other Eastern Europeans who had waited on the back stoop for their turn with the gypsy, rolling cigarettes, smoking and talking, anxious to hear about their families in the Old Country, if they would get a job on the General Motors assembly line, if their child or old mother would mend.

Hermano smiled. "If we may, we will wash and bathe as you do? And there is no need to be embarrassed by your hippie custom of nudity. In Europe, we bathe as you do." He began disrobing while Aaron dipped the bucket in the tub and proffered the Dr. Bronner's. Ghost Bear too undressed, and Raven down to her thin cotton shift.

Syd, one arm around his mother's neck, pointed at Hermano's tattoos. Catching his eye, Hermano laughed and pirouetted in the lantern's light as Aaron threw the first bucket of water over him. "My body is a map of the entire world. See, on my back is the East—Russia, the Middle East, India, China, Japan, with Africa on my left buttock and Australia on my right."

Ariel and Syd clambered out of the vat for a closer look.

"And on my front are your Americas, Greenland, Western Europe, with Eastern Europe under my arm making the bridge to the Middle East."

"Like Bradbury's *Illustrated Man*," Aaron grunted.

Even in lantern light, the colors shone lustrous, as if with a light of their own. Marveling, the children traced mountains, deserts, rivers, and oceans as Ghost Bear and Raven settled into the vat. Syd followed migrating birds, spouting whales, winds and currents blowing ships and aircraft over the sea and land, all the way to the outline of the great tree sprouting from Hermano's groin and over his belly.

"Yes, child," Hermano smiled again, "the Tree of Knowledge of Good and Evil, the Wakah-Chan rooted in the universe from which all living things evolve."

Syd traced the taproot down Hermano's left thigh to the tip of his big tope while Ariel traced the branches up to his heart and out along his arms to hundreds of pale green leaves burgeoning from his veins.

All business, Ariel turned Hermano around and leaped back with a shriek. Writhing up from his coccyx through Northern Africa and into the Middle East and Russia, up and over his shoulder blades toward the Arctic Circle, was a two-hooded, two-crowned cobra. Hermano crouched down so both children could see the heads. Gingerly, Syd reached to touch them but thought better of it.

From the vat, Seven pointed. "What is over your heart?"

Hermano beamed, pointing to his stomach. "Here is Mexico," then moving his finger up to his heart, "and this Four Corners on the Colorado Plateau, where the US Geological Survey crossed the heart of America with four states, where the Hopi say their Emergence from the Fourth World occurred, a place not so far from where the Bomb shattered Earth Time 25 years ago."

41

The magical moment of the Illustrated Man turned ashen grey at the mention of the Event no one wanted to remember so as to retain the illusion that it was over and done with and nothing could be done about it. Hermano followed Aaron and children into the vat.

"We must not turn away from the fact of the Bomb simply because it is unpleasant," he continued. "Under your 33º Freemason President Harry 'True Man,' those three acts at White Sands, Hiroshima, and Nagasaki constituted a three-fold alchemical ritual under Sirius known as the Creation and Destruction of Primordial Matter. The guns of Europe and the South Pacific were scarcely silent when the world's womb was ripped open to give birth to *Rosemary's Baby.* Your generation is the first to follow Antimatter's opening of a kingdom historically consigned to the shadows of Nature's counterspace."

Seven recalled her neighbor the Colonel's description of the V2 rocket traveling at 5,000 kilometers per hour about to fall on London in October 1944.

"What did 'about to fall' mean?" the Colonel had rhetorically asked. "From the point of view of the radar operator reading waves that travel at 300,000 kilometers per second, the trajectory of the V2 was a *fait accompli.* For him, everything had already happened. Nothing could now intercept that engine of death, no warning, no second thoughts. For him, Time was different than for those about to die. In radar Time, they were already dead."

She wished the Colonel could meet Hermano.

"I need a joint," Aaron grumbled, sloshing out of the vat. Talk of the Bomb had awakened the ball of fire in his belly and made him yearn for the soothing, forgetful powers of *mallihua.* Aaron prided himself in not believing in anything, not in his family's Jewish G-d nor in the order of society. The topic of the Bomb had taken him by surprise.

As Aaron left in quest of his stash, Barbara explained to Hermano, "He can't handle bad trips very well."

Ariel sidled up to the big brown man sitting quietly in the vat. "Why are you called Ghost Bear?" she asked.

The native man's black eyes twinkled. "If I tell you, will you tell me why you are called Ariel?"

"Yes," the little girl promised somberly, putting her hand on Ghost Bear's shoulder as Syd inched up to his other side.

"So it is this way, Ariel," he nodded. "I am from the Black Hills we call *paha sapa*—sacred, ancient hills that from the air have the shape of the human heart. Long ago, when the Cheyenne, Lakota, and Arapaho were all parts of the Star Nation, *paha sapa* was a Garden of Eden. Near the Bell Fourche River is a sacred mountain that was once a volcano. We call it *Mato Tipi* or Bear Lodge, though *wasichus* like the ones who mined and logged *paha sapa* call it Devil's Tower. Its top is like a GI haircut," he sliced the air horizontally, "and its steep sides are almost as straight as those of a skyscraper but have up-and-down scratch marks on them." He scratched the air vertically. "*Mato Tipi*, being the heart of the heart of *paha sapa*, has a strong medicine star story about how those scratch marks got there."

By now, Ariel and Syd were on Ghost Bear's lap. "Tell us, Ghost Bear," Ariel commanded.

Ghost Bear nodded again. "Once there was a chief with seven beautiful daughters," he drew his head back and looked Ariel, "almost as beautiful as you. Every young man wanted to marry them, but the sisters could not imagine ever being separated. One night, as they danced in the moonlight by the Belle Fourche River, near where the great Cheyenne chief Sweet Medicine once lived, a grizzly bear saw them and leaped into the clearing. The girls bolted for the mountain, their long black hair flying behind them."

Worried, Ariel pulled Ghost Bear's chin around toward her. "He won't get them, will he?"

Ghost Bear smiled. "The sisters ran toward the sacred mountain as if to their mother and climbed her steep sides as nimble as monkeys with the bear right behind them. But when the grizzly began to climb, he was so big and heavy that he kept slipping, his sharp claws gouging the mountain. The girls made it to the top and cried out to Sky Father to save them. Just as the bear finally made it up to the mesa, the seven sisters were swept up into the sky. Even then, the grizzly didn't give up. He leaped into the sky after them and chases them to this day."

Pointing up to a tiny but brilliant cluster of stars, Hermano said, "There they are, up in what we call the Pleiades, a tiny dipper of girls riding the back of the Bull of Heaven, Taurus, just below the warrior Perseus' foot."

Ghost Bear swung his finger toward the center of the sky. "And there is the Great Bear with his long tail, Ursa Major, what you call the Big Dipper. It is the Great Bear's fate to chase the beautiful Seven Sisters forever but never to catch them."

Ariel stared up at the Sisters forever safe in the bejeweled, humming heavens.

Ghost Beat smiled as he watched the little girl. "And I am called Ghost Bear because I once stood in the Bear's Lodge, dancing the Ghost Dance with my people whose spirits still wander the Earth because they love it so."

"How do you get up there to dance with them?" Ariel asked, thinking of the steep sides.

"Well, that's the funny thing. Part of me flies up there while my body sleeps." Ghost Bear chuckled. "That's getting into a national monument the cheap and easy way."

"I do that sometimes," Ariel said excitedly. "I go and watch Barbara sleep, then sometimes I fly up by the Moon and take my little brother with me, don't I, Syd?" Syd nodded vigorously. "Sometimes I'm afraid and so I wake up."

She dog-paddled out into the middle of the vat, held her nose, and went under. Heartbeats later, Seven felt Ariel's little hands moving up her legs. When she surfaced and blew out her breath like a baby whale, Seven pushed the blond curls out of her face.

"Now it's your turn, Ariel," Ghost Bear reminded her.

Syd dog-paddled over to his sister now on Seven's lap. Ariel smacked her lips self-importantly.

"My name is from the play called *The Tempest* about a shipwreck off the coast of America, down where Christopher Columbus landed—"

"In the Caribbean Sea," Barbara amended.

"Uh huh, the Caribbean. The magician Prospero was banished there and caused a storm to shipwreck the men who had banished him to the New World. Ariel is a spirit and has to serve Prospero until he lets Ariel go. But that doesn't happen until the end, right, Barbara?"

Barbara nodded.

Hermano said, "Indeed, Ariel, Prospero the European Druid was exiled to these shores long ago and grew ugly and devious here, as many Europeans have become. The man who wrote *The Tempest* was staring Death in the face—not just his own death but the death of his long-cherished dream that beautiful Atlantis might be resurrected in the Americas from her full fathom five grave in the Caribbean."

Ariel began reciting—

Full fathom five thy father lies;
Of his bones are coral made;

45

Those are pearls that were his eyes;
Nothing of him that doth fade
But doth suffer a sea change
Into something rich and strange . . .

The company applauded.

"Bravo, Ariel!" Hermano cried. "For so the playwright saw sunken Atlantis in the Caribbean. Prospero's final speech indicates that he wisely let go his dream of an American Atlantis come again, unlike Freemasons who still pursue it—

And, like the baseless fabric of this vision,
The cloud-capp'd towers, the gorgeous palaces,
The solemn temples, the great globe itself,
Ye all which it inherit, shall dissolve
And, like this insubstantial pageant faded,
Leave not a rack behind. We are such stuff
As dreams are made on, and our little life
Is rounded with a sleep . . .

"'Leave not a rack behind,'" Seven murmured pensively.

Ariel paddled over to Ghost Bear who lifted her high over his head where she extended her legs and arms and flew as a sprite in the night, the stars her backdrop, the Moon her floodlight.

Seven got out of the vat, dried off and dressed so she could warm food for the travelers while Barbara bedded down the children. After Raven ate, she and Barbara retired, leaving Seven to wander the starlit canyon with Hermano and Ghost Bear. Much was said that Seven would mull over for the rest of her life, for some things come only once and never again.

Finally, they all lay down to rest until just before dawn when the three travelers returned to the International. It was time to push on to Indio before continuing to Four Corners where Ghost Bear's son

White Bull was languishing in a Fort Defiance jail along with other American Indian Movement resisters. Ghost Bear took the wheel and Hermano rode shotgun. Seven was there to say goodbye but found herself saying something different.

"Take me with you," she pleaded. Suddenly, nothing seemed more important than being near Hermano. But he shook his head.

"No, *Lilya*," he said. Seven had no idea how he knew her birth name. "You must not miss your appointment with destiny. You and I are members of a very large and old family that is now spread thin. Clinging to each other while humanity plunges into darkness is not for the likes of us." He gestured to Ghost Bear and Raven. "Even we three will not be together much longer. We must accustom ourselves to doing with little, treasuring each moment we are together, basking in whatever light there is wherever we are. There is much to do and little time. Ten thousand hearts beat with yours, so learn to carry what you must carry and see what you must see. I will be wherever you go, be assured." Smiling ecstatically, he squeezed her hands. "Fear not, my Slavic sister." He kissed her cheeks and Ghost Bear started the engine.

She waved goodbye, her heart dragging behind the headlights threading into the dark preceding dawn. When she slept again, she dreamed her first dream of the old woman and a coming flood.

3
St. Martin
2019

*In the Great Plains are the Sand Hills of Nebraska,
200 miles east to west, from the Valley of the North
Platte in the south to the Black Hills and Badlands in
the north. The American Rub al Khali or Gobi Desert.
Dig beneath the green prairie and you'll find sand. Dig
beneath sand and you'll find an ancient sea, 156,000
square miles of the Oglala Aquifer with more water
than Lake Huron. Crazy Horse died in the Sand Hills.
Denver, Wichita and Lubbock flushed their toilets and
watered their lawns with that aquifer and it's drying
up. Welcome to the new Afghanistan.*

- Rob Schultheis, *The Hidden West*, 1996

*Perpetuation of the great plan was secured by secret
tradition among an inner group of initiates unknown
to the outer Order at large, and patterned...in
[Francis] Bacon's* New Atlantis. *This inner group
counts a small number of members in all the
countries of the Western Hemisphere. They have kept
the lamp of the Muse burning during the last three
hundred years.*

- Marie Bauer Hall, *Francis Bacon's Great
Virginia Vault*, 1940; *Quest for Bruton Vault*,
1984

Setting out on the Oregon Trail had not been a
rational decision. On the 22nd of July 2019 at
precisely 3 a.m., old Seven awakened from a dream

she'd had intermittently since that night at Wheeler Springs 49 years before when she had first met Hermano and was young and untried. *A wall of water as high as the sky towered over her, wet and churning as the Red Sea, arrested in midair, anxious to be loosed. Opaque shadows hurried back and forth behind the wave. An arm shot out, fingers caught her by the throat and sought to pull her through the wall of water.*

Twisting and writhing, she awoke sweating and panting, the sheet in a wad, the acid taste of fear in her mouth. It had been a world dream, not a personal dream. Catastrophe was on its way. Her pact with Thomas and Vince had always been that if Humpty Dumpty finally fell and shattered, they would rendezvous in Rocky Mountain National Park where the three rivers met. Mannie and Ray knew, but Baby Rose—well, who knew where, and if, she was anymore.

So all these years Seven had lived low to the ground, teaching until they required fingerprints, writing under aliases. Most recently, she'd lived in a little Pacific Northwest town, traveling only for low-profile talks and small-press book signings. Domestic travel had become increasingly difficult after 9/11 and the surveillant 21st century ground into gear with its identification checkpoints at airports and along toll roads, satellite surveillance, and ignition systems doubling as transponders. She'd fabricated cover stories and fictitious identities replete with birth certificates, mother's maiden names, SSNs, and latex fingerprints, thanks to an old hacker friend who'd picked up such useful arts while languishing as a prisoner of war in Hanoi where (according to official records) he had officially died in 1973. He had even gone to his own funeral and felt bad that he couldn't comfort his mother. Political death appeared to be lonelier than real death.

Eluding detection had long ago lost its 007 appeal for Seven, but what could she do? Thomas' original enemies were long dead, but the NSA and other agencies were still interested, so Seven surmised she was still on watch lists. True, she was a fading luminary in the house-of-mirrors American underground, due to her writings and late night KMAE guerrilla call-in show, but beside Thomas and Vince, she was small potatoes. KMAE was just a little AM station with a 40-storey tower owned by a man named Alex and his South American parrot Huitzlipochtli (Whiz for short). Alex rented out daytime frequencies to pay for primetime night frequency. Small operations like KMAE were rare birds, indeed; one by one, they had been picked off over the years by corporate raptors. "Seven at 7" was streamed throughout the world of strange fare, some disinformation, some legitimate, all sending flares into the increasingly rarefied atmosphere of an ever-tightening global fascist night.

Everywhere Seven went, the desperate young either clung to her or castigated her for her generation's failure. To all, she was a Sixties survivor of Big Brother's decimation of America beneath the megacorporate heel. However she was viewed, she was a willow bending and dodging, doing whatever it took to keep her taproot buried deep in the subterranean waters that continue to run beneath the driest of times, clinging to mental snapshots of those who had been her beacons—Martin Luther King, Jr., Mae Brussell, James Shelby Downard, journalists like Danny Casolaro, Jim Keith, and Gary Webb. She accepted her troubled era as unavoidable and her business as keeping a perspective by which she and others might survive and thrive.

Thus she had obeyed the dream. First, she'd paid her next month's rent, telling her landlady that she was going to California for a few weeks. The woman suspected nothing; her kooky old renter was often gone. Next, she'd packed her essentials in two duffle bags—camping gear, clothes, food, maps—then packed up her old Mazda, dropped stuff at the Goodwill and duffle bags at the bus station. She'd driven to her mechanic's, a sharp old Libertarian she had known for years. That he was from the right and she from the left didn't matter: a common enemy and love of the truth create unforeseen alliances. Glancing at the surveillance camera across the street, they spoke about the Mazda needing a tune-up and her visit to California; he would park it in the yard until someone came for it. Seven felt bad about not telling him the truth, but she knew it was safer for him not to know her movements.

Jimmy arrived as planned to give her a ride to KMAE. He was a nice enough leftist college kid, but she had her doubts, having learned long ago that people who just pop up out of the blue and seem to reflect your ideas to a T may simply have studied your file. Nor did his poor struggling student status match his spending and travel habits. Jimmy made it his business to know everything about Seven and never missed her show, though until now he hadn't figured out where she transmitted from week to week. In short, he'd been compromised, perhaps because of a pending drug charge or family threat. He had lost himself and didn't see what a waste it was to spend life excelling at deception. Thomas used to say that the man who said *Ignorance is bliss* had tears in his eyes. She had Jimmy's number, so he was easy to get around. His handlers probably didn't even care; in fact, they probably wanted her to know they were keeping tabs on her.

Not all dissidents need murdering; some are allowed to live to attract other dissidents. Under constant surveillance, her life hadn't been her own since those early days. She played the mouse and

51

they played the cats—isolation, suspicion, never sure of who was who, all of it a double game. Some were driven mad, particularly if psychotronics were used. Others like Jimmy were turned and used, yet others marginalized and discredited. Seven had long ago accepted the house of mirrors and had learned not to get too close nor divulge too much. Loving Thomas had meant drawing a line in the dirt and training herself not to cross it so she wouldn't drag him down. Not having their own child was but one of the prices they had paid for their political life.

Jimmy dropped her at KMAE and she shooed him away. Hopefully, she would never have to see him again and witness the slow, incremental dismantling of his humanity. Overhead, a chopper from the north inscribed a low, noisy circle: tax dollars at work for an old woman flyover. For some, the show of power was everything. The America she had known and loved, if it had ever existed, was dead and gone.

Saying goodbye to Alex without really saying goodbye would be harder, nor could she tell her listeners. Long ago, her Gaussbuster had registered serious bugs in the station and no way would she risk putting Alex in harm's way. The ever-watchful Whiz squawked as she entered. Alex was cuing up the digital jukebox in the sound booth. Other than her show and the occasional taped historical speech—like Lindbergh's 1938 warning to maintain neutrality toward the escalating war in Europe—Alex played nothing but music: early 20th century, old Broadway tunes, arias, swing, country, and early blues—his way of saying that since the Bomb, America had gone to hell in a hand basket. About Lindbergh, he'd said, "It's easy to destroy a dead man who can't defend himself. He was a maverick like Kennedy, and his little boy was taken and killed on March 1, 1932. I for one won't forget *or* forgive . . ."

As soon as he spotted her, prescient Alex put on "Good Night, Irene." Too casually, Seven told him that she was going to treat her old bones to a few days at a hot springs on the Wind River, then head for a California radio interview, would Alex play her old shows or those of Mae Brussell? Listening and nodding, sage Alex looked around the station as if to acknowledge the bugs.

"Wind River, huh? They say the wind blows where it will." He took her hand, his old eyes sad. "See you later, 'gator."

From his perch, Whiz cried, "Take care, take care!"

Seven's throat tightened. Life was one long hello and goodbye. She couldn't even warn him of the coming cataclysm. "Alex, did you know you're on the endangered species list?" She grasped his hands and silently mouthed, *Thank you,* then left without looking back, grateful for the walk to the bus station.

In Vancouver, she caught another bus east along the Columbia Gorge, the Sun setting behind her. All her thoughts went to her last meeting with Thomas three years before at the Whale's Tale in Florence, Oregon. *It's coming down like we always thought it would, Thomas,* she thought. *Will you be there, my love?*

Just past Carson, she got off the bus and hitched a ride in a pickup to Berge Road, then walked in the dark the rest of the way to the hot springs, stopping at last at the little cabin the St. Martin's or whatever corporation pretended to be the St. Martin family rented by the night. The St. Martin's had owned the access to Carson Hot Springs since the 1800s. She would sleep, then spend the day soaking in the hot springs until dark, when she would embark on the famous Oregon Trail.

That night in the St. Martin cabin, she slept like a saint, awakening at dawn in the midst of a conversation with someone she knew but couldn't recall. Over the years, she had learned her way around the dream world, but more as a savvy sightseer than a card-carrying resident. Since California in 1970, she had become like the servant in the Black Forest fairy tale who dined on a white snake and gained occult access to the languages of creatures. No doubt like her grandmother's clairvoyance, her gift was a curse and a blessing, her senses having become creatures in their own right, cohabiting her body along with the point of consciousness she called herself. Wherever she went, the dead and phantoms joyously showed themselves to her and spoke, the eye being much older than the neocortex and the ear older yet. It was not the senses that deceived, but the judgment.

In the morning she signed the guest registry at the trailhead, then walked through the clearing where Lonna St. Martin had once been the guardian of the Wind River and the hot springs bubbling up from the Underworld below. The Multnomah, Willamettes, and Klickitats had lived along the banks of the mighty Columbia, crossing back and forth over the bridge of the gods called *Tamaniwas*. The concrete pretender further downriver was nothing like the great natural stone bridge that had once arched over the Columbia like Bifrost, the flaming rainbow bridge built by the gods long ago when the world was young. What it must have been like to walk over such a bridge, the stone vibrating like a tuning fork to the hooves of ponies, the roar of the mighty Columbia below. The Willamettes' fate was tied to their *tomanowos*: when the white man came in numbers, the Great Spirit had toppled them and their bridge.

Laying her clothes aside, she slipped into a steaming sulphur pool, her burden of old age already slipping downriver to the Columbia and out to sea. All morning, she drifted among veils of cloud and thought, mentally mapping her trek east, thinking back to when Washington Territory was a *terra incognita* etched in the American imagination, and South Pass a mindmark like the Pillars of Hercules for the Greeks.

Seven hundred thousand white settlers had gobbled up all of Ohio, Indiana, Illinois, Alabama and Mississippi even before stalwart European stock barely one generation American and desperate for roots had snatched at the Pre-Emption Law of 1842, then the Oregon Donation Land Act of 1850. Troopers and trappers, desperate seekers and refugees had already opened Washington Territory, a country so wild and glorious that tears stood in the burliest of men's eyes for having not seen such virgin wilderness in Europe for centuries. In Independence, Missouri, families long on desperation prepared to plunge into two thousand miles of Indian country. They listened carefully to tales of wintry deaths in the Rockies and took special heed to make Independence Rock by Independence Day.

That the land promised to them by their adopted republic had been mother to brown-skinned Others for fifty thousand years was beyond their reckoning. Accustomed to scrabbling at the bottom of the pecking order for crumbs falling from the chins of those dining at the great oak table of Manifest Destiny, the desperately poor couldn't afford to think of Indians as being anything like themselves, nor could they contemplate being but the plow breaking ground for distant masters. Such thoughts were so much subtext to the societal law of gravity their parents, grandparents, and great grandparents had been bent to as to a law of God: theirs was not to question why but to seize opportunity when it raised its fatuous head.

The Welshman Captain Merriwether Lewis and Scotsman William Clark—Freemasons both—had preceded the settlers in 1804, sent by then-President Thomas Jefferson after he had brokered the best land deal ever with Napoleon and doubled the size of the United States. No matter that France did not own the land it was paid for; to Europeans long accustomed to conquest, possession was the better part of property, whether purchased outright or stolen. In 1775, Jefferson himself had amended the first resolution of the *Declaration and Resolves of the First Continental Congress* to read "life, liberty and the pursuit of happiness" instead of "life, liberty and property" due to the outcry among propertied Freemason Brothers on both sides of the Atlantic. The American poor of European stock may have taken pride in equality before the law, but in the end their destiny still belonged to the few the Maker had cut from finer cloth, men destined to be treated more equally than most.

And so like their oxen the people had toiled west over the Great Plains and Rockies, three hundred and fifty thousand of them, their seventy-five thousand covered wagons a great white snake slipping through a sea of sweetgrass. Sweet Medicine had warned his people the *Tsistsistas* (called by the Lakota the Cheyenne) that a people with white skin and hair on their faces would flow like a river from the east in canoes moving over dry land. Thus in the 1850s and 1860s, men the color of earth sat on their horses watching speechlessly from hills and groves as the dry supernatural river flowed west. The Shoshone called it the River of Destruction, the Lakota *Wasichu Canku*, the White Man Road. Oxen, horses, mules, milk cows, and sheep plodded through country made sacred by Elk and Buffalo.

The earth-red men studied every detail of the River of Destruction, and when their tongues were finally loosed, discussed it endlessly. Perhaps, they said, it was a sign of hope that the faces of the pale women swaying on the buckboards were smooth like theirs and not hairy like those of their men. But the sign proved insubstantial. Over the course of the next half century, get-rich-quicks, underpaid soldiers, liberated slaves, Civil War soldiers paid in Western land, bounty hunters paid for Mexican or Indian scalps locked horns with those they were taught to call Stone Age heathens and devils, cursing them for the heathenish practice of scalping when in fact the devilish practice began during the French and Indian War of 1755 when both French and British paid Indians for enemy scalps and recorded the numbers as conscientiously as Nazis. Sadly, the new republic had not thrown off the tired old European determinants of skin, blood, flag, and almighty money-hoard. In fact, greedy vengeance doubled due to the vast resources seemingly there for the taking. All who balked and insisted upon the more humane were condemned as mad, evil, impractical, disobedient, or downright womanish. Fewer than four hundred pioneers died at the hands of Indians, while disease and accidents claimed ten thousand.

Luxuriating in the hot sulphur waters, Seven turned her thoughts to something Hermano had said at Wheeler Springs so long ago: that Columbus had called the Indians *In Dios* not because he thought he was in India but because he found them to be as religious as children, so unlike the jaded, rapacious Europe he hailed from. The supernatural white river sent many *In Dios* to the bosoms of their gods. In 1500, they had been 150 million strong, and by 1890 they were a scattered diaspora of three million.

"What nonsense schools teach!" Hermano had railed. "Just as the naming of the Americas had nothing to do with that Italian navigator Amerigo Vespucci, Columbus had excellent maps of Baconian ciphers saying exactly where the Americas were, ciphers now in the rare books section of your Library of Congress. He knew exactly where he was going, and to what end. The much more interesting question is why so much effort has gone into propagating a 500-year-old lie among the American people. Discover the answer to that and you will go far . . ."

In the afternoon, she finally poured herself out of the hot pool and took one last cool dip in the river before returning to the cabin to eat something and prepare to embark. While eating her unyeasted bread and cheese and lamb—the last meat she would have for months—she studied a topographical map of the Oregon Trail. She would pick it up at The Dalles Dam. At last, she loaded her pack with the forty to fifty pounds of essentials she had brought and settled it onto her back. Everything shipshape in the cabin, she left a St. Martin saint card on the table, closed the door, and hiked back past the trailhead as the Sun was sinking in the west. Swinging toward Highway 14, she caught a glimpse of a small-boned someone with a nimbus around her head moving among the cottonwoods. After the concrete Bridge of the Gods, she picked up the Oregon Trail at The Dalles, mile 1820, and thus began her autumn of 2019 hiking through what had once been British territory. Three months and one thousand miles later, she would cross the Continental Divide and reach Independence Rock at Mile 838 in Wyoming.

Traveling by day meant too much attention, not to mention that without her Polartechs, direct sunlight dried her eyes out and made them burn. Night vision was easier on her eyes, sensitive after so many years of *seeing*. Had she chosen to travel in the day, she could have cut through the dead and phantoms like a hot knife, the way everyone all day long cut through the invisible electromagnetic worlds pulsating thick about them. But she preferred nights.

What she didn't yet realize was that traveling the Oregon Trail east would mean encountering a wave of the American past hurrying westward, ghosts on every side with haunted, harried eyes, ghosts of Indians, settlers, soldiers, rising out of thin air or old makeshift graves along the Trail, mingling with phantoms of Seven's own past. Come dusk, when the sun's fiery ball no longer ate up the subtle light emanating from all living things, when day was no longer day and night not yet night, her eyes relaxed and the windows to an entirely other Earth began to fly open. Everything peripheral lay in shrouds, but whatever she looked at swam in a rich green-white glow, as if her eyes were twin alien flashlights able to illuminate the overflow of light locked in matter. And so, like a possum or lemur with lantern eyes, she nosed her way eastward along silky nocturnal trails where the living had once scattered their light like Hansel spreading breadcrumbs. To her fairy lantern eyes, the Oregon Trail, bisected by modern highways and interstates, was at once a historical trail through Space for the living and through Time for the dead.

Crossing the dark Deschutes River, she caught sight of a ghost floating a Murphy farm wagon around the submerged rocks, his ghost oxen pulling for all they were worth, while his terrified ghost wife crossed on an Indian pony behind a phantom Indian rider who cried in English, "Wicked woman, put your trust in God!"

4
Initiation

In the morning after the Wheeler Springs happening, Barbara and the children had driven back to Santa Barbara with Seven; Aaron would pick them up at Rhea's that evening, after he finished his "business" in Ojai. Neither of the women asked what his "business" was.

Ariel and Syd loved Seven's VW bus with its snug double bed, foldout table, tiny refrigerator and sink. Seven relished the freedom the bus afforded, having lived in it while driving across country from the Midwest and even in San Francisco while topless dancing in a North Beach club to get enough money for a cheap room in the Panhandle where smack addicts were still tying off at six in the morning when she'd stumble into the kitchen to make tea and cook cereal before her temp day job. Living in the bus had honed her survival skills—paying close attention to where she parked for the night, keeping to strict criteria of personal safety, anonymity, water, proximity to freeway onramps or highways, and finally beauty and quiet on a promontory or lakeside, in a field, but always with an eye to the fact that too much isolation might be dangerous. One frosty night in the Midwest, she'd parked in a quiet neighborhood ten minutes from the freeway and was contentedly sleeping in her bus cocoon, the curtains drawn, when she was awakened by someone jimmying the lock. Willing her breath to deepen, she'd envisioned a ball of fiery iron in her belly, risen to her knees, and howled like a banshee. Immediately, she heard the soft, rhythmic pad of the invader's swift departure. Knowing she would sleep no more that night, she'd heaved herself into the driver's seat and driven on through the night.

So Syd and Ariel hopped about playing house while Seven filled Barbara in on her late walk with the night visitors. They both agreed that whatever mystery surrounded Hermano, it had nothing to do with drugs; he was not, as Aaron had sneered, a burned-out acid freak.

In line for food stamps at the Santa Barbara post office, they'd continued their analysis. Other hippie women waited with small children in tow and babies on their hips, slender young women tanned by the California sun in halter tops and madras and paisley skirts, their hair long and woven with flowers and feathers, beads around their necks, wrists and ankles, their half-naked, longhaired children running about shouting and laughing. Most had emigrated from other states and countries, but some like Barbara were native Californians—native, at least, since the 1800s. Barbara's Catholic parents would have nothing to do with her or their grandchildren, mostly due to her Jewish husband and his justification for a lazy existence so his wife had to turn to welfare. Aaron's insistence that screwing the government was revolutionary and all the while dealing pot was not unusual. White barefoot hippies with long hair, unbuttoned rumpled shirts and muslin drawstring yoga pants were in line, too. A few Mexican *familias* stood among the flower children, deep brown from days in the California fields and orchards, the men's jeans and short-sleeved cotton shirts neat and clean, their hair short and slicked back, and the women and serial children wide-eyed, quiet, and colorful.

With the month's food stamps in hand, the hippie mothers and children then headed for the nearby health food store for treats they'd been doing without. They would wait to go to the natural food store out in Isla Vista on the University of California campus to get their bulk organ grains, beans, oil, honey, and vegetables. As Seven headed the bus for Rhea's, Ariel gobbled Dr. Bronner Corn Chips and savored a ginseng cola while Syd slurped a blueberry yogurt.

Seven had met Rhea through a want ad that read, *Have you a kingdom for a Siamese prince?* Intrigued, she'd driven up into the San Ysidro Foothills at sunset, reds and oranges spilling like tinny liquid gold over the dusty yellow hills, musing on how the Golden Age and Renaissance had loved such light. She'd parked between the low walls at 1549 Hillcrest and raised her hand to knock on the *rancho* screen door when she was confronted by a bigger-than-life painting hanging in the foyer of a naked hot-pink girl falling down an Alice in Wonderland vortex, her eyes surprised, her mouth a tiny *O!*

That first visit, Seven had brought away much to ponder but not the eunuch Siamese cat soon to be immortalized on canvas, large and regal, staring out through inscrutable eyes with pregnant Barbara beside him, whispering with Isis, *I am the Past, the Present, and the Future, no mortal hath yet lifted my veil.* Until the day Rhea died, the uncanny Siamese prince sat sentinel inside the screen door, guardian of the temple within, just as he did that immortal day Ariel and Syd bounded in, slamming the screen door behind them, stroking and squeezing him with small, sticky fingers. When Rhea died, he would sniff at her pale, still form on the bed, affirm that his tour of duty was indeed over, and vanish.

Ted was out selling copy machines and Rhea was in the living room setting up for Barbara's session. Easels and tubes of paint were everywhere amidst magazines, half-folded laundry, and evaporating cups of *bancha*. Ted and Mina dealt with Rhea's Promethean sprawl by delighting in ongoing projects of their own, which tended to be half-finished and shunted to the side. Bamboo shades and spindly tripods with bulbs for heads stood ready to adjust lighting. The furniture was late Salvation Army painted over with brightly colored cubes, cats, calla lilies, heart-faced anthuriums with red tongues, and beady-eyed staring pigs. Black and white photographs of nude Barbara, Aaron, Ted, Mina, and Seven were tacked on walls as rich with umber as the hills outside, and beneath their feet were the cool cerulean blue and marigold terra cotta tiles. The entire house was cool, despite the Southern California midday raging outside.

As usual, Rhea's coal black hair with a few grey scouts was restrained in a bun at the nape of her neck. If her hair was coal, her eyes were flinty obsidians smoldering with uncanny darkness. Her skin was more olive than Seven's and Barbara's, the tone deeper, bequeathed by high-steppe Russian Jews. Her severe dark beauty had now turned dry, the softer beauty of the girl lingering only at the edges for a backward look. The lips were a little cruel, perhaps from long-suffering.

Rhea and Ted were night and day. Everything about Ted appeared average, except for his impish, wide-eyed face that gave a hint to the stalwart individuality he was. Though gray and losing his hair, he was several years younger than Rhea. He ate as Rhea commanded and took care of the money scene while Rhea supplied the dramatic context. He was the rock, she the storm, for better *and* worse. As for love, Seven surmised it must have weathered the fifteen or so years they'd been together, but she did not pretend to penetrate the veil behind which marriages hid. How much was habit and how much love was hard to say. Rhea once said she had given Ted an ultimatum in order to get him to marry her, and sweet dark-haired Mina may even have been her ticket to staying home to paint—a hard-hearted thought, but not once had Seven seen Rhea hug or kiss her daughter.

"Mina! Mina!" the children clamored.

"In the garden," Rhea pointed sergeant-like, and Ariel, Syd, and Seven were off, leaving Rhea and Barbara to their session.

The garden. Somehow, Rhea had commanded the elements and coaxed paradise from a tinder-dry half acre of chaparral, scrub oak, and rock. Mina was weeding in the shade of the Joshua tree, crouched among a throng of bracken fern and white poppies, *Canbya candida,* flocking like tiny sheep around her ankles, while three exquisite purple irises rose up among them. Desert candles stood Red Guard about the little white village and elven thirteen-year-old as she jabbed and yanked at intruders, her arms too thin, her pointy chin and ears out of proportion to her pale face and large brown doe-like eyes. Rhea had poured more of her maternal power into the garden and her paintings than into Mina.

The children crouched around Mina, already intent on a fat tiger-striped caterpillar nibbling at milkweed, laughing at its tiny bites. Seven kneeled beside them, examining the tiger stripes.

"Is it a monarch? Pretty soon, it will make a pupa, a little sac to hang in for a while, and when it comes out—"

"—a butterfly!" Ariel cried excitedly.

Seven looked about at the Ione wild buckwheat, manzanita, blue-flowered gilia, goldfield, lilac, flannel bushes, mountain mahogany, purple sage, bracken ferns, juniper, sycamore, blue-green, long-needled spruce, *piñon*, walnut, buckeye, date palm . . . On and on the list went, a Mediterranean Garden of Eden coaxed from rock. How could they all thrive year round in the serpentine soil of a climate whose rainfall was a few inches a year at best? Rhea had indeed called *Lazarus! Come forth!*

In Greek mythology, Rhea had been the Titan married to her brother Cronos who devoured each child as soon as it sprang from her womb. Phrygians called her Cybele and claimed she taught her rites to Dionysus, the ever-youthful Christ-like god of the Mysteries that the Reptile King Jim Morrison adored. Like her namesake, Rhea seemed more phenomenon than mortal, and all—husband, daughter, friends and followers—circled her orbit like willing and unwilling moons. When she died, hundreds attended her wake to witness her ashes being scattered in the dry California hills. But looking down at Mina patiently showing Ariel and Syd how to pull weeds up from their roots, Seven winced. It was hard when your mother was a Mother of the Gods, adored by many near and far, when all you wanted was a warm, human-scale mother.

She stood and began strolling counterclockwise around the house to where the vegetables were growing—carrots, chard, lettuce, chicory, cabbages, eggplants, peppers, artichokes, asparagus, a cornucopia of every vegetable imaginable clinging happily to the narrow path spiraling into an island of roses, a rainbow haven of liplike and salmon pinks the color of the soul, icing yellows, bride whites, velvet reds, and at the very center uncanny *blue roses* cloistered like vestal virgins around a ten-foot night-blooming Cereus not yet in bloom. Rhea had planted Bavarian gentians around the Cereus because

65

of D.H. Lawrence's visit to America when he said the
American soul was isolated and a killer—

> *Bavarian gentians, big and dark, only dark*
> *darkening the day-time, torch-like with*
> *the smoking blueness of Pluto's gloom,*
> *ribbed and torch-like, with their blaze of*
> *darkness spread blue*
> *down flattening into points, flattened*
> *under the sweep of white day*
> *torch-flower of the blue-smoking*
> *darkness, Pluto's dark-blue daze,*
> *black lamps from the halls of Dis,*
> *burning dark blue,*
> *giving off darkness, blue darkness, as*
> *Demeter's pale lamps give off light,*
> *lead me then, lead the way...*

But instead of gentians, Rhea had gotten *blue* roses. It
was impossible, of course, but there they were. Seven
had taken solitary nocturnal strolls along this Edenic
spiral to the blue heart from whence a strange,
unearthly glow emanated to keep tabs on the Cereus.

Now she followed the arc of fruit and nut trees, the
saving arbor whose tall shade relieved the green
citizenry facing the late Mediterranean afternoons.
She plucked half a dozen figs and munched their
gritty sweetness as she climbed beyond the tree line
where Rhea's civilization ended and the San Ysidros
resumed their dry rollercoaster to the south and east.
The white-hot sun was already beginning its slow red
descent.

Shielding her eyes, she turned to survey the
dimensions of the garden and house and their
orientation to Hillside Drive, running a visual plumb
line up to the three tipis and yurt tucked among
chaparral and yucca. It was a never-ending puzzle.
Why did the house look so much bigger at night, and

why was its orientation to Hillside so skewed? She looked again up to the tipis. Ray was the only one staying up there now. His VW bug was gone; he was probably out at Isla Vista. Her eyes followed Hillside Drive up to where the pavement ended and there were no more houses, but she could still see the turnout seven or eight miles further up to where a final rustic dwelling was tucked. *Thomas.* A stab of longing divided itself between her heart and the V between her legs. Perhaps tomorrow night she would drive up. Turning to descend, she wondered what he would think of Hermano.

Back in the living room, Barbara and her naked belly and breasts were perched on a stool and Rhea was painting away. The radio was playing *The Green Door—*

> *Midnight*
> *one more night without sleeping,*
> *Watching*
> *till the morning comes creeping,*
> *Green door*
> *what's the secret you're keeping?*

"I'll go out to The Source while you're working," she announced to Barbara. "Where's your grocery list and food stamps?"

"In my purse," Barbara mumbled so as not to move.

"A quart of sunflower oil for me, please," Rhea yelled as Seven slammed the screen door.

She stopped at her apartment on State Street to check her larder and grab a few containers, pausing in front of the Colonel's apartment next door. She could hear his television and fan thrumming away and made a mental note to check on him later. He had a sister in Texas, but his family had been the Air Force. Now, he had her chauffeuring him on Sundays in his pale yellow '59 Eldorado Biarritz Cadillac designed by Harley Earl, the father of modern automotive design. The Colonel had explained that the Caddy's outrageous tail fins and jet pod taillights came straight from the twin-boom, twin-tail P38 "Lightning" fighter plane powered by two GM Allison V12 engines. "From headlights to tailfins, she has a P38 line," the Colonel had crowed. First, they took their drive, then went for a lobster dinner out on the pier. War was generally the topic of conversation, given that the old man had been in several, from World War One to Two to Korea to Vietnam, and was haunted.

Desolate and transient Isla Vista had grown up around the university: a few stores, cheap student housing, cars, bicycles, packs of bristling mongrel dogs. In exchange for a little cooking and cleaning, she parked outside a student housing unit and used the bathroom and kitchen on the nights she didn't want to drive back into Santa Barbara. It had only been a month since Rashidi Ali, the Black Student Union and United Front leader, had been arrested and the Chicago Eight lawyer Bill Kunstler had flown in with Abbie Hoffman's wife to give a speech that riled up the students. After they left, Seven watched as the Bank of America burned to the ground. Students had roasted hot dogs and marshmallows, waiting for the police and lockdown that must follow, hotly discussing whether or not revolution had to be violent. Ray had seen three guys who didn't look like students pour gasoline from canisters already there. When the fire ignited, he'd tried to follow them, but there were too many people rushing around, cheering, tipping over a police car.

The vigil over the burning bank had lasted deep into the night, marijuana wafting over the unreal scene of war come home to roost. All the next day, the Bank of America smoldered into smoke and ash while Isla Vista was ominously silent and rumors flew—the

pigs would torch Isla Vista when night fell, professor
Bill Allen, already censured by the Board of Trustees,
would be blamed for the fire, and on and on. Ray was
his teaching assistant. Seven had walked around with
Ray while he made inquiries.

Exhausted when night finally fell, she had crept
into her bus to sleep. Hours later, National
Guardsmen had torn her from her sleep slamming
her up against her bus while they searched it. Shouts
and the sounds of rotors assaulted her ears, and the
night sky was filled with helicopters and searchlights,
a loudspeaker shouting, "All right, you fucking
assholes, everybody out. We're going to find you, you
bastards, and tie you up by your balls . . ." A giant
garish light was mounted on a tank rumbling down
the street. Hundreds of soldiers in gas masks with
bayonets on their rifles and grenades hanging from
their belts were everywhere. Apartment after
apartment was shredded. Later, Ray said he'd
foolishly told the FBI about the three pyros and they
hadn't even seemed surprised but became more
interested in him.

But all that seemed a long time ago in the Source
bristling with activity, the Moody Blues singing—

> *Timothy Leary's dead*
> *No no no no, he's outside looking in . . .*
> *Along the coast you'll hear them boast*
> *About a light they say that shines so*
> *   clear*
> *So raise your glass we'll drink a toast*
> *To the little man who sells you thrills*
> *   along the pier . . .*
> *He'll glide his astral plane*
> *Take you trips around the bay*
> *Bring you back the same day*

69

Young women with babies on their hips and small children clinging to their long skirts were furrowing their brows over bulk grain bins, organic vegetables, and shining California fruits while their hippie men lounged outside around the picnic tables, smoking Drum mixed with marijuana, catching up on the news of the continuing curfew and National Guard perimeter, waiting for their women to finish shopping and join them for a big garden salad and chapatis smeared with miso and peanut butter, stuffed with brown rice and pinto beans, topped with melted cheese, tamari, cayenne, and brewer's yeast, all cheap and plentiful and healthy, vegetarian peasant food loaded up with rich condiments paid for by food stamps. They ate what their bodies told them to eat because happy bodies meant happy minds free of the gluttonous meat industry that was even importing beef from Costa Rica for fuck's sake because America couldn't produce enough for its fast-food, fast-road mania for feed-lot burgers and steaks loaded with steroids making the cancer that profited the medical and pharmaceutical industries. The cutting edge of an entire generation had discovered something too simple for mainstream America: just eat the grain directly and leave eating the animal that ate the grain out of the equation. Low on the food chain, man, while the Third World these white middle-class rebels idealized were thrilled when they saw McDonald's and Burger King opening in their countries. To these thin explorers of consciousness, redressing the bad national karma of slaughterhouses began with aligning food with international brothers and sisters who had been and were still being robbed and raped and dominated by colonizing carnivores. And yet Ray had sneered when Seven insisted that food was more Marxist than theory.

Then there was the radical act of robbing the robber-baron culture of their labor. They would not work for war nor eat the food of war nor espouse the values or beliefs of war, and if they couldn't help the twist of fate that had made them white and American, at least they could sit at the table with the rice-eating poor whose brown and yellow and black skin was tribute enough to the Earth's nonviolent bounty. That their unpolished unprocessed grains were purchased with government food stamps and grown in the oil barons' Texas Panhandle were ironies that eluded them like a fart on the wind or a politician's promise, nor did it dampen their self-righteous, mythic sense of solidarity with the poor. For them, food stamps and welfare ripped off the System and like a slow tide would eventually magically wear away the rocky shoals of greedy, rapacious capitalism. The less revolutionary truth was that they were post-war babies accustomed to being handed everything and may indeed have discovered free-from freedom but hadn't yet discerned how it differed from free-to freedom.

Seven had compassion for food stamp and welfare hippies with children, but Ray didn't. Both he and Seven demanded of their radicalism that they pull their own weight, though Seven made exceptions, like the grueling State of California abortion she had when she first struck the West Coast. She admired Ray for trying to build a revolution, especially given the holier-than-thou pleasure addicts like Aaron who preferred acid and dope and a welfare check over the labor of plowing through *Das Kapital* and getting a degree or two. Ray maintained that the only thing that could save honkies and blacks from capitalism's sickness was real work, whether of the head or body or both, not waiting for Uncle Sam to buy your Third World food for you so you wouldn't have to taint yourself with the compromises that living in America constantly required. This was why hippies were despised by the very people they wanted solidarity

71

with. Ray had two advantages over them: he was from a real blue-collar single-parent family, and he was black.

Seven splurged on a black cherry yogurt and listened vaguely as talk moved from the Bank of America to how a year had passed since the oil spill in Santa Barbara Channel, when they had walked the beach with candles, playing a dirge on their drums and flutes, stopping before each little clot of crude oil like blood on the shore to curse Exxon, Texaco, Gulf, Chevron, Mobil, Shell, and British Petroleum, the Seven Sisters of greed. The young men's minds worked over possible connections between the Skull & Bones flag that Texaco flew over its headquarters and the Chicago Eight trial, the Kennedy and King deaths, Vietnam and the Golden Triangle, the bad acid and heroin suddenly so plentiful and cheap on the streets of San Francisco and LA. Power was an octopus, man, with its tentacles everywhere. Yeah, but even an octopus has only one head. What or who could that one head be? The Pentagon sending 17-year-olds to the psychedelic hell of Vietnam? Nixon? Kissinger? Shit, they were all cut out of the same polyester, like the president of Union Oil who said he didn't like to call the oil spill a disaster because, after all, no human lives had been lost, and what was all the fuss over a few birds, anyway? *A few birds,* they sneered, smoking and grumbling, waiting for their old ladies. Seven asked after Ray but no one had seen him.

After shopping, she set out back along Hollister Road where a squat little Indian woman flagged her down. When she pulled over and opened the passenger door, the tiny woman climbed in, turning her broad brown face smiling a big toothy smile toward Seven. She looked more Mongolian than either Ghost Bear or Raven, and her dress was little more than feathers and what looked like bird skins. Seven had never known a Native American in her life and now she had met three in two days.

"Where are you going?" she asked, smiling back.

The grinning little woman struck her chest. *"Chupu. Wot Chumash,"* she announced proudly, nodding toward the road ahead. So Seven drove on, watching out of the corner of her eye as the *chupu* woman took up the flute hanging from around her neck, shut her eyes, and began to play.

Seven knew the word *Chumash.* California had incorporated many Chumash names: Matilija, Ojai, Sisquoc, Lompoc, Malibu. This old woman's people had once numbered in the thousands from Malibu Canyon to Morro Bay—peaceful, well off, with an advanced system of trade and taxation between Alta and Baja California. Even the Mojaves had traveled hundreds of miles from the Colorado River to trade fruits of the earth for those of the sea. Salinans, Yokuts, Tubatulabal and Kitanemuk, Alliklik and Shoshonean Gabrieliño had swapped white pigment for black, abalone for antelope, shell beads for *piñon* nuts, ironwood for soapstone. Of them all, the coastal Chumash had been the richest, attested to by the rings of clamshell money necklaces they wore, fashioned by artisans deft at drilling tiny holes with sea lion whiskers and stringing them with gut. Seven stole another glance; the old woman wore such a necklace. Chumash artisans had painted, sculpted, and built 30-foot *tomols,* seaworthy pine-flanked canoes found only in California and southern Chile among the Araucanian Indians.

The flute music sounded remarkably Celtic and melodic. The flute looked to be made of bone. Seven suddenly remembered an anthropology professor saying that the last full-blooded Chumash had died in the 1950s.

A wave of nausea passed over her as something hard gave way in her chest. She kept driving but in a daze, the music boring into her. Pictures rose and fell before her mind's eye—the Eagle and Sun in the East, Coyote and Morning Star in the West. *Life is a circle, the music sang, an eddy upon Alampauwauhani the Abyss. Human souls are the stars winnowed at night by the winds of cosmic war up and down the star ladder, while here on Earth, Xolotol the Death Dog and his eight brothers run wild, Plague, Earthquake, Drought, Famine, Incest, Insanity, War, and Betrayal. Here the fragile soul fights to escape the chaos left in the wake of each night's battle so as to grow wise as a serpent and discern god from god, until the veiled language of the Great Plumed Serpent is again unlocked. Arise, stars strewn among these hills and mountains, valleys and forests! Arise! Chinigchinich comes again!*

Music poured from the flute and Seven drove. The *chupu* woman pointed at Seneq Peak and stopped playing long enough to say, "*Asiqutc.*" Movie star governor Ronald Reagan had sent the National Guard to Isla Vista and would buy a big ranch on Seneq Peak four years later.

Up the narrowing road toward Painted Cave Seven drove, the flute music in charge. Suddenly, a mule deer bounded into the road and she braked, his 10-point antlers wide and still as a tree. He stood in the middle of the road and stared at them, his face strangely round and brown, then bounded up the bank and looked back before disappearing into the brush.

"*Sa'alahsaiyai!*" the *chupu* woman cried delightedly, gesturing toward the disappearing buck as she opened the passenger door and got out.

Groceries and Rhea and Barbara forgotten, Seven too got out, vaguely wondering how the bus had tilted itself on the edge of the road. Like a sleepwalker, she

74

hurried after the spry old woman up the embankment in the mule deer's wake and into the brush over lichen-covered rocks, through scrub oak and ferns, her breath laboring in the thick, resistant air, her feet like lead. A sudden mist made everything slow, every step a giant's feat. The breath in her ears sounded like someone else's. The old woman was out of sight and Seven was following the melody.

> *One day in the forest, the bird Elepaio appeared and called out to her from amongst the leaves. Elepaio's notes made words in her mind:* Wend to Wai-a-hao, wend, where the fish is fine and the fruit. *To her attendant she said, "Is it a bird calling?" And her attendant said, "Oh, it is a branch scratching against a branch, or the wind going amongst the leaves." Again the notes of Elepaio made words in her mind,* Ye mists that creep toward the uplands, ye mists that creep toward the sea, come!

A terrible clacking and roaring assaulted Seven's ears, like bullroarers and ten thousand insects scraping their legs together. The *chupu* woman appeared ahead, then melted away again. Arduously, Seven pulled her way up through the undergrowth, drowning in the thick moist air, an animal crouching in her chest, its breath keeping time to the buzzing and clacking and roaring growing louder, the breath belonging to another, something she could not see.

The *chupu* woman came in sight, perched on a ladder descending into a *temescal* sunk into the earth where, Seven uncannily knew, others were waiting. The melody continued beneath the deep drone of the bullroarers, but it was no longer coming from the old woman's flute. Around her, she saw a dozen or more round houses with thatched roofs of tule, carrizo grass, wild alfalfa, and fern. Children playing shinny paused to stare at her. Women in antelope skirts with magpie and roadrunner feathers in their hair pounded abalone and ground seeds and acorns for *pinole*. One was mixing Jimson weed with hot water for *toloache*. How did she know all of this? She looked over her shoulder, but the thick mist had cut off any exit. She didn't belong here, and yet she had been called.

The bullroarers stopped as the woman preparing the *toloache* handed a gourd to the *chupu* woman.

"*Xihuiqui nican!*" the old woman commanded.

Seven obeyed and began her descent on the ladder into a darkness filled with hissing and spitting steam. Already, her lips and lungs were burning.

Tiny Chumash men sat around the perimeter of the underground circular chamber playing whistles, rattles, clapsticks, and bone flutes to the resolute rhythm. No one looked at Seven or the *chupu* woman. Stones glowed in the fire pit. Across the chamber was a *sipapu,* a two-foot-square window framing the cool blackness of Earth. Seven's stomach lurched as she looked at it. Instinctively, she turned to ascend, but the *chupu* woman was already undressing her, lathering her with soap plant bulb and crushed ceanothus blossoms, scraping her skin with a sweat stick made from the jaw of a porpoise, rinsing her with cool water. While she worked, she grinned and sang.

Purified at last, Seven drank the bitter *toloache,* shuddering. The fear that had gripped her gut softened and drifted away. Now seemingly far below, the old woman was painting something on her palm. Then, stroking Seven's hair like a mother, she led Seven to the *sipapu.* A cool underground breeze wafted over her. *Alampauwauhani, alampauwauhani,* she heard again and again, and was hoisted up and through the window into blackness.

5
Chindi Witchery

The glacier knocks the cupboard,
The desert sighs in the bed,
And the crack in the teacup opens
A lane to the land of the dead.

> - W.H. Auden, "As I Walked Out One
> Evening," 1937

Night after night, old Seven threaded her way along interstates and highways, holding fast to the trail of history, locating out-of-the-way campsites and landmarks, keeping her eyes on the luminous river of ghosts pouring past her like a terrestrial Milky Way. Despite the fact that Celilo Falls had been inundated in 1960 by the Dalles Dam, she stood on the basalt bluffs above and watched Indian phantoms dip-net fish in the water below. In the phantom world there was no Dalles Dam, just young brown men fishing for salmon at the Cascades Portage and women scaling and drying fish, singing salmon songs, strands of brass beads sparkling around their necks like loons. Everywhere along the Trail, she read messages left for family and friends, bits of ribbon and cloth pinned to trees and brush, names carved into rock, codes like *GTT*, gone to Texas so the law won't get me. Tacked to a Sierra pine was, *President Lincoln has been assassinated.*

Over the years, ghosts had become as normal for Seven as night itself. After her California initiation, the parallel ghostly world had faded in and out like bad reception or *pentimento* beneath the thick pigment of daily life, an abandoned city beneath its

77

modern, bustling clone, there and yet not there, a holographic *maya*. Had the initiation somehow triggered all that happened after they left Santa Barbara for Dallas? Thomas' explanations of quantum physics made the presence of phantoms seem less mystical, and slowly over Time the world had revealed itself to be a great electromagnetic preserve housing both fantastic creatures and a multilayered diary or museum or library inscribed by everything and everyone that had ever been and perhaps would ever be. The Book of Life was no metaphor.

Over time, Seven had grown adept at relaxing while paying attention so the doors of perception would fly open and reveal the 3D tableau of each kingdom of Nature and super-Nature with its own peculiar, exquisite signature of *light*. Creatures great and small crept forth. To Seven, human light was the most beautiful of all, complex and multilayered, each layer encompassing the light of other kingdoms like a fugue. Each human ghost also retained its unique cast, a species unto itself.

It took years to sort it all out, not just one signature of light from another but the multitudes of presenting new categories. Infrared film could discern some, but what was this kingdom of crawling, zooming, and oozing shapes like inhuman phantasms from medieval paintings and bad acid trips? At first, she had thought she was hallucinating, but no, there they were, thick as thieves in some places, some as benign as Casper the Friendly Ghost, others distorted, malign, and voracious, for whom human fear was a particular delicacy, all coveting the energy of strong human emotions, all offering a whole new frequency subtext to the neat model of heaven, purgatory, and hell.

Thomas explained that matter had an antimatter and space had a counterspace lying beyond, beneath, within, or behind the kingdoms of nature and seeming density of the world. Both antimatter and counterspace were populated by inhabitants not limited to material bodies, and able to take on shapes and sizes (form) according to frequencies. They perceived themselves to be the *true* inhabitants of the Earth, living *in* the planet and its atmosphere and not just *on* it, requiring neither sunlight nor air nor any materiality whatsoever, excepting plasma, the gaslike ionized substance. They were *conscious*, Thomas assured her, and moreso than humans in some ways, due to not being burdened by material bodies. What they lacked was any moral sensibility whatsoever.

At first, Seven trembled when she caught a glimpse of them grazing on the light locked in animal or human bodies. They grazed everywhere, passing effortlessly in and out of bodies, even trees. Like the ghosts of the dead, they were acutely aware of Seven, and when they crawled or floated or flew by in their strange UFOs, they would slow down to coldly behold her humanness, perhaps checking one last time for an ingress. It was startling to look into acutely aware *inhuman* eyes, and yet early on she intuited that she, the conscious human being, was in command. When they approached her by dream or thought, she made sure to compliment them on their brilliant and analytical intelligence, not dwelling on how narrow and cold it was, nor how she preferred the imperfect warmth of human consciousness. Had she been less firm, they would have set to grazing on her, but as it was they had no access. One evening, while meditating on Grünewald's painting *St. Anthony's Temptation*, she realized that these phantom creatures could not touch truly Christ-filled human beings.

She walked through phantom rain drifting earthward in sheets and evaporating before it hit the ground. In late autumn, snow began to fall, so dry that a hundred inches equaled just an inch of rain. Static electricity bounced between the horns of phantom cattle. Ghostly stagecoaches thundered by, their horses' chafed mouths so close Seven could hear phantom teeth rattling against the bits. Phantom frames of freight and mail wagons lay like castaways beside the rib cages and hollow-eyed skulls of horses and oxen. Pony Express riders hurried west with messages. Pack horses and mules, Mormon handcarts, Confederate Army stragglers, wild mustangs, all running and plodding and walking and riding and stumbling west all night long, every night until dawn, like some great Egyptian exodus.

Everywhere were trailside graves, some with phantom headstones, others with a hasty cairn or cross bound with colored yarn like a God's eye. Most of the ghosts took no notice of her as they flowed past her, perhaps seeing her as one of their own. Now and then, one stopped to ask, *Is it true there ain't no snow out in California, and you can just throw out a handful of seed and it'll grow year round?* or *Is it true that the soil in Oregon is so black it ain't got no bottom?* A freed slave stopped to ask if it was true that George Washington Bush, an ex-slave and trapper, hadn't been allowed into Oregon because he wasn't white, and did she think they might turn him away, too? A little Irish girl told her she'd been sold for debt to a family coming West but had died falling out of their wagon during a snowstorm and was run over by the wagon behind before anybody took notice.

More and more tremors from west to east rippled beneath her feet, reminding her that her dream was true and she must hurry.

Outside of Pendleton on the Umatilla Reservation, she had visited with Cayuse, Umatilla, and Walla Walla elders who had known Ghost Bear. One of the grandchildren had seen him in a dream a few years back, but that was all the news she'd been able to glean. They'd brought out some tasty deer stew and fry bread and then guided her to the Nix Ya Wii (Place of the Quaking Aspens) Warriors Memorial where a Cayuse medicine woman was fasting and praying beside the Wallula Stone, a six-ton basalt rock that had been watching over her people for 15,000 years.

Kennewick Man's spirit had come to the Stone and told her how his 9,300-year-old bones had been stolen from at the University of Washington Burke Museum in Seattle by soldiers with faces painted black and triangles on their chests, and that they'd substituted another skeleton. His *Caucasian* bones with red-gold hair still on the skull had been found in July 1996 in the Columbia River shallows of Kennewick, Washington. The Yakima, Nez Perce, Colville, and Wanapum joined the Confederated Tribes of the Umatilla Indian Reservation (Cayuse, Umatilla, Walla Walla) in rallying around the NAGPRA law of 1990 (Native American Graves Protection and Repatriation Act) that allowed excavators only 48 hours to uncover, photograph, and measure skeletons. But scientists representing the Ásatrú Folk Assembly believing in *metagenetics* of related peoples filed suit to allow extensive research on Kennewick Man. From DNA analysis of a tiny sliver of bone, the Bering Strait emigration theory was used to make Kennewick Man into an Ainu. Then Senator John McCain, the Arizona Republican chairing the Senate Indian Affairs Committee, introduced Senate Bill 536 to change the definition of Native American to *of, or relating to, a tribe, people, or culture that is, or was, indigenous.*

While the argument over SB 536 continued well into 2010, Kennewick Man's bones had been quietly removed from Seattle to a secret city under the desert in the Southwest. The Cayuse medicine woman described the sign she had seen when Kennewick Man's spirit had flown hers down there to see—

81

Nellis Bombing and Gunnery Range
RESTRICTED AREA
NO TRESPASSING BEYOND THIS POINT
WARNING
U.S. Air Force Installation

She said she saw *chindi* men in white coats shaving
slivers of bone from Kennewick Man and putting
them into silver machines to make his body over
again, *chindi* witchery that had been going on for
years with extinct animals and dead bodies, even
mixing men with animals. The old Cayuse woman
sighed. Because of all the witchery, Earth Mother
would now take back Her ancient son's bones and
much else that had been stolen.

Mene mene tekel, Seven thought as she listened.
During King Belshazaar's feast so long ago, the words
had written themselves on the wall, foretelling the
end of the Babylonian Empire. Vince told her that
Mene mene tekel u-pharsin in the older language of
Mayan was *Mane mane tec uppah,* Thou hast been
weighed and found wanting. Swiftly wilt thou be
broken in two, parceled out not to the Persians but to
merchants and moneylenders, profane *nouveau riche*
who choose dollar signs over signs from God. America
would now have to answer the haunting Renaissance
question, *What is the role of free will in a divinely
ordained world? Man in the image of God, or man as
god?* She could still see Hermano looking up at the
stars and musing, "Whoever wrote *The Tempest* saw
the writing on the wall, tolled the death knell, and
never wrote again."

Beside the Wallula Stone, Seven recounted her
dream about the wall of water and the rest of the
evening was devoted to working out her dream and
the old Cayuse medicine woman's vision, both having
taken place in the Northwest.

"Surely the Cascades would hold off a great wave," one elder said, speaking the worry in everyone's mind.

"But what about the old Wasco story of Plain Feather?" another elder countered. "He disobeyed his guardian Great Elk by killing more than he needed, then even wounded his guardian and tracked his blood all the way to the Lake of the Lost Spirits, where Great Elk lay in the shallows. They both sank, and when Plain Feather awoke, he was surrounded by the dead moaning in terrible pain. 'Draw him in,' 'Draw him in,' and finally a third time, 'Draw him in and cast him out.' The law is firm: lose your guardian spirit and you wander in the land of the dead forever."

The elders' wives brought more food, after which Seven curled up and catnapped while the others continued to hash over the dreams. By the time she awoke, they had decided to ask a Wasco brother to join them in an immediate pilgrimage to the Lake of the Lost Spirits where they would inquire of Mount Hood what they should do. If a wave was coming, many would have to evacuate to higher ground.

At dusk, she set out southeast along Interstate 80, heading for Idaho, picking her way off road. The 19-year silent war begun by Clinton/Gore on January 20, 1997 had come to an end in 2017. Now, one of two signs put out by the International Union for Conservation of Nature (IUCN) was posted on all public lands—

PROJECT WILDLIFE CORRIDOR
Wildlands Buffer Zone
This is your world –
Care for it.
- IUCN Directive

PROJECT WILDLIFE CORRIDOR

Wildlands Core Zone
Pristine
Ancient
Nature
Commune with PAN.

- IUCN Directive

Congress never passed the Global Biodiversity
Assessment, but so what? All 1,140 pages of it
outlined national policies that would implement the
UN Convention on Biodiversity presented at the 1992
Earth Summit in Rio de Janeiro, virtually abolishing
private property rights and committing one-half of
CONUS landmass to a biodiversity preserve under the
Wildlands Project—in other words, a vast eco-park for
the global green elite. In the guise of liberal
"sustainable development," the 42nd President
granted the IUCN diplomatic immunity from all the
lawsuits that followed from people being forced off
their land. In the thousands of pages of *Sustainable
America: A New Consensus*, the masses
("overpopulation") were blamed for global warming
and pollution. Those who saw through the ruse were
deemed right-wing nuts.

Protected areas—wilderness, national parks,
wildlife refuges—now included small private
properties that had once belonged to thousands now
evicted with partial financial compensation.
"Bioregional management" had merged with law and
military enforcement and was the new feudal fiefdom
under the "bioregional councils" that appointed the
governors of FEMA's ten CONUS regions. The
President's Council on Sustainable Development
("reinventing government") picked up the land that
the Environmental Protection Agency and
Department of the Interior didn't. Scientists and
resource managers ran the strange global-local brew

of state, county, and federal workers for whom constitutional law was now historical.

National borders were disappearing, all in the name of bioregionalism. Sovereignty was passé under the centrally planned global economy. Under the North American Cooperative Security Act, Mexico and Canada would bring North American bioregions to 21. UN-accredited councils reported to the Petitions Council under the IUCN. In the name of gender equity and economics, the family was dismantled. War, weather engineering, and poverty were quietly reducing population while a pre-industrial standard of living had been foisted onto those who managed to escape the reduction. By 2050, the population would be "stabilized" at nine billion. While UN visions of a new world order were being cobbled together, societies were being carved up for corporate gods under the vast canopy of trade blocs superseding nation states.

Rolling her eyes over another one of the signs, Seven shifted from contemplating the brave new world to staring through the *sipapu* window framing the old *chupu* woman's face like a portrait on the wall of Time. She remembered the *ocote* fatwood torches illuminating the stream at her feet and the glow of a telluric current winding along the underground streambed. She heard again the clacking and bone flutes as she walked upstream, feeling but not seeing large wings sweeping over her head. *Tzopelote the condor,* a little voice clarified, *your guardian scouting ahead so the Dark Lords or their ajmotocnihuan minions won't eat your heart.* At the brush of Tzopelote's dark wing, she did begin to *see,* really *see,* and the first thing she *saw* was a shadow tethered to her body, gliding in front of her through the subterranean land of dusk and dawn, guiding her ever southward.

85

She intuited that she had walked these recesses of America before but had doubted her intuitions. Not even her *roma* blood had saved her from years of denial. Why had the old Chumash woman brought her there? *You are necessary to the Great Work,* Hermano had said. She remembered looking down at her palm where the *chupu* woman had painted a four-petal dogwood blossom and glimpsing little Lilya sitting in a wooden chair in the East Detroit kitchen, swinging her legs, watching and listening to her *roma* grandmother stir *chocana* on the stove, inhaling the double elixir of stew and the story of Queen Mu and her brother-husband Prince Coh, the beloved king stabbed in the back by his own brother, the jealous Aac. *And Queen Mu fled east to her Mayan colonies on the banks of the Nile where she was called little sister or Isis,* her *roma* grandmother had recounted. How had she known that story?

The kitchen disappeared and the stream had hardened into an asphalt street lined with palm trees and glowing street lamps, a street sign reading, *Fifth Helena.* The shadow led her up a walkway to a Spanish-style bungalow with bougainvillea dripping from the lintel. Three men in suits had hurried past her, unseeing. On a shallow stone wall she read, *CURSUM PERFICIO,* I complete the race. The front door was ajar.

Inside, a calendar on the wall read *Saturn's Day, August 4, 1962.* A statue of a slender Egyptian woman with a cow's head and horns stood in the hallway, her stone mouth saying, *Hail, Isis!* On a big-screen color television in the adjacent living room, Elizabeth Taylor dressed as Cleopatra triumphantly entered Rome with seven thousand Catholic Italian extras crying, "Liz! Liz! *Baci, baci!"*

Continuing down the hall, Seven had passed a laundry room where the housekeeper was bent over a washing machine. Further along was a sparse bedroom with little more than a bed, a night table, and a lamp. A man in a shimmering green suit was bending over a platinum-blond woman sprawled on the bed, her arms streaked blue. The green man turned and smiled unctuously at Seven. *He is evil and can see you,* the little voice said. She watched him withdraw a needle from the woman's chest and calmly wipe it off. Phantoms drifting around the bed whispered, *Norma Jeane from the Los Angeles Orphans Home!* Hiram "Hank" Williams was there, Robert Johnson, Buddy Holly, the Big Bopper, and Ritchie Valens. Hank was singing the last lyrics he ever wrote, found on a scrap of paper clutched in his hand when he was peeled out of the wreckage of his 1952 Cadillac convertible—

> *We met, we lived, and dear we loved,*
> *Then comes that fatal day,*
> *I love you still and always will,*
> *But that's the poison we must pay . . .*

James Dean and Elvis Presley joined the vigil, then Lenny Bruce and Jane Mansfield. Brian Jones was there, Janis Joplin, Jimi Hendrix, Jim Morrison, along with Cass Elliot, John Lennon, Bob Marley, Jerry Garcia, Tammy Wynette . . . John Lennon leaned toward Seven and whispered, *Some of us are dreaming, but we'll all be like Norma Jeane soon.*

The shimmering green man snapped his deathbag shut and strolled out without even glancing at Seven. Elvis brushed a peroxided curl from Norma Jeane's childlike face and Janis Joplin said sadly, *They called me Pearl.*

Then Norma Jeane's eyes opened and looked at Seven, the dead lips saying, *The sons of Sam are out back having a Southern-style barbeque.*

With those words, Seven felt as if she were being pulled on a conveyor belt out of the bedroom and down the hall toward the back of the bungalow and "the sons of Sam." *Did she mean Sam Giancana, her mafioso lover some said was involved in the Kennedy brothers' assassinations, or Uncle Sam the government?*

The hallway was a thick magnetic field as difficult to navigate as the Moon. She felt like she was space-walking in a pressurized suit and weighted shoes, tethered to *terra firma* by the flimsiest of umbilici. If she'd known that she was about to encounter Baby Rose, it all would have made more sense.

6
Baby Rose

*The state of the brain continues the remembrance;
it gives it a hold on the present by the materiality
which it confers upon it: but pure memory is a
spiritual manifestation. With memory, we are in
very truth in the domain of the spirit.*

- Henri Bergson, *Matter and Memory*, 1896

How long she wandered in the *chupu* woman's
world before awakening in the cave on Painted Cave
Road was hard to say. She blinked. Above her on the
cave ceiling were four horsemen on white, red, black,
and transparent horses. Immediately, she thought of
And an old white horse galloped away in the meadow
by the American poet who had fled America for
England.

Standing up, she staggered, tentatively feeling for
her face, almost afraid it wouldn't be there. Hovering
near the horsemen was a huge bird woman with
breasts, wings, and spiky feathers. Primitive
drawings and paintings of people who had been
having visions for millennia surrounded her: a black
disc surrounded by an aureole of white, a comet with
a long streaking tail, a man with a deer's head, a fish
with a human face, geometric shapes, caterpillar-like
creatures with big eyes swimming through the air . . .

She stumbled out of the cave into the dry grass.
Day was in decline, but still she didn't know how far
she had fallen out of Time nor how she'd ended up in
the cave. She followed the cord of a dusty trail
winding through the rocks. When she passed what
appeared to be desolate ruins of a village, she

remembered in a flash the *temescal* into which she'd descended. The line between past and present, between one reality and another, was still thin. Seeing something move in an old burial ground out of the corner of her eye, she started. The Chumash had cremated their dead so their hearts could return to Chinigchinich. The people's hearts roamed the hills and valleys they had loved, but the chief's heart became a star.

At Painted Cave Road, she searched the deepening blue for Venus, first star of the night, the word *sacred* suddenly palpable. Miraculously, her bus was sitting where she'd left it. Still, nothing was the same. The door handle felt strange, but once the engine started up, she had no trouble driving. When she turned off of Painted Cave Road and onto Highway 154, she saw a towhead barefoot girl in a torn mini-slip staggering along the road.

Hesitant but concerned, Seven slowed down to call out the passenger window, "Need a ride?" But the girl kept stumbling along as if she didn't hear and had walked too far to care.

Seven pulled over and got out to stand in the girl's path. She couldn't have been more than seventeen. Her face, arms and legs were bruised and scratched, and her upper lip crusted with blood from her nostrils. She looked fearfully over her shoulder, whimpering like a terrified animal, some of her long hair matted with dried blood. Gently, Seven took her by the hand. "Come with me where you'll be safe." She helped her into the back of the bus where she curled up on the bed, trembling like a rabbit. Seven covered her and in seconds she was asleep.

Between 154 and Hillside Drive, Seven must have seen half a dozen police cars. Rhea would know what to do; she and Ted had been on FBI lists for years for having artist friends.

It was deep dusk when she pulled into Rhea's. Leaving the girl asleep, she got out and looked for the groceries. Where were they?

Rhea was in the kitchen. The homely smells and sounds of dishes clattering and television in the family room were a welcome relief; it felt like a hundred years since she'd been there. Busy cleaning up, Rhea explained that Aaron had picked up Barbara and the children hours ago but she'd saved a little dinner for her in the oven.

Seven's eyes were on the jar of sunflower oil on the table. Her tongue thick in her mouth, she mumbled, "Did . . . Barbara get her groceries?"

Rhea looked up. "Oh yes, they were on the table when we finished our session, with the food stamps on top. We figured you'd dropped them off, then gone. Seemed a little weird, but the radio was on and . . ."

Seven didn't hear anymore. The Prince of Cats was watching her closely. *I am the Past, the Present, and the Future, no mortal hath yet lifted my veil.* From the sunflower oil, she moved her eyes to the large in-progress painting of Barbara.

Both Barbara and Rhea would be dead in a matter of months.

Rhea left the sink and frowned into her face. "Are you all right? You don't look so good."

Seven shrugged, taking her dinner out of the warming oven. Everything was so *different.* She wanted to talk about the events of the afternoon, but she couldn't. Besides, Scorpio Rhea was not the one to tell. She was like the Scorpion Woman living on top of Scorpion Woman Peak, the one the Chumash said would meet them when finally it was their turn to take the Path of the Dead. Ted had come to terms with her double-edged nature and adored her for her passion, art, and dark beauty. He had learned to live with her *noli me tangere* brand of arm's-length love. Years later, he'd explained how he'd tried to get away

91

from her but found himself coming back again and again, like the men who keep returning to the desert or the sea.

Mina was slouched on the couch in the cluttered family room, thumb in her mouth, hypnotized by *The Prisoner*, one of the few television shows Rhea let her watch. Seven sat down next to her. Mina popped her thumb out and caught Seven up: The hero was Number 6, a British ex-secret agent abducted to a remote island run by a secret society called The Village. Rhea said secret agents never really quit, Mina went on excitedly, and that they're given three choices: to be *secret* secret agents for life, die, or end up in places like The Village for reconditioning.

> *Number 6:* *Where am I?*
> *Number 2:* *In The Village.*
> *Number 6:* *What do you want?*
> *Number 2:* *Information.*
> *Number 6:* *Whose side are you on?*
> *Number 2:* *That would be telling. We want information ... information!*
> *Number 6:* *You won't get it!*
> *Number 2:* *By hook or by crook, we will.*
> *Number 6:* *Who are you?*
> *Number 2:* *The new Number 2.*
> *Number 6:* *Who is Number 1?*
> *Number 2:* *You are Number 6.*
> *Number 6:* *I am not a number! I am a free man!*
> *Number 2:* *[Laughs]*

Mina whispered, "Number 6 doesn't know it but his dreams are being monitored by a machine that translates the electrical impulses of his brain into images, then reprocesses them and gives them new, brainwashed content. But Number 6 saw the needle marks on his arm and realized that he's being drugged, so he gets around his next dosage and confronts his controllers *in his dream state.*" Mina was gleeful. The hero was getting the better of his cybernetic masters.

Seven marveled at the plot's sophistication, like *Brave New World* and *1984* rolled into one—brainwashing and the far-out idea of confronting controllers in a dream state . . .

Some months before, Hugh "Wavy Gravy" Romney and his psychedelic Hog Farm Collective waifs had spent a few days with Rhea. Rhea loved it when Wavy Gravy dropped by. They'd laugh about the old days in Pasadena and she'd make sketches of his menagerie. One night after she'd gone to bed, they had toked up and watched *The Prisoner.* Stoned, they'd held forth on the revolution, sure that the pigs would lay down their arms, the Establishment crumble neatly like a house of cards, and the Age of Aquarius commence. The exact mechanics of how it would all go down were as hazy as the marijuana smoke. As soon as Wavy Gravy's psychedelic bus pulled out of the drive, Rhea would shake her head and say, "I love Hugh but I don't trust him farther than I can throw him. Look at all those drugs. Do you think for a minute the pigs would allow him to flaunt all of that if he wasn't somehow useful to them?"

Barbara and Seven secretly wondered if any of the old Beats—Romney, Kerouac, Burroughs, Ginsburg, Kesey, Cassady, even Rhea—could be trusted, or for that matter anyone over thirty.

Seven glanced at Mina. By the time Mina was her age, the television trance would be widespread. How brilliant to implant the future in the name of entertainment—as sinister as it was brilliant. Somewhere behind the dialogue and plot, in the shadows of CBS, were writers and producers with agendas extending far beyond good ratings. *Norma Jeane! Norma Jeane!* In her mind's eye, she still saw the tousled platinum-blond hair spilling over the bed. Suddenly surfacing in her mind was *a little Legong dancer lying at the foot of a tree with meek, bejeweled hands over her chest, around her grunting men in animal masks, three-piece suits, military Class A's . . .*

Where did that come from? Mina looked too much like the little Legong dancer and the girl asleep in her bus. Seven leaped up.

The girl was gone. Alarmed and irritated with herself for being so spacey, she scanned Hillside Drive, then circled the house to check the garden. It was cool, now that darkness was washing over the land. The Moon was arcing low, spreading a sheen over the dreaming vegetation. The Prince of Cats joined her, proud of the lizard squirming in his jaws. Seven smiled grimly; he might be a prince, but he was still a beast.

Another lifetime, surely not just hours ago, she had walked this same path. Somewhere, Crosby, Stills, Nash and Young were singing, *And we've got to get ourselves back to the garden.* Into the spiral she walked, trailing her hands through the moonlight, marveling at the soft green-white light emanating from everything. She looked up toward the tipis; Ray still wasn't home. Recalling the police cars, she wondered what was happening out at Isla Vista. *We are stardust, we are golden, we are caught in the devil's bargain.*

In the dark, pastels peeked electrically from sleeping petals. Had she seen these nuances of light before? She'd always loved the dark, from nestling into corners and closets in her grandmother's house to listen to daylight sounds like a detective, to catching fireflies in jars on her grandfather's farm to study their distress signals like Morse code, the signals growing weaker and weaker, knowing the fireflies were dying, seeing how close she could get to death, more often than not failing to recognize the exact moment . . .

Nearby, a childish voice was singing—

Ring-a-ring-a-rosies
A pocket full of posies
Hush! Hush! Hush! Hush!
We all fall down!

The girl was circling the tall night-blooming Cereus with its thick blue-green stalk all aglow, the blue roses below pulsing like little alien transmitters. The girl's hair shone silver in the moonlight. Hearing Seven's approach, she stopped singing.

"Remember me?" Seven asked gently. "I'm Seven, what is your name?"

Pointing to herself, the adolescent answered in a little girl's voice, "Baby Rose."

Was she mentally retarded?

"Remember when I picked you up on the road . . ."

The girl sank to the ground beside the glowing *Cereus* stalk like a puppet with cut strings. Seven sank beside her and hugged her, cursing her curiosity. No more questions tonight. She rubbed the thin arms and scanned the stars. Were the stars hollowed-out spaces? The Great Bear was rising, Ursa Minor was pointing the way to the Pole Star, the Moon was climbing to her zenith, God was in his heaven and all was right with the world—or was it?

"Ohhhh!" Baby Rose cried as she leaped up.

The night-blooming *Cereus* was preparing to give birth. Seven stood and touched the smooth blue-green stalk of the noble queen of cacti: the buds were opening. In the soft light, Baby Rose *was* the Legong dancer. Seven ran back along the spiral to the house to get Mina and Rhea. By the time they returned clutching blankets and pillows, Baby Rose was asleep again, curled around the *Cereus* stalk amongst the blue roses like a cabbage baby. As they too snuggled around the blooming stalk, Seven whispered the little she knew about Baby Rose and they wished that Barbara and the children could be there to watch the three white blossoms unfold in the starlight, illumined by a light all their own.

Seven stayed awake, promising to wake Rhea and Mina when the blooms were open. Musing on the story of another famous night garden scene, when Jesus spent his last night on Earth in the Garden of Gethsemane and his disciples, worn out by grief, fell asleep, she must have dozed, for she found herself under a sky streaked with the thick pigment of Van Gogh's suffering. A dogwood Cross of the World stretched from Earth to Heaven, the Ecliptic arcing through its branches. Nailed to the Ecliptic was a man, and beneath him a weeping woman in black kneeled. Every breath he breathed labored like a bellows, every drop of his sweat and blood was consumed by millions of tiny Earth mouths. She knew this place, this time, this dying man, and this woman on her knees at the base of the Wakah-Chan, but she resisted knowing. *No, not Him! Not Christianity with all its hypocrisy and cruelty! Do not tell me that the myth is true. Not Him . . .* Breathing his last, the man cried out and turned wearily toward her, pouring into her some sort of knowledge.

She awakened, her face tight with dried tears. The Great Bear had hardly moved, but the sweet, dizzying fragrance of three white saxophone-like blooms trumpeting to the heavens swept her to her feet.

"Wake up, they're here!"

Rhea, Mina, and Baby Rose stood to marvel at the three beauties for whom the Moon was their Sun. They breathed in the perfume again and again, rejoicing that the Earth was indeed a spiritual house behind whose doors dwelled many mysteries. Baby Rose and Mina held hands and spun around and around, singing *Ring-a-ring-a-rosies*, falling down and getting up and singing and falling down again, laughing and squealing. Finally, hand in hand, blankets trailing behind them, Mina and Baby Rose followed Rhea inside for sleep. Baby Rose needed a bath and rest for now; they would talk about what to do later.

Seven remained at the foot of the *Cereus*, inhaling its perfume again and again, touching the white wonders with trembling fingers. Thomas would have loved this nocturnal birth. While Mina and Baby Rose danced around the stalk like nymphs around a maypole, two feelings had pierced her: the mystery of the little Legong dancer image and a longing to see Thomas. Kissing each redolent blossom, she set out for his eyrie high in the hills.

7
Things Fall Apart
2019

*Airplanes, jets, and rockets were already
malfunctioning, crashing and exploding.
Electricity no longer obeyed the white man. The
macaw spirits said the great serpent was in
charge of electricity. The macaws were in
charge of fire . . . The macaws said the battle
would be won or lost in the realms of dreams,
not with airplanes and weapons.*

> \- Leslie Marmon Silko, *Almanac of the
> Dead*, 1991

*Everywhere predictions were being recited and
oracles being chanted by such persons as
collect them, and this not only in the
contending cities. Further, some while before
this, there was an earthquake at Delos, for the
first time in the memory of the Hellenes . . .*

> \- Thucydides (460-395 BCE)

*. . . Taken together, the prospects for space war
or 'cyberspace war' represent the truly
revolutionary potential inherent in the notion
of military transformation . . . [F]or the US
armed forces to remain preeminent and avoid
an Achilles Heel in the exercise of its power
they must be sure that these potential future
forms of warfare favor America just as today's*

air, land and sea warfare reflect United States military dominance.

- "REBUILDING AMERICA'S DEFENSES: Strategic Forces and Resources for a New Century" (RAD), Project for a New American Century (PNAC), 2003; after 9/11 rewritten as "National Security Strategy of the United States of America"

Making her way carefully along the outskirts of towns, old Seven sometimes lingered to hear news reports. Television, Internet, and radio were apparently down, so people with shortwaves were opening their doors and turning up the volume so neighbors could listen in, though even shortwaves were fading in and out. *Vancouver Island . . . Cape Mendocino, California . . . Chile . . . 319 years ago land from Neah Beach to Astoria sank under a wall of water 100 feet high . . . Long Beach . . . Willapa Bay . . .*
BBC reported high water in the Thames Gateway. *Dungeness and St. Mary-in-the-Marsh, gone,* a shortwave operator in a service station whispered.
"Serves them right," an old woman grumbled, "them and that 1783 Treaty of Paris. All them flags in our courts with gold fringe on them, most of our money gone to that Satanic British Crown all these years . . ."
But the words "Tsunamis generally follow a 500-year rhythm" sent a shaft of fear into every listener. "The great flood of January 1607, the BBC announcer was saying, may not have been caused by high tides and severe storms, but by a tsunami, which means we have had earthquakes here in the United Kingdom, due to an ancient but still active fault off southwest Ireland. 17th century eyewitnesses described huge and mighty hills of water advancing faster than a

99

greyhound can run and not receding for ten days. Deposits brought in from the open ocean at Cardiff's Rumney Wharf support this contention. Seven thousand years ago, a 70-foot wave hit Scotland . . ."

KBOO in Portland mentioned MIDAS, the Missile Alarm Defense System, making Seven wonder if the military was reading this cataclysmic weather as an attack. Had the 66 Iridium satellites in their pole orbit detected something in the magnetosphere? Had the Earth's magnetic field finally gone haywire, due to the HAARP weather warfare technology? Ionospheric disturbances could cause massive power blackouts.

". . . the Larsen Ice Shelf in Antarctica for 12,000 years . . . an intriguing mystery in the Arctic. Twenty years ago, we noticed melting around the edges, and yet nothing tied the ice loss to any man-made or natural global warming. The behavior of Atlantic currents is off, as well, and yet the US Navy's Scientific Ice Expeditions, SCICEX, which has sent research submarines under the icecap, won't release detailed Russian and US measurements of ice thickness made over the past seventy years due in part to continuing secrecy regarding acoustic signatures of specific American submarines . . . UFOs sighted again at Lake Jacqueline in Custer, Wisconsin . . ."

Was this then the fifth Earth cataclysm ending the Fifth Age of the Mayans? The first had been Hyperborea at the end of the 2nd root race; the second caused Lemuria to surface for the 3rd root race; the third came geologically from within Lemuria; and the fourth was Atlantis. All but the third were sidereal cataclysms. Was this one?

Speaking of Atlantis, Jacqueline Kennedy's New York apartment faced the glass-enclosed wing of the Metropolitan Museum of Art and stones stolen from the ancient Nubian Temple of Dendur south of Aswan. Once dedicated to Isis, Osiris, and of course

Harpocrates, the god of silence who became Horus, the temple stones had been lifted from Egypt in 1963, the year Jackie's Osiris was slaughtered in Dallas and hacked up en route to Washington, DC. Equally interesting was that the temple had been famed for its zodiac carving of the Earth's axis at an entirely different angle to its current position, and for the designs in subterranean chambers of what appear to have been electrical devices—snakes inside oblong tubes. Had one smart electromagnetic system crossed purposes with another, like Aegis destroyers hitting their own satellites?

Jackie kept *The Urantia Book* on her coffee table.

Now that televisions, cell phones, and computers were silent, people were seeking information from others. Schools were cancelled, so children were among the talking adults. Some adults still went to work but those whose jobs revolved around communications didn't. A Mexican woman recalled *dichos* to an Anglo neighbor she had not spoken to for months. Another woman told her grown son about a September 1997 earthquake in Italy that destroyed the upper St. Francis basilica but not the lower basilica that centuries before had been destroyed by yet another earthquake.

In a grocery store in a tiny mountain town, Seven skirted the closed-circuit camera at the checkout stand and made her way to the back of the store where people were listening to a shortwave, their shopping carts bulging with what they might need in the days to come, before everything ran out. ". . . Kashagan at the mouth of the Ural River dividing Europe from Asia . . " The geologist being interviewed was close to tears. "Emptying the oil and gas from the reservoirs under the Caspian Sea has triggered these devastating earthquakes!"

The shortwave operator edged the dial clockwise. ". . . upper atmosphere detonation of nuclear weapons in the 1950s and 1960s. Physicist Nicholas Christofilos of the University of California's Livermore Radiation Laboratory harnessed the energy released in hydrogen fusion reactions by using magnetic confinement fields. Speculating that an artificial radiation belt could be made intense enough to destroy satellites in orbit . . ."

The band faded so the operator continued dialing.

". . . where earthquakes hit, arcane mysteries buried will rise again. These are the end times . . ."

". . . and this happened just three or four years after HAARP went fully operational."

". . . While western Siberia has turned into a watery landscape of lakes due to an increase in average temperature of some 3° Celsius, in eastern Siberia thousands of lakes have disappeared." A man with a thick Russian accent spoke. "These are basically peat bogs filled with methane gas, 70 billion tons. If the bogs dry out, all is well. But if they remain wet, the methane will rise into the atmosphere . . ."

Had ionospheric heaters and CERN finally burned a hole in the ionosphere and thrown the magnetosphere into turmoil? Were solar winds blowing satellites out of the sky? Was the electric potential of the Poles shifting? The HAARP acronym had been well chosen: as the Earth rotated, HAARP pulsed each longitudinal magnetic string with harsh high and low frequencies out of harmony with the Schumann resonance. Perhaps more than a few strings had finally broken.

Two old-timers were talking. "Jim says the North Pole's about to flip. Molten iron in the Earth's core is shifting and triggering a switch. Magnetic reversal, they call it. Physicists of the Globe Institute in Paris and Danish Space Research Institute in Copenhagen say the molten iron at Cape Horn is already moving. Right, Jim?"

Jim the shortwave operator was deep in conversation with someone else. "I pick up the HAARP or Brookhaven transmissions at night bouncing off the F layer in the ionosphere. Two frequencies, 3.39 MHz and 6.99 MHz in a 6.25 second pulse with 15 to 30 seconds between. Sounds like a buzz saw. They've been making an awful racket the last few weeks. A lot of activity."

"You think that's what this is? The Poles flipping?" the second old-timer asked the first.

"You got me, Charlie, but it sure as hell ain't 'climate change.' If I hear that poor excuse for science one more time . . ."

A woman was saying to the man behind her, "I'll never forget July 15, 1982, when that rainstorm in northern Colorado was threatening the dams and that mine was detonated at the base of Lawn Lake Dam, and they blamed Russian weather modification. Estes Park flooded—my sister lived there . . ."

The man nodded. "World Commission on Dams should just decommission *all* the dams instead of lettin' the World Bank loan countries money to build more. Remember when hydroelectric power was going to solve all our energy problems? Foolin' with Mother Nature, that's what's brought this on, whatever it is. Can't leave well enough alone . . ."

". . . snowpack in the Sierras is twenty percent down and all we hear is water shortage like in Africa and India where those folks got no water rights left. Now they want to run ours. Well, just let them try to get a-hold of *my* well . . ."

The woman nudged him in the ribs. "But what about the Missouri? No snow pack in the Rockies and it's dryin' up. Thirty-nine of Montana's 52 rivers are dry. Nuclear plants don't have cooling water and can go to hell for all I care, but I *do* care about rivers and forests."

The water rights man's face reddened. "What's melting the Antarctic ice sheets is geothermal heat from the volcanoes under there."

Another old-timer said, "Well, if they're so goddamn smart, why not bring us a little rain and snow? A *little* rain, I said, not a flood to wash out the dams we're stuck with."

The water rights man said the word no one would say. "It's Armageddon."

The word sounded out over the gathering in one of those odd moments of silence in a talking room and sent a shiver up the collective spine. *Is this it, then?* everyone was thinking, wanting to laugh or shrug it off but unable to.

Tiberius Caesar saw flames and smoke over Ostia, not knowing it was only the aurora borealis. The night of October 8, 1871, when Mrs. O'Leary's cow supposedly burned down Chicago, firestorms were moving horizontally through the Northwest sky and laying forests flat.

Had the Moon been at perigee, and the Earth, Sun, and Moon in syzygy? Had the outer planets awakened the subterranean forces that command earthquakes and volcanic eruptions?

Repair my Earth. Tikkun olam.

During the San Francisco earthquake of April 18, 1906, Uranus and Neptune had been in opposition, Uranus in 15° Sagittarius, Neptune 14.5° Gemini. In 1991, 1992, and 1993, there were three earthquakes, all under Neptune and Uranus. In the Philippines, when Mt. Pinatubo erupted and vented 19 million tons of sulfur dioxide, Uranus was 18° Sagittarius, Neptune 21.5° Sagittarius. An undersea 6.8 earthquake in Indonesia caused tidal waves when Uranus was 22° Sagittarius and Neptune 23° Sagittarius. On Hokkaido, Japan, a 7.5 earthquake occurred when Mercury 25.5° Sagittarius was conjunct Uranus and Neptune 24° Sagittarius.

Sagittarius, the great bowman shooting his arrow into the center of the galaxy. Was the Earth undergoing a cosmic event, or manmade? Seven voted manmade and wondered how Thomas and Vince were viewing it.

Seven looked around, wondering when the fear would truly strike the American soul as it had in Mexico when the priests spilled all the blood they could to stave off the inevitable—first, people of light complexion, then thousands of captives, then their own blood. *Nenacazteco: auh in teteupan, susuchcuico, tlachalantoc: ic mitoaia, intla tlamiz, in qualo tonatiuh: centlaiooaz: oaltemozque, in tzitzitzimi, tequaquiui.* (It was thus said: If the eclipse of the sun is complete, it will be dark forever. The demons of darkness will come down and eat men.) Night and day, the temples had throbbed with chants while outside the war cries of fierce and hopeless men had flown into dark nothingness. What, who, could they fight? The demons of darkness, the eaters of men, were coming, to whom muscle and weapons meant nothing. Poseidon was coming to shake the Earth until teeth and bones rattled. St. Elmo's fire would lick the ground under their fleeing feet, demonic smells of sulfur, nitrogen oxide, and chlorine gas would burn in their wake.

". . . the Arctic ice-free by summer 2100 has infuriated Inuit hunters now complaining to the 34-member Organization of American States about HAARP and its microwave heaters percolating from Alaska up to the ionosphere and back. 'That's what's taking our livelihood,' an Inuit woman shouted into the microphone. 'This weather is the scientists' fault, not our cars! And they know it, but they're not telling us. The UN threatens us with droughts and floods and storms and says the melting icecaps will drive up the sea levels and swamp our coastal areas and low-lying islands. If that happens, HAARP did it, not climate

105

change. They're all in this together against us, the people . . .'"

The Inuit woman's speech moved listeners with its ring of truth. As the Canadian station faded, the operator moved the dial to *The Voice of Russia—*

Interviewer: This is Science and Engineering on the Voice of Russia. I have with me a plasma engineer to anonymously answer listener questions regarding the High-frequency Active Auroral Research Program in Alaska known as HAARP, an immensely powerful geophysical weapon whose objective is to influence the solid, liquid, and gas layers of the Earth for military purposes. How could such a microwave generator or plasma weapon be used in warfare?

Plasma engineer: First of all, let me say that geophysical weapons are far more powerful than nuclear weapons. That said, the HAARP generator would fire a plasmoid, a blob of plasma, into the path of an incoming missile, warhead or aircraft. By effectively ionizing that region of space, the aerodynamics of the flight of the missile, warhead or aircraft would be disturbed and its flight terminated. This makes such a generator and its plasmoid a practically invulnerable weapon... In 1993, at the Russian-American summit in Vancouver, the Russians proposed a joint experiment in testing such generators - or plasma weapons, as they are called here - as an alternative to the Strategic Defense Initiative, SDI. In such an experiment, to be code-named Trust, the system would be used to repulse a missile attack . . .

Interviewer: Could tectonic plates be moved dynamically if these scalar weapons were applied at resonant frequencies? And would this have anything to do with Project Vulcan?

Fade to white noise. "A lot of blocking going on," Jim explained, puzzled.

Vince had been right. Technical black magic rituals had enslaved and disgruntled the subterranean powers forced to drive elemental powers of air and water over and over to loose catastrophic weather. GWEN arrays and phased arrays had been disrupting the Earth's magnetic field for half a century, damaging bodies and brains, and exerting power over minds. The scales of justice would begin the rebalance with weather chaos, Vince said. An electromagnetic pulse would show up on weather radar maps as an anomaly, or a government test would go wrong and set off a chain reaction, or an EMP warhead like the Hermes II particle beam fusion accelerator used during the first Gulf War would send out RF shockwaves stacked on hundreds of 20-trillion-watt pulses lasting 20 billionths of a second and burn out one electrical system after another. A nuclear explosion 100 miles up could produce such an EMP and shut down power systems, destroy missile guidance systems, computers, and communication systems. Whatever the physical scenario, it would be Atlantis all over again. Hubris. Naughty, naughty child of Man.

Earlier, Seven had walked a short way with a middle-aged Balkan geologist who had come to America to hike a section of the famous Oregon Trail and muse on what America could have been. They'd compared anomalies in animal and bird behavior they were seeing. He said he'd heard that mice were drowning themselves by the hundreds of thousands in the steppes of northwest China, then joked about the American novelist Tom Robbins' Clock People in the Great Burrow. Seven asked what he thought of the catastrophic theory of Earth development.

"Oh, I am sure it has happened over and over again," he said. "Truthfully, I think the ice cap of the Ice Age is a professional lie. Certainly there was a magnetic *lurch* in the north that caused the oceans to slosh into the south. For days, not thousands of years, mountains of polar ice and rock tumbled southward, pulverizing everything over the mountainless plains of Western Europe, Canada, and the United States. Imagine the roar of such water! Then over thousands of years volcanic gas belts raised the surfaces into mountain ranges."

He laughed. "Had the Labrador Peaks towered 60,000 feet into the air, with an icecap of 20,000 feet, the mountains would have been fifteen miles high! No, the geological story of such an ice cap around the Northern Hemisphere down to the 40th parallel is simply not possible. There was a flood, certainly, but not an Ice Age. The proof lies in Siberia along the Lena River Valley and watershed. There it is evident that at the end of the Pliocene or beginning of the Pleistocene, between two and five million years ago, when the supposed ice cap of tens of thousands of feet was covering the northern part of the Northern Hemisphere, a flood from the *south* rolled north over the plains of Manchuria, Mongolia, and Siberia to the Arctic Ocean. Water at the same parallel as an ice cap? Hardly."

Then he had stopped. "The question is, why would intelligent men who know better want to deceive history in such a way? Surely I am not the only one who has discerned this far-fetched fabrication you still find as fact in textbooks."

After the geologist had gone his way, Seven had listened briefly to a silver-bearded prophet in clean jeans and a lumberjack shirt doing some street preaching in a tiny farm hamlet. A dozen or more anglos, Mexicans, and Shoshone had gathered to hear him out, now that everything was collapsing around them. His quote of I Kings 19, 11-12 sent shivers up her spine—

> *For the Lord was passing by: a great and strong wind came rending mountains and shattering rocks before him, but the Lord was not in the wind; and after the wind there was an earthquake, but the Lord was not in the earthquake; and after the earthquake, fire, but the Lord was not in the fire; and after the fire, a low murmuring sound. When Elijah heard it, he muffled his face in his cloak and went out and stood at the entrance to the cave.*

It had been 21 years since 1998, 666 x 3, when the Sorath-Ahriman being had fully entered the Earth. Was this then Its coming of age as the Shatterer in the Eighth Sphere surrounded the Earth's planetary core? Vince said it was from the Shatterer that black magicians summoned their primal forces. The Etheric Christ was now passing through the Shatterer's territory. Was a Surfaceworld catastrophe part of the battle against the Etheric Christ?

8
Thomas

The shadows of reality in the mind are closer to reality than the shadows of life in the lower world.

- Giordano Bruno, *De umbris idearum*, 1582

The Wright brothers? A catapult!

- Waiter at a Rio restaurant

Seven had met Thomas while exploring the San Ysidro Hills up Hillside Drive. Around a bend, the road leveled off into a grassy plateau where a little sprawling *rancho* was tucked. Curious, she'd parked, wondering if the *rancho* was occupied, given that she saw no cars or trucks. All she heard were insects in the dry midday meadow and the trickle of the brook below.

"Hello!" she'd called, heading down the footpath to the *rancho*.

Over the door were wings of either a California condor or an eagle, huge and meticulously preserved.

"Hello!" she called again. Then she looked up.

High above, a man with wings was gyring. Shielding her eyes, she walked toward the dry meadow he was circling. Gliders were intrepid, leaping from cliffs, catching updrafts, tethered to planes and then unhitched, but this man was *flying*. He must have seen her because he began narrowing his gyre and descending, an Icarus with a hopefully happier fate.

She squinted. How agile he was, tilting and flexing in the peculiar harness. She could hear the wind in his pinions. At last he landed, running hard, exhilarated, dragging his wings awkwardly like an angel unaccustomed to the Earth. As he disengaged from the harness, a huge black dog with golden eyes big as Asian teacups bounded out of nowhere to greet him, then bounded toward Seven to unceremoniously bury his nose in her crotch.

"Sirius! Where are your manners?" the young man scolded, laughing as he pulled at the dog's ruff and met Seven's eyes.

His features were rugged and square with deep-set blue-gray eyes, a thick shock of coarse blond-red hair. Stroking the feathers he had painstakingly sewn in place and petting Sirius with her other hand, Seven tried to still her heart as she stared at his quivering bare arms, half-listening to how he had studied Leonardo da Vinci's drawings of wings while lying in the meadow watching birds soar and glide, accelerate, decelerate. Nodding and petting, she'd stolen glances at his face, almost afraid to believe he was real. Young as she was, she knew as did he that they were two long lost friends overjoyed to find each other at last. It was, as he would say later, a once in a lifetime.

While the Sun plowed the western sky, they'd jabbered in an ecstatic daze, then later over a lantern-light feast of brown rice and vegetables in his rustic kitchen they'd peered into each other's eyes. Even Sirius, a Tibetan mastiff, was vegetarian! By the time the Sun returned in the east, they had made love and hardly slept on the porch over the garrulous brook, professing their astonishment a hundred times over having found each other, especially given that Thomas rarely left his mountain stronghold, choosing instead to spend his days in the laboratory he'd built beneath the house, deep into the hill.

After breakfast, he gave her the tour. Into the arch over the entry to the lab he'd carved,

Know, O all ye investigators of this Art, that the spirit is all, and that unless within this Spirit another like Spirit is enclosed, no good will come of anything.

"How long did it take to excavate?" Seven asked, agog at the sheer labor digging into the hill must have required.

Thomas shrugged. "Not long. Acoustic physics has been around for thousands of years, the knowledge that all matter has its own peculiar geometric, *fractal* structure and frequency. Compute the harmonic values and build a sonic generator that can attune to those values and you can stimulate the molecules along those fractal lines to resonate, and if they resonate fast enough and long enough—Do you follow?"

She did: he had weakened the rock until it had crumbled along a million tiny fractal lines, then shunted the debris down a chute into the ravine. From the air, it would look like a small rockslide. He'd smoothed and waxed the chute so that all he had to do was keep the wings tucked, shoot down head first, and out he soared. The thought of such faith made Seven shudder.

Laboratory, library, computer room, and shop were packed to the rafters with blinking, glinting hardware and books. Monitors watched the road, the entryway, the hills below, the sky, as if he were expecting danger. When she asked how he ran so much equipment offgrid, he'd smiled and said he'd gained a secret method from the old alchemists. "A whole science, Seven, that Yale never mentioned," he'd said mysteriously.

On the rocky ceiling of the lab, an angel cradled a spinning atom, a verse from Psalms winding about them in flowing script, *When I consider Thy heavens, the work of Thy fingers, the moon and the stars which Thou hast ordained, What is man, that Thou dost take thought of him, And the son of man, that Thou dost care for him?*

That first day together, he could not tell her enough about his passion for science. He leased the entire hilltop from the Los Padres National Forest for a hundred dollars a year.

"I've immersed copper in certain organic solutions so as to make my instruments hard and penetrating. And here's the lightweight vest once worn by the Gauls in battle, simply by treating a wool-cotton amalgam with certain acids." He plucked the vest from a shelf. "Not only is it bullet- and fire-proof, but with the copper mesh I've added, it will withstand modern electromagnetic weapons as well."

Little did Seven know that one day she would be wearing one of these very vests.

He pointed to the walls. "They're lined with copper mesh, too, as is the roof, partially for grounding, partially as a shield against eyes in the sky— satellites, U2s—but especially as a control for the constant traffic of telluric current or electromagnetic force from the Earth that my research tends to awaken."

"What's that room for?" she asked, noticing a tiny, insulated room off the laboratory.

"That's a . . . a collection chamber for telluric current, some of which I harness to supplement the solar energy I collect in the non-reflective solar panels on the roof. Energy is not so much about quantity as quality. Some of my . . . experiments call for both solar and telluric, or only telluric . . ."

He trailed off, quickly launching into an impassioned speech about metallurgy and how it hadn't taken him long to discover that chemically pure salts would not work. The ancients had used only impure natural compounds because of how magically and catalytically they worked. Excited, he added, "I was even able to create a simple instrument for making all the heavy water I would ever need for nuclear fusion, not fission. Fusion builds, fission destroys.

"*Quality* determines everything, Seven. While pondering this thought, even I was catalyzed and transmuted. Suddenly, I didn't feel like a little ethical guy up against big bad technology. Not only do I not need big superconductors and lasers and military grant monies to pursue real science, but I realized that I was probably saving my soul by eschewing complex machines. My soul and life itself. Human scale is qualitatively superior . . ." A cloud drifted over his face. "The corollary of the great alchemical secret *As above, so below* set me free. *As below, so above.* What occurs in my crucible also occurs in my soul. Every scientist who works for universities and labs that take money from the military is doomed to split his soul into a Jekyll and Hyde. Believe me, I know."

Seven wondered just how he knew but would wait for him to tell it in his own time.

Beyond his extensive shop was a wide entryway. He slid the tall ceramic door open to the canopy of trees overhanging the brook below the porch they had made love on. A beige pickup that had seen better days was parked under the trees, while along both sides of the brook and terraced along the hill as far as she could see grew flowers, edible plants and herbs.

"I experiment with various growing conditions," Thomas said, throwing his arm wide, "from shade- and water-loving plants to those I cultivate as

114

naturally and randomly as possible, everywhere reworking the soil with this or that variant, according to moonlight, starlight, planetary alignments, wind, condensation, etc. It's called biodynamics and is based on quality." He laughed. "Again, *As below, so above.* The question that guides me is, how can I align the healing properties of this or that plant with the healing properties of the body? And some plants give me dyes like da Vinci's that will outlast cloth or canvas."

She recalled the tiled floor in his kitchen. "Is that how you made the kitchen floor so red that I feel like I'm floating in red?"

He smiled and touched her dark hair. "By introducing gold at the moment of fusion, yes."

By her second visit, he had fashioned two silver bracelets infused with copper, one for Seven and one for himself. "Quality, Seven. May these bracelets connect us, wherever we are," he said softly, kissing her.

She felt the silver on her wrist; he had crafted their communion into the bracelet, though the words *wherever we are* worried her. Was he planning to go somewhere? Surely he would not leave behind such an elaborate laboratory. Would the people he sought to protect himself from come for him? Whenever she drove up and the pickup was gone, she would think, *Is this it?* But he was always there the next time.

Now, it was almost dawn and she was driving up to Thomas with revelations whose meanings lay beyond her grasp. An old Indian woman had given her something to drink, drawn a dogwood blossom on her hand, hoisted her into a hole in the Earth, and the first thing she had seen was Norma Jeane's murder that history claimed was suicide and a girl named Baby Rose. Why?

And the crucifixion thing. Maybe it was what Jung called a collective unconscious memory. Baptized

Russian Orthodox, Seven had only gone to church maybe half a dozen times in her life. Her mother had despised old country ways and superstitions. Seven recalled sitting beside her grandmother in the pew of the dark Eastern church filled with sad icons and drapery. The liturgy had been high drama with the priest's ornate cassock and wiry, angry eyebrows. Magic Russian words had issued from his black curly beard as he swung the frankincense burner to disappear with the altar in an infernal cloud of smoke like Faust.

She had gleaned wisps of *Sophia* and *Christos*, but her knowledge of the man called Jesus was limited to literary allusions and old movies in December and March. She looked down at her palm; the dogwood blossom was gone. Had it been connected to Christ hanging from a dogwood tree under a freaked-out, unnatural sky? But the old *chupu* woman was Indian, not Christian. During her walk under the stars with Hermano and Ghost Bear, Ghost Bear had said there were many stories throughout the Americas of an ancient visitor, a Pale God commanding the winds and seas who taught the people. Like Quetzalcoatl, he had departed to the East—toward Europe, toward Palestine—promising to return.

"Which is why Venus, the Morning Star, is still sacred to these continents," Ghost Bear had explained. "She rises in the east as a promise."

To which Hermano added, "For the ancient Hebrews, Jupiter was the eastern star, not Venus, and they called him Zadoc, the righteous one. Jupiter is the same as the ancient Sky Father Jove whose concerns were with oaths, treaties, and brotherhoods. Most philanthropists consider themselves Jovian, as do legislators, bankers, and lawyers. And when Freemasons came to the Americas and saw thousands of petroglyphs of the Eastern Star, they saw Jupiter, not Venus—authority, not love. But Jupiter can also mean reason, perspective, generosity, and expansion."

Ghost Bear continued. "But of the Pale God, little was said—"

"—at least publicly," Hermano interjected.

"Yes, publicly," Ghost Bear agreed. "Wherever there was a story about the morning star, there was also a story about the Pale God's visit and departure and promise of return. My people called him *Waicomah*, the Yakima *Tahoma*, the Hawaiians *Wakea*, the Hopi *Bahána*, the Algonquins *Emeeshetotl* the Feathered Serpent, even *Chee Zoos* or Dawn-God."

"Gothic, perhaps from the Vikings," Hermano surmised. "Even now, the Pueblos in Acoma burn a light every night to welcome him, should he choose to return."

"Didn't the Indians think Cortés was this god?" Barbara had asked.

"Moctezuma did, yes," Ghost Bear nodded. "Whenever a white man came—Drake, Cook, Columbus, Cortés—Indians had to at least get close enough to see if it might be him in another incarnation. But it didn't take them long to realize their mistake, and by then it was usually too late."

Ghost Bear had looked at Raven. "The Hopi did not become as bitter as the rest of us; they were even willing to consider that *Bahána* might be one of your *hipi* nation." He paused and smiled. "Old signs are hard to read, hard to interpret in times that look different from the old times. At first, I thought it was all nonsense, the Pale God and everything, a story seeded by Christians and Mormons. I saw you white kids as spoiled middle-class brats indulging in sex and drugs and the easy white life. But Hermano has changed my mind. He is the first truly civilized white man I have ever met." He smiled at his friend. "No, you *hipis* cannot save us from what must come, and yet Hermano says that you, like the Indian, are being targeted by the two-hearted."

"The two-hearted?" Barbara asked.

Seven had interrupted. "Ghost Bear, are Indians still waiting for—the Pale God?"

He smiled. "Everyone is waiting for something, aren't they? The Jews, the Christians, the Hopi . . . Many of my people don't believe in the old stories anymore. They have fallen under the white *chindi* spell of believing only in what they see." He shrugged. "Appearances are deceiving. Raven, tell the story of *Ptesan-Wi*, White Buffalo Calf Woman."

Raven nodded and began in a soft voice. "Two young men were sent out to hunt. Halfway up a hill, they saw a beautiful young woman approaching. She had a round red dot on each cheek and was dressed in fine white buckskin embroidered with sacred porcupine quill designs in rich, unearthly colors. Her blue-black hair hung loose, except for a strand on the left tied with buffalo fur. Her eyes were dark and sparkling, with great power in them. She was *lila wakan,* sacred, and both young men stood transfixed by her beauty, one in awe, as was proper, the other overcome by desire. When this one reached out to touch her, some say lightning burned him to a crisp and left his blackened bones on the Plains, while others say that he was filled with snakes and eaten from the inside out, until there was nothing left. White Buffalo Calf Woman then followed the good brave back to his people and taught them the art of being human, then departed, saying, *Toksha ake wacinyanktin ktelo,* I shall see you again."

"She taught them that the buffalo represents the universe and four ages of creation, and was put in the West to hold back the destroying waters of another flood," Ghost Bear explained. "Every age the Great Buffalo loses a leg, every year a hair, and when all the hair and legs are gone, water will again cover the

118

Earth. Yes, appearances are deceiving, and yet we must learn to be ready to discern the spirit when it chooses to reveal itself.

"If the Pale God is returning in the ethers today as my white brother Hermano says, who am I to say it cannot be true? But who will recognize him? Only those with second sight." With two fingers, he drew a line from his eyes.

"I now understand how the long war against Christianity has confused everything. Christians have been two-hearted since they came to these continents, split between God and property, bending and twisting their stories for gain. They are why many of my people despise Christianity. Hermano has helped me to see that if there is a Pale God, he will not return in a body. My white brother assures me that the Pale God's return has begun and will take a hundred years to complete. Is the Pale God the same as Jesus Christ? I don't know. Even in the Yucatan, Indians still discuss whether or not Quetzalcoatl and Jesus Christ are the same. *Wasichu* history says nothing about Jesus coming to the Americas. Perhaps he came in a dream body. Perhaps his resurrected body flew on the wind across Africa and the Atlantic and he came in a cloud of light. Perhaps the Pale God is returning like that.

"But I don't think I would believe in such a vision if it came in the sky like a movie. Hermano tells me that *wasichu* science witches have technology that can make visions appear in the sky because they believe the Great Spirit is dead and like kids whose parents aren't home fearlessly do great mischief. My son tells me that even photographs can lie, like the one on the cover of *Life* magazine of Lee Harvey Oswald holding the rifle. My son said, 'Look at the shadows, Dad, they're all wrong.'" Ghost Bear sighed and shook his head. "Such two-heartedness is foreign to my spirit. No, it is all mixed up now, like wool tangled in Spider

Woman's basket. The vision quest may be the only way left to tell the true from the false. Jesus was a good man, Pale God or not, as badly treated then as those who believe in his churches."

Barbara had then shared a dream from that very morning. "I was standing in a hot dry field somewhere in the Midwest. Several men and I were standing around a pregnant buffalo lying on her side, rolling her eyes and bellowing. Suddenly, her body shuddered and out came a white calf with the cowl draped over its head like a mask. Someone said, *A miracle! Not since 1933.*"

Ghost Bear shrugged. "If an Indian dreamed it, I would say one thing, but a *wasichu*—what do you think, Hermano?"

Hermano smiled. "Blood is no longer as important as it once was. At one time, race said a lot about who brought what to the human drama, but now not so much, particularly in America. The Hopi may be right that the *hipi* family of consciousness, not blood, is pointing the way into the future. That Barbara has dreamed a native dream," he shrugged, "is like the postman delivering a letter. Would you require that the postman be of your race or family? We must not ask *who* dreams the dream, but where is the dream from, and does it bear relevant information? Hers does. The white buffalo calf of 1933 is coming again."

Ghost Bear sighed. "I was a boy when that white buffalo calf was born in Colorado. My father and other Lakota elders took me along with some of the Ho-Chunk buffalo clan—Winnebago—to welcome White Buffalo Calf Woman's messenger. But when the calf died ten years ago and things only got worse, we did begin to look for another birth . . ." He shook his head. "But the old signs and ceremonies don't work the way they used to, and it is difficult to see what means what."

"Yes, my brother," Hermano had said gently, "like the blood. You and I know that we live many lives, sometimes in a red skin, sometimes in a black or white skin. What is skin but the cover of a book we have read but forgotten? We must build discernment and no longer look to race or genetic line. White Buffalo Calf Woman, whoever she is, began her return in 1933, when the Second Coming began. The calf died sixteen years later, four times four. Numbers still determine signs, but we mustn't forget that the left-handed Brotherhoods do not hesitate to manipulate those numbers to deceive us. The calf Barbara dreamed will be the first of six to be born before the close of the millennium. Examine the circumstances of their births so as not to jump to the conclusion that White Buffalo Calf Woman necessarily sent them. It could just as well be genetic manipulation."

Gripping the steering wheel tight for the turns on the coil of road leading up to Thomas, Seven struggled with the *terra incognita* of yesterday's events, her head swirling with double meanings. Barbara's dream, the *chupu* woman and her vision quest, the drug as the map and the blossom as the key, or was it vice versa? *The map is not the territory*, Alfred Korzybski said. If a drug was a key, what did it unlock? A *bardo*? Her own DNA? The twin spiral of DNA looked like a caduceus, Hermes' healing staff of two serpents intertwined, insignia of the medical profession. Doctors dispensed drugs . . .

At last arriving at the clearing near the *rancho*, she turned the engine off and got out, inhaling the balm of the stream running beneath the porch and down into the ravine far below. She scanned the dark horizon. Light was slowly blinking out the stars. Dawn was on its way.

She picked her way down to the half-moon garden, wondering where Sirius was. If Rhea's garden was a

Shangri-la, Thomas' was an exotic biosphere. Thin rods calibrated to centimeters and millimeters stood beside some plants; others grew beneath porous domes of different hues and yet others out in the open, each specimen enjoying its own unique soil of sedimentary, igneous, and metamorphic rock, metals, nonmetals, and rare earths. Like the Augustinian monk Mendel, Thomas crossed traits and strains, subjecting descendants to varying cosmic proportions as well as rainwater bombarded by gamma rays, x-rays, ultraviolet, and infrared. Measuring, always measuring, hypothesizing, discounting, adjusting, repeating. He had tripled the stream's flow by dowsing for its source and coaxing water with sound up into the writhing serpentine water forms based on sacred geometry that he'd sculpted from soapstone. The water forms changed the water's quality, he said, after which it ran into the pond he'd dug, then trickled out again on its merry way down the mountainside to nourish stream, soil, air and sea with new quality. The freshwater fish he'd stocked the pond with seemed content to reproduce and be studied while Thomas ate them as a kind of communion, like the Martian Michael Valentine Smith in Heinlein's *Stranger in a Strange Land*.

Seven nibbled a sprig of watercress before circling back up and around to the door under the condor's wings. Thomas had left a lantern burning for her. The gold in the kitchen floor glistened and wriggled in the blood-red glass beneath her feet. He wasn't on the porch. Was he up at the old fire watchtower where he kept his telescope?

Turning, she almost ran into the mastiff who patiently went toward the door and looked back, expecting her to follow. Outside, he led her across the road and up the hill. At last, she saw Thomas' silhouette bathed in starlight, waiting for her. How she loved him. The men she had known so far had been interested in the comfort of her body and ministrations, but not that interested in the winding ways of her individuality. Thomas was different. For reasons of his own, he had asked her to be discreet about their relationship and where he lived, telling her it was better she did not know the details of his past because knowing might put her in harm's way. She had accepted his terms, loving him as she did. But now something had turned her world inside out and she must lean on him in a way she hadn't yet. She wondered how he would respond. What if he found her fears to be a drag? Should she risk losing him?

For his part, he had been wondering much the same. He loved the integrity he sensed in her, all too rare in women, and yet how much of his past could he burden her with? It wasn't fair to be involved with her, given that he couldn't promise her any semblance of a normal future. He was a marked and hunted man, and anyone associated with him would no doubt be hunted, too. But all resolutions to give her up had evaporated. Love made him irrationally hopeful that things might be otherwise, like lighting the lantern in hopes of her arrival. Now, as she climbed the hill toward him, he could already sense that she was burdened by something.

Approaching his silhouette, her body thrilled to their yearning for each other. She could hear his breath, or was it hers? Silently, she raised her arms as he stood and peeled her shift up and over her shoulders. Silently, he lifted and cradled her as she ran her hands over his cool, smooth skin and felt the ache of loving the one she would love forever, come what may. For a thousandth time she wished she could escape the weight of this love she felt, but knew she didn't really mean it. Besides, you can never go back. Love, that strange and solitary creature obeying no one, visits very few. From Thomas she learned the meaning of *swoon*, and this she now did as he lay down with her on the mattress on the hill just hours after she had been changed forever but didn't know how. *You can never go back,* she thought as she swooned, *but you can lay your burden down for an hour here and there.*

9
Burned Over

*In the future, humanity must be guided beyond
many things with whose karma mankind is
heavily burdened in our present grievous and
painful times. Today mankind is burdened with
the karma of the dream life of the past
centuries. This mystery must first be grasped
in its depths; then it will be easier to
understand our sorrowful present and also to
understand how humanity must gradually
prepare a different karma for the future.*

- Rudolf Steiner, October 1, 1916

*"Look," Betonie said, pointing east to Mount
Taylor towering dark blue with the last
twilight. "They only fool themselves when they
think it is theirs. The deeds and papers don't
mean anything. It is the people who belong to
the mountain."*

- Leslie Marmon Silko, *Ceremony*, 1977

*There is always a gate to any history. The
Indians entered a certain gate, one which
Columbus opened when he presented to Castile
and to León a New World. On this imagined gate
there was to be carved the verse from Dante:*

125

"Through me thou enterest into endless sorrow.'

- John Collier (1884-1968), US Indian Bureau, 1933

The ghosts of two mountain men named Joe and Bob joined up with Seven in the Blue Mountains, vanishing at first light and returning at dusk. Back in '40, they told her, they had been the first to prove that a wagon could make it over those mountains. Joe showed Seven a 1906 phantom silver half dollar commemorating old Ezra Meeker's preservation mission from Puyallup, Washington to the Missouri River, Meeker on one side with Twist and Dave pulling a prairie schooner, and a handsome Indian on the other side. Seven listened with half an ear, long accustomed to talkative ghosts with narrow ranges of self-interest, incapable of moving beyond their electromagnetic geography.

Ghosts with too much Time on their hands reminded her of the Burned-over district in New England in the 1840s, when the Freemasons and Madame H.P. Blavatsky's *mahatmas* launched an astral campaign to take American souls by storm. From Philadelphia to upstate New York, they concentrated considerable remote occult skill on stirring up disoriented emigrants and cutting a broad swath through what came to be known as the Burned-over district—burned over, that is, by the fire of the spirit. Sensitives, later known as channelers, sprang up overnight—among them the Fox sisters and Joseph Smith—and with them a blizzard of séances and special effects by which the dead sought to communicate with the living. Unbeknownst to the sensitives, their communiqués were often manipulated by occultists from Philadelphia to

Veracruz and London to the banks of the Brahmaputra. By 1851, one hundred mediums in New York City alone were tabletapping and reading everything from tea leaves to Tarot cards and entrails.

The impact of this movement paved the way not only for spiritual materialism and New Age religion but for the nihilism for which history will remember the 20th and 21st centuries. Mediums and their hopefuls saw no heavenly kingdom beyond this life but only an eternity of shades, a waiting room filled with ghosts of the restless dead, like Beckett's post-Bomb *Waiting for Godot*—

> *Vladimir:* Ah, Gogo, don't go on like that. Tomorrow everything will be better.
> *Estragon:* How do you make that out?
> *Vladimir:* Did you not hear what the child said?
> *Estragon:* No.
> *Vladimir:* He said that Godot was sure to come tomorrow. What do you say to that?
> *Estragon:* Then all we have to do is to wait on here.

Nihilism and ennui went hand in hand with the Cold War and National Security State that welcomed the Paperclip Nazi scientists. Paperclip came from a deal cut by Allen Dulles, Director of the new Central Intelligence Agency (CIA), and SS Commander Karl Wolff, head of the Gestapo in Italy, slaughterer of 300,000 Jews at Treblinka. Nixon and Reagan both had Nazi friends looking forward to the great fascist shift in America, the transferred Third Reich.

One night, Joe and Bob melted into the ground and popped back up to confirm that yessiree, there were catacombs of roads and chambers under I-80 snaking south and east through a huge military reserve from Oregon into northeast Nevada and beyond, from

Unity Lake to Crowley, Burns, and Rome. They surmised that the concrete and steel underground complex led to yet another underground lair stretching from San Diego to Denver, a spaghetti of highways, railways, and waterways connecting missile sites, laboratories, and relay stations. *A great flurry of activity down there*, the ghosts confided.

In the ruins of a stagecoach station, Seven found a plunder box with a ragged sock doll inside, a black baby with black button eyes. Tenderly, she touched it, remembering Baby Rose and Mina singing *Ring-a-ring-a-rosies*. Near the Powder River, a phantom was cutting down a tall phantom pine over and over. What did the repetition signify? Why that scene and not another? Thirty miles beyond the summit of Flagstaff Hill, at the mouth of Kitchen Creek near the headwaters of the Burnt River, a wagon train massacre was being played out. Indians who had once helped pioneers now slaughtered them, killing women and children or taking them for wives and slaves. All Seven could do was watch since the *mano a mano* slaughter had already taken place two hundred years before. Now the slaughtering was from ionospheric heaters heating the outer core and mantle of the Earth, torquing up the crust and tectonic plates.

It was dawn and she'd been hiking all night. At Farewell Bend, she caught her first glimpse of the Snake River. Joe and Bob faded, their last words the hope that she'd be at the annual get-together of trappers, mountain men, and Indians down at Lombard Ferry on the Green River. *You'll take a shine,* their disappearing phantom lips grinned, *to the races and story-swapping, venison biscuits and gravy, maybe even get to meet Kit Carson or better yet Baptiste, Sacajawea's half-white son.*

Planes were patrolling from the north. She clicked her binoculars to daytime and made out *AWACS* on the fusilage. Airborne Warning and Control Systems from the 552nd Air Control Wing at Tinker in Oklahoma, which meant NATO.

She thought about how the mountains had been islands of refuge during the Flood and wondered if it would be that way again. Mountains had ever been sacred beings to whom prayers were offered and pilgrimages taken, with gods and goddesses communing at the apex and gnomes and Earth beings in the recesses of caves. Earth tremors indicated that the great *devas* magnetizing the Earth and guarding its sacred portals—the *sidhe*, shining, opalescent beings—were on the move.

Before resting, she paused to bless the south and west with a bit of tobacco, points of reference for the energies of the four sacred mountains of the Navajo: Sisnajinni, sacred mountain of the East (white), called Pelado Peak in Bernalillo County, New Mexico; Tsodsichl, sacred mountain of the South (blue), Mt. Taylor, the Woman Veiled in Rain Clouds of the San Mateo range; Doko-oslid, sacred mountain of the West (yellow), the San Francisco peaks in Arizona; and Depenitsa, sacred mountain of the North (black), peak on the La Plata or San Juan range. The bones of giants had been found in a cave on Black Mesa in the Tewa Valley between San Ildefonso and Santa Clara pueblos in New Mexico and inside a Cuchama initiation chamber by missionaries.

She raised tobacco to Cuchama, Mt. Tecate in San Diego County, sacred to the Cochimis (the *Ku-tcan*) in Baja California and Yumas in the lower valleys of the Colorado and Gila rivers, Imperial Valley, and southern California. Pizarro burned the Incan chieftain *Chall-cuchima* alive. *Mohave progentor Mastambo,* Seven uttered under her breath, *Ku-tcan progenitor Kumastamho, may you walk again, now that the Earth shifts once again. Manco Capac, founder of the Inca dynasty of the divine Children of the Sun; Chinigchinix, leader of the San Juan*

Capistrano Indians of Southern California, walk again!

In 1947 near Sonora, Mexico—about 90 miles south of Alamos in the Rio del Fuerte, north of San Blas near the border of Sinaloa—a lost city of beehive huts was found. In the huts lay mummies of giants eight to nine feet tall wrapped in saffron robes. Blue pyramid-like shapes and white dots in the cloth signified the Mayan time cycle or Platonic year of 25,000 years. Both Yaqui and Seri on Tiburon Island say the giant race came from Mu long submerged. Two other giant skeletons were found in a cave in the Arroyo de Los Yglesias of Chihuahua in Tarahumara Indian country.

Lifting tobacco to the west, she envisioned Lassen Volcanic Forest and Lassen Peak, inactive since 1914, where the Cascades met the Sierras and wove into the underwater chain of 1,100 volcanoes along the Eastern Pacific Rise extending south from the Baja Coast down to Chile and Antarctica, some simmering under thick blankets of ice. Five plates meet there, the Pacific, Antarctic, Nazca, Cocos, and North American, all moving apart, converging, and overlapping like the Symplegades, the Pacific moving northwest, the Eurasian east, and the Indo-Australian north, squeezing the Philippines and Japan on the easternmost edge of the Eurasian Plate. The deep underwater trenches ringing the Pacific Ocean—the Pacific Rim of Fire from Chile to the Aleutians to Japan down to New Zealand and around through Easter Island to Antarctica and back to Chile—call tsunamis like dragons to flick their tails while the Cascades with their 600 miles of snowy peaks sleep.

Long ago, the Pale God's servant with the red cross on his white tunic once stood on Tzatzitepec, the Hill of Loud Outcrying, and tried to warn the priests of Tula that an earthquake and volcanic eruption would soon tumble its temples and rubble its houses. Would he come again now to do the same? In El Salvador, magic dogs called *cadejos* live on volcanoes like Tecapa the beautiful lady and Chaparrastique the handsome man and eat *olotiuqui* seeds extracted from the blue calyxes of the morning glory *Ipomoea violacea*. On the Pacific coast of Guatemala are the seven fiery Cané (Mayan Vukup) gods Tacaná, Tajamulco, Gagxanul, Atitlán, Pekul, Chikac, and Cajol-Juyub.

A phalanx of fighter jets streaking north cut short her ministrations, after which she heard engines grinding on a road nearby. She needed shelter and sleep. Creeping away from the road to a relatively dry thicket, she then arranged her space blanket and fronds. The last image to visit her mind before sleep was Thomas, when he and she were young and the pilgrimage was being set in motion.

That night on the hill after making love, then had stared up at Cygnus, the Northern Cross Swan soaring high overhead. She had so much to tell him but still resisted telling him. Like all who are in love before the work of love has really begun, she wanted him to only see her at her best. Besides, there was so much she couldn't recall, like the sons of Sam backyard barbeque and what the vivid image of a little Legong dancer signified. They lay naked in each other's arms, talking of Ophiuchus grappling with the Serpent in the southwest sky, of Thomas' constellation the Centaur, half-man and half-beast, of Seven's constellation the twins Castor and Pollux, one striding inside the Milky Way, the other outside. They puzzled over how constellations light-years away could affect personality.

Below the conversation, angels and demons wrestled. Neither was sure of how much to reveal, Seven fearing Thomas' disbelief, Thomas fearing putting Seven at risk. He hugged her nakedness and buried his face in the nook of her neck to breathe in her scent, remembering the last woman he had allowed himself to love, his old Jamaican nurse Winona, more of a mother than his mother ever was in her elegant pale beauty and manicured nails sharp and red as those of the wicked queen in *Snow White*, always distant, traveling or cloistered in her rooms, self-medicated to the gills. When she half-heartedly touched his cheek, he recoiled at her alien touch, her watery eyes of vast distance and utter defeat. He even doubted that that he had come from that poor, anesthetized woman of old American stock, she was so frail and insubstantial.

Thomas had been three when his uncle sent Winona away. Everyone he ever loved had been taken from him in obeisance to *der Wille zur Macht*, to which his father, uncle, grandfather, and great grandfather had submitted before him. Winona had loved him as her own, privileged orphan that he was. With Seven, something in his chest relaxed. It struck him as strange and wonderful that loving her made him want to tell her everything. But should he? He raised his head and gazed upon her in the starlight.

For her part, Seven was stuck on the word *safe*. Her reality had been torn asunder and now she knew that something else existed, but what? Not even her few LSD and *peyote* trips had been so *real*. And how had the green man bent over Marilyn Monroe's body known she was there? And the sunflower oil on Rhea's table? *We are such stuff as dreams are made on, and our little life Is rounded with a sleep.* Whatever had happened to her defied the laws she had previously believed to be absolute.

Taking a deep breath, she began telling Thomas everything, beginning with Hermano and Ghost Bear and Raven, then on to the *chupu* woman, the *temescal* and *toloache* and *sipapu*, Marilyn Monroe and the sons of Sam having a barbeque, and of course the leering doctor in green. At that point, the memory door flew open and she saw herself stepping out the back door into a salty African Caribbean inland. She remembered flying and looking down on the Gulf states whizzing by at lightning speed—Florida, Alabama, Mississippi, Louisiana, Texas and into Mexico, all the way around the giant Caribbean G to Veracruz at Coatzacoalcos, Place of the Serpent. She saw the Coatzacoalcos River moving north through the Gulf of Campeche to merge with the Mississippi River at the mouth of New Orleans.

A gathering was underway. *Was this the barbeque?* People in animal masks—possums, lemurs, raccoons, marmots, bobcats, leopards, wolves, coyotes, dogs—were dancing wildly by torchlight. Effortlessly, she landed in a top branch of a dogwood tree. When she looked at her palm, her hand had become a condor's talon.

The revelry and chatter died away as a huge jaguar cut a slow, regal swath through the crowd, his finely chiseled head swiveling to survey his awe-struck minions. Having garnered their attention, he rose up on his hind legs and changed his frequency to that of a man with piercing dark eyes. Similar transformations occurred in the political and societal luminaries who were his minions: the Vice President and National Security Adviser, the Senator chairing the powerful Senate Appropriations Committee, US Attorneys, Mafia bosses, Warren Commissioners, Prime Ministers, Supreme Court judges, Boston Brahmins in $2,000 suits from Louis of Boston, governors, Pentagon brass, and UN Security Council members. The director of *Rosemary's Baby* was there, his pregnant wife sacrificed the year before by the mind-controlled Manson girls. Magazine and newspaper agenda-setters were there, science fiction writers, scientists. Prince Hall Lodge Brothers who had tacitly approved of the assassinations of Malcolm

X and King hobnobbed with a Rothschild from RAM London, penurious Gnomes of Zurich, Nobel doctors, Anglican and Lutheran ministers, pedophile Catholic Archbishops. The evangelical Iron Lady of Britain was heard to say to Queen Elizabeth, *I am in politics because of the struggle between good and evil.* A Saudi prince and the President of Mexico flanked Nazi General Reinhard Gehlen and his famous compatriot, the handsome NASA rocket scientist Dr. Werner von Braun. Kowtowing to them were old SS friends, generals and heads of state in Brazil, Bolivia, Paraguay, Uruguay, Argentina, and Chile, as well as a doctor flown up from the South Pole by Raytheon Polar. The guest list went on and on, including the deathbag doctor of the deathly green hue.

Smiling unctuously, the Jaguar high priest glanced up at the condor in the dogwood tree, making her feathers bristle. He then turned to the crowd and raised a Satanic salute, which they returned . . .

"Seven, what is it?" Thomas was shaking her.

Breathless, she recounted what she had thus far recalled of the sons of Sam barbeque in the Place of the Serpent. Thomas sucked in his breath when she described the Jaguar high priest and named some of the men and women she'd recognized from the news. His body became rigid with what it didn't remember about having been at such a "barbeque" in Veracruz with his uncle several years before.

"Since meeting Hermano, nothing's been the same," she sighed, kissing Thomas on the cheek, "except you."

He turned and kissed her fervently. He must tell his story, if for no other reason than that it was already interwoven with hers. The time was now, while dawn still eluded them. He would pull from the East the light that would illuminate the memories eluding him so the night could finally depart.

134

10
The Green Door

*...The Lord God made tunics of skins for Adam
and his wife and clothed them. He said, 'The
man has become like one of us, knowing good
and evil; what if he now reaches out his hands
and takes fruit from the tree of life also, eats it
and lives for ever?' So the Lord God drove him
out of the garden of Eden to till the ground from
which he had been taken. He cast him out, and
to the east of the garden of Eden he stationed
the cherubim and a sword whirling and
flashing to guard the way to the tree of life.*

- Genesis 3:21-24, *The New English Bible*

*When Churchill spoke of a world 'made darker
by the dark lights of perverted science,' he was
referring to the revolting experiments
conducted on human beings by Nazi doctors in
the concentration camps. But his remarks
might with equal justice have been applied to
the activities of the CIA's Sidney Gottlieb.*

- Obituary, *London Times*, March 12,
1999

At last free of Interstate 80, old Seven walked the
authentic Oregon Trail along deep ruts left by prairie
schooners almost two centuries before. For the first
time since leaving The Dalles, she felt safe walking
during the day if she chose, warmed by the autumn
Sun and nibbling at the pemmican the Umatilla had

gifted. At dusk and dawn, ghosts still swept West—
white pioneers and black soldiers, Freemason
explorers and naturalists, Shoshone, Bannock,
Paiute, Nez Perce, and Coeur d'Alene, some herding
glowing cattle that in life had died after being
mutilated and shot up with radiation for secret
genetic projects. The phantom world was converging
past with present.

Just before dawn one night, she replenished her
water in an all-night laundromat on the edge of Vale,
Oregon. Hovering near the faucet was a ghost named
Henderson who said he'd died of thirst just east of the
Malheur in the spring of 1852. Clasping his throat
and working his mouth, he'd followed her for a while,
asking if she was *sure* she had enough water for the
twenty miles of desert between the Malheur and the
Snake. Repeatedly, she assured him she did, touched
by his concern.

East of Vale, she found the hot springs pocket
she'd been seeking, tucked behind a shack whose old
pipes and flooring reminded her of Wheeler Springs
so long ago. She spent the day soaking the Oregon
miles away, napping and eating and poring over her
maps. The ground around the pool was too hot for
bare feet, but she managed to scoop up some of the
salty residue she'd read about in John Fremont's
1843 journal to replenish her salt supply. In the
evening, she continued southeast to where the Boise
and Snake Rivers joined. The original adobe Fort
Boise founded by the Hudson's Bay Company—still a
big corporate player in the 21st century—had been
swept away by floods.

As per the old alchemical law *As above, so below*,
the conjunctions of rivers correspond to planetary
conjunctions. Watery conjunctions were still sacred to
Satanists and pagan esotericists seeking back roads
into the underworld and land of the dead, down into
the bone mountain of *Miquitalan* where the dead

enter the Most Holy Earth and the Lords and Ladies of Death eat the phantom flesh of dead and living alike. Caves, streams, pools, sinkholes, and wells where *Natura* and Subnature converge are still where the Nine Lords throw fêtes for those sacrificed, the main dish being souls.

David Berkowitz admitted to being one of thousands if not millions of Sons of Sam and lived near Wicker Street in Yonkers by the aqueduct that carried drinking water down from the Catskills that old Rip Van Winkle once fell under the spell of. The aqueduct flowed past the once-lavish estate of Samuel Untermyer, a practicing Satanist. In Untermyer Park was Devil's Cave, an old pumphouse at the bottom of the Thousand Steps leading down to the Hudson River. Half a mile away was the old Stillwell estate on North Broadway, and nearby in central Westchester the former Warburg-Rothschild estate. Further up the Hudson is West Point, then Sleepy Hollow where the Rockefellers bury their dead. All of the 1976-77 Son of Sam serial (cereal) murder victims were Roman Catholics from Italian sectors of the Bronx, Queens, and Brooklyn, all the way from Gravesend Bay to the old aqueduct.

In the morning, Seven packed up and went to visit the site of the old British fort. Besides the heraldic lion's head sculpted in concrete by Yaden and Yensen on 18 October 1971 (shades of Yubela, Yubelo, and Yubelum), she recognized the Masonic sigils on the pedestal. The lion's countenance was distinctly Mithraic, celebrating either Zurvan, the lion-headed god of Infinite Time, or Ahriman, eternal enemy of Mithras/Christ. Was this a Lion's Gate boundary between Oregon and Idaho, like the one leading to the Muslim sector in Jerusalem? Running her hand over the lion's cold stone mane, she guessed that the bust marked the ascension of "Yaden" and "Yensen" to the 4th degree of Mithraic initiation called the Lion, reserved for those who renounce water in favor of fire. *Firewalk with me . . .* Or was it celebrating the Lion of Judah descendants in Freemason England and acknowledging an American debt to Brothers in the Hudson's Bay Company?

The night before, she'd watched Perseus' Y-shaped constellation climb the star fields of the Milky Way in eternal pursuit of the plummeting Andromeda three million light years away, Perseus' sword poised to smite the chains that bound her, the Gorgon's head swinging from his left hand. The Colonel once said that Zurvan was to Mithras what the Gorgon was to Perseus and what Satan is to Christ. *Only the stars tell real Time*, she mused, with their Platonic year of twelve Platonic months, each 2,160 years long. Human time was so relative, like the Masonic calendar beginning 4,000 years before Christ when the Sun was still rising in Leo on the day of Sirius' first heliacal rising, so that for Freemasons the millennial year 2000 read 6000 Anno Lucis, the year of Lucifer. For Freemasonry, there was no Christ Turning Point.

After examining the sigils carefully, she surmised that there was probably a cave or grove north of the fort, perhaps near some old Phoenician settlement or Celtic *menhir*. High-level Masons adored the old gods, and hadn't Hiram Abiff's people been Phoenicians and Aramaeans? She sighed, tired of sniffing out the myriad ways Masonic cuckoos laid their eggs in others' nests. Once noble, the Masonic Brotherhood had been usurped by Illuminati and grown evil, stinking to high heaven and now trapped in a mercantile mentality, *an alien people clutching their gods.* Plotting against History had made them devious instead of wise, trying with sheer numbers to storm the gates of the gods and reverse the Will of Time. Their hubris had dishonored the very name of the old Mysteries they claimed to adore and tightened the snares set by Satanists dedicated to inverting what was truly human.

She had spent the better part of her adult life tracking the death littering the wakes of Brotherhoods beating a vicious, power-hungry swath through the 20th century, the century beginning with the end of the Kali Yuga in 1899 and thrown 33 years later into the struggle over the commencement of the Second Coming. Western left-handed Brotherhoods had thrown in with Eastern efforts to divert the Etheric Advent by fomenting two world wars, the Bomb, Korea, Vietnam, endless wars in the Middle East—and technological mind control. The Bomb had been a direct assault on the 12-year Jupiter pulse through Leo and sidereal Virgo to make way for the Etheric Ingress all the way to the Moon Sphere. The decree of Time was to expand the old vertical Mysteries of the law into new horizontal Mysteries of liberation and love. No more priests, no more initiatic Brotherhood degrees, no more bloodline clairvoyance. *Generic, not genetic!* To Freemasons and the Catholic Church, the immanentizing of the Eschaton was terrifying and merited joining forces.

As Seven searched for the Masonic landmark she was sure couldn't be far from the lion, she reviewed how the Freemason Enterprise in America had once been invisible to her but began falling into place after that night in the San Ysidros, thanks to her Veracruz vision, Baby Rose, and the past Thomas chose to bare to her. They were all entwined with America's post-World War Two, Cold War nightmare and nothing short of uncanny.

She and Thomas lay on the hill overlooking the *rancho*, talking their way into the elusive dawn. Hesitantly, Thomas opened up.

139

"My identical twin and I were born in 1943. Supposedly, he died at birth. I used to believe it, but now I'm not so sure." He sighed. "My childhood was shrouded in secrets, half-truths, and pregnant silences buried like landmines. My paternal grandfather and grandmother had two sons, my uncle Hiram and my father Laurence. Both my grandfather and Hiram served in high military and civilian capacities during the re-shaping of Germany after the Third Reich 'fell.'" He laughed darkly. "Only it didn't fall, it simply emigrated to Canada and the Americas, which was the plan all along. World War Two was intended to finish what the First World War hadn't finished, namely the destruction of old Central Europe, and move the still-intact Third Reich instrument of Nazism to the resource-rich Americas."

Seven understood. The Colonel had said much the same.

"Had my twin not died or been taken . . ."

Seven nestled closer and kissed him. Her touch cracked the alabaster vial of grief buried in his chest.

Tears coursing down his cheeks, Thomas whispered incredulously, "Did you know that Elvis had a twin, Jesse Garon? They said he died at birth, too."

Hercules kneeled overhead and Ophiuchus crushed the Scorpion's head with his heel while wrestling the Serpent. *How frail we are,* Seven mused, stroking Thomas head and recalling Poste's translation of Aratos—

And all the signs through which Night whirls
*   her car,*
From belted Orion back to Orion and his
*   dauntless Hound,*
And all Poseidon's, all high Zeus's stars,
Bear on their beams true messages to man.

Her eyes on Ophiuchus, she recalled Ray telling her about a friend from Stanford who went down to the Amazon to do field work in forest pharmacology under a Merck Pharmaceuticals grant. The friend knew that Merck would take his research and give nothing but heartache back to the indigenous peoples from whence it came. While among the Ashaninca, he ingested *ayahuasqa*, the vine of the soul, with an *ayahuasqero* or shaman, and the trip changed his life. Huge twin psychedelic serpents telepathically informed him that they lived deep in his cells and could answer any question he put to them. Dumbfounded and terrified, he asked if Darwin's theory of evolution was true. Their answer was laughter, leaving him with a life-long enigma. When the drug wore off, he'd asked the *ayahuasqero* if the serpents were real or not. The *ayahuasqero*'s answer was to ask if radio waves were real. *Aayahuasqa*, being high in dimethyltryptamine, may have put him in touch with his DNA helix entwined like twin serpents. So how had the serpent gone from wise DNA to being the enemy of Western man?

Thomas hadn't wept in a woman's arms since his old Jamaican nurse. Wiping his eyes with the back of his hand, he said, "Did you know that many gestations start out as single-egg twins, but in the first weeks of pregnancy one twin simply vanishes? Either its tissue and amniotic sac are 'devoured' by the other twin or reabsorbed by the mother's body. Sometimes, when a surviving twin is born, a fetus papyraceus or incomplete infant is found in its abdomen. Sometimes, a cyst or teratoma on a woman's ovary is actually the remnant of a twin she has carried since she was born . . . What I mean is I can understand why scientists would want to study twins. What I *don't* understand is how they sleep at night, doing the things they do to children and embryos and the poor young women who carry them.

141

Like what happened to my mother, the vacant, drugged woman I address formally as 'mother.' Lineage! That's all I heard as I was chauffeured from one tutor or training program to another."

In the silver predawn, he stared into her eyes. "My life was like that show *The Prisoner*, Seven, and my uncle is deep in it, whatever it is. Somehow, it's going on all over the country—on military bases, NASA installations, hospitals, universities, churches. And I don't mean just twin research. I mean children, Seven, children, women, men, rich and poor, Catholic and Protestant, Native American, white and black, young and younger . . ."

He grew silent with the horror he couldn't communicate, pain driving him to the crux he had never given words to.

"Did my uncle broker a deal to separate my twin and me at birth for Cold War twin research? Sometimes, I sense he's alive, I can feel it. And my father . . . I can't even hate him for what he's allowed my uncle to do to me and maybe my twin. He's as much a pawn as I was in the games of men like those you saw in your barbeque vision. I wouldn't be surprised if my uncle had been there. And your green man, I think I know who he is."

Seven stared back. "The doctor in my Norma Jeane vision?" Were visions connected to reality? "What did I see, Thomas, and why? If it weren't for the sunflower oil . . ."

Thomas shook his head. "Does the human nervous system create everything it sees, or is it like a receiver, picking up what is there, if you can only fine tune it enough?" He smiled. "Come on, I want to show you something." He threw off the blanket and leaped up.

Naked, they made their way down to the brook with Sirius leading the way. Taking care not to turn on any lights, Thomas led her into the lab to the window of the tiny insulated chamber she had asked about. It was dark inside. His hand on a switch, he looked at her.

"Ready?"

Her belly tightened.

He grinned. "I once told you that I catch telluric current in this chamber. Well, under thermal infrared light . . ." He flipped the switch.

At first, all Seven saw was vibrating muted light, but slowly she discerned movement. Something elfin and ill proportioned, with head and torso, legs and arms akimbo, was moving about the chamber, cautious and curious. Seven could see through its body.

Sirius whimpered and wagged his tail as he beheld the creature.

"It's Gollum from *The Lord of the Rings*," she murmured.

Thomas whispered back, "Exactly what I thought when I first saw it. In quantum mechanics, he would register as a potential or composite of potentials or result of potentials of an accelerated charged mass, but not mass in the way we're taught to think of it. This Gollum may be a hyperspatial, virtual being infolded from a zero point. Maxwell would have said he is scalar because if we can see him, he has magnitude. With the right measuring device, I could measure him, just like I could measure an invisible gas. Magnitude and direction, moving through space in some way, translating spatially, makes him a vector or having internal vectors. His physicality is not matter as we define it but plasma, the fourth state of matter. Spatial magnitude, internal spatial vector structure, hyperspatial, virtual, energy trapped in a local medium . . . His presence induces electromagnetic changes—I've measured them— though he himself doesn't exhibit his own electromagnetic force field. That's the Aharonov-Bohm effect," he added absentmindedly.

Seven hardly heard or understood a word he was saying, so captivated was she by the little Gollum Thomas had lured into his chamber.

"Does he live here?" she asked.

"He comes and goes, depending upon the electromagnetic field in the chamber." Thomas said. "I couldn't hold him if I wanted to. But you see how curious he is. Curiosity means intelligence."

Gollum stopped near the glass and peered at them.

"Does he see us?"

"I think so, or senses us. I think he can adjust his frequencies more easily than we can. Since 1959, quantum mechanics has known that EM potentials are primary agents, not force fields. But then, what does 'primary agent' mean? A being? Is this little creature a potential from the eternal Æther?"

Seven laughed. Quantum theory was explaining what the *chupu* woman had bestowed upon her. "So this is the secret of shamans, mystics, and sages," she whispered, "sensory awareness, the doors of perception." She hugged Thomas impulsively. "You've gone through the doors of perception with your instruments, and I've gone through the old way."

It was true. Thomas had located Gollum on his instruments while constructing a wind and water free energy device down by the stream. The Geiger counter had indicated radioactivity in the soil. Following his hunch that natural radioactive metals like uranium-238 were connected with stream and hot springs sacred sites, he began digging, after which synchronicity was loosed. First, he found Indian artifacts. Then a Serrano Indian who stopped by from time to time verified that there had once been hot springs here and that shamans came annually to confer with beings from other worlds, other dimensions—beings whose watery, airy forms traveled to the Surfaceworld by means of the springs. "He said the beings are exceedingly clever," Thomas explained excitedly, "and they conversed with shamans not in words but in mental pictures, revealing to their minds how this world of matter is constructed like a grid or web or net with enormous meshes, like the Spider Woman myths say. He said that we surface creatures live in these meshes caught in dense matter while wind and water, being made of finer matter, flow through the meshes we're stuck in. When we look out over our mesh, most of us cannot see or hear or feel anything moving through it, other than the slight friction of wind and water. To us, space is empty and our world solid, but the truth is that the space between the meshes is ten thousand times more real and more powerful than all of our 'substance.'" Thomas pointed to the window. "Gollum's no hallucination. He's a citizen of a dimension existing *inside* our material world."

Scientific ciphers often hide in legends and myths, Thomas reasoned, particularly when they're about spirits arising from subterranean spacetime. So he built his lab underground by the spring, leaving as much as possible as he found it, meanwhile camouflaging the air duct through which he collected planetary and stellar light for the vacuum chamber. Shamans and Druids, Egyptians and Mayans had coaxed solstices and equinoxes, star and planetary influences into subterranean sacred chambers. Thomas assured her that scientists at observatories like Palomar and Arecibo were testing and measuring these influences just as he was. No sooner had he captured the light of Sirius than little Gollum came sniffing around.

"Sirius!" Seven laughed, petting the Tibetan mastiff's giant head.

145

Since then, other creatures had revealed themselves in rolls and rolls of infrared film, and not just in the chamber but outside in the sky—caterpillar shapes, cigar shapes, half-moons, triangles, discs, globular critters with close-set eyes, all swimming through the air like an ocean. Thomas had penetrated Stanford Research Institute's computers, then those of Lawrence Livermore Laboratory, and struck pay dirt. Livermore had files and files on occult lore, papers by Sir Isaac Newton, Aristotle, Kepler, Giordano Bruno, Marsillo Ficino, Cardinal Nicholas of Cusa, Roger Bacon, Albertus Magnus, Al-Kindi, Abbot Trithemius of Würzburg, even Cardinal Pierre d'Ailly and Kepler horoscopes of Jesus Christ. The extensive collection pointed to Jesuit interest in scouring Renaissance literature for information regarding perception of the finer levels of the electromagnetic spectrum.

In the *Qur'an*, the Muslim holy book, Thomas found highly detailed descriptions of *jinn*, creatures with organic "ships" popping in and out of our atmosphere for centuries in various ephemeral shapes, but suddenly appearing in large numbers when radar—microwave radiation—began flooding the atmosphere in the 1940s and 1950s.

"Their bodies appear to be in the infrared spectrum," Thomas surmised, "and our microwaves, being just below infrared and just above radio waves, are disturbing their medium, the interplanetary Æther."

Heatedly, they discussed the endless array of questions that opening doors of perception unleashes: Is awareness utterly dependent upon perspective? Is that why the East has always said that the world is *maya?* Were the gates of Eden that the Cherubim guarded with flaming swords about not opening the doors of perception before one is prepared?

"Surely, 20th century science with all of its discovered and rediscovered technical genius and technology has *seen* into this infrared realm as you have, Thomas. What has it done to the Newtonian worldview?"

"Shattered the Enlightenment schizophrenia between mechanistic and alchemical—the mechanistic for the masses, the magickal for the elite." He sighed. "But are we ready? I don't think so." He put his arm around her shoulders. "I think this is the problem now. Moral development hasn't kept pace with technological discovery."

Seven stared at the creature staring back. Was this then the forbidden fruit of the Tree of Knowledge of Good and Evil? How was the problem of good and evil bound up with human perspective and awareness? She thought of the convocation of men in animal masks down in Coatzacoalcos. Certainly the Jaguar priest knew of this etheric world. Were such esotericists able to manipulate æther with their rituals and sacrifices, their aberrant sexual acts?

Just as she had this thought, her lifelong relationship with the dead commenced. Beside Gollum, a young man drifted out of the infrared soup toward the window, staring at Seven with profound sadness.

She clutched Thomas' hand. "Do you see him?" she asked breathlessly.

"Who?" Thomas saw only Gollum.

"The dead human boy," Seven whispered.

Thomas shook his head, puzzled. He had never seen a human in the infrared mix.

Words from the boy arose in her mind. "He says he was . . . shot and killed today out in Isla Vista by a Santa Barbara police officer. He says they're going to pin the blame on Ray." She glanced at Thomas. "I've got to go and find Ray."

When she turned back to thank the boy's ghost, he was gone.

"I'm going with you," Thomas decided quickly as he turned off the infrared. He had never met any of Seven's friends; it was time he got involved.

The hill was now bright with dawn. They dressed quickly, gave Sirius a swift hug, and jumped into Seven's bus. Weaving down the mountainside, they continued to talk, first about how the dead boy's ghost could have been in the chamber, why Thomas couldn't see him but could see Gollum, then about the Mexico vision and the little Legong dancer that reminded Seven of Mina and the girl Baby Rose.

"Baby Rose?" Thomas was puzzled. Seven hadn't talked about her.

He was all ears when Seven mentioned how terrified the girl was and the dried blood from her nose. "I've seen MK-ULTRA files about mind control experiments, hospitals and laboratories, drugs, electroencephalograms, electroshock." He glanced at Seven and decided not to go any deeper for now. "Baby Rose may be one of the girls programmed at Nellis, Point Mugu, Vandenberg, Goldstone, Lockheed, Northrup. Maybe she's an escapee."

The tranced-out little Legong dancer, Baby Rose singing nursery rhymes and looking over her shoulder in fear . . . Seven glanced at Thomas. "On the run?"

"Possibly. If my twin is alive, he and I could have been experiments, too—who knows? When I first drove up through Ojai, I had the strangest feeling that I had been there before, only by helicopter. Nothing firm, mind you. Just a sense." He stared out the window, his jaw tight. "Men like those in your vision, men like my uncle, have a plan for the future, Seven, and it's not pretty."

Seven furrowed her brow. Hermano had mentioned the CIA. "Your CIA has been as busy as bees since its creation at the end of World War Two. Study the CIA, Lilya, how it began, who was involved, what its agenda was and is, and you will find that a cuckoo has laid her eggs in the United States 'national security' nest, and when each egg hatches out, it will devour whatever is still good in your nation . . ."

She gripped the wheel tighter.

Thomas was dipping into her thoughts. "'And the truth shall set you free.' Imagine that: Jesus' words engraved on the wall of CIA headquarters in Langley, Virginia.. I've seen records of children going back to the early Fifties. Brainwashing, reprogramming, reconditioning—something your green man knows a lot about." His face clouded. "I think he is the Dr. Greenbaum who signed off on a lot of those records, he and the CIA chemist Sydney Gottlieb. Dr. Greens, Dr. Whites, Dr. Blacks—generic colors for doctors who did what Greenbaum and Gottlieb dictated."

Seven reached over to touch his sweet face. "How did you learn all of this?"

He shrugged. "Partially through my uncle, partially through university data banks I've broken into. When I 'disappeared' a few years ago, I made good use of the names and entry codes I had heard and seen all those years of being a *Wunderkind* lab rat. I've even hacked into J. Edgar Hoover's Political Sex Deviate Index. Now there's a juicy file worth millions in blackmail money and backroom deals—detailed rosters of preferences far beyond Joe Kennedy's penchant for having a woman three ways. It was from that Index that I learned how Marilyn Monroe was an MK-ULTRA sex slave assigned to sleep with Robert Kennedy and Sam Giancana the whole time she was married to Arthur Miller."

"Did . . . Dr. Greenbaum murder her? The police said it was a suicide."

Thomas laughed darkly. "Suicide is the convenient, all-purpose cover for eliminating

149

problems. Maybe she was discovered, or her programming was unraveling and she was becoming a liability and so was terminated. As an MK-ULTRA slave, they would have thought of her as theirs to do with as they wished.

"The Fifties were the early days of government mind control and a 'sexpionage' agent wasn't allowed to live much beyond thirty, unless she was programmed for more than sexpionage. If Baby Rose has been programmed, she would be second generation programmed for more than sex, maybe with cybernetic memory capabilities, mathematics, athletics, acting—whatever might be useful."

Uncannily, he started whistling the very song Seven had heard on the radio at Rhea's the previous afternoon—

> *Midnight*
> *one more night without sleeping,*
> *Watching*
> *till the morning comes creeping,*
> *Green door*
> *what's the secret you're keeping?*

"But how could such a secret be kept for decades without public knowledge? All it would take is one journalist, one politician—"

"—and *boom!*" Thomas cried. "Oh my, the poor man had an 'accident,' his airplane blew up. Or he 'committed suicide' because he was 'depressed.' Or his children are abducted. 'How *violent* life is becoming in America.' A lone nut is paraded across television sets. He had a bad childhood or was mad at his boss and look what happened. *Tsk tsk.*" He glanced at Seven. "There *have* been people who've tried to speak out. All the dead Warren Commission witnesses? John Lennon. The 'Paul is dead' thing? There's so much under the surface . . ."

150

He sank into silence.

Seven reached over to squeeze his hand. "I'm sorry, Thomas. You've been living with this all your life, but before yesterday, I never thought much about things like mind control or Satanic rites in Mexico or doctors killing Hollywood stars or military programs using children like you and Baby Rose . . ."

Suddenly, she could see Dr. Greenbaum's cold eyes staring at her from the corner of her mind. Was it just a memory, or was he somehow able to see her even now?

She released Thomas' hand and gripped the steering wheel like it was her fear. "But I know one thing: not only is Ray in danger but Baby Rose and you are, too. I can feel it. We've got to hurry."

And with that they were silent, willing the bus to get to Rhea's as quickly as possible.

11
Ray

Mr. Weinglass: Will you please identify yourself for the record?

The Witness: My name is Abbie. I am an orphan of America.

Mr. Schultz: Your Honor, may the record show it is the defendant Hoffman who has taken the stand?

The Court: Oh, yes. It may so indicate . . .

Mr. Weinglass: Where do you reside?

The Witness: I live in Woodstock Nation.

Mr. Weinglass: Will you tell the Court and jury where it is?

The Witness: Yes. It is a nation of alienated young people. We carry it around with us as a state of mind in the same way as the Sioux Indians carried the Sioux nation around with them. It is a nation dedicated to cooperation versus competition, to the idea that people should have better means of exchange than property and money, that there should be some other basis for human interaction. It is a nation dedicated to --

The Court: Just where it is, that is all.

The Witness: It is in my mind and in the minds of my brothers and sisters. It does not consist of property or material, but rather of ideas and certain values. We believe in a society --

The Court: No, we want the place of residence, if he has one, place of doing business, if you have a business. Nothing about philosophy or ideas, sir, just where you live, if you have a place to live. Now, you said Woodstock. In what state is Woodstock?

The Witness: It is in the state of mind, in the mind of myself and my brothers and sisters. It is a conspiracy. Presently, the nation is held captive, in the penitentiaries of the institutions of a decaying system . . .

- Opening testimony of Abbie Hoffman at the Chicago 8 Trial, September 24, 1969

Seven was right: Ray was running scared, heading north for home. Sitting in the San Francisco bus station on the corner of Stockton and Clay, trying to get hold of himself, he wanted to call Rhea and find out what was going on but figured her phone might be tapped by now. He scanned the *San Francisco Chronicle* and came up with nothing. If something was up, it was going down quietly. The good news was, being black, he blended in a hell of a lot better in downtown San Francisco than in Isla Vista or Santa Barbara, and the bad news was he was running on automatic. Going home was a bad idea, given that the pigs had his file and knew all about his family. But he wasn't really thinking. He was running.

In a way, he was already home because it had all begun in Oakland across the bridge. As far back as he could remember or wanted to remember, he'd been split down the middle, a coffee-and-cream nigger, white family in Tacoma, black family in Oakland. His mother was a Jamaican beauty, his father a hotheaded Scots-Irish.

Politics was all he'd ever known. From the time he was ten, he'd grown up in Tacoma, Washington, a workingman's town on Commencement Bay between Seattle and the state capital at Olympia, reared on stories of ships three deep crowding the docks in Commencement Bay, lumber schooners, single-decked, broad and long with square sterns, their hatches ready for Douglas fir en route to San Francisco, Chile, Australia, Liverpool. By the 1880s, all that was left of Great Lakes old growth was bought

153

up by German-American Frederick Weyerhæuser, whose St. Paul and Tacoma lumber companies then bought up ninety thousand acres of timber from Northern Pacific Railroad, the biggest private land deal in American history, barring the ongoing theft of Indian land, of course. Then in 1900, Weyerhæuser bought a dozen times what he'd bought from Northern Pacific, thanks to the president of Great Northern, his one-eyed Canadian friend, James Jerome Hill.

Ray had been the apple of his stormy white grandfather's eye and therefore heard every litany of the past ten times over that his thick brogue could tell. *Dico tibi verum,* his grandfather made him recite over and over, *libertas optima rerum; nunquam servili sub nexu vivito fili,* assuring him that if William Wallace had learned it by heart, he too could learn it. "Don't forget, lad," his Scottish grandfather stressed, "Northern Pacific was owned by Germans, not Americans, so all the money went back to Germany. International trade spells the death of nations."

Black-powder men commanded a high wage, particularly after Tacoma Smelting and Refining began processing bullion. Ray's grandfather was a powderman from England by way of San Francisco. The Panic of May 1893 dashed his New World hopes and those of three million other men and women. The tide of emigrants carried steadily west for fifty years suddenly reversed and drowned thousands of starving families. Ray's grandfather and other men made common cause with one another, calling themselves the industrial army, and petitioned the powers-that-be for food and transport to possible jobs. They elected officers, issued meal tickets, and assured each man an equal portion of whatever the group came up with. Then Jacob S. Coxey of Massillon, Ohio recruited them to join the

Commonweal Army of Christ and march to Washington, D.C. to petition the government to create what President Franklin Delano Roosevelt later would call the New Deal.

Ray's grandfather believed in the industrial army, but not in Coxey's agenda or his Commonweal Army. He foresaw only grief in a 4,000-mile march to petition the federal government for anything, having figured out that fat cats only get fatter from stock market crashes, and that each one of them probably had two or three legislators in his back pocket. That a thousand or more poor men, women and children starved here or there made no difference to them; there were more where they came from. What was it preachers were so fond of quoting? *The poor are always with you.* Oh, what the wolves had made of that naive, bleeding Carpenter! Ray's grandfather liked to say he'd squeezed the curd from the Scottish Calvinist tradition and left the whey. He had no argument with John Calvin or the Carpenter; it was their bloody followers who had done the damage and ground the poor into dust with religion. *Pernicious predestination!* Ray's grandfather would thunder, his face flushed, the silver hairs in his eyebrows a-bristle.

Strong individuality ran in the family. Ray's white great grandmother, God rest her soul, had hailed from Arundel where she'd sat at the feet of the only preacher she would ever care about when she was but fifteen. He was a MacDonald and the deacons had got rid of him two years later because he didn't preach enough hellfire and damnation, preferring instead the dangerous Christian idea of *Love* to fall from his lips like pollen. When he left the pulpit and went to write his faerie tales, she had wiped the dust from her feet and left the religious persuasion that prided itself in saying that Christ had died only for the elect.

So when Coxey's Tacoma contingent of the Commonweal Army started for Washington on Easter

Sunday 1894, Ray's white grandfather, then about
Ray's age, wished them well and stayed behind. When
he heard that Northern Pacific had refused to let the
men fire up the engines and boxcars just sitting in the
hands of receivers in Seattle, Ellensburg, Yakima, and
Spokane, he had shaken his head and sighed. In
Puyallup, as the numbers of the army of the poor
swelled to thirteen hundred, police trigger fingers had
begun to itch. On May 9, three men and two US
deputies were wounded outside of Yakima and fifty-
some men arrested and shipped back to Seattle for
trial. The rest pressed on by foot through the
Bitterroots and Rockies to Great Falls, Montana,
where the Commonweal Army finally collapsed, only
to be saved by Charlotta Cantwell, the best woman
alive, save Ray's grandmother. With her St. Bernard
Colonel at her side, she practically single-handedly
fed, clothed, and sheltered twelve hundred
bedraggled men, putting on daily fundraising rallies
across from saloons, singing songs, selling poems,
even addressing the Fourth of July American Railway
Union picnic to make enough money to hire a freight
to Minneapolis. Of the original twelve hundred, a few
hundred finally made it to Washington only to be
ignored by Congress.

This sad little paragraph in American labor
history reminded Ray of Martin Luther King's
planned Poor People's Campaign scheduled for the
summer of 1968. When he heard about it, he
prophetically thought, *They'll never let him get away
with it.* And they didn't.

After the bitter end of the Commonweal Army,
gold in the Yukon boosted the economy and perpetual
control over the Panama Canal was coming, so
Weyerhæuser bought up the remainder of western
Washington. Once Tacoma became too big and too
busy, Ray's grandfather moved to Centralia and
signed on for the 160-acre timber claim he might

156

have if in three years he could clear acreage for crops, build a house, and live on the land. As chief powder man for Eastern Railway and Lumber, he was paid well to travel from camp to camp. Everywhere he went, he saw living conditions even a dog shouldn't submit to. The company not only paid no insurance against injuries, but work days were long, the men isolated in camps deep in the woods and disallowed to leave sometimes for months, sleeping and eating in tattered tents or cabins with wide chinks in the walls and little opportunity to bathe or wash their clothes. One horse doctor sufficed for dozens of camps. Loggers were hired, fired, paid arbitrarily, and if they made a stink, ended up having an "accident" while another hungry man took his place for less. Everywhere in the woods, in the sawmills, the mines, and the smelters, Ray's grandfather heard the tramping of the ghosts of the Commonweal Army, the opening and shutting of boxcar doors as they scuttled in and out of shadows on their way to where they'd heard there was a job. He worked his land and tried to stay out of harm's way but had no peace with so many poor men of all colors tramping through his heart. Meanwhile, the rich grew richer.

He had heard of the IWW's success in organizing textile workers back East and that they were coming to Centralia. Wondering if they lived up to their high-sounding creed, *An injury to one is an injury to all*, he went to an early IWW meeting where his Celtic blood drew him to Eileen, a third generation Irish Catholic American covering the meeting for *The Centralia Daily Hub*. Her grandfather had fled the potato famine in 1846 and come to America because of a handbill he'd seen in Galway about land in Oregon Territory being given away under the Pre-Emption Law of 1842. Instead of milk and honey, he'd found more hardship than ever he'd endured in Catholic Ireland. Just short of his eighteenth birthday, he made it to

157

Kansas City in time to head west with a wagon train of folks who'd seen similar handbills.

It would take him a few years to figure out that the potato famine had been a Freemason ploy to get cheap labor to America. The *phytophthora infestans* was true enough, as were the needless deaths of one million Irish, but shiploads of good potatoes had still found their way to England, for Christ's sake! One and a half million Catholic Irish had to leave their beloved Éire and emigrate west as indentured slaves for the building of the Freemasons' New Atlantis, while the British Opium Wars of 1839-42 and 1858-60 thrust 100,000 penniless addicted Chinese up onto America's western shores. *Empire building needs cheap labor,* Ray's grandfather would sneer, *just ask any ancient Egyptian or Roman.*

At this point, he would pause in the story and ask Ray, *What would have happened had I not gone to that meetin' and met your grandmother? Why, you wouldn't be here now, lad.* And little Ray would ponder this mystery, his brow knit over how lives hinged on chance encounters, which meant you might miss a crucial turning point if you turned right instead of left, or changed your mind. (Or was that part of fate, too?) And the old man would sit and smile as he watched the little brown bairn's stormy face struggle over the age-old problem of fate and free will.

Then he'd go on about Eileen's honey-colored hair at the logger camp meeting that night, her slight, tough frame, her Irish blue eyes with a hint of the green hills in them, and how unflinching savvy she'd been about what it would mean if laborers united against the bosses and brought their guns in case of trouble. Her questions toward the close of the meeting were forthright and to the point, laying open the will hiding behind those faerie-fine female features. Like all men, he'd seen his mother in her, the only other woman he had given life-long love to. A deep river ran through her that he wanted running through his children and his children's children—and here he would poke Ray's chest and Ray would feel wanted and loved by his white grandfather and bask in the fact that great events had him in mind before he was ever born. His grandfather decided then and there in that logging camp that if she would have him, she was the woman he would love until death do us part. He was forty-six and she twenty-six, an old maid by the standards of the day. But she was the first daughter of a large Catholic family and had had to raise the rest of the brood as they came up, raging over the unwritten law that said sons were assets and daughters deficits to be relieved only by marriage. Still, the worst for Eileen was a terrible family secret and she vowed to marry only a man who once he heard it would weep for her and what she had endured under her own father's hand. Ray's grandfather had passed the test of tears.

"But Granddad," Ray would whisper, "what was the terrible secret?" and his grandfather would look him over with a measuring eye to see if he was old enough yet to swallow the bitter pill, then shake his head.

"No, laddie, not yet. But I promise you that someday you will know it all and be man enough to weep for what helpless womenfolk and children have had to put up with for too long. Many families like your grandmother's are crippled by such secrets, and if I were a prayin' man, I would pray right along with that bleedin' Carpenter that the poor and oppressed— and no one is more oppressed than women and children, whether rich or poor—be spared such God-awful things, for what it done to my beloved wife was not healed yet when she was taken from me," and here he always sighed.

Ray had never known his white grandmother Eileen, and only his grandfather spoke of her. Not once did his father mention her, perhaps blaming her for taking the light out of his father's eyes. But whatever caused the shadow that hung over him, Ray's father had been a hellion, his grandfather would say, shaking his head, and had gone off for years, only to suddenly come home worse than ever after leaving Ray and his Jamaican mother and her two little girls from a previous man.

Sitting in the bus station, himself now on the run, Ray didn't want to heap more trouble on his father who'd refused to fight when the second European war in his lifetime came along and he was sent to Washington State Penitentiary in Walla Walla. After they let him out, he disappeared, ending up in Oakland with Ray's mother and her daughters. Ray was born in 1944 and six years later his father left. Ray didn't see him until he was ten and had saved enough bus money to make it to the Tacoma address he'd found on an envelope in his mother's bedroom.

While thinking he didn't want to think about the night his father left, he found himself staring blankly at a face across from him in the bus station. An older white man with dark hair and eyes was smiling as if he knew him and before Ray knew it was getting up and crossing over to him.

"Ray, isn't it?" The ageless man proffered a pale hand.

"Do I know you?" Ray asked gruffly, not taking the hand.

Sliding into the seat beside him, the man said, "I believe we are common friends of a young woman named Seven?"

Ray stared at him. The accent was from Europe somewhere, the clothes straight. He'd talked to Seven?

The man shook his head, smiling. "I have alarmed you and I apologize. No, I am not an intelligence agent, at least not in the way you might think. But I have come to intercept your present plans, if possible. This much is true."

Ray could only stare, his mind rushing. "What do you mean, 'intercept'?" He checked the exits. He still had a few friends in Oakland who could help.

The European said, "Forgive my brevity, but there is not much time." He too looked around. "You are correct in assuming that certain parties are looking for you."

How did he know that?

The European leaned forward. "*Te está encaminando mal.* You are taking the wrong path, Ray. I know you do not love prayers like your grandmother did. Living in the land of materialism weakens the ability to converse with divine beings without whom we cannot draw one breath or savor one political insight. Thoughts are what make us human, but today it is very difficult to experience your own thoughts, isn't it? Most are the result of modern media sorcery filled with spellbound images to ingest. Follow them back to their lair and you will see if they devour or nourish, poison or heal. But this is difficult."

Ray sat dumbfounded, wondering where the ageless man was going with this.

"Similarly, you are blinded by anger at religion because the big churches and temples and synagogues are dying institutions, it is true. But anger only blinds and won't keep us safe from further pain.

Ray wanted the old man to shut up about pain. His words were messing with the dam he'd built against memories of childhood ghettos with drugs on every corner, overworked mothers, absent fathers, holes in his shoes, pregnant little girls and tough little boys and the white man's heel, always the white man's heel on the black man's back. He had good reason to be angry and yet the man was right: anger was killing him slow, eating him like cancer. Wasn't it one of the seven deadly sins? He couldn't remember

The European took a long cool drink of his Perrier and smacked his lips appreciatively. "How I miss these French waters." He gazed on Ray. "You are right to not trust large hierarchic institutions. However, it is not just money and secular power that men at the top of these organizations want. They want power over *souls.* Your grandfather understood this. First, they convince you that there is no such thing as the soul, then they devour it with maws of consumer nothingness." He chuckled. "Then Sartre celebrates *Being and Nothingness.*"

Power over souls. The ache always just a word or gesture away was getting away from Ray. The dam was breaking behind which was walled the six-year-old boy and his memory of a particular night.

Like a midwife, the European gently placed a hand on Ray's. "Let him out, Ray, he can't breathe in there. Once he is out, you will have only memories and not a death sentence."

The European's touch sprang the lock and Ray saw that little Oakland boy once so full of piss and vinegar and joy, not anger. Then there it was: the night his father left. *Went back to his people,* his mother hissed while washing dishes like she was punishing them. He could still hear the door slam after she and his father had argued. Beside him, his two half-sisters slept the sleep of innocents. He waited until his mother had gone to bed, then crept out to look for his father, knowing the bars his Irish friends frequented.

Ray could still hear the boy's bare feet slapping the pavement, the wind whipping through Oakland just before Christmas, the cars whizzing by, the music and loud talk at The Caribbean and smell of urine and alcohol outside mingling with the smell of smoke and sweat inside. But before he could look to see if his father was there, the big black bouncer said to be involved in voodoo chased him out. Crestfallen, he'd moved on to check another bar. Just as he was passing an alley, black hands grabbed him, taped his mouth and covered his head with a pillowcase and bound his hands behind his back. His pants were yanked down, he was slammed frontwise against the wall, and—

"I can't, I can't," Ray gasped, his face wet with tears he didn't know he could produce anymore, his body shaking. Sobs twisted his chest and gut, knots of resistance, but still he forced himself back to the scene, helpless to stop what those three men did to that good little boy looking for his daddy. The rhythmic grunts, the whiskey and bad breath, the sour sweat. All over again, he felt the red-hot knife of rape.

He had come to later on an unfamiliar floor beside other bound boys and girls, some unconscious or maybe dead, the pillowcases gone, their mouths still taped. In the semi-darkness, the awake children stared at each other, listening to adult voices beyond the tattered curtain separating the storefront from the little storage room they were in. The accents were Caribbean, Oakland, Southern, and they were haggling over price.

The older boy hog-tied behind little Ray wriggled until they were back to back, then worked the twine cutting into little Ray's pencil-thin wrists. Once they were loosened, Ray pulled his hands free and turned to free his liberator. But the laughter in the other room indicated that the price had been decided and footsteps were moving their way. The older boy nodded vehemently toward the dog door in the bottom of the back door. With a backward glance at his savior and the other children, Ray crawled toward the door, his anus burning. Houdini-like, he squeezed his head and long limbs out, casting one last look at the boy who had bought him his freedom, a glance that would last a lifetime.

Outside, little Ray jerked off the tape and ran until he finally found two cops, one black and one white. Breathless, he explained the situation and tugged at their uniforms to come quickly. They put him in the back of the squad car and followed his directions to the Houdou storefront. *Stay in the car,* the white cop said, and went in while the black cop went around to the back. Peeking out the car window and through the storefront window, little Ray watched as the cop talked to the witch doing business in the middle of the night. When her slow eyes turned toward the squad car, Little Ray scrunched down as low as he could, trembling. When the cops got back in the car, the black one turned and said, *You sure this was the place?* He was sure. The two cops glanced at each other, then took him home. He was ashamed to tell them or his mama what had been done to him and had been running ever since.

Back in the bus station, Ray looked down at the white man's hand on his, the man who knew Seven. He took a deep breath. The rock he'd been carrying in the middle of his gut for twenty years had softened, the rock that made him smoke too much dope and drink too much wine and burn with rage. He'd never found out what had happened to the children he'd been unable to save, but at least he knew he'd done the best he could. Suddenly, he understood that his politics came straight from that older boy tied up on the floor. His eyes teared up again for all the hardness in the world. Had he known how gently and quickly healing could come, maybe he could have done it sooner. Ray smiled into the European's dancing eyes.

"Welcome back, Ray," the man beamed. "Believe me, we need you strong and whole. There's a lot to be done."

12
Didymus

Arise! Arise! he cried so loud with a voice without
*   restraint,*
Hear me out, ye gifted kings and queens, and hear
*   my sad complaint.*
No martyr is among ye now whom ye can call your
*   own,*
Go on your way accordingly, but know you're not
*   alone.*

I dreamed I saw St. Augustine alive with fiery
*   breath,*
I dreamed I was amongst the ones that put him out
*   to death.*
Oh, I awoke in anger, so alone and terrified,
Cut my fingers against the glass and bowed my
*   head and cried.*

- Bob Dylan, "I Dreamed I Saw St. Augustine,"
1967

As Didymus Hauser and FBI Agent Simon Iff
exited northbound 101 at Santa Barbara, a Los
Angeles radio station was playing the Bob Dylan song
about the watchtower for early morning commuters.
Didy liked Bob Dylan. He didn't let any of the other
agents know he liked him, though. Dr. Greenbaum
had always told him to keep things formal, so Didy
made sure he was always addressed as Agent Hauser
by everyone but Simon Iff. Nor did he partake of
needless stakeout chitchat. After all, he was a Chosen
One, as Dr. Greebaum had said a thousand times. Didy
didn't understand what Dylan was trying to say, but

he liked how it sounded. *Outside in the distance a wildcat did growl, Two riders were approaching, the wind began to howl* . . . Dylan was a lot better than all the drivel about momma and my baby left me in the country music Simon Iff preferred.

What Didy didn't know was that his partner knew a lot more about him than he knew himself, including his *real* surname. Iff was a veteran agent carefully chosen and briefed about Didy being the unknowing identical twin of a wanted fugitive named Thomas Gardner, and that Didy was some sort of futuristic Bionic Man because of how he'd been handfed by a lot of Agency docs since he was a baby. The classified report Iff read said Didy had several personalities, most designed for exceptional performance in the field. For the most part, Iff didn't need to worry about it, his field officer had said; the personalities could only be triggered by a phone call from either Greenbaum or Gottlieb. All Iff had to do was keep Didy in his sights and make reports to the docs about how their Bionic Man was doing.

At which point the field officer had hesitated. "But there is *one* thing, one situation that's *sensitive,* and if it comes up will call for your utmost alertness. Agent Hauser knows nothing about his twin whose disappearance six or so years ago has brought some high-ranking CIA project to a screeching halt." He lowered his voice and smiled. "The Company still has its panties in a wad over it."

The two veteran agents smiled knowingly at each other. The CIA was the prima donna, not meat-and-potatoes like the FBI. The Company didn't just *have* a Weird Desk, it *was* the Weird Desk.

"And you know who their uncle is," the field officer added, "*and* who their grandfather was."

Yes, Gardner was a name well known in intelligence circles, and yet despite the combined efforts of FBI, CIA, DIA, ONI, Interpol, you name it, not a hair of the missing twin's head had been seen in six years.

The field agent went on in a whisper. "Talk about embarrassment. The Gardner kid is some sort of genius who can hack his way into the Pentagon, for Christ's sake, and wipe his trust fund clean, millions, without a trace. Some sort of miracle kid who can walk on water, the eggheads' worst nightmare." The field agent chuckled. He hated Nazi spook doctors like Greenbaum and Gottlieb thinking they were God. And the trust-fund rich? Piss on them. "So he's somewhere out there," he continued, pointing to a world map on the wall, "scrambling information in NSA data bases it takes months to retrieve and re-order."

The two agents laughed again, shaking their heads. Some criminals you just had to admire, especially if they got the best of spook doctors.

The field agent got serious. "It's a snowball's chance in hell that you and Hauser would come across him, but if you do, the shrinks say that *your* twin shouldn't bat an eye, even if he's looking straight at his spitting image, because of something they call mirror programming." He shrugged. "Anyway, Gottlieb says to observe Hauser carefully. The Gardner twin has really messed up Gottlieb's twin research, and boy, is he ever hot about it." He chuckled again. "I wouldn't want to be that whiz kid twin when Gottlieb gets hold of him."

So Didy was Iff's real assignment, whatever cover assignments he might be given. What the FBI field agent didn't know was that Iff *was* CIA with an FBI Agent cover. He'd been recruited straight out of Brigham Young University. His great uncle worked for the General Authorities or Brethren, the living oracles of Mormonism, and had recommended him to one of his political friends as good Company material. That was all it took. The Company liked Mormons, preferred them by far to Protestants, though Knights of Malta were still the kingpins. Mormons understood the value of absolute belief and obedience, and without a testimony, *no one* could get a Temple recommend to get into the Celestial Kingdom. Mormons were exceedingly patriotic, hating Communism and socialism and worshipping capitalism. Hell, they basically owned four states.

At nineteen—right after the Temple ceremony received him into the Melchizedek Priesthood—Iff had gone with his family to a CAUSA International convention where Reverend Sun Myung Moon of the Unification Church was speaking, along with Dr. W. Cleon Skousen, ex-FBI and Salt Lake City chief of police heading up the Freemen Institute his father was a member of. Young Simon had been dazzled. Scientists, top Pentagon officers, conservative political leaders were all there, murmuring, *We affirm that the God of Judaism, Catholicism, Protestantism, the Mormons, the Unification Church and the God of all religions are one and the same.* Beautiful words, but how could they be true? The Church of Latter-Day Saints believes there is no salvation outside the Church. But he silenced his nagging doubt and was recruited by the CIA just before setting out on his mission to the Yucatan, where the events of *The Book of Mormon* had taken place. "We'll see you when you get back from your mission," the handsome Mormon agent had smiled, slapping him on the back. Such blessings!

Now, after ten years in the Agency, he wasn't so sure. He'd seen things, *done* things . . . But he'd clung to his faith in the Church, his testimony, the Temple recommend he and his wife and family needed for their life together in eternity. Ideals and religion didn't have to go together. Tough choices, that's what life was about. Ideals were the childish things he had to put away.

Iff and Didy stopped at The Olive Tree for some breakfast before heading out to Isla Vista. Iff had eaten there in February when the pinko students had burned the Bank of America to the ground and Reagan had called out the National Guard. Now there was new trouble. The night before, Santa Barbara FBI had called to report (as per COINTELPRO instructions) that local PD had jumped the gun and killed some kid. There would be hell to pay in the press without a mop-up.

It had been so simple when CIA meant *international* espionage. Operation Chaos had changed all that, bringing the Agency home and making cover-ups more complex. *Possible outside Communist agitation* might cover for some Agency presence—that was how Director Hoover had backpedaled out of the Congressional inquiry into Martin Luther King's tapped phones—but it was getting thin. Iff believed almost everything the Agency churned out and was proud to be part of the joint CIA-FBI COINTELPRO team operating out of Los Angeles under Operation Chaos. He was committed to undermining in every way possible and by any means necessary the so-called Sixties generation and their dope, sex, and Marxist anti-war, peace-and-love bullshit. But the "Communist leaning" story was getting old.

He made another phone call to the agent handling media, then slid into the booth at The Olive Tree, rubbing his eyes. They'd been on the road since five-thirty or so to beat rush hour in Los Angeles.

Unlike his partner, Didy could care less about Mom or apple pie. Anti-Communist fervor had been a minimal part of his programming. His had been geared to the coming era when petty nationalism would give way to huge trade blocs and one-world governors, when the elite no longer had to play footsy with the self-deluded democratic masses and could dispense with staged elections to rule as the benign dictators they had always perceived themselves to be. Didy's neurons were not clogged with patriotic crap. Dr. Greenbaum had programmed him for efficiency, stamina, and superior reactions. The avenging angels of man's quest for dominance—doubt, fear, and anger—could not weaken his capacities, nor had he been raised by a neurotic mother or family. Everything had been done scientifically, methodically, quantitatively. Didy did not know what it was to be divided against himself because he did not actually think of himself as a self. He was a locus of perception, acutely sensitive to all taking place around him and therefore able to act instantaneously, incisively, and ruthlessly if necessary.

But even Greenbaum and Gottlieb knew that Didy's extraordinary capacities were spun together by a thin thread of programmed amnesia. As long as he did not remember, he would not know that the very nature of programming was being shattered into a thousand personalities like the mirror in Hans Christian Andersen's *Snow Queen*, the story Dr. Green had read to him over and over again when he was little—

> *. . . and a demon invented a mirror in which every good or beautiful thing shrank away to almost nothing, and every bad and good-for-nothing thing looked its worst, in which the most beautiful landscapes looked like boiled spinach, and the best people were hideous, and if a good thought passed through anyone's mind, it turned to a grin in the mirror. The demon thought it all immensely amusing. After showing it all over the Earth, the demon flew up to heaven with it to mock the angels. The*

higher he flew, the more the mirror
grinned, until at last he couldn't hold it
anymore and it fell to Earth, shivering
into a million pieces which then flew all
about, and into people's eyes, and even
into their hearts . . .

Didy remembered nothing of being split and
nothing of all he was privy to, including US Navy
experimentation databases of hundreds of thousands
of children and women and men programmed in the
name of national security. Chosen Ones acted as
backup memory banks so that "sensitive" data was
not committed to a paper or computer trail.

Except for that worrisome thread, Didy was an
impervious, consummate cyborg. Iff thought the
binary memory system of a fractured psyche as a
repository of national security data, a veritable Fort
Knox, sounded pretty worrisome. On the other hand,
his hothouse of personalities was undistracted by the
silly self-doubts and yearnings and ponderings of
typical youth. Didy was like the dysfunctional village
on that series *The Prisoner*, each inhabitant
remembering only a sliver of the collective day or
minute.

As for how strong the rest of the threads were that
bound Didy the baby and Didy the boy to what
Gottlieb and his lab-coated minions deep in the
mountains on the parched plains of national security
had done to him, no one really knew and certainly not
Iff. Each persona had risen up like a bright-helmeted
angel from Didy's jerking, pain-racked body in the
laboratories deep in the Snow Queen's palace. During
each incident of trauma and terror, one angel or
another had risen up armed with shield and spear to
hold at bay the icy Cold War memories of what
medieval science had done to drive his soul from his
body and numb his heart and head. Each angelic alter

had taken the pain as he lay under the surgical lights, electrodes plastered to his temples, the stun gun on his genitals; as he witnessed adults doing unspeakable things to him and was forced to do unspeakable things to others in turn or be killed. Each persona tried to shield Didy and other Chosen Ones from feeling how alien and utterly unhuman Dr. Gottlieb and his Nazi "research" were.

Such was the village that was Didy.

Agent Iff had been briefed on only one of Didy's split-off angels, the one programmed as a sleeper that just a few trigger words could turn into an automaton killer, a psyops nightmare come true. It had been explained to Agent Iff that those trigger words were worth thousands and thousands of Operation Sleeping Beauty dollars and could, for the right price, be acquired by private citizens with something the military or intelligence wanted, like public silence or complicity, in exchange for the death of a public figure foreign or domestic. A sleeper was an ace up the sleeve, a Manchurian asset, a kamikaze pilot nose-diving the plane on cue, a spree killer at the office waiting for the trigger, a sex-crazed serial killer working at a daycare. The assassin sleeping under Agent Hauser's skin was gold to those who orchestrated national security. Didy might pick up a phone or pass someone in a crowd and hear the trigger words that awakened Sleeping Beauty to do their will, even unto self-destruction.

But a sleeper like Didymus was rarely commanded to self-dispose; too many millions of dollars had gone into building Delta sleepers. Plus Didymus was half of a Mengele twin research project temporarily shelved until the other half was found. Intelligence brass were confident that one day Thomas would slip up and they would have him again, so they kept Didymus on ice under Simon Iff, their veteran West Coast handler.

Didymus had been programmed from infancy to be the hardened warrior, while Thomas had been sleep programmed for physics and biochemistry under his handler uncle. When Thomas disappeared, Dr. Greenbaum had argued with Gottlieb that his thought processes had been programmed to be too complex, too inquiring, too self-reflective—definitely a problem when programming for more than functionaries. They could produce genius intelligence and superhuman Olympic athletic performance through trauma-based mind control, yes, but in the more sensitive the programming didn't necessarily remain *fixed*. Just the right amount of self-consciousness was the problem. That brilliant rocket science kid Jack Parsons had gone off the deep end, and British intelligence had always been on less than firm ground with Aleister Crowley. But *without* self-consciousness, cybernetic humans might be gifted but remain somewhat stupid and mechanical, much like binary computer simulacra.

Outside of MK-ULTRA, Freemason initiates had traumatized and programmed the childhoods of thousands over the centuries, from killers to actors like Fonda, Streisand, and Brando, musicians like Robert Johnson and Hank Williams, Baez, Barrett, McCartney, Hendrix, the Grateful Dead and other Laurel Canyon types, and virtually all of country music. Mind-controlled celebrities were easy to pass off on a public already conditioned to think of drug and alcohol problems as the norm for performers. Commercially speaking, they were a better investment than free-will artists. MK performers could tour and tour and never grow tired, never complain, produce film after film and never break stride, needing only a little tune-up at a rehab center now and then. And when they start to age and really break down, like Monroe and Elvis, Hollywood pundits dropped the drug problem or depression gambit to cover an untimely death. Entertainment moneymakers weren't the least interested in free will and were therefore deeply indebted to MK-ULTRA's trump of *Masonic apoplexy.*

Thomas proved that the programming allowing for a certain amount of self-consciousness was less predictable. From the beginning, he'd been smart, quick, and impenetrable. Still, they hadn't foreseen that he would have the wherewithal to deceive them for years, then gut his trust fund. He was simply too self-conscious. Once Greenbaum got him back, the re-programming would fix that.

Agent Iff smoked a Winston while watching Sleeping Beauty run his fingers over the bark of the huge old tree growing up through the restaurant roof. Was this his child personality? Iff made a quick scan of his investments in the business section of the *LA Times,* took a last drag and stubbed out his cigarette. "Let's go, Didy."

In the car, Iff glanced at Ray Kofi's FBI file. Before Isla Vista, he'd take a look at the residence on Hillside. According to Santa Barbara PD, Ray would be their doer for the Bank of America fiasco, a political troublemaker tied in with that camel jockey Rashidi Ali. Two birds with one stone were counted as good Agency coup, and it might serve to cover the PD snafu, given that Ray was living at the residence of a Commie sympathizer from Pasadena. A real rat's nest.

Agent Iff drove between the low walls at 1549 Hillcrest. Agent Hauser should scout around back while he went to the door. He checked his watch: 0711, an auspicious time. He liked to catch people early and a little off-balance. He knocked at the screen door and, like Seven before him, stared at the Siamese sentinel with saucer eyes and the hot-pink girl spiraling down the vortex. *Weird,* thought Mormon Agent Iff.

175

Didy slipped around to the back of the house, the thick viscous bouquet of morning organic life barraging his senses much as the great olive tree at the restaurant had overwhelmed his fingertips. While his eyes scanned the chaparral, his skin said *Come hither* and temporarily melted his warrior mode. His ears listened for movement while his feet followed the spiral in and further in, enticed by the scent of roses, roses, roses, part of his hippocampus now in upstate New York and Glen Cove, Maine, part at The Olive Tree touching the bark. *Mill ponds, beaver dams, honeysuckle, katydids . . .* Rounding the last tiny arc, he gaped. Before a towering blue-green stalk stood a girl with spun white-gold hair who neither saw nor heard nor sensed him, so intent was she upon a wilting white flower.

Didy gaped. Females were foreign to him, other than in connection with certain acts that his programming forced him to perform, none of which he remembered. The girl's slender form, cradling the blossom as if she feared to damage even a cell of its fading beauty, nudged loose a great stone long ago heaved onto his stunted heart.

She turned to look over her shoulder at him, her eyes brimming with tears. Her beauty, her spun-gold hair . . . *He knew her.*

His mind and throat constricted like a snake. Terrified of the cry forming in his throat, he turned and stumbled back along the labyrinth, finally careening off the spiraled path and out of the garden up toward the bare yellow hills. At last standing in front of the tipi he knew to be Ray's, he looked back down but saw only the tip of the blue-green stalk.

In control again, he snooped through the tipi. Either Ray didn't own much or he had cleared out. By nose, Didy could tell that no one had been there in maybe three or four days. Satisfied it was a cold trail, he descended and skirted the garden, cut around the

176

house, and almost ran directly into an irritated Rhea with Mina peeking from behind her.

Didy flashed his credentials. "Just looking around a bit, ma'am."

Rhea scoffed at the card. "Young man, I know my rights and you need a search warrant. And what is the CIA doing in California, anyway?"

Agent Iff walked up. He'd already encountered the old Commie.

"Sorry, ma'am," he said, nodding toward Didymus, "new kid on the block along for training. Thank you for your time." Smiling, he guided Didy by the arm back to the car.

Once they were driving out between the low adobe walls, Iff asked, "Find anything?"

Didy shrugged, the blond girl in his mind's eye. "Not really," he heard a new part of himself lie. "Looks like the suspect cleared out three or four days ago." He was breathless with the effort of hiding something from Iff. "How about you?"

Iff glanced at him. Hauser was uneasy, but why? The witch doctors would have to know; he'd put it in his report.

"That pinko bitch wouldn't cop to anything. She said a lot of people stay up in the tipis, how's she supposed to keep track of one young black buck. We'll put a stake-out on her place, he may be back." He shook his head. "Weird paintings inside, nudes and stuff.—I need to stop at the station, then we'll head out to Isla Vista and build our case. We don't need the 'young black man' for that, anyway. By the time he's picked up, we can just slip him into our case like a hand in a glove, then give the DA a heads-up."

Agent Iff lit a Winston. He liked these open-and-shut cases that allowed for a little creativity. Operation Chaos was full of them. *The truth shall set you free.* Once in a while, his conscience piqued him, but only when he was weak enough to doubt what he had to do for his patriotic duty and Temple recommend.

While they stopped by Anacapa Sciences at 301 East Carrillo Street, Didy eyed Iff's briefcase. He was sweating over the authoritative voice in his head chanting *No No No*, his fingers flexing and unflexing. Agitation was a rare state in Didy's programmed life, and disobedience unheard of. Already today he had told a lie and now was contemplating a second rebellious act.

Screening out his handler's voice, he commanded himself to go into secret agent mode. Courage flowed into his hands as they snapped open the clasp on the briefcase. Didy fanned open Iff's *LA Times* while the other hand flipped through the files to a butterfly logo and *MON322*. He opened it to a photo of the girl with the white-gold hair, a second-generation Presidential Model. Mother was terminated, national security memory banks transferred to the daughter. Functions: sexpionage, drug mule, "bionic woman," database. She escaped Bob Hope's Jordan Ranch almost a week ago while Hope and friends were playing "Virginia Dare," a night-hunting game with the Monarch "kitten" as prey. She had slipped right through their razor wire, hounds, and helicopters. She had believed them when they said they would kill her if they caught her. In reality, they would have done no such thing, given her immense value for the data stored in her neurons and the millions that had gone into building her. But to a Monarch butterfly, words are reality, and part of her remembered the last time they had caught her in a drugged delirium and stun-gunned her until she'd passed out from the pain.

Didy smiled. Kissinger (K.) and his European masters must be furious about losing a national security sex kitten. Those stoned big wheels shouting Monarch triggers through megaphones to shut her

178

down must have sobered up real fast when their hounds flailed at the cyclone fence topped with electric razor wire and their helicopters cast spotlights every which way over the dark compound and found nothing. SWAT teams had been called in to continue the search. A boy was even shot out in Isla Vista as a cover for the roadblocks and shakedowns. It was a full-scale manhunt not for Ray Koffi but for the girl Didy somehow knew.

Didy knew K., too. K. believed in the future of mind control but wouldn't be caught dead being drugged out of his gourd and playing boys' games with national security assets. He wouldn't be that stupid. Didy smiled again, thinking of how angry K. probably was. Something deep down in Didy liked it when things went wrong for his masters.

Underneath the *MON322* file was another file. *Gemini. FOR YOUR EYES ONLY.*

Didy peeked over the top of the newspaper and through the window of Anacapa Sciences. Iff was still talking to someone. Didy opened the file right to his name and another name below it: *Thomas Gardner.* Beside his Agency photo was another photo of himself taken several years ago. He didn't remember it, but then he didn't remember a lot of things. He stared at it, willing himself to remember.

Hearing Agent Iff's voice, he frantically slipped the files back into the briefcase and snapped the clasp just as the driver's door opened. Studiously, Didy pretended to be deeply engrossed in the *LA Times.* Never had Iff seen his little robot take an interest in the news. Two unusual behaviors in one day. He glanced down at his briefcase and experienced a moment of doubt, then shrugged it off.

"Isla Vista it is," he announced briskly, edging out of the parking space. "This'll be like shooting fish in a barrel."

Didy smiled disingenuously as he folded the newspaper and looked down at his hands, happy to see that they were calm. He didn't know it yet, but he had just taken two toddler steps toward freedom.

On the way out to Isla Vista, he thought over the previous night's episode of *The Prisoner*, his favorite show. He wasn't supposed to watch any television, but Agent Iff had left their motel room to see a woman friend. Didy didn't consciously know that *The Prisoner* was about Chosen Ones like himself, especially the part about Number 6's dreams being monitored by a machine that could translate electrical impulses into images and reprocess them. Didy had been hooked up to that very machine. Dr. Greenbaum said he should be proud of making history, but Didy's great hope was that Number 6 would finally be cunning enough to escape the Village. He had to keep watching to see if, and how, he did it.

13
Wrapped in a Mystery
Inside an Enigma

*"We're an empire now, and when we act, we
create our own reality. And while you're
studying that reality – judiciously, as you will –
we'll act again, creating other new realities,
which you can study too, and that's how things
will sort out. We're history's actors...and you,
all of you, will be left to just study what we do.*

- Bush Administration aide, from
"Without a Doubt" by Ron Suskind, *New
York Times*, October 17, 2004

At Souls Rest east of Boise, old Seven took the
Goodale Cutoff over the Snake River Plain. The Cutoff
was an old Shoshone migration trail, now mostly
plowed under and running along Highway 20.
Sacajawea had been Shoshone, and Seven wondered if
she'd walked this way with Lewis and Clark. The trail
between Souls Rest and the skull-like Cathedral
Rocks had been closed off to the public ever since a
fire 25 or so years before, one of many white-collar
arsons plotted by energy industrialists to kill two
birds with one stone: skyrocket electrical rates and
profits, and sequester national forest land for elite
global playgrounds as well as the occasional secret
camp or underground facility.

She was already accustomed to weaving on and off
the Trail to search out fragments of the old trail,
gingerly pick her way across private land, or warily
hike along public roadway. Highway 20 was an INEEL
conduit, which meant keeping an eye out for Idaho

181

National Engineering and Environmental Laboratory (INEEL) patrols. Military and private security presence meant no fire for cooking or warmth.

The ancient sanctuary at the heart of the Great Rift was known among the Shoshone as the Lost Valley but rechristened Craters of the Moon National Monument in 1924. East of Craters of the Moon stood the two glowing bookends of the 1950s Atomic Energy Commission: Atomic City, "1st City in the World to be Lit by Atomic Power," and Arco, named for the British petroleum giant. Once the public began whispering downwind that atomic energy was not the godsend they had been assured it was, the AEC Reservation was rechristened the National Reactor Testing Station and the Atomic Energy Commission the Department of Energy. Meanwhile, the two radiant cities surrounded by nuclear silos perched precariously on the edge of the deepest known open volcanic rift on Earth slid into the nation's memory landfill along with the rest of the absurdly naïve post-World War Two 1950s.

Late fall on the Snake River Plain was cold and windy but still relatively easy hiking, at least until the hardened volcanic soil from recent flows known in Hawai'i as *pahoehoe* and *a'a'*. It took Seven almost two weeks to cover the hundred miles into the Lost Valley, what with the *a'a'* digging into her boots, staying vigilant for bubbles and *pukas* from the last flows, and evading the occasional Humvee or unmarked chopper. During the brief winter day, she curled under brush or in a campground or abandoned shack, then set out as the Sun sank behind a mantle of cloud and mountain. Even while slipping exhausted into her sleeping bag, often as not repeating Eliot's poem like a mantra—

"A cold coming we had of it,
Just the worst time of the year

For a journey, and such a long journey;
The ways deep and the weather sharp,
The very dead of winter" . . .

—a ghost or two might hover, waiting for her body of light to drift into their frequency so they could talk. Past Souls Rest, she looked for Inscription Rock but it was on private land and too far removed from the Cutoff to make trespassing worthwhile. Besides, she doubted that Thomas or Vince would have left a message there for her.

As the Sun sped to the other side of the Earth, a spirit with the pale features of a little pigtailed pioneer girl named Nellie wafted up from a cairn entangled with wild roses. Nellie had died of a rattlesnake bite back in the 1840s and her folks had buried her out by the buttes at Martin's Cove, then sadly continued west. Nellie took the long nocturnal walk across the Camas Prairie with Seven, chatting about all that she had loved in her brief life—how her ma kept a pail of milk behind the sideboard sloshing and churning up butter and clabber for biscuits to sop up the gravy she'd make when the wagon train finally stopped for the night, and how good the gravy was if her pa got fresh meat, but how she hated it if it was nothing but salt pork and flour, and how she and her little sister would sit on the back of the wagon swinging their legs and singing *Froggie Went A-Courtin'* while they scanned the hills and groves in hopes of seeing a real live Injun. They'd started out in Missouri with but the meagerest of provisions, two hundred pound of flour, a side of salt pork, twenty pound sugar, ten pound salt and coffee, castor oil and peppermint essence for the summer complaint, and how by the time they got to South Pass most families was roasting parched wheat for coffee and tired out from agonizing over how much to share with the less fortunate Browns or the Clemens or the Martins and how much to let their children eat or save for after Independence Rock, and how little they could get by on until Fort Bridger or Fort Hall or Fort Boise where they might buy coffee, sugar, and cotton for two or three times what they was worth, or firkin butter made in New York and come by ship around Cape Horn up the Pacific Coast to San Francisco or Portland and then inland by pack train. Nellie knew every grave they came across and how many there was along the Trail west of South Pass and how quiet everyone got in the wagon train while passing grave after grave.

Seven had *seen* the dead before she'd learned to *hear* what they had to say. When the Isla Vista boy's ghost approached the window in Thomas' Gollum chamber, he had just died and still had the energy to jam her brain's frequency. But later, hearing ghosts long dead meant learning to relax her gaze and empty her mind like a Buddhist. At first, it was frightening to feel the loss of separateness, but when she was finally able to wipe the slate clean and listen, the dead's thoughts "played" on her brain like it was their own instrument, given that all thoughts are spoken, whether said out loud or not. Private thoughts only appear to be silent; actually, they're playing in a vast amphitheatre only requiring an instrument to "tune in," whether a psychic or NSA synthetic telepathy technology or the dead or, in Thomas' case, an identical twin.

Now that the electromagnetic soup was so thick and the Second Coming plowing deeper into the Earth, the dead were a considerable populace, along with strange airy critters she saw more and more of with her own eyes (and even better through the infrared lens of her binoculars), now that the Earth was disturbed. The truly dead were generally what they seemed, given that the spirit world brooked no deception—for example, the dream warning her to

184

flee east had come from them. It was the *living dead* whose words she had to weigh carefully against the feather of intent. And then there were the dreamers, always the dreamers. The Age of Air was quite crowded.

One grey, freezing early morning little Nellie faded as Seven entered a tiny sleeping town with a Town Crier monitor in a grocery window. Isolated towns kept Town Criers encased in safety glass going night and day "in case of emergency." They reminded Seven of the old phone booths and kiosks that were no more. Town Criers generally ran weather disasters and CCTV wars and street crimes going on somewhere else. Now that nations were subject to giant global trade blocs, private corporate armies were commonplace, and once in a while a nation had to be brought back into line. Corporate elites were more and more moving from their sky castles to underground mansions while maintaining Space Fence eyes and ears on all fronts—economic, cultural, social, political, medical, psychological operations, telecommunications, security.

Town Crier war footage of supersoldiers and Humvees and SCUD bombs decimating buildings kept people in *1984* entertainment-fear mode, regular warfare having been abandoned since the Revolution in Military Affairs in the 1990s. Trouble generally merited little more than a SWAT team and maybe a few laser zaps, after which robots did the rest, along with QUEEMS communications or RATT radar rigs regularly spaced on urban roofs to microwave restive neighborhoods just enough to keep their central nervous systems agitated and disoriented. If dissent reached rebellion proportions, QUEEMS and active denial systems (ADS) frequencies were amped up to boil blood, melt flesh, and make crowds flee in terror. Ultra- and infrasound generators, high-intensity strobes, holograms, sleep-inducing agents mixed with dimethyl sulfoxide (DMSO), area-denial chemicals, electrified human capture nets, blinding lasers, LED incapacitators, isotrophic radiator shells, thermal and magnetosphere stun guns with paralyzing UV radiation were just a few of the surprises awaiting protesters. Meanwhile, Humvees with mounted ADS patrolled. Asymmetric warfare was far more terrifying and effective, just as white-collar crime was more profitable ($500 billion per year) than street crime ($8 billion). Satellites and computers were what the military now protected. Thomas had spent decades concentrating on the linkups.

On this particular morning, the Town Crier was running taped PackBot police robots patrolling somewhere far away with stun guns while mini-disc drones armed with Tasers cruised through the financial district canyons. Occasionally, a Spy Drone or cyborg moth or dragonfly or beetle flitted or scuttled into a building (Hybrid Insect Micro-Electro-Mechanical Systems). Right of last resort targets were being hunted down by UAV Predators and Reapers armed with Hellfire missiles. Gang members reared in target slums, their brains wired in prison by TMS (transcranial magnetic stimulation), slunk through alleys while being downloaded by Global Hawk ground patrol. Whether conducting gang sweeps or Raytheon's Integrated Sensor Suite—synthetic aperture radar (SAR) with electro-optical (EO) and infrared (IR) sensors—in ground moving target indicator (GMTI) mode, Global Hawk could determine exact coordinates and order up precision strikes with little or no collateral damage. Urban Resolve provided digitized 3D maps of terrain, building interiors, sewers, city rhythms, etc. With SWORDS (special weapons reconnaissance detection systems), micro-aircraft and sensors for heat, light, movement, and sound, Automated Target Recognition software could keep up a steady stream of sensor

SIGINT (signals intelligence) comparisons with ground control data before "deciding" to fire. *Keeping America safe,* the Town Crier boldly asserted in block letters.

Seven scanned the grey sky, wondering what drama was unfolding in near-earth orbit and if Thomas had anything to do with it.

Outside of town, Nellie rejoined her and together— the old and the young, the living and the dead—they made their way out onto the forlorn Snake River Plain. Little Nellie's silky luminous form and childish chatter were a comfort to the old woman whose time had not yet come to cross over the thin line between dimensions.

It was hard to believe that beneath this Ring of Fire of 25 volcanoes and lava, cindercones, spattercones, *pahoehoe* and *a'a'* flows punctuated by sturdy timber pines lay an aquifer the size of Lake Erie. The last eruption had been when Jesus Christ walked the Earth and Vitzliputzli wrestled with the Black Magician in Teotihuacan, and the next was due any day. Except for the occasional steam vent that Seven warmed her hands and feet at, it was calm. Snowdrifts testified to the bone-cold winds sweeping south in staccato blasts, ice coating anything and everything attempting to survive, and sagebrush skeletons shivered among the fierce clumps of wiry grass bent on eking out a piteous shred of life from the lichen soil. Suspended over lakes of fire and water, death clung to life. The valley was truly a crossroads of spiritual power.

Seven skirted Fairfield and tiny Picabo, population 50—pronounced like Tikaboo, the Nevada valley where Groom Lake and Area 51 were, where the old Cayuse medicine woman said Kennewick Man's bones were taken. The further in she walked, the more ghosts she encountered, ghosts of settlers, rascals, gold diggers still obsessed with the itch to strike it rich, outlaws still on the run. Nellie's ghost avoided such roust-abouts, but when Tim Goodale and his Indian wife joined them, she cuddled between them like they was her ma and pa, and when Goodale and his wife faded one dawn, Nellie faded with them and did not return. Seven missed her, just as she missed Mina and Baby Rose, forever young in her mind, despite the fact that Mina was now an aging woman with grown children, and Baby Rose—well, she hadn't yet seen Baby Rose among the dead.

Not all of the dead were chatty. Some showed up only when needed, but most clung to the Earth and remained much as they had been in life with the same concerns and yearnings, restless, peace and resolution still eluding them, talking on and on about themselves like the *Snow Queen* roses that could only dream their own dreams, never venturing beyond their own self-centered sphere. When she awoke from her own earthly dream, would she be like them and remember only what had meaning for her?

And so she listened and pondered and slept and listened some more, all the time trudging eastward over the lava fields, her escort of Indian ghosts increasing—Shoshone and Bannock, Kutenai, Paiute, Ute, Arapaho, Crow, even a few Okanagan, some from long ago carrying hand axes with flaked obsidian blades, crying, *Bahána!* and making her wonder if Ghost Bear had preceded her here, too, just as he had in the Umatilla Reservation child's dream.

At Silver Creek, she drank snowmelt and the Indian spirits drank, too, light streaming down their spirit throats. Her breath made clouds in the cold air almost as dense as the phantoms. She listened to the drone of helicopters and scanned the horizon where daylight lay like a thin southeast thread. Wearily, she smiled at the eager, whispering throng that pressed insistently about her, hungry to be near the *Bahána* who could see and hear them. Being dead, they had no fear of heat sensors on helicopters and had all the time in the world to rest.

Near Lava Lake, she found a hot springs bubbling up from the volcanoes below. Briefly, she wondered how the volcanoes under West Antarctica were holding up. Their collapse would mean sea levels rising six meters and the collapse of densely populated waterfront cities like New York City, Los Angeles, New Orleans, Tokyo, Hong Kong, Bangkok. Dungeness and St. Mary-in-the-Marsh had already gone under . . . Without ice, the West Antarctica crust would resemble Nevada, Arizona, and New Mexico, its heat conducting from the Earth's interior. The Antarctic ice sheets had not always been there, nor would they always be there. Everything on the Earth was in flux.

Bone-weary, she spied a lava bubble near the hot springs. After determining that it would make a cozy little cave and dissipate smoke, she dropped her pack inside it, immediately struck up a fire with the brush and sticks she'd been collecting, then dug in her pack for her pot and rice and salt. Along the way, she'd also collected camas bulbs, dwarf buckwheat roots, plantain, shriveled berries, and her last piece of Umatilla pemmican. Gratefully, she lowered her old bones onto her pack like a stool to prepare her food. Women ghosts drew near to inhale again the fragrance of her cooking pot while she continued to envision Antarctica and what must be going on down there.

The *portolan* map of Piri Re'is, dated 1513, depicted Antarctica as it was more than six thousand years ago. When Antarctica was ice-free, all the continents were in a different relationship to the Earth's poles. The Piri Re'is map seemed to have been copied from an even more ancient map belonging to an advanced maritime culture of more than 10,000 years before. In *The Lost Continent of Mu*, James

189

Churchward dated human beings to have been on the Earth since the end of the Oligocene epoch, 33.7 to 23.8 million years ago. West of the Rockies was the Lemurian past, east of the Rockies the Atlantean past—the two pillars of the American Freemasons bent on passing off the snake oil that human civilization began just 10,000 years ago instead of *re*began. And what of the melting ice sheets and Ice Age that the geologist she met said had never taken place? Every era one chose to incarnate into had its garbage and gold that one must wade through to determine the difference. Life certainly wasn't all *maya.*

Ghost protocol required listening to many death stories replete with attendant circumstances: he or she was shot, strangled, crashed, fell, cholera, smallpox, hepatitis, syphilis, AIDS, fetal alcohol syndrome at birth or while giving birth in the desert, on the sea, in the air, on the reservation or in a tavern in Coeur d'Alene, Bozeman, Salt Lake City, Detroit, Tampa, Ottawa, Juarez, by their own hand, in the bed they had been born in with five generations of family standing around to see them off, in endless white man wars, the Civil War, the Spanish-American War, the World Wars in Europe and North Africa and the Pacific, Korea, Vietnam, Iraq, Kosovo, Afghanistan. Old Seven listened, nodded, grunted, wept, and laughed as she cooked and finally ate, swimming through the sea of memories washing over her. They who had once scouted the trails of Space now scouted Time, from the ghost canyons of the Past to the metallic glint of the Future, while the old woman's shadow danced between them and the shadow of a great horned owl passing out of the *puka*. She was comforted by the visit of a living bushytailed woodrat that crept near, nosing about for grains of rice.

Once Seven had finished eating, she leaned against her pack and tamped a bit of tobacco into her pipe as the men ghosts took out their *chanunpa* and passed it among themselves, leaning in to savor the aroma of Seven's smoke, the two smokes crossing the divide between spirit and matter, chasing each other up into the vault of heaven. Finally, it was time for stories from the long ago whose clues and hints might help to face the now of *koyaanisqatsi* and hard Days of Purification to come.

A young Kutenai in cowboy boots and blue jeans began, his western shirt blue as the Montana sky, his string tie clasp an iridescent hummingbird. The Blackfoot had named his people *Kutenai* for their wavy hair, light skin, and slight beards, and the Okanagans called them *skelsa'ulk,* water people, because their white ancestors had come from the sea. Pointing down instead of up (Space being inverted for the dead), he said that the North Star was no longer where it should be, which meant that Coyote had finally shot his arrow into the Sun's face.

A moan went up from the ghost people. Fire and flood must now come out of the West. A Ute grunted assent to Seven's thought that this must be why so many ghosts were hurrying west, then explained, *Ta-vi the Sun-god will scorch the shoulder of Ta-wats the Hare-god again and flee beneath the Earth to his cave. Ta-wats will then shoot him in the face and burst his head into ten thousand pieces and set fire to the Earth. Then Ta-wats' eyes will burst and his tears gush over the Earth to extinguish the fire.*

The Shoshone who had died in a tavern in Juarez added, *Once, Ta-vi was tied to the Intihuatana, the hitching post in Chaco Canyon.*

Ta-wats reminded Seven of long ago when the Moon was torn from the Earth.

Yes, said the Ute, looking down into the sky, *Ta-wats still lives in the Moon.*

The Kutenai said, *An old medicine man in Gallup once told me that the Apollo moon flights were* wasichu *witchcraft to make the spirits living in man-made things rise up and force the Eater-of-Souls into a body.*

Seven shuddered. *When last did Ta-vi wander?* she asked in her mind.

Before the last flood, whispered an Okanagan, *when our homeland Samah-tumi-whoo-lah sank, what* wasichus *call Mu.*

Great canoes had once landed on the shores of islands now known as Mount Baker, Mount Rainier, Mount Jefferson, and Mount Shasta, all at least 1,800 meters above sea level. Ta-wats' arrow might come from Sagittarius, the Brave on horseback whose sky arrow was aimed at the galactic center of the Milky Way and the Scorpi Black Hole beyond. How long had Sagittarius been barraging the Earth with his shooting stars and wavelengths even more intense than those of the Sun?

Finally, Seven carried her few dishes to the hot springs sulfuric waters, rinsed them, then shed her winter layers and slipped gratefully into the dark, bubbling pool, watching her breath mingle with the steam in the cold air as the miles fell away and Draco slithered above the horizon through the early winter vault. Taurus rose with bright Aldebaran, Castor and Pollux strolling nearby. The thought of Twins sent Seven's mind like an old hound to Thomas.

When Seven and Thomas arrived at Rhea's, Baby Rose tore around the side of the house squealing with joy and ran up not to Seven but to Thomas and hugged him fiercely. Bewildered by the girl's display of affection, Seven and Thomas were still staring at each other when Rhea and Mina came out, brimming with edgy news about the recent visit by Agents Iff and Hauser and that Ray was in trouble. But before they could speak, they too stood with open mouths, not so much because Baby Rose seemed to recognize

Thomas as that Thomas looked to be Agent Hauser in different clothes.

Prying himself loose from Baby Rose, he held her at arm's length to get a good look at her. "Do you know me, Baby Rose?"

Then Baby Rose caused more gaping.

"Baby Rose?" the girl said haughtily to Thomas, ignoring everyone else. "It's me, Alice. Don't you remember me?" She looked around. "Where are we? Who are these people?"

Baby Rose was no longer talking baby talk; her entire demeanor had changed.

Rhea peered about apprehensively. "Let's go inside," she said. It wasn't nine yet and already more than the Southern California spring day was heating up.

They all sat down in the living room *cum* art studio. "Alice" was night and day from Baby Rose in that she was self-possessed, mentally quick, and in charge. Mina stood behind Seven's chair, a little afraid of her new friend's shift. "Alice" knew all about Baby Rose and held her in the lowest contempt.

As Thomas stared at "Alice," the shadow of a memory began to take shape. *Fort Detrick. New York State Psychiatric Institute. Awake, drugged. A three-year-old strapped to a gurney, an operating theater, the teenager in the balcony forced to watch . . .*

"Alice," he said in a commanding voice he scarcely recognized, "I need to talk to Baby Rose."

Her eyes glazed over.

"Baby Rose?" Thomas asked gently.

Everyone waited for the miracle to occur.

"Uh huh," came the baby voice. "Alice" was gone.

"Baby Rose, do you remember me?" Thomas asked.

Baby Rose nodded. "This morning, out in the garden you surprised me, then went away, and now you're back . . ."

Thomas looked quizzically at Rhea.

"Either you were here a couple of hours ago, or Agent Hauser is your twin," Rhea confirmed.

Seven gasped.

Thomas sat stunned. "Agent Hauser . . ."

Rhea recounted the visit from the agents looking for Ray. Agent Iff said they just needed to ask Ray some questions, but Rhea hadn't believed him.

The dead boy in the Gollum chamber had been right.

Meanwhile, emotions were buffeting Thomas— elation that his brother might be alive and near, fear regarding what his brother had been made into and what his coming here might mean. Had his enemies gotten wind of where he was and were now using his twin to get to him? He had hoped a thousand times that his brother might be alive, but that he seemed to be working with the feds made him a potential danger.

Thomas explained the little he knew about how "Alice," a more controlling personality, could co-exist with Baby Rose, thanks to MK-ULTRA and the use of drugs, hypnosis, and pain induction.

"Then Baby Rose is an MK-ULTRA victim?" Seven asked. Seeing it in person made it much more real and frightening.

"I'm guessing yes," Thomas said, still confused by his own vague memories. "I discovered MK-ULTRA while probing NASA and National Security Agency files for information about my birth. There were hundreds of subprojects, some of the files under codes I couldn't follow that may even have been about Baby Rose."

"Why would she gouge herself here?" Rhea asked, gently pulling Baby Rose's hair away from her right ear.

Thomas examined it. "Baby Rose, how did this happen?"

"I took it out and threw it away so they wouldn't find me," she said sheepishly.

"Very brave, Baby Rose," Thomas said approvingly, then turned to the others. "It was probably some kind of transponder so they could keep track of their property—an ID with her birth date, where she was programmed, birth order, maybe even the number of generations in her cult. My twin probably has one, too. I must not or they would have come for me by now." He turned back to Baby Rose. "When I saw you this morning, Baby Rose, did I remember you?"

Baby Rose nodded. "Uh huh. It scared you and made you run away."

Thomas sighed. Everything was happening so fast. "It's possible that Ray is their real target and that . . . my twin just stumbled across Baby Rose. But it's just as possible that Ray and maybe the entire Isla Vista event are a smokescreen for a dragnet to get Baby Rose . . ."

". . . and you," Seven finished for him.

Thomas nodded. "Either way, they can't afford to make either of us a news event. But if Baby Rose, my twin, or Ray are bait for me . . ." He looked at Seven.

Baby Rose wandered over to the window seat overlooking the garden and began petting the Prince of Cats. Mina went over and joined her.

Rhea said, "But if Agent Hauser exposed her to his partner, wouldn't they have come back by now?"

Thomas said, "Maybe he didn't say anything, or they'll be back soon. Baby Rose is worth a fortune. They don't spend millions building 'Monarch butterflies' and then let them fly away . . . My guess is they didn't come here looking for her. Besides, if . . . Didymus—that's my twin's name, or at least it *was*—" he said, savoring saying the name"—if he's MK-ULTRA, too, and I have no doubt he is, and he was here, once his handler accesses his memories, Baby

195

Rose will come up and they'll be back. There's probably a nice little bonus, if not a promotion, for whoever brings her, or me, in . . ."

Then they all sat staring in that numb way people do when too much is unfolding too fast. Rhea had known cloak-and-dagger, cat-and-mouse danger in Pasadena, but not MK-ULTRA, handlers, triggers, etc. Mina felt like *The Prisoner* had descended upon her home.

"The one person we know they're after is Ray," Seven finally said. "He didn't burn the Bank of America to the ground or kill that kid—" She really didn't want to go into Gollum and the dead boy's ghost or sunflower oil and condors in Veracruz.

Thomas nodded. "Right. Whether Ray's being used or not, he's our top priority. He's innocent . . ."

"How do you know he's innocent?" Mina suddenly asked. "Why would the agents lie?"

Seven smiled wanly. Mina was too young for all of this. "It's like on *The Prisoner*, Mina. They lie to Number 6, don't they? And we know Ray."

"Ray didn't kill anyone," Rhea scoffed. "He may be a political hothead, but he's no killer. It's the old one-two: cover for a trigger-happy pig, eliminate Ray as a political player and discredit his politics all in one. It's what the FBI and CIA do best."

Mina's little brow was still furrowed. As Rhea's and Ted's only child, she had heard all manner of political rants by Beats, Communists, ex-Communists, socialists, union leaders, and New Left intellectuals like Ray. Some had sung bedtime lullabies to her and were just people with strong opinions, though she didn't really want them to visit her at school.

But talk about MK-ULTRA and Ray made her think of the *Superman* reruns with George Reeves. In the last show George Reeves ever did—just before his strange death in Benedict Canyon—Jimmy Olsen said, "Golly, Mr. Kent, you'll never know how wonderful it is to be like Superman," and George Reeves replied, "No, Jimmy, I guess I never will," and winked at the camera. Superman was white and wore red and blue, all the colors of the American flag. Rhea said that back in the Forties Superman was a comic book hero who spent his time saving people from natural disasters and corrupt businessmen, especially weapons makers. Then, after nine years as the television Superman, George Reeves—drugged and drunk, hero of millions of children—shot himself. Ted said there were three bullets and he was murdered, two in the wall and one in his right temple, and three bullets were missing from the German Luger magazine. "Think about it," Rhea had said, "what would killing the hero of millions of kids do to an entire generation?" Build up a hero on television and in the movies, then *bang!* it was the magic bullet all over again.

Rhea and Ted used to curl up and watch *Dragnet* and *I Led Three Lives* and laugh hysterically at the Cold War propaganda. *I Led Three Lives* was modeled on the life of triple British spy Kim Philby who had managed to work for and against America, Great Britain, and the Soviet Union all at the same time. The real Philby "disappeared" in 1963, but Rhea had known an old Trotskyite in New York when she was a young anarchist artist in Greenwich Village in the Fifties who had told a different story. In his thick accent, he'd said it was well known in the Soviet Union that Philby was alive and well in Moscow at Patriarch's Pond. *There ees no Cold War,* he'd ranted, waving a Gauloise in the air, *eet's a deal between Langley and Lubyanka. Same elite puppet masters running both shows! And who will pay? Little people, of course. Dat is why I quit de Party, eet's a sham.* The gruff old Russian had then wept.

While Mina thought of Superman, Rhea was remembering how numb she'd felt when Kennedy was

197

killed and she and millions of Americans sat watching the television images of his murder over and over again, the shots striking him one after the other, *bam! bam! bam!* and Jackie in her pink suit crawling over the trunk to retrieve his skull, and Governor Connelly jerking backward. The images had played over and over, retraumatizing and numbing millions. Eventually, she'd picked up the threads of her life and gone on under Johnson, then Nixon, but things were never the same. Just two years ago, Martin Luther King on April 4 and Robert Kennedy 33 days later— *11/22, 4/4, 6/6* . . . The numbers spooked her.

After the President was murdered in Dallas in broad daylight right on television in front of God and everybody and the murder covered up overnight, strong opinion began to mutate into whispered plans of action among Rhea's and Ted's friends. Rhea had tired of being called a Red simply because she had figured a few things out and was trying to speak out before it was too late, so they'd decided to leave Pasadena and move to sleepy little Santa Barbara to raise their child. Besides, they couldn't afford to go on associating with people who might unintentionally drag them down with them. Look what happened to Ezra Pound and Wilhelm Reich. Oh sure, the U.S. had no political prisoners. What a joke. *Thank God the war is over, let's get back to the business of making money and raising families,* people sighed in the late Forties and early Fifties, while the CIA and National Security Agency were just revving up. It would be decades before middle America left off congratulating itself for winning the war and awoke to smell the same Nazi stench from the Pentagon and its elite corporate masters.

And look what the media were doing to the huge upsurge of political dissent brought on by civil rights and Vietnam. Ray was right: the corporate media circus would rewrite the Sixties as sex, drugs, and rock'n'roll, rarely if at all mentioning how political those years were. Mario Savio and the Free Speech Movement, gone. The sit-ins against corporatized universities, gone. Abbie and Jerry would make the Chicago Eight trial into a circus. Future high school students wouldn't read about the millions in doubt about what had really happened to the Kennedy brothers and King, or how the CIA was shipping heroin home in body bags with dead soldiers, or that Eisenhower foresaw a fascist take-over by huge American and international corporations that had made millions during the war, or how Nazi and behavioral science were kissing cousins, or how not only trade unions but American industry in general was being shut down and moved abroad as farmers were driven to cities or stalled out on subsidies as agri-corporations took over.

Ray, Rhea, and Ted had argued incessantly about violent versus nonviolent revolution. Rhea and Ted knew violence would be no solution at all; once the smoke cleared, the men willing to exercise violence for political change would be their new masters. No, violent change was an oxymoron. America was being dismantled and the Sixties generation felt it coming, but being young and traumatized by the murders of their heroes, they were caught in words and ideologies that couldn't agree on action and America was decades from detecting the Nazi viper that US military and intelligence officers, Freemasons, and Knights of Malta had invited into American schools, hospitals, military bases, state and federal government positions, and communities, all paid for by American tax money. The easy cover-up of Kennedy's murder confirmed for many that it was already too late, and for those who wavered, the cover-ups of the King and Robert Kennedy assassinations four and a half years later settled it.

Many older radicals who saw the writing on the wall were withdrawing from the field of action so they could live what lives they had left and watch from the sidelines as the nation descended deeper into the maelstrom that must come. Rumors flew like brushfire that the CIA and FBI under COINTELPRO and Operation Chaos were infiltrating radical and conservative groups, black and white. Everyone the least political was looking over their shoulder, doubting cohorts, and turning people in. Bad drugs were flooding urban and rural streets. Rhea thought she should paint another *Guernica* but instead found herself painting flowers and pigs and cats and geese and naked pregnant Barbara.

"Ray will head north," Seven said resolutely, "he'll head for the white Wobblies side of his family. Maybe even go to Canada along with the conscientious objectors."

They pictured Ray heading north, first to San Francisco, then Arcata, Eugene, Portland . . .

"Can we help Ray?" Mina asked, petting the Prince with Baby Rose.

Thomas sighed. "No, you should lay low. Your house will be watched now, your phone tapped, inquiries made, satellite photos . . ." Silently, he wondered what it would mean for all of them. "They'll be back. Finding Baby Rose is but a short step to finding me, especially if my twin is involved." He followed Baby Rose's gaze out the window to the garden. "Strangely, I can now *feel* him, as if your telling me he is alive has triggered my twin sixth sense. And if I can feel him, then he can probably feel me . . . What I'm getting at, Rhea, is you and your family could be in a whole world of trouble. I'm sorry. Certainly, I never would have brought this on you intentionally . . ."

Rhea leaned forward and squeezed his hand. "You don't know who you're talking to. I'm an old hand at this sort of thing. They've got a file on me the same as they've got a file on you." She smiled.

"No, Rhea, these people—the people who programmed Baby Rose and used her for their entertainment and criminal enterprises, the people who feel they *own* her and me and my brother—they're ruthless, above the law, and I think all three of us were caught in the Artichoke Program that goes far beyond bipartisan politics and persuasions. If they think you know *anything* about us . . ."

Rhea interrupted. "Don't you know anyone who can help you?"

"Connections? No. They have my father, my mother, and my brother, and if I went public and started talking about Baby Rose and mind control, who would believe me before I was dead or muzzled? To decent people accustomed to their small lives, the story of evil is always unbelievable. Say it got national coverage. Then would come damage control. Media attention wears off and suddenly somebody—my father, my brother, me—has an 'accident,' maybe a plane crash, killed in the line of duty, witness has a bad day and kills himself by overdosing." He shook his head. "I'm under no illusion about my situation. Either way I go, I'm bound to my past. What is it they say? 'Wherever you go, there you are.'

"My choice has always been to live as anonymously as possible, and now a monkey-wrench has been thrown into that plan. Truthfully, I don't know what to do yet. I do know one thing, though: Baby Rose comes with me. If they come back with my brother and ask about the girl in your garden, tell them you don't know what they're talking about, the only girl here is Mina." He looked at Mina. "Do you understand, Mina? We think Baby Rose is in danger, and her danger puts all of us in danger. That's why we have to lie. I hate having to tell you to lie, but there are lies and there are lies. Do you understand?"

Mina nodded. For Baby Rose, she would learn to lie.

"What should I do?" Seven asked. At this point, she was the most invisible of all.

He shrugged. "For now, go to school as usual."

Seven stared at him. "How can I do that when all the people I care about are in danger?"

Thomas smiled, picking up Rhea's *Tao Te Ching*. "Let's see what Lao Tsu says." Without looking, he opened the book and handed it to Seven who read—

> *There is a saying among soldiers:*
> *I dare not make the first move but would rather*
> *   play the guest;*
> *I dare not advance an inch but would rather*
> *   withdraw a foot.*
> *This is called marching without appearing to*
> *   move,*
> *Rolling up your sleeves without showing your*
> *   arm,*
> *Capturing the enemy without attacking,*
> *Being armed without weapons.*
> *There is no greater catastrophe than*
> *   underestimating the enemy.*
> *By underestimating the enemy, I almost lose*
> *   what I value.*
> *Therefore when the battle is joined,*
> *The underdog will win.*

Seven looked up. "How did you do that?"

Thomas grinned. "The *Tao Te Ching* knows and sees all."

Laughter lightened the mood.

"All right," Seven said, "I'll go to school, but where will you and Baby Rose go?"

"Up to my fortress, at least for now." He looked at the girl. "Maybe I'll see who besides Baby Rose and 'Alice' is behind that pretty face."

Baby Rose jumped up from the window seat and hugged him from behind. "Alice is *mean*," she whispered, "she's telling me right now to shut up or she'll shut me up for good."

At that point, no one knew how effective "Alice" would be.

"And how long will this plan stay in effect?" Seven asked, worried about all the hidden variables.

Thomas shrugged. "Like good Lao Tsu soldiers, let's watch for the enemy's move, then decide. Meanwhile, we keep our eyes and ears open."

"And Ray?"

"No one looks for him. We wait to see where he pops up, then think everything through again."

So they all hugged, uncertain as to what might come next. In emergencies, they would leave messages on the health food store bulletin board downtown that Rhea would check every other day. Seven would listen at school for rumors about Ray.

Thomas checked the house perimeter; the coast was clear. Mina walked Baby Rose to Seven's bus. She would miss her new friend, despite her nagging doubt about who Baby Rose really was.

14
Zwillinge

The land! don't you feel it? Doesn't it make you
want to go out and lift dead Indians tenderly
from their graves, to steal from them—as if it
must be clinging even to their corpses—some
authenticity, that which - .

> - William Carlos Williams, *In the*
> *American Grain*, 1925

But the divine revenge overtook not long after
those proud enterprises. For within less than
the space of 100 years the Great Atlantis was
utterly lost and destroyed; not by a great
earthquake, as your man saith, for that whole
tract is little subject to earthquakes, but by a
particular deluge, or inundation; those
countries having at this day far greater rivers,
and far higher mountains to pour down waters,
than any part of the old world. But it is true
that the same inundation was not deep, nor
past forty foot, in most places, from the ground,
so that although it destroyed man and beast
generally, yet some few wild inhabitants of the
wood escaped. Birds also were saved by flying
to the high trees and woods. As for men,
although they had buildings in many places
higher than the depth of the water, yet that
inundation, though it were shallow, had a long
continuance whereby they of the vale that were
not drowned but perished for want of food and

other things necessary. So marvel you not at
the thin population of America, nor at the
rudeness and ignorance of the people; for you
must account your inhabitants of America as a
young people, younger a thousand years at the
least than the rest of the world, for that there
was so much time between the universal flood
and their particular inundation.

- Francis Bacon, *The New Atlantis*, 1624

Old Seven was still dozing in the steaming pool,
listening to the mumblings and whisperings of ghosts
and revisiting memory trails through the great
drama Hermano had alerted her to and the *chupu*
woman had initiated her in preparation for. *We are*
members of a very large family, you and I, but spread
thin. Seven smiled ruefully, an old woman alone on
the Great Rift in the dead of winter with ghosts for
company and not a friendly living soul for miles . . .
    She dreamed Ghost Bear was whispering *Sleep*
and his ghost people were turning to him as to a Sun.
Hearing the cry, *Tunkashila! Tunkashila!* she'd
drifted deeper into the arms of Hypnos, beloved son of
Night and brother of Death, listening to the chants of
the dead somewhere below. She sailed out over the
Snake River Plain, over the glowing nuclear reactors
and substations scattered over the Great Rift where
secret genetic and radiation experiments had taken
place. In the lava womb south of the 44° north
parallel and a few minutes west of 113° longitude, in
the time of 13 Incense 4 Ancestors, tremors were
marching like a Roman phalanx from west to east,
shuddering the spine of the Americas. Bright day
waned and the air grew still. Nature was holding Her
breath and the phantoms standing guard over the
flesh-and-blood woman's sleep trembled for their

Mother's labor pains. Fire and flood were on their way.

Somewhere over the Atlantic Ocean, Olaf Asteson was rolling over in his deep winter sleep as old Rip Van Winkle in New England did the same, their beards commingling somewhere over the Atlantic like branches of the hoariest tree in the darkest of darks, its veins pulsing, its branches a luminous web of humming memories and dreams. Chagall could have painted the nocturnal commerce between sky and land that Seven was *seeing.* People were flying without umbrellas, wings, or broomsticks upon the sweet balm of sleep. Still in their beds, middle-aged men with financial and marital problems were still savoring the mint from their toothpaste as *up* from their problems they flew, *up* from their beds and through their roofs, breaking free. Like Portuguese Man o' Wars trailing silky light, Americans wafted up into a sea of dreams as Europeans were waking up. Diaphanous, they rose, already reconsidering what they had done or not done for one god or another.

All along America's Mercy Street, neighbors were popping through their roofs, their eyes open and their worries cast aside, giving up their ghosts, surfacing one after another like buoys or balloons. *Anchors away!* Off on nocturnal voyages, one rising effortlessly, another begrudgingly. Across town, across the tracks, they slipped out of dark and pale bodies trailing filaments of light, some brighter than others, like stars.

Dreaming Seven stared in wonder. The night sky was suddenly a freeway filled with buoyant passengers. *Up, please.* A child paused to peer at her, then was off like the white rabbit late for the tea party. The Twelve Holy Nights were on their way, the Three Kings, the Sun in the Goatfish. What would all of these dreamers do between January 10 and 14 when the Sun hurtled through the Greater Void and

Earth through the Lesser Void? The Centaur Archer, Tu-wit on his pony, was poised to shoot his arrow into the center of our galaxy on December 19 while Earth transited the Twins.

It was then that Seven noticed Ghost Bear's phantom adorned with a bear's head beside her, his eyes two dark stars.

"Ghost Bear," Seven whispered, scarcely hoping to believe. "Am I dead?"

He laughed, his light pulsating, delighted by her surprise and confusion. "No, old one, not yet. But you always were good on ghosts."

She smiled. "Then you are dead?"

"Dead on my feet, you might say," he chortled. "Unlike my brothers and sisters here, where I go is not limited to where I lived or died. Messengers like us travel the spirit road wherever it leads."

She jumped up to hug him, wondering how she'd gotten so spry. Then she looked back and saw an old woman dozing in the pool. From her dream body, she no longer perceived insubstantial wraiths but colorful, vibrant people crowding around her body and Ghost Bear.

"So much has happened since the Matilija, Ghost Bear," she said wistfully.

He glowed. "Yes, Lilya, but apparently not enough. I have come to the ghost zone of the Lost Valley to prepare my people for what approaches."

A lump rose in Seven's throat as Ghost Bear turned to the upturned faces.

My people, he said, *Utes were once fierce warriors able to withstand Comanche, Arapaho, Kiowa, and Cheyenne.*

The ghost people nodded and grunted. It was true.

Once, Utes and Azteca grew from the same branch, until the Azteca priests became twisted. Bad chindis meant abandoning Chaco, Mesa Verde, and the Aztec Ruins. Ghost Bear wrenched the air with his hand and the ghosts cried out as though he had twisted the hearts from their chests.

This was all long ago, when the faraway planets wasichus *call Uranus and Neptune lay just beyond the Scorpion's claw.* He pointed to the Scorpion roiling beneath their feet. *Before then, these twin messengers brought only beauty and new ways. But then we entered the Scorpion's claw, and by the time the European Cristóbal Colón came to the Americas, the twin messengers were locked in the Scorpion's heart where Antares shines, and when Hernán Cortés docked at Coatzacoalcos in Veracruz, they rode the Scorpion's tail.*

Ghost Bear sighed and his people sighed with him. *I show you the script of the stars and planets because I want you to see that it is not enough to blame* wasichus *for our woes; they too are caught in the snares of the Scorpion's claw.*

Again, he pointed below. *See, Uranus and Neptune now leave the elbow of the Brave on horseback. Soon he will loose his arrow into the Scorpion's heart.* He shook his big head. *The Azteca Old Ones did not die. They waited in the Black Lodge for this doorway in Time to live in* wasichu *bodies and prey upon two-hearted and one-hearted alike, seeking as many spirit deaths as their voracious appetites could claim.*

The ghost people looked east toward Arco and Atomic City and trembled.

Ghost Bear followed their gaze. *Yes, the nuclear dead now mingle with the beings driven from the Earth by* wasichu *nuclear and electromagnetic technologies. Our dances and rituals no longer hold them at bay.* Chindis *summon them against their will, witchery is on a scale we have not seen in many ages.*

The people breathed with him. *Many of you remain blinded by hatred, eaten up by what has been taken from you, stumbling through Time, looking over your shoulder at what has been, grinding your teeth. Some of you do not even acknowledge that you are dead and therefore do not move on, wasting your deaths on resenting what the spirits governing the stars and planets say must be.*

Some of the ghost people blinked their spirit eyes and looked about. Were they truly dead? Was this not the Lost Valley of their ancestors?

Skin and religion no longer tell who is brother and who is enemy. So how will we know the difference? Ghost Bear beat his fist against his chest. *By this heart with its eyes, its ears, its thoughts. What unites us is deeper than what divides us. Whatever our skin or gods, those who love what is human and good now share the same spirit heart* and the same enemy.

Open your spirit eyes. Is there a one-hearted people left on all the Earth who have not felt the death rattle of the two-hearted? Wasichu *witchery from Europe has found new power here among our own undead Azteca Old Ones. The European witches did not just seek gold or minerals but the ancient power, the serpent energy buried in our long chain of mountains that is the spine of the Earth, protected by Mayan and Quichuan brothers and sisters for thousands of years before the Azteca. It was this serpent energy that the priests and alchemists of Europe sought when they opened Turtle Island with soldiers and priests. Now the Tibetan Chief in the mountains on the opposite side of the Earth has been hounded from his stronghold to loose more serpent powers. Does all this not strike you as necessity, instead of a matter to fester for blame and hatred?*

*Once, each people had their own road to the spirit. Their legends and rituals protected them—Indians, Christians, Buddhists, Jews, Muslims. But as I said to my European brother Hermano many years ago, he whom both Seven and I love—*he stole a glance at Seven*—the old ways no longer work as they used to, and the evil brew the two-hearted* wasichus *have* stirred up is more than they can handle. *Now, we all must drink it and by drinking transform it.*

He looked out over the throng with love. *We are all two-hearted now, our hearts cut in two. This is a fact. And you who are dead, tell me, how is it now for our Mother the Earth? The rain forest, the desert, the islands, the Black Hills, Black Mesa. Where shall we flee? No longer is it simply a matter of millions of buffalo rotting on the prairies, or the Smithsonian arrogance that desecrates the bones of our grandfathers and grandmothers. No, my people, something new has arrived on the Earth, released by the atomic bombs of the white* chindis *whose Azteca desire has been to prematurely open the gates between our world and other worlds. For thousands of years, we have danced, fasted, sacrificed, and sent our seers into those realms to honor their greater powers while protecting our realm of life.*

A murmur of assent from the older ghosts.

Now, white and Asian chindis *seek to invert the return of the invisible Pale God by forcing what early Christians called the harrowing of hell in all the Earth.* He shimmered, looking at Seven. *When our Bahána sister walks further east, she will see for herself what has become of our sacred Lost Valley.*

A catastrophe is coming, my people, brought on by chindi *black magic. It is time to shed the hatred for* wasichus *that you have dragged around too long. Shed it as you have shed your red skins. Wasichus are but messengers of a terrible necessity, and the poison of race will do no good. We have all known bad Indians just as we have known good* wasichus. He paused to smile at his old friend. *Skin is a garment we put on and take off, each race bearing a gift and a burden. Long ago, after the last flood, the Aryans of India were great, then the Mongols, the North Africans, the Iranians, the Greeks, the Romans. The tide of human evolution swept ever west and now we are to be torn from our child's dream.*

How fortunate we were to have slept at our Mother's bosom for so long! But the Europeans have kicked us awake and engaged us in a struggle for our Earth and for humanity itself. Is it not time to dry our tears and look about? We are swept up in a great struggle swirling around everyone, a struggle that began with the great war that raged in Mexico more than a thousand years before the Azteca ever came to the Valley of Oaxaca. My European brother Hermano told me of the fierce battle that ended in a volcanic eruption that completely covered the city Cuicuilco and the cone pyramid temple dedicated to another dimension's god. What caused this battle? The fate of the Pale God half a world away.

No, Ghost Bear has not fallen prey to the Jesuit priests. This Pale God does not belong to those who bow their heads in white churches and cry, 'Jesus, Jesus.' The Pale God has been spoken of everywhere among our people. You have heard the stories about when he came among us, each time with a different name.

The ghosts murmured their assent. They remembered.

At the very same time the Jew Jesus was born in Palestine, another child was born in Mexico. Both were born of virgins and feathered beings from the heavens. Thirty years later, when Jesus was baptized as a great shaman in the River Jordan, down from the heavens flew a bird, sign of the Sun god entering the shaman Jesus to remain with him for three years.

The ghosts peered down into the pool of stars at their feet.

It was during those three years that all the trouble came to a head between Cuicuilco, where Mexico City stands today, and Teotihuacan, fifty kilometers northeast of Mexico City on a high plateau. As the

211

man-god half a world away began his journey into the kingdom of the Lords of Xibalbá, Vitzliputzli, then also about thirty years old, had to fight the chindi Moon priest Tezkatlipoka . . .

New arrivals from the South drawn by Ghost Bear's history drifted up from the *Jornada del Muerto.* Shorter and stockier, with moon faces like Vince's, they stepped out of the darkness and into the shadows around Ghost Bear's shimmering light.

The horns of the tired old Moon had long set when Seven finally forced herself from the hot pool, her old body smooth and steamy, her fingers like prunes. In the icy night, she returned to the lava bubble and squirmed into her layers of clothing and shouldered her pack, determined to press on toward Big Cottonwood Canyon. The whole way she contemplated Ghost Bear's story of the battle between Vitzliputzli and the *chindi* Moon priest Tezkatlipoka. The first Europeans to come to Turtle Island from the Land of the Midnight Sun had believed in four Suns or Ages: the Axe, the Sword, the Wind, and the Wolf. During the Wolf age—known to the Azteca as the age of the Earthquake Sun—the wolf Skoll would swallow the Sun and spatter blood and gore upon the walls of the house of the gods. The Moon would be torn asunder, the stars would disappear, and the Earth would shudder as the sea reared up and Jormungand the Serpent twisted and writhed toward the land. When Ghost Bear mentioned the Serpent, the ghost women had rocked back and forth, wailing and tearing at their phantom faces. Ghost Bear whad been relentless; he was, after all, the messenger.

Old Seven remembered the Fifties plan for an atomic doomsday. Under Outpost Mission, the 2857th Test Squadron would fly out of Olmsted Air Force Base in Pennsylvania with nuclear decontamination kits and radiation bodysuits impregnated with lead while the *USS Northampton* was poised off the

Atlantic Coast. Outpost Mission was moved to Dover Air Force Base and operational until 1970. Elementary schools played duck-and-cover films over and over, and high schools boned up on their radiation-monitoring kits. Everyone carried wallet-sized instruction cards, families built bomb shelters in their backyards. The horror of nuclear war was everywhere, the assumption being that martial law, food rationing, censorship, and suspension of civil liberties were just over the horizon.

Vince had told the Aztec story about the Fifth Sun long ago out in the desert. It was remarkably like that of Ta-vi. "After Water Sun departed—the *fourth* sun the Earth had known—the world was again dark and the four creator gods asked each other, 'Who will be the fifth sun?' They came down to the Earth and built a big fire, but none of them wanted to sacrifice himself for the Earth. Who could they get to jump into the flames to become the next sun?

"Nearby stood poor Nanahuatl covered with sores, the most inferior of the 1600 gods they had created. Should Nanahuatl be the sun? They much preferred Teucciztecatl, but he was as frightened as they were. So there was no choice: they told Nanahuatl to purify himself. For four days and nights Nanahuatl fasted and pricked himself with spines and needles, much as the great Oglala Sitting Bull did to defeat the Yellow Hair Custer.

"Once Nanahuatl was purified, the creator gods chalked his body and pasted feathers on his arms. 'Don't be afraid,' they said, 'you will soar through the air and light up the world.' So Nanahuatl closed his eyes and jumped into the fire. When his body was completely burned to ash, he descended into the Dead Land and traveled until he reached the Earth's eastern edge. With Nanahuatl gone, Teucciztecatl took courage to run around the fire four times and jump in to become the Moon.

"When Nanahuatl finally brought the new dawn, it lay bright red on the horizon and burned everything in sight. No one could look at it without being blinded. The fact was that the new Sun refused to rise into the sky. So the creator gods sent a falcon to beg him to keep rising before everything burned up, and the falcon returned to say that the Sun would continue to rise only if the gods allowed their hearts to be torn from their bodies.

"Angry and frightened, the four creator gods told Morning Star to shoot an arrow at the Sun, but the Sun ducked and retaliated, and Morning Star fell into the Dead Land. One by one, the four gods had to allow themselves to be sacrificed for the sake of the Fifth Sun, Earthquake Sun, the one who one day would bring earthquake and hunger."

Northern Europeans believed that earthquakes and tidal waves and floods would be the beginning of Ragnarok, when the old gods would have to die and the sons of the Fire Giants in the south would storm the gates of the north and they would have to battle giants, elves, dwarves, monsters, and all the denizens of the Nine Worlds beneath and behind the Earth. All would burn, the myth said, and from the ashes would rise a new green Earth, a Fifth Age out of the water, and the gods who survived would sit in council to set a new and better world in motion. A man and woman, Lif and Lifthrasir, would survive fire and flood by hiding in the trunk of the great World Tree, the Wakah-Chan, and eat morning dew and light from the hand of the daughter of the devoured Sun and make many new children to populate the purged Earth.

Old Seven sighed. The birth of the Fifth World would be preceded by the breaking of the waters, like every child's birth. They had all broken their waters beginning in Santa Barbara, back when everything was mythic and a month a year and a year a profound chapter of an epic that shaped the rest of their lives.

214

It was a surprisingly hot day, even for spring in Southern California. Thomas, more wary than ever now that he was Baby Rose's protector, watched two wanderers climb the desert hill toward the *rancho*. Baby Rose and Sirius were cooling in the stream. After not even a week, she and the mastiff were inseparable.

Two middle-aged men greeted him, one with a European accent, the other a Native American. The European reminded Thomas of a man he'd encountered in Los Angeles a few years before, or perhaps it was that he felt familiar. Sirius ran up and gave them the sniff test, so Thomas brought out the lemonade and four glasses and they sat under the willow's shade by the stream near Baby Rose. The European—Tzarogy or Ragoczy or something Hungarian-sounding— chatted briefly about weather and geography, then plunged into relevance while his native friend listened intently.

"You are a thoughtful young man, Thomas, so I put it to you: Surrounded as we are by lies and ersatz paths, how can we know the truth? The lies, of course, are understandable, given how the old ways are dying and their adherents exploiting anything to keep them going . . ."

"'The old ways'?" Thomas asked.

On tapered fingers, Ragoczy enumerated, "The Catholic Church, Protestantism, Judaism, Islam, Freemasonry, Satanism." He shrugged. "The old ways. Once, the Mysteries meant liberation and bound initiates to serving their people. Now, those who were unable to grow beyond the old blood laws, like the ancient Aztecs and Jews and Freemasons like your uncle—"

Thomas started. "My uncle? You know him?" His face grew hot.

Ragoczy shrugged. "Not personally, but I am very old, Thomas, older than I look, so I have known a great many people. In this life, your uncle has chosen again to swim with the sharks."

Thomas looked at the Indian whose name he hadn't caught. His face registered no surprise.

"Your father, on the other hand, is not a former Aztec, though he is weak in ways that his brother has been strong. At this moment," Ragoczy pensively looked east, "your father is planning to visit Europe and may yet remember what he is about." Turning back to Thomas, he smiled. "Do not give up on him yet."

Despite his shock over the turn the conversation had taken, Thomas begged to differ. He had already given up on his father.

Gently, Ragoczy continued. "Then there is your mother and—your brother."

Thomas started again. "My brother?"

"Yes, your twin in Santa Barbara with the FBI man who is really CIA."

Thomas' heart thundered. "So it's true. He didn't die at birth. Did—my uncle take him?"

Ragoczy's face remained impassive as he nodded.

Cursing his uncle and his shadowy Freemason associates, Thomas asked, "What did they do to him? Where has he been all these years?" Hot tears welled in his eyes.

Respectfully, Ragoczy indicated Baby Rose. "She knows what happened to him, but she doesn't know that she knows because what was done to him was also done to her. Neither of them at this stage can remember much of anything."

Wiping his eyes, Thomas stared at Baby Rose. "Poor Baby Rose, poor—Is he still named Didymus?"

"Yes, nicknamed Didy. As you know, Thomas, it is an evil, magickal technology intended to break the will, the holy of holies in the human soul. In large part, this technology is why I am here, now." Ragoczy smiled wearily. "The human journey is long and arduous, Thomas, taking many turns over many epochs. Your brother does not know it yet but he is looking for you. Be cautious. He has been trained to kill in a way that is absolutely mechanical and obedient."

"My brother Didy . . ." Thomas murmured, savoring the sound of *brother*.

"Did you know that the name Thomas is the Hebraic sobriquet for twin?" Ragoczy smiled. "Thomas and Didymus, Thomas the Twin. In the Acts of Thomas, it is written, *Come, Holy Spirit, Holy Dove that bearest the twin young. Come, Hidden Mother.* Long ago, there was a Mediterranean cult called Dioscuri, the Divine Twins. An altar to the Heavenly Twins Castor and Pollux ruled in the hippodrome during the Olympic games. Rome had the twins Romulus and Remus, Turkey Momin and Aziz, then Jesus and Judas Thomas. Poussin painted twins, da Vinci's *Last Supper* depicts twins. At Rennes-le-Chateau in France, two Holy Families grace the one altar for the two Jesus children. Siamese twins like Chang and Eng were exhibited in the 19th century by the showman Phineas Taylor Barnum. Now, sonography, fetoscopy, and amniocentesis have revealed that we all may begin as twins. The mystery of twins runs deep, Thomas."

Thomas nodded. "I was just talking about vanished twins a few nights ago. I've *felt* Didymus for years, but always just out of reach."

Ragoczy's Indian friend joined in. "My people know something of loss. Spirit songs look for what has been lost by what Yaminahua shamans call *yoshtoyoshto* or language-twisting-twisting that calls out for the lost twin or *double* wrapped about us, like the DNA helix."

217

Ragoczy agreed. "Relations with spirits are elliptical, multi-referential, mirror subject-object twoness-oneness. The spiritual-DNA side to twins, including the *double*, has something to do with why the Nazis were so intrigued by them, and why some cultures still kill twins at birth. After the Black Death in the 14th century, fertility increased exponentially and there were thousands and thousands of twin births, very few of whom had full sets of teeth, as if they even had to share *teeth* in order to assure their birth. Twins that have shared the resources and risks of one womb have tremendous powers of endurance, Thomas, and prescience. You might say that having a twin *doubles* one's earthly chances."

He hesitated, then went on. "Under Ottmar Freiherr von Verschuer, Josef Mengele ran terrible *in vivo* experiments on twins—*Zwillinge*—that SS guards retrieved for Mengele from boxcar arrivals at Auschwitz. They were known as Mengele's Children, one twin the control, the other the guinea pig. Once Mengele found out all he could from a set of twins, then it was death by injection. You and Didymus are such Mengele twins under a CIA program known as Artichoke, and your bloodline has determined the methods used on both of you, though certainly more extensively on Didymus."

Thomas put his face in his hands. He knew the man spoke the truth.

Ragoczy continued. "I myself have seen a telegram dated May 30, 1932— 3/30/32 in the Julian calendar—sent by the Rockefeller Foundation to the Kaiser Wilhelm Institute for Anthropology, Human Heredity and Eugenics in Berlin, detailing the funding of a three-year project on twins and the effects on later generations of substances toxic to germ plasm. After the war, American and British press blamed the Nazis for such experiments, omitting the fact that they were secretly funded by American and British

218

foundations and corporations. Eventually, *eugenics* was renamed *human genetics*—the American Society of Human Genetics, the Institute of Human Genetics at the University of Münster, the Italian Society of Genetics, the Anthropological Society of Vienna, the Japanese Society for Human Genetics. In America, a 20-year program under the National Institutes of Health is separating twins and triplets and having them raised separately with no knowledge of each other to answer the nature versus nurture questions that still stand in the way of human engineering. California remains the center of the American eugenics movement . . ."

Thomas looked up. "But Didy is here?" Sad hope flickered bright.

Ragoczy smiled. "Forgive me for digressing. Yes, Thomas, he and the agent acting as his handler are at this point looking for Ray and Baby Rose. Soon, they will add you. They will use Didy to track you down."

Thomas nodded dully. *He had a brother.* "It was my uncle."

Ragoczy nodded again.

"My father and mother? Did they know?"

"No," Ragoczy said emphatically, "and they still do not know." He looked east. "Soon your father will, though. Do not give up on them yet."

"'Honor thy father and mother'—isn't that what your Bible says?" the Indian asked. "It does not say love them, for love cannot be forced, but *honor.* They too are clumsy and finding their way."

Honor, not love. Thomas hardly knew his parents. So many nannies, boarding schools, tutors. But honor . . . Perhaps.

Science had always been his security. As a boy, he'd wondered about the free energy everywhere going untapped. Who could believe it? And not just transverse waves but longitudinal, scalar waves in the time dimension! The tutors his uncle hired hadn't

219

wasted time on the Newtonian model but had gone straight to the physics that oil, weapons, debt, and drug money were quietly bankrolling for the Enterprise. Westinghouse, General Electric, and other military contractors jealously guarded the physics Tesla gave his life for, handpicking and funding bright minds, suppressing it at mainstream universities. For them, society was a hive in which the worker bees were destined to slave for drone Brothers jealously guarding Queen Isis of the Mysteries by withholding secrets that might have eased and enlightened the lives of millions and given meaning to otherwise endless, ignorant, debt-ridden toil.

How excited Thomas had been as a boy! But soon enough his tutors guided his love for science toward weapons potentials and away from easing human woe. Initially, he thought that perhaps his mentors didn't see the relief that æther technology could grant, but when he'd finally asked why this physics was being withheld from other bright minds, his tutor made the mistake of sharing how generations of "Wise Men" had been waiting for just this particular turning point in Time.

"'Wise Men'?" Thomas had been born the year Tesla had died and was all ears.

The tutor glanced anxiously at the closed circuit camera that filmed their sessions. "A decade before you were born," he murmured, then dropped the issue entirely.

Thomas computed. Hitler. Roosevelt had ordered the U.S. off the gold standard in 1933.

He hadn't heard a word in his Yale physics classes about two American greats: John Worrell Keely in Philadelphia and Nikola Tesla in Colorado and New York. It was as if they wanted his generation to believe that the electromagnetic spectrum and periodic table were all there were. John Jacob Astor had been involved in backing their research. Was he a

"Wise Man"? His lap dog Thomas Edison had prevented Keely and Tesla from meeting. Nor had he heard a word about James Clerk Maxwell's EM potential equations, and certainly not about Dr. Wilhelm Reich languishing in federal prison while his research into life-giving æther was stolen. He had heard a few snippets about how life-draining thermal electromagnetic energy was but nothing about the effects of nonthermal.

"So knowledge is used like a weapon against the masses," Seven had responded when he'd told her about his privileged education.

"Just like the Wise Men want people to think that oil is all there is for energy," Thomas had fumed. "My uncle directed the course my tutors set for me. Some things they wanted me to know, some not yet." He had looked up at the studded stars that supposedly faded millions of years ago, which he also no longer believed, and chuckled. "They probably think that given enough time and power they can set the course of the stars, as well, or at least make us think they can. The Wise Men should be called the Pretenders."

His uncle and father, like his grandfather and great grandfather before them, were members of elite Freemason Lodges to whose rituals and blood oaths they were bound.

"Freemasonry isn't like the Rotary Club or Chamber of Commerce," he had explained to Seven, who later would learn that her father too had also belonged to a Lodge. "You can quit the Rotary Club but not Freemasonry—no way out but death or obloquy. And should a member inadvertently or intentionally betray certain secrets, he will either die, ringed about by certain words and numbers and sigils to warn other Brothers, or his family or those he loves will pay." He'd kissed her sweetly and sighed. "Men initiated into the high degrees wield the faith of their fathers like a weapon—Christian, Jew, Catholic,

Muslim, Buddhist, pagan, Satanist—but they sit at the same table, drink from the same cup, and share the same worldly objectives. Beliefs for them are a means, not an end, and are used to set believer against believer for distraction and controlled wars . . ." He'd tapered off dully, exhausted by the sadness of the past that had torn him and his family in two.

Thomas made a simple supper for Ragoczy and his friend, though Thomas noticed that Ragoczy did not eat and only took water with fresh mint. Thomas was ecstatic to discover that Ragoczy too was a scientist and seemingly fascinated by Thomas' studies of Kirlian photography.

"The Kirlian process is a high-voltage AC field between two condenser plates," Thomas explained, "but when photographing a person, only one plate is needed, since the human body acts as a condenser. I began by copying the optical discharge capacitor plate that the Kirlians employed, then experimented with all sorts of power sources as well as voltage, harmonic frequencies, pulse, and radio wave."

"I must see your apparati," Ragoczy responded, equally excited.

And so Thomas took both men down to his laboratory, which Ragoczy swore was the noblest laboratory he had ever seen.

"Here is the basic Kirlian set-up," Thomas announced, pointing to the apparati, "a Tesla coil, both the spark gap and vacuum tube models, piezocrystals, a Van de Graaf generator, a charged capacitor, even low-frequency induction coils coupled to a capacitor discharge system. I ranged frequencies between one cycle per second and megacycles, pulsed and unpulsed sine and square waves. Voltage and frequency could go quite high; what I had to be careful of, as Tesla warned, was amperage."

Ragoczy nodded. "Yes, Tesla took voltage extremely high, bathing himself in a sheet of flame at a million volts. Even two hundred thousand volts alternate in irregular intervals a million times a second, so imagine a million volts! Vibrate it faster, take a hundredth of it and direct it, up the amperage, and you have a weapon that will cook whatever it is directed at." In *sotto voce*, he added to his Indian friend, "This weapon is coming."

Thomas didn't hear the aside. "I set out to duplicate the Kirlian experiments, looking for the geometrical patterns they'd found in various organisms. One day, while staring at a photograph of a dead condor whose wing had been gnawed off, I suddenly realized what I was looking at."

He placed a photograph before his guests, a black and white phantom of a condor's luminous body, black showing up where physical matter was densest. The missing wing, relieved of its density, revealed a wing of light—not light emanating from the body but the light that the matter of the wing had clung to for a time in order to allow this bird to fly in 3-space.

A current of understanding passed among the three men. Thomas' eyes teared. Why was such intimacy among men so rare?

Ragoczy laid a fine-boned hand on his shoulder. "It is the divine you are showing us, Thomas. Only those who seek to exalt the innate divine can hope to be authentic scientists. My friend and I are honored to meet such a scientist, for they are rare in any age, but particularly in this one." His dark eyes shimmered. "This Kirlian photography is a remarkable technology, bioenergy being more subtle than electromagnetic waves, especially human bioenergy. Whereas plants retain their color schema unless injured or, more happily, while feeling the frequency intervals of a Mozart or Bach, human skin alters according to the complex interweaving of the varied biological systems."

"Yes," Thomas responded eagerly, "even the consciousness of an observer staring at the skin can make the electrical discharge disappear entirely. Kirlian photography converts nonelectrical properties into electrical properties and captures them on film. When the subject is human, these properties shift in color, pattern, and intensity."

Ragoczy laughed. "As I recall, adolescents are highly charged, like human storage batteries. The human being is like a gyroscope constantly trying to maintain an internal and external balance of forces and energies. These same non-electrical properties are evident in the nimbi around saints' heads, the blue flames hovering above the ship masts of St. Elmo, church spires, airplane wing tips. They are the Dioscuri Castor and Pollux, Fermi's fire, the *corpo santo* or holy body."

Thomas was transfixed. "Yes! When the Tesla coil built up voltage, a strange ghostly blue light arose and the coils flamed with masses of fiery hair. Everything in the building grew flaming needles of light, and I could smell the sulfurous odor of ozone."

"Photographs of the heart no doubt show an intense blue," Ragoczy said, "the forearms blue-green and the thighs olive green. In the presence of fear or illness, only the degree changes.

"Yes," Thomas nodded, "how did you know?"

Ragoczy's friend laughed. "He does Kirlian photography with his eyes."

Ragoczy smiled. "So Thomas, tell me about the vacuum chamber you constructed."

Thomas stared at him; he had said nothing about Gollum's chamber. He began walking toward it, explaining, "It's a vacuum chamber to keep out atmospheric 'noise,' my premise being that the radiation field of the body of light that Kirlian images capture is *transdimensional* and that high-frequency current cracks the 'doors of perception, open."

In front of the chamber, Ragoczy stopped smiling. "You have realized, of course, that once the Russians reached this point, the American military made research into Kirlian photography and acupuncture disappear in scientific circles, and catalogued human beings under higher animal open systems. This is why the technology was not allowed to go public in 1939."

Thomas was puzzled. "1939? I thought Kirlian photography was invented in 1958 by Semyon and Valentina Kirlian."

"No, it had been discovered nineteen years before by Prat and Schlemmer, two Czechoslovakians who photographed the corona discharge or bioplasma through a celluloid English fabric supposedly impermeable to infrared. Both inventors vanished overnight, just as Léon Theramin was spirited away to a Soviet *sharashka* or secret research lab nineteen years after inventing the theramin, an instrument generating a tone whose frequency is modulated by a capacitor."

"I never heard of Theramin," Thomas frowned.

"I am sure there are many inventors of whom you have never heard, Thomas, including the Brazilian Alberto Santos-Dumont who invented the airplane before the Wright brothers. His plans were stolen and he was thwarted at every turn by the same Lodge Brothers who thwarted Tesla and Keely while rewarding the inferior Lodge Brother Edison. Santos-Dumont, like Tesla, wanted to build airships as instruments of peace, figuring that if people were able to travel to other nations more easily, their fear of differences would evaporate. Instead, he was driven into madness by those who use and abuse genius. Once flying machines based on the design he refused to patent were employed in the 1932 Brazilian Constitutionalist War, he was found hanged in his hotel room. Where inventions are concerned, Thomas, glory and profit go to those who steal the inventor's

225

fire.—The Beach Boys use the theramin in their apt song 'Good Vibrations.'"

The three men laughed.

"Now," Ragoczy smiled at Thomas, "I would be pleased to see the guest you draw into your infrared chamber?"

Thomas shook his head in amazement. "He comes and goes as he pleases."

"He will come if I call," Ragoczy said confidently.

15
The Gardner Brothers
East Coast

*There is sufficient evidence that a number of
Societies of the Illuminati have been
established in this land of Gospel light and civil
liberty, which were first organized from the
grand Society in France. They are doubtless
secretly striving to undermine all our ancient
institutions, civil and sacred. These societies
are closely leagued with those of the same
order in Europe; they have all the same object
in view.*

- Rev. Joseph Willard; Sermon,
Lancaster, New Hampshire, 1812
(Houghton Library, Harvard University)

Hiram Gardner despised democracy. Whenever he
went abroad and returned to La Guardia or Dulles,
nothing—not escorts, dark glasses, or smoky
limousine glass—protected him from having to peer
into one stupid American face after another at
intersections, in car parks, elevators, even in the dim
lighting of private clubs.

Like the face that had leered at him years before in
a Dallas traffic jam. The limo couldn't move and he
became almost *frightened* that he was just another
among the sweating masses holed up in their
automobiles, creeping along in abysmal little lives. An
old man hawking newspapers at an intersection had
pressed his grotesque nose up against the window
and squinted through the smoky glass in quest of
contact with the beings who drove through the

streets in their long dark vessels like gods. Shrinking back into the upholstery, Hiram had felt like he had been lowered into shark waters. The horror of the teeth, the red, cavernous mouth, the blackheads on the bulbous nose, hairs in the nostrils, grime and mucous. Their eyes had met, despite the glass designed to avoid just such encounters. Finally, the limo had moved on, leaving the alien being in its wake. A sheen of perspiration had formed on Hiram's forehead and upper lip.

Driving the memory from his mind, he picked up the threads of the speech he was scheduled to give. He loved all things active and despised all things passive. His was a religion of *will,* not the bleating faith of sheep. He waited for nothing and went after what he wanted. If those around him were asleep at their posts, that was their problem: he would take what they were too stupid to keep.

He dialed his brother Laurence to make sure he would be at the meeting. Not that he needed him there, but family solidarity was good window-dressing. The Lodge Brothers wouldn't mind, even if Laurence had refused to go beyond the third degree. Laurence had paid in spades for his foolishness, so no one would say anything.

The reminder delivered, he returned to his notes, sifting through the words to make sure he didn't go too far. He wished he and his brother were more like the Dulles brothers. Allen Dulles was Hiram's hero. He'd worked for Prescott Bush, was legal counsel for Fritz Thyssen and I.G. Farben, the chemical cartel described by the head of Gestapo counterintelligence as a state within a state. Both Prescott Bush and Herbert Walker had worked for Thyssen, and Thyssen and the chemical cartel were early supporters of Hitler's rise to power. During the war, Dulles had headed up the Swiss office of the OSS, then after the war became director of the new CIA. Some chose to see no cause and effect to his career, but others knew better. Fortunately for American and European banking and industry dynasties, Dulles had gone from Bern to post-war Germany as U.S. intelligence chief.

Hiram was sure he wouldn't go too far today. *The Cold War will go down in history as we wish it to be remembered . . .* He'd touch lightly on what a godsend the Federal Reserve Act of 1913 was, how without it they could never have swung the February Revolution *or* the Cold War, and how now men like Jacob Schiff no longer had to support Brotherhood enterprises from their own pockets. Schiff had poured $20 million of his own money into the Bolshevik Jews, with $10,000 to Trotsky alone on his return to Petrograd in May 1917. Then there was the Rothschild money and Kuhn-Loeb, now part of Lehman Brothers. Should he mention that his grandfather had been at Carnegie Hall on March 23, 1917 to celebrate the abdication of Nicholas II and the success of the Revolution? Schiff hadn't been able to attend but had sent a congratulatory telegram. High-mindedness—no need for fanfare or accolades. Schiff's generation of Brothers was truly the selfless generation. How different it was now. He wouldn't mention it, but *slime* called themselves Brothers now. Still, the annual dues were useful.

Then came the era of interlocking big business and banking run by old families and ambitious men sitting on each other's boards, owning each other's stocks, marrying into each other's families . . . His smiled: he wouldn't add diddling each other's children, buying elections and academic and research positions for those willing to do their bidding, controlling the networks, news outlets, the Hollywood star machine that kept people's minds occupied . . . He wouldn't say any of that. *How far our think tanks and research laboratories, military and civilian, have come, all of which are essential to the technology needed for our greatest bid yet to power on a global scale. NGOs and foundations are proliferating—the outreaches required for guiding and shaping government and economic policy, influence legislation, and to offer direction to the United Nations.* NGOs were the real change agents behind the Punch 'n' Judy show called democracy. The Punch 'n' Judy metaphor was good, but did it go too far?

He would praise the computer for its rapid cross-referencing and organization of vast stores of data that availed them of greater centralization of power and delegation of oversight of various population sectors. For example ... Immediately, he thought of an example he shouldn't use, namely the culling of children through the Talent Identification Program (TIP)—scanning fourteen-year-olds for cutting-edge, futuristic programming, and at the other end Justice Department tracking of young throw-aways for other programming needs. In the right hands, both ends were useful. Of course, the public couldn't know that some of their brats were being recruited. Stats going out to the public proved that violence in America was rising: nine out of ten young people murdered in industrial countries were slain in the U.S.; homicides for youths 15 to 24 were five times the rate in Canada; U.S. poverty rate for children was more than double that of any other industrialized country. Only the U.S. and Great Britain were not concentrating on bringing children out of poverty. A student a day was being sexually abused by a teacher or school staff member ...

People stupid enough to become breeders owed the State its due. If the State needed their children, so be it. Solon had required military families to eat in common so as to overcome illusions of a wasteful private life. Parents should thank their lucky stars that the State didn't take all of their children. Weapons were in the making that would mean fewer of the poor's sons would be needed for wars, but they would still be needed for other programs. Besides, if a youth had what it took, he'd find a way to counter whatever the State did to him.

Hiram wasn't quite sure about "what it took," but he had done all right, considering what his grandfather had done to him as a child in the boathouse and at the Lodge to "prepare him for the power he must one day wield," as his grandfather put it. And it had prepared him; the old man had been right. That he had no deep relationships or friendships and that the thought of women was repugnant were small prices for the power circles he traveled in. Such amenities as friendship and love belonged to another world and were antithetical to the world he'd been prepared to thrive in. Why, he had even been able to make use of his own weak, ineffectual brother's family.

Satisfied he knew the meat of his speech by heart, he tucked away his notes as the chauffeur pulled the limo to the curb outside a small elegant building wedged between two skyscrapers.

Laurence Nile Gardner rose up early that morning in Philadelphia and embraced his routine. The thought, *I will be fifty this year,* almost wedged itself between him and the fleeting comfort of his routine, but he fought it off. He stripped off his pajamas and entered the bathroom. A good piss, then a shower, shave, deodorant, underwear, clean shirt and tie, suit. The man in the mirror with thinning hair made him think of J. Alfred Prufrock.

> *There will be time, there will be time*
> *To prepare a face to meet the faces that you*
>   *meet;*
> *There will be time to murder and create,*
> *And Time for all the works and days of hands*

Caroline wouldn't be up yet. Why after all these years did thinking of his wife make his chest ache? Enough. He re-busied himself. *Keep in motion, don't think.* He slathered on his skin bracer, the only time all day he would touch himself other than to urinate.

Whistling Mozart's *Requiem* under his breath, he willed himself not to look at his wife's bedroom. Downstairs, his breakfast of toast, marmalade, and Irish tea was laid out nicely at the end of a table that always looked too big, given that he and Caroline rarely had guests. He felt like a tiny boy sitting at the adults' table, surprised that his feet actually reached the floor. *The Wall Street Journal* was where it should be and Mrs. Potter was where she should be, jut as Jimmy and the limo would be where they should be. *Meeting at ten in New York,* he reminded himself, munching wholegrain toast and sipping tea, perusing the headlines, feeling almost normal.

When the phone rang, his stomach twitched. He knew who it was.

Mrs. Potter bustled in, gesturing to the telephone on the table. "Good morning, Mr. Gardner. Your brother, sir."

He picked up and waited to hear Mrs. Potter's click, then said, "Good morning, Hiram."

"'Morning," the voice he had come to loathe said peremptorily, "don't forget, meeting at ten. I'll do the talking." *Click.*

"Right," Laurence said into the empty receiver.

Thoughts ambushed him during the drive into the City, returning like old dogs to the same old wounded places. His brother telling him that he lacked mental discipline and should practice out of sight out of mind, such as Veracruz a decade ago, the same week that Thomas was to undergo the secret Dickey (Delta Kappa Epsilon) initiation known as The Agony.

232

Thomas had changed, and Laurence hadn't been there.

At Harvard, he'd been a Porcellian. Founded in 1791, the Pig Club—the elite of the elite—made its selections from Dickey boys and other boys who'd gone to the right prep schools: Groton, Andover, St. Mark's, St. Paul's, St. George's, Middlesex. Cousins were in Scroll and Key and Wolf's Head, some by marriage, some by blood. Vaguely, he wondered how many senior fraternities the Order had its claws into. Fraternity initiations and hazings had always been grueling, but as the world power game became more brutal, so had the preparation of new helmsmen. *What kind of initiation could Thomas have been subjected to?* Thomas had simply withdrawn, refusing to talk about it.

Laurence didn't remember most of whatever had happened in Veracruz, either, which must be why his mind constantly took him back there, back to the boat ride at dusk with the grinning German and Finnish ex-patriates in white linen suits. He remembered the underground *cenote* bathed in blue light, drinking something in an oddly inscribed cup, and awakening the next afternoon in his hotel room with his heart beating erratically and the ghost of a sickeningly sweet smell churning in his stomach. It was terrifying not to remember. Hiram was gone when he awoke. When he got back home, he told Hiram in no uncertain terms that that was it, no more trips for *that* sort of thing, and when he had asked Hiram just what kind of politics he was involved in, his brother had laughed and responded flippantly that Laurence needn't worry, he wouldn't have to go again, that it was done. *What was done?* he had wanted to ask but hadn't, afraid of the answer. He suspected that Hiram's insistence that he go had been to get him out of the way during Thomas' initiation. That's when the panic attacks began and things went from bad to worse between Thomas and himself.

Then Laurence had found something in the back stacks of his club library, something he didn't want anyone to know he was reading and so hid it like a schoolboy. *Ancient and noble families are prone in special measurement to degeneration, and degeneration can only occur because of a separation from the spiritual world.* This one sentence had made him think of his grandfather and his military and Nazi cronies, his brother's political intrigues and the riff-raff whose company he more and more preferred, a South and West criminal element wallowing in oil fields, arms deals, and Mexican rituals, all consorting with shadowy cartels and CIA agents who had spent too many years in Central and South America.

Ancient and noble families called to mind the trip to Edinburgh with his grandfather, when they had rendezvoused with Hiram at his boarding school in Edinburgh and a gaggle of Scottish and European cousins he had never met before, all with their nannies and governesses and tutors in lieu of parents. He remembered how windy and cold it was on Princes Street, and the pubs on the Royal Mile where men with rough hands and red faces reeled into the street with whisky oozing from their pores.

Before dawn, the boys—where the girls were, he wasn't sure—had been trekked to Holyrood Park and up to Arthur's Seat, an ancient and extinct volcano, to look north and east along the shore toward Bonnybridge and North Berwick. While the youths waited and watched for they knew not what, Hiram's tutor, a strangely intense man, stood beside his grandfather explaining how between the Castle Rock that Edinburgh Castle stood upon and Bass Rock beyond Craigleith Island were no fewer than six extinct volcanic plugs; and how Melrose Abbey and Craigleith Island lay due north of Glastonbury along

234

the same ley line. At some point, his grandfather proudly announced that Edinburgh was the capital of the *Old Religion*, at which the tutor pointed to Calton Hill and its unfinished acropolis and promised that one day soon Beltane would again be celebrated openly there, with fire. The man's tremulous intensity had embarrassed and mystified the youths, all but Hiram, who was entirely under his spell.

It was Thomas' disappearance six years ago that had galvanized Laurence to begin the painful work of comprehending his true condition. From birth, he had succumbed to the demands of privilege. First, his parents and tutors, then his brother had told him what to do and what not to do. Wealth, lineage, and position had ever been the masters of his fate. He knew that what galled his brother most about Thomas' vanishing act was not that he had given the world's best intelligence agents the slip, nor that he had been ingenious enough to know how to take his trust fund with him and continue to access it under a variety of names not even FinCEN could ferret out, but that Thomas had walked away from what Hiram had handed him on a golden plate. Thomas was right, of course.

Laurence had done nothing to protect his son from Hiram. He had never been a father in the true sense of the word. *Is my brother my keeper?* Yes, he had allowed Hiram to be Cain from the very beginning. *The sons of Cain,* words from a Freemason ritual he'd undergone.

Had he ever known a moment of freedom? The summer fortnight with a few school friends in Yosemite. Sneaking away from his watchers at Oxford to meet Jill in Paris after which they had hitchhiked deep into France, to Languedoc and the Pyrenees. *Jill.* After all these years, he still felt the loss. Jill had not been in the family plan. When his father had suddenly died of an aneurysm his junior spring at Harvard, Hiram had made a passionate appeal that as a loyal son he must postpone his personal life for a while, at least until their father's affairs could be sorted. As usual, he had gone along, putting himself and Jill last, and months had turned into years, until Jill was history. From afar, he had followed her life itinerary. She had studied in Paris, then Istanbul and Rome; now, she was a curator at some museum in the south of France near where they had been that summer. She had never married.

After Harvard, he had married Caroline Sinclair, a woman he did not love. But she was a Sinclair, the bloodline that would connect Thomas to the old Templar days of Robert the Bruce. Hiram had arranged the marriage, a good move for his political career but bad for Caroline, Thomas, and Laurence, the ones who would have to live a loveless marriage. Thomas and the twin who had had the bad luck to be born dead would be their only issue of their unholy union, to unmarried Hiram's chagrin. Caroline had gone from pain medication and alcohol to various other over-the-counter addictions.

Like himself, Caroline was well-intentioned woman and went along with what her father and brothers decided was good for her. Her older sister had "mental problems" and was in and out of hospitals, never marrying, living alone with her dogs in a cottage on her family's Connecticut estate a stone's throw from her parents. Caroline, like Thomas, was therefore the golden child, a stable, calm, pleasant, dependable, gracious hostess with impeccable taste. It did not matter as much that she was utterly unapproachable by husband or son, what her Harvard therapist termed *affective* being virtually absent. Her physician—the one who delivered Thomas but couldn't save his twin—was a Bonesman friend of Hiram's.

Making love to her had felt to Laurence like he was raping a compliant victim. She simply vanished. Vaguely, he wondered what could have happened to her to make her that way. Was she too in love with someone else? For the erections he needed when he initially tried to fulfill his marital obligation, he had conjured up Jill's face and lips and how they had loved each other once when the world was still fresh and new and had not exposed its poker hand. Poor Thomas, never to have seen love leap the synapse between his parents. But then Laurence had never seen it between his parents, either. Had anyone he knew? He reviewed the faces of the Pig Club initiation that spring night so many years before. Hiram had been a Bonesman, as had their grandfather. Both had been cut from the same mean cloth.

But their father had been a gentle fool, frail, leaving his boys to his domineering father, a stern man with a brogue and no heart under his ribs, rankled that his son lacked the "fiber" that at least one grandson would have when he was finished with him. Blaming their parents for making them "soft," the old man had summarily whisked Hiram off to Edinburgh so that for the rest of his youth he saw his mother just three weeks every summer. Laurence had stayed at Groton and thus had seen his parents more. Had *they* loved each other? He thought so, but like himself they hadn't the mettle with which to withstand the onus of privileged blood. His grandfather had been right: they were both soft from suffering defeats they couldn't recover from. Both his father and mother died from lack of joy, much as he imagined Caroline was in the process of doing while he stood by, helpless.

Why was all this worth remembering? Since boyhood, he'd been surrounded by elite cadres of males whose vicious initiations had been conjured up centuries before to hone the will by pushing them beyond humane limits, toughening them for the hard decisions wielding wealth required, driving them to draw and erase and draw again the shifting moral line necessary to the destiny before them. Living double truths and telling double lies—what kind of life was that? Laurence told grey and white lies to get by and stay safe, in the end thinking that telling the truth was more about who you were telling it to. He was sure this was why his life had become stale, flat, and cynical. How many flagrantly indulgent hotels could one really enjoy? How many professionally executed blowjobs or expensive meals? It wasn't the eating that counted, but who was doing the eating. His life was being conducted without him. Living lies had made him weak and his brother strong.

Looking out the tinted bulletproof windows onto the Avenue of the Americas, he felt like he was watching a distant movie. An old man was picking through trash. What was he looking for? Food? Yesterday's news? Truth? Strange how when one begins to lose the self, one of the first things to go is awareness of appearance. Why does the old man even go through the motions of living? Something had obviously gone seriously wrong, so why didn't he just return to Go, even without collecting the two hundred dollars? *Life clings to life, as if it has some inherent meaning.* Here he was in his limo, whining about his vacuous padded life, while an old threadbare man in the wealthiest country in the world was picking through garbage. *Drive on, Jimmy!* he wanted to yell. *Run the light, I can't bear it!*

He was coming apart. Perhaps he should make an appointment with Caroline's Skull & Bones shrink over on Fifth Avenue and pay him to put Humpty Dumpty back together again. *I hate my brother, my son has disappeared, my wife is on happy pills, and yet I must finish all the peas on my plate because somewhere, everywhere, someone is starving, being tortured, or dying because of this weary old world where the rich get richer and the poor poorer, except for those who learn to sell their souls sell their souls sell their souls the way their masters do.*

Jimmy pulled over to the curb, got out, and opened Laurence's door. As he stepped from the limo and wished Jimmy the good day he himself wasn't going to have, he looked up at the small elegant building wedged between two skyscrapers. As usual, Hiram would do the talking and he would grin and bear it until he was on his own again to continue his own personal Inquisition.

16
The Dragon Cometh

The essence of true myth is to masquerade behind seemingly objective everyday details borrowed from known circumstances.

- Giorgio Santillana and Hertha von Dechend, *Hamlet's Mill*, 1969

When the bomb fell on America, it fell on
people.
It didn't dissolve them as it dissolved people in
Hiroshima.
It did not dissolve their bodies,
But it dissolved something vitally important to
the greatest of them and the least.
What it dissolved were their links with the past
and the future.
There was something new in the world that set
them off forever from what had been,
Something terrifying and big, beyond any
conceivable earthly dimensions . . .
It made the earth that seemed so solid, Main
Street that seemed so well-paved
A kind of vast jelly, quivering and dividing
underfoot . . .
What have we done, my country, what have we
done?

- Hermann Hagedorn, from "The Bomb That Fell on America," 1946

Ruminating on Ghost Bear, old Seven left the Cutoff and set out across the iridescent Blue Dragon

Flows looking for all the world like a moonwalk to Oz with their magnetic lines of crystallized titanium magnetite sculpted in fire and arrested in glassy rock by the snaky subterranean flows of long ago. She'd asked Ghost Bear about Hermano, but all he would say was that she knew Hermano was a Time Traveler. *Push on to the three rivers! Dokshé,* he'd responded gruffly, to which she could only whisper *Dokshé.*

Phantom ponies clopped over the *pahoehoe.* Shades of children with moon faces clung to their mothers' buckskins. Unearthly phantoms wriggled up from myriad small sutures in the *a'a',* phantoms worthy of Hieronymus Bosch moving among the dead, some faceless, others with triangular chins and big ears, wings and scales, some round as a ball with one unnerving eye, most with two eyes animated by a cold, inhuman intelligence. If surface-dwellers only knew that "primitive" beliefs were true and they shared the Earth with multitudes of plasma beings, with radiation creating more. Seven wouldn't have batted an eye if the Great Pan himself had arisen before her.

The Roman historian Plutarch recorded an incident that occurred in the seventeenth year of Tiberius' reign, in 32 or 33 CE—the time of the Crucifixion. Plutarch's teacher Epitherses was sailing from Greece to Italy on a ship carrying freight and passengers. It was evening near the Ekhinádes Islands when the wind dropped and the ship drifted near Paxoí. Almost everyone was awake, many not even finished with their after-dinner wine, when suddenly from the dark shores of Paxoí a voice loudly called the name of the ship's Egyptian pilot, *Thamus! Thamus!* Even the passengers did not know his name. Twice Thamus made no reply, but the third time the voice called, Thamus answered, at which the voice commanded, *When you come opposite to Palodes, announce that the Great Pan is dead.* All stood on

241

deck, astounded, whispering among themselves whether it would be better for Thamus to carry out the order or refuse to meddle in affairs of the unknown. At last, it was decided that if there was a breeze when they reached Palodes, Thamus would sail on and keep quiet, but if there were no wind and a smooth sea, he would speak. When they finally came opposite Palodes, there was neither wind nor wave, so Thamus cried out from the stern toward the land, *Great Pan is dead!* There then came a great cry of lamentation from out of the darkness, not of one voice but of many, to the marvel of the passengers.

Small stone circles made iridescent by the Blue Dragon Flows were everywhere, sacred, wise, and old. The ghostly steps and flutters and whispers accompanying old Seven grew thicker, as did the sing-song vowels rolling from spirit tongues, shaping the names of all that the dead longed for, now that their sensory gateways to their Mother's house were closed: *dawn, sleep, breasts, the small of a man's back, a baby's sigh, fire in winter, wind in the poplars, the tang of pemmican, first snow, cold beer in July, spring wind, mountain, dancing, the feel of the bow.* On and on they chanted their mass of the dead, and Seven, still an inhabitant of a different country in space and time, listened and nodded as was proper.

At Indian Tunnel with its thirty-foot opening, the acrid smell of bat guano from deep in the cave almost bowled her over. Lava stalactites dripped from the ceiling, lichens and moss clung fiercely to the walls and carpet-like soil. The Blue Dragon had slithered this way, suffusing the cave's icy darkness with its telltale light. As her ghostly escort disappeared into the cave, Seven followed. In the high-vaulted chamber, sacred images danced on the walls: buffalo, elk, wolves, the Morning and Evening Star, handprints, birds, men with wings, snakes like lightning. One image in particular caught her attention: a huge wave curling over a big boxy modern city. She left the cave and pushed onward.

The night was black and brittle cold. By the light of the Dragon's veins, she could see where Murphy farm wagons had run their ruts across the lava flats almost two hundred years ago. *Kapukas* glowed like distant cities or stars, while overhead Orion hunted, wheeling bright Betelgeuse and Rigel westward. Soon, the Twins would follow, then the Crab. Would Thomas be at the three rivers tryst? If he was alive, he would come.

She stopped to breathe deep, leaning on her walking stick and looking up. The Crab had been a scarab for the Egyptians, a tortoise for the Babylonians—a hard-shelled creature for all, ruled by the Moon and tide, symbol of the soul. Cancer always looked so *nebulous*—thus the Cancer nebulae—no head or eyes, the fuzzy Beehive Cluster at its heart on the ecliptic. For the ancients, the Beehive was the Gate of Man, *Praesepe* or Manger through which souls gained entry to the Earth. *Cancer, the Mother sign* . . . Just before dawn, Leo's sickle-like head would rise with Regulus glowing in his heart. One of the Persians' Four Guardians of the Heavens, Leo in a month or so would swish his tail and scatter Leonids over the Earth.

The night was clear but the air charged. Foreboding gripped her chest. Tongues of lightning lapped at the overturned bowl of the sky, just as they had in the early hours of the Moon Day July 16, 1945, down the snaky spine of the Rockies, the Blood of Christ and Sacrament Mountains, all the way to Alamogordo. Arthur C. Clarke said that any sufficiently advanced technology would be indistinguishable from magic, and what had occurred at Alamogordo was magickal—not sleight-of-hand parlor tricks but the real magick of advanced technology prematurely *cracking open* the future and thus transmuting it. Isaac Newton, the last of the great alchemists, was one of the three men Thomas Jefferson had most admired. Newton was a cabalist first and physicist last, cabalists being superior to physicists due to their ability to wield the unseen forces or powers that *prima material* unleashed, whereas physicists only believe in what they see, mesmerized by what to cabalists are mere means. Alchemy wove through Los Alamos, White Sands, and the American tragedy that shattered matter and began the premature, violent storming of the Threshold gates with neither caution nor moral development.

Vince had explained how Spilling the Gourd of Ashes was a crisis rivaled only by Atlantis twelve thousand years earlier. It marked the beginning of the Hopi Day of Purification foretold on the stone tablets that some said were older than the Book of Revelations. The Creation and Destruction of Primordial Matter had been a public ritual of cosmic proportions, an event for all spacetime—the annihilation of *prima materia* a dark god's achievement or, as Illuminists preferred to think of it, the cataclysmic liberation of Light, *luxor e tenebris.* The Age of the Pale Horse had culminated at the Trinity test north of Alamogordo at the 33rd North parallel in the Malpais Lava Beds of the Sacrament Mountains near the Three Rivers Petroglyphs. It had breached Space and Time by means of a knowledge coveted by the few since Atlantis. At the very nanosecond of detonation, the Italian Enrico Fermi let drop his scraps of paper on which he had planned to jot his observations and Robert Oppenheimer clung knuckle-white to a table top, reciting from the *Bhagavad-Gita—*

> *If the radiance of a thousand suns*
> *were to burst into the sky,*

that would be like
the splendor of the Mighty One . . .
I am become Death, the shatterer of
worlds.

By the light of St. Elmo's fire, Seven read a sign marked with an atomic sigil—

Idaho National Engineering and Environmental Laboratory
National Reactor Testing Station
Operated by the Lockheed Martin Idaho Technologies Company
RESTRICTED AREA
NO TRESPASSING BEYOND THIS POINT
!!!DANGER!!!
ORDO AB CHAO
By Order of the Department of Energy and U.S. Navy

Ordo ab Chao. The US Navy had once trained submariners here in simulators. Were they still here? Seven's father had been a Navy Intelligence scientist, Navy meaning Navigators with a capital N, Argonauts with a capital A—Freemasons, Knights of Malta, Dragon Court, ONI Psyops—their creed being out Order from Chaos. Create the Chaos and you control the Order coming from it.

Was it dawn yet? It was hard to tell night from day in this radiated penumbra quivering like fretful protoplasm suffused with electrical impulses jumping invisible synapses. It all reminded Seven of the gelatinous blobs of biological material that had been raining down on small rural towns since the end of World War Two, filled with bacteria and eukaryotic cells that made people sick for months.

A *wasichu* ghost arose and pointed imperatively at the ground, glancing north over its shoulder before disappearing. Seven followed its gaze and caught the distant *whop-whop-whop* of an approaching patrol. By the halogen lights crisscrossing the desolate plain, she guessed they were Apaches. Deftly, she heaved her pack into a *puka* and crawled in after it. Pulling the space blanket and fronds over herself, she lay absolutely still, figuring they had motion as well as heat sensors on board.

After the rotor whispers faded, she got out her ion chamber survey meter and tested for radiation. The numbers she saw made her press the Takyon amulet around her neck. Instantly, a three-inch orgone shield sprang up around her body. She was too near the dragon's lair to rest, so she rummaged for the last of the Silver Creek snowmelt, reprogrammed the meter for magnetometer function, re-shouldered her pack, clamped a Dune filter over her nose and mouth, and crawled out of the *puka*.

The LCD grid on her ghostbuster registered a wavering electromagnetic dome overhead, like the wall of energy she had seen years before running north-south through Chaco Canyon that had been activated by a military jet from miles above. Faintly, she could hear a Dantean chorus singing, *Lasciate ogni speranza, o voi ch'entrate. Abandon all hope, you who enter.* Hesitating for the briefest of moments, she strode forward.

Immediately, she was joined by the ghost of John Collier, Commissioner of Indian Affairs for President Franklin Roosevelt from 1933 to 1945. She was grateful for his presence as the heat rising through thousands of tiny fissures in the volcanic rock began to increase. Her magnetometer picked up the contours of a huge rectangular chamber below that John Collier said was a metal-lined vault fitted with fiberoptics and chemical alarms and packed with thousands of railcar containers in which plutonium 239, cesium-137, strontium-90, and tritium was cooking. *Underground base, too,* Collier confirmed, pointing to multiple levels filled with chambers, interlocking tunnels, and corridors, even a four-lane highway with a monorail. Seven turned off the magnetometer. Sixty-six research reactors out on the Snake River Plain, one of the least stable rifts in the entire North American continent. Why so many, and why here? John Collier repeated Oppenheimer's words: *I am become Death, the shatterer of worlds.*

Time was still in the dead zone, always between midnight and dawn; even the dry lightning was out of season. The Bitterroot Range should have been funneling a wicked north wind, but instead the sub-zero air was uncannily paralyzed. Nothing lived here, not even wind, and the further in she walked, the heavier her load felt. Her breath labored, and John Collier kept breaking up.

. . . field too strong . . . sorry, he transmitted.

Collier! she transmitted back, not wanting to be left alone. *Is this all that is left of the Lost Valley?*

What they have made of it, he whispered, and was gone.

For the first time in all the months on the Trail, she felt utterly bereft. How dependent she had grown on ghostly company! She could die out here and no one would know. Her walking stick pulled her over the *pahoehoe,* her steps echoing over whatever and whoever was below. She reactivated the magnetometer; she was still over the subterranean base, passing through a door, along a corridor. Suddenly, she discerned life form blips hurrying down the corridor toward her position. Quickly, she disconnected, her heart racing, her eyes scanning the terrain and skies.

Hurrying east, her thoughts returned to the Bomb. Roosevelt had died suddenly on April 12, 1945, just a few months into his War Powers *fourth* term. Germany surrendered on May 7. Hitler hadn't had the Bomb, after all, but the Strangeloves weren't about to close down the Manhattan Project. In fact, in the weeks following the end of the war in Europe, the work pace doubled so a bomb could be detonated once the dog days of July got going—when Sirius and our Sun were in conjunction—and another two ready for Japan at the end of the dog days in August. Everything in three's.

1945 plus 55 is 2000. 55 signifies death and destruction. James Franck and six other scientists tried to stop the Bomb, meeting like thieves in the night in the bowels of the University of Chicago, hammering out the famous Franck Report that history would minimize along with Franck, despite his 1925 Nobel Prize. He forwarded the report to War Secretary Stimson on June 11, and on June 16 it was repudiated by the Interim Committee of twelve: Stimson; Harrison, his deputy; Byrnes, head of the Office of War Mobilization and Truman's man; Ralph A. Bard, Navy; William L. Clayton, State Department; Bush, Compton, and Conant, scientists; Oppenheimer, Fermi, Compton, and Lawrence, atomic experts. With the 32nd President out of the way, Truman was the unelected 33rd. In 1933, Roosevelt had worn the regalia of the Georgia Grand Lodge and raised his son Elliot to the degree of Master Mason at Architect Lodge 519 in New York City. *Thirty-three.* Truman was a 33° Freemason.

Years before, Ray had dreamed of the Shatterer deep in the Earth and the primal forces that black magick adepts summon for devious deployments. Seven now knew much more about the Shatterer and the Earth Severer. In China after the millennial change, Shatterer adepts had ordered electroshock for Internet-addicted youths aged 12 to 24, along with drugs, hypnosis, and "military discipline" (torture) to create PTSD'd Chinese automatons who would lead the way to machine consciousness. The West was doing the same to its youths with violent video games. In the Spring 1998 issue of the Army journal *Parameters,* the article "The Mind Has No Firewall" went public about *strategic personality simulation,* the most invasive of all covert tactics of containment, including the *shattering* of the human soul.

Seven sighed. Loneliness was cutting her to the bone as she trekked deeper and deeper into the National Reactor Testing Station. She was too old for this. All she wanted was lie down and sleep the Big Sleep.

She paused to breathe. Back before the pilgrimage to Dallas, Thomas had had very little idea of the future he would have to resist with all his being.

A week had passed since Seven and Thomas had agreed to go on as usual until news of Ray surfaced. Seven had spent the day wrapping up the academic quarter out at Isla Vista and arrived at Rhea's for a late dinner, discretely avoiding the stakeout out front by parking up behind the tipis and approaching from the back of the property. On her way through Rhea's kitchen, Seven fondly remembered the sumptuous macrobiotic meal she'd prepared for a Japanese *roshi* who had profusely apologized for only eating a little white rice and miso soup, as was his ascetic habit.

In the living room, Ted and Mina were crouched over what looked like a model Hopi village for Mina's sixth grade project. They'd mixed fine sand with pigment and were covering the *kivas* with symbolic designs signifying Hopi Sun and Coyote clans. Excitedly, Mina showed Seven the tiny baked bread she had made for inside the small clay oven. *Native America again,* Seven thought. Something was trying to tell her something.

At about ten o'clock, they all sat down to steamed greens with carrot slivers, millet, beans, and *masa harina* tortillas. Chewing and digestion were like communion for Rhea, so the meal was quiet. Only when the *bancha* was poured did Seven begin to recount some of what had happened at Wheeler Springs, which now seemed like eons ago. Both Rhea and Ted listened carefully to everything she said about the tattooed European, Ghost Bear and Raven.

Rhea finally said to Ted, "Do you remember that guy in Pasadena, the computer whiz we always thought took too much acid? What was it he said about saying too much?"

Ted was not just Rhea's money bulwark; he was the memory keeper, as well.

Ted nodded. "He was moving around with Hugh and the Farm in that big school bus. I couldn't tell if he was strung out or simply had a really big scare, but he sure was paranoid. He talked about being a CIA operative, then laughed to make us think he was joking. Later, he said something about being in 'Nam to set up fly-over drug deals for the CIA, and that they were out to kill him because he knew too much. He smoked a lot of pot." He shrugged. "I didn't really know how much to believe. I mean, the CIA drug connection is common enough knowledge. Hugh might know what happened to him."

"I don't mean that," Rhea snapped. "Didn't he say he met a guy who looked like a monk?"

Ted's face brightened. "Yeah, he said he was driving out of Camp Nelson past the Tule River Indian Reservation when he picked up an old hitchhiker. He said he usually didn't pick up hitchhikers after dark, but something in the guy's face made him pull over. He was dressed in a cassock, no beard but hair like a Druid. The old guy told him that he'd been heading east but had taken a detour to catch a ride with him so he could tell him something.

"There they were, driving away from one of the biggest military installations in the country, down a little highway toward Porterville in pitch dark, and this guy tells a paranoid nerd that his life really *is* in danger because he knows too much, that a little accident is being planned for him, and if he wants to live, he should maybe take a new identity and *next time*—this computer guy was really bothered by 'next time'—he should know better than to get involved with government covert operations. The guy got out near Porterville."

"Did . . . did the older man have an accent?" Seven asked breathlessly.

Ted furrowed his brow. "I don't remember. Do you, Rhea?"

Rhea shook her head.

Maybe it had been Hermano. After all, he was a Time-traveler, whatever that meant. Whoever he was, he wasn't a sneaky, two-faced spy. But her American education had methodically drained her of confidence in her gut feelings. Truckloads of information had been shoveled into her with no way to gauge the truth of any of it, much less integrate it. Juggling facts and figures and her personal life was like 52-card pickup. The mark of the beast was probably already behind her forehead, and the media was glutting everyone with entertainment like *The Prisoner*. What a trip America was.

She swallowed and plunged. "The man I met does sound a lot like the man with Druid hair." Her eyes drifted to Rhea's face. Why was she, like Mina, so desperate for Rhea's good opinion? "The Indian man with him said he's is a Time-traveler . . ."

No one laughed.

Ted put down his chopsticks. "Why not? I've seen a lot of strange things since I left Chicago as a young man, not the least of which are some of Rhea's friends." He smiled. "In the Philippines during the

War was the first time I'd ever been around an utterly different culture. One night, I was awakened by a Filipino boy who worked for us. He wanted me to follow him into the jungle. I knew it would mean trouble if we were caught, but I went anyway, more scared of poisonous snakes than my CO.

"He led me to a hut on stilts guarded by a man with a torch. We went inside where a dozen or so people were standing around a pallet with flashlights and lanterns, all looking at an unconscious girl about Mina's age."

Mina slid onto Ted's lap as he went on. "Standing over her was a man as beautiful as a woman, his eyes closed in rapt concentration, trembling, small beads of sweat on his brow. I had two thoughts in quick succession: that the air between the pallet and me was full, pregnant, not empty, and that he needed our presence in order to do whatever he was doing for the girl. It was the first time I had seen a shaman conduit unseen energies.

"The shaman opened his eyes really wide and breathed in and out through his nostrils like the *kundalini* breath of fire, then gently pulled the sheet down and unbelievably quickly, with his palm flat, traced an incision on the girl's abdomen—and *her skin opened.* Blood and fluids seeped out as he deftly reached into her viscera and pulled something out, put it in a bowl, rearranged something else, then with his palms resting on the two sides of the incision, looked up, rolled his eyes back in his head, and closed them. The room was crackling and popping with energy, like during Barbara's birth-ins.

"When he took his hands away, it was as if the skin had never been opened. No scar, nothing. The boy had to lead me out, I was so dumbfounded. Outside, other patients were waiting on litters, surrounded by relatives ready to offer up their energies. Silently, we returned to camp. The next day, I tried to say something to him about it, as he understood some English, but he quickly put his hand over my mouth and told me white men must learn what needs to be said and what doesn't, as words are power. I knew that what he said was true. It wasn't about secrecy or the authorities not approving of 'primitive' healing— by the way, the healing I saw included an invocation to Christ—it was a matter of spiritual discretion. I had been a guest in another world and was expected to respect the laws of that world.

"All the time I was in the Philippines, I never heard anyone refer to the psychic surgeons, though I'm sure every night the 'hospital' was open for business. Since then, healing for me has been a spiritual matter, not technological, and loved ones are not to be banished because of hypothetical neuromedical antithetical pathogenical germs." As he sang each Gilbert & Sullivan term, he tickled the giggling Mina.

Rhea's obsidians burned. "Intelligence, miracles, *charismata*, strange occurrences—all are really daily fare, and yet most of us are clogged up with nonsense hitting us from every direction." She looked at Mina. "What was it you were reading to me from Willa Cather just today?"

Pleased to be called upon, Mina collected *Death Comes for the Archbishop* from the couch, opened to the passage, and read aloud—

> *Father Vaillant began pacing restlessly up and down as he spoke, and the Bishop watched him, musing. It was just this in his friend that was dear to him. "Where there is great love there are always miracles," he said at length. "One might almost say that an apparition is human vision corrected by divine love. I do not see you as you really are, Joseph; I see*

you through my affection for you. The
Miracles of the Church seem to me to rest
not so much upon faces or voices or
healing power coming suddenly near to
us from afar off, but upon our
perceptions being made finer, so that for
a moment our eyes can see and our ears
can hear what is there about us always."

Rhea nodded. "Being a spiritual warrior these days means pushing distractions far enough away so you can think. History is being eradicated like in *Fahrenheit 451.* In ten years, you won't find any truth about Vietnam or the Sixties in any high school textbook. Ted and I moved here so we could concentrate like that Filipino healer, so we could feel the Earth and hear the plants growing and see the stars at night before our heads began leaking and the blood in our arms and legs turned to lead.

"But even in quaint Santa Barbara we're under fire. Santa Barbara is the patron saint of mariners, and yet Union Oil's Platform A has coated the beaches with oil and killed the birds, fish, vegetation, and virtually destroyed Santa Barbara Channel, and now they're still drilling five miles offshore. Before that, the fire up at Painted Cave. In 1925, a 6.3 earthquake leveled just about everything, and over the rubble they rebuilt Hispanic red-tiled roofs, arched façades, central patios, pastel exteriors. Even back in the early 1800s, a 'quake wiped out everything around Santa Barbara Mission, the so-called queen of missions—dams and aqueducts from Mission Creek, fields of wheat, corn, barley, beans, hillsides of orange groves, olive trees, grapes. And in 1942, a Japanese submarine got close enough to shell Goleta Beach.

"Ages past knew that everything has intelligence and is connected. Those quakes were justice for Jesuits and Franciscans building the queen of missions on the whipped backs of Chumash labor, the people who had reigned supreme from Malibu Canyon to Morro Bay. Like your old *chupu* woman, Seven, they were not 'savages' but keepers of the Earth with a highly distinctive language, trade and taxation, artisans and boat builders, living on the bounty of sea and land with more leisure time than anyone has today. Instead of idling away their leisure, they created stories, textiles, paintings, sculpture, pots, all in a climate of peace.

"At least we should keep the story straight.—After the Spanish priests and soldiers enslaved them, the US Marines landed and took over Santa Barbara on Christmas Day 1846. California began with a military governor and we still have one. Our military governor sent his helicopters and soldiers with grenades swinging from their belts to Isla Vista to remind us of how they want our college kids to behave, right?" She glared at Seven. "You saw them. The Marines guaranteed free passage for the settlers who took over Mexican and Indian land. The Treaty of Guadalupe Hidalgo and disenfranchised were brushed aside. A drought ruined the remaining Mexican *ranchos*, and Chinese immigrants—many of whom had been addicted during the British Opium Wars— came to work on the railroads and gold rush, then moved into the vacant houses and started restaurants and laundries, brothels and gambling houses. When the Chinese got to be doing too well and getting too settled, a 1912 law forbade them to own land, along with the Mexicans and Chumash.

"It's a conspiracy against history, that's what it is. What did your Time-traveler say? That you're necessary to the Great Work? If he's traveled the past, he's right: remembering the truth is the first order of business because in the end the truth won't be quiet. I hear it asking, *What are we allowing to be done in our name? How will it end?*" She pursed her lips. "If another big 'quake is coming, and I have no doubt it is, it won't be any 'freak of nature.'"

Rhea looked up at the seven-foot painting of nude Ted, Barbara, and Aaron playing volleyball. "Maybe your European friend has come to do what he can about our *seventh* direction, our human direction of inner imagination, feeling, and thought. *In* is the new direction and we Westerners are terrified of going *in*, despite all the psychological snake oil and old religions that founded this nation and are now freaked out about all the Sixties trail-blazing and experimentation. How else are to discover the possibilities of the seventh direction in a land steeped in materialism? Sure, we can get lost in vast inner space, but it may be even more dangerous to navigate by the old charts. Self-navigation is clumsy because it's the new frontier," she pointed upward with a smirk, "not up there with our orbiting hunks of iron and male projectiles."

"I'll toast to that," Ted laughed, holding up his Japanese cup of *bancha.*

As they raised their cups to the advent of the seventh direction, they heard a rapping.

Mina ran to the garden window and mouthed silently, "It's Ray!" Bug-wise Rhea had told her not to say Ray's name out loud. Mina was learning.

17
The Lost Valley

If much in the world were mystery the limits of that world were not, for it was without measure or bound and there were contained within it creatures more horrible yet and men of other colors and beings which no man has looked upon and yet not alien none of it more than were their own hearts alien in them, whatever wilderness contained there and whatever beasts.

- Cormac McCarthy, *Blood Meridian, or The Evening Redness in the West*, 1985

For they have sown the wind and they shall reap the whirlwind.

- Hosea 8:7

You place a tall bone-covered hat on your head just so, and whisper the long, convoluted incantations just so . . . And then you rise, slowly at first, up through the smokehole, out into the bright night sky. Clouds drops from your hands like icy handkerchiefs. You tear through the ultraviolet shrouds of oxygen, soaring toward the Land of the Dead, where you must go to be reborn.

- Rob Schultheis, *The Hidden West*, 1996

Old Seven's thoughts continued to darken as she tramped further and further into the cotton-candy pink haze surrounding the glowing reactors out on the National Reactor Testing Station. Her magnetometer indicated multitudes of underground chambers honeycombing the plain. *Abandon all hope, you who enter,* she sulked, the mood of the place having invaded her soul. She must hurry through.

Wading deeper into the nuclear haze, her breath laboring through her air filter, she discerned a blacker than black disc floating three fingers above the horizon where sky should have been, a negative space peephole.

The Midnight Sun, a disembodied voice nearby sneered.

Seven jerked around to see who had spoken so cynically, but saw nothing. A comet streaked from around the back of the disc with six aureoles orbiting its fiery head and more coating its streaming hair. *Kometes,* the ancient Greeks had called them, the longhaired ones. In Longfellow's "Hiawatha," they were *Ishkoodah.*

> *Eight things there be a comet brings*
> *When it on high doth horrid rage:*
> *Wind, Famine, Plague, and Death of Kings,*
> *War, Earthquake, Floods, and Doleful Change.*

The Great Comet visits every 3,065 years. It last accompanied Napoleon's birth in 1769, then returned from its journey around the Sun when he was 42; when its tail split, he marched into Russia. One Saturn pulse later, in 1840, *four* comets streaked through the heavens, heralding to occultists everywhere the advent of a great War in Heaven in which the Time Spirit of the Age, the Archangel Michaël, struggled to save the Heavens from Ahriman the Destroyer. On Earth, human spirits were buffeted as by invisible solar winds. Comet Tebbutt arrived in 1861 with eleven aureoles, then Donati's Comet passed in front of the Great Bear on October 5, 1878, not seen (according to Seneca) since 146 BCE. Finally, Brorsen's Comet paid its fifth visit in 1879, when, according to Western occultists, Michaël succeeded in throwing Ahriman down into the Earth to save the Heavens. Then in September 1882, the Turkish Scimitar gave birth in the skies to a second comet, bright Tewfik's Comet, appearing over Egypt during a solar eclipse, then ominously fleeing behind the shadow where the Sun should have been. Pope Leo XIII (1878-1903), versed in the occult significance of cosmic visitations, made his coat-of-arms a comet streaking over the Wakah-Chan world tree framed by two fleur-de-lys.

The 19th century teemed with comets, thirteen naked eye, three hundred sightings in all, streaking through the Heavens like aberrant thoughts leaping the synapses of a strange and difficult brain spawning one –ism after another: nationalism, industrialism, materialism, spiritualism, Freudianism, Marxism, behaviorism, Darwinism. Accompanying the –isms was the onslaught of technical inventions: electricity, radiation, the telegraph, radio waves, the automobile and airplane.

Was it just a fluke of cosmic nature that most comet sightings occurred in the 1940's while World War Two raged in Europe and the Pacific Ocean? Finally, three comets one Jupiter pulse apart rounded out the end of the second millennium: Kohoutek in 1973, Halley in 1985 for its 29th round and second visit this century, and dubious Hale-Bopp four times the size of Halley in 1997, cutting a swath close enough to Spaceship Earth to merit a terrible sacrifice of 39 (13x3) mind-controlled souls christened Heaven's Gate.

But the comet over the National Reactor Testing Station at the end of 2019 was like nothing Seven had ever heard of, even in holotheaters. Its fiery fuchsia head obstructed half the dome of heaven, its garish unnatural hue like the viscous fog sucking at her trembling legs. Its tail wasn't smooth and long but wiry, charged, helter skelter. This Medusa was an unholy *Wundererscheinung*, a demonic Star of Bethlehem foretelling the birth of a new terror. Or was it a technomagician high-powered microwave hologram of *War of the Worlds* in living color? HPM holograms were useful for diversions and social control. Jesuits favored the Virgin Mary or Jesus, angels and devils; Pentagon buffs preferred elaborate fleets of flying saucers, aliens, reptoids, and greys to be belabored by panels of Disclosure experts until the inchoate pablum settled into the mass mind and drifted half-digested down the Memory Hole. This apocalyptic messenger, however, was no holohoax. This *Ishkoodah* was the genuine article.

Hurrying along under the still life Medusa, Seven almost missed the old B-29 bomber buzzing like a mosquito in her path. She squinted. *Enola Gay* was inscribed on the fuselage and the ghost of Brigadier General Paul Tibbets was in the cockpit, observing the popping and sizzling Medusa hurtling toward the Earth. Nothing could stop it now, certainly not the *Enola Gay*.

The nasty whisperer hissed, *Cukra, flying on board a high-powered vimana, hurled onto the triple city a single projectile charged with all the power of the Universe. It was an unknown weapon, an iron thunderbolt, a gigantic messenger of death that reduced to ashes the entire race of Vrishnis and Andhakas . . .*

The garish light of ten million night flares from Medusa's head flooded the plain and x-rayed the horrors living beneath the blanket of pink fog.

Mustard-green Boschian creatures with unblinking cavernous eyes moaned, screamed, howled, scrabbled, and tore their way up through *pahoehoe* cracks, their skin stretching like chewing gum as other desperate creatures dragged them down to usurp their place. Millions of mouths with little rows of sharp teeth sucked and gulped the radioactive light in the sludge. Gaunt faces—human at another, happier time— had mouths fixed in terrible little O's. This then was Bedlam, hell, the netherworld Seven had been taught didn't exist.

... *An incandescent column of smoke and flame, as bright as ten thousand Suns, rose in all its splendor* ... The whisperer snickered.

Finally, the Medusa struck. Seven winced, expecting shockwaves and a tortuous death by fire, but the Earth, raped by the psychic specter's penetration, only buckled and writhed and heaved up a vortical abyss. Was this, then, what Dante had envisioned? Particles of pink dust flew about like the dust Little Boy sowed in Hiroshima and Fat Man in Nagasaki, like the dust that 333 above-ground H-bombs sowed in America. Up, up the little atomic Tinkerbells whirled, flinging their magic death dust with abandon, up the smoky shaft of the blossoming World Tree of Fire, an Atomic Tree crowned with a diabolical halo, beating its black wings over the wide world. Miles below, the Medusa's last electromagnetic shock of hair slipped into the abyss.

... *Corpses were so burned as to be unrecognizable,* the voice whispered hurriedly, *hair and nails fell out, pottery broke without any apparent cause, birds turned white. In a few hours, all the food was contaminated. A fine dust settled over everything, and then—the experiments.*

Seven shivered.

What was once a plain was now a chasm a half mile across with the *Jornada del Muerto* spirit road running north-south through it, from the Arctic Circle down the Mackenzies and Rockies to the Sierra Madres and Cordillera de los Andes and Antarctic in the south. Up and down the road, the dead were walking, naked, in finery and rags, their numbers glutted with the nuclear dead hailing from the Nevada Test Site and the nuclear triangle made by the Mescalero Apache Reservation, the Waste Isolation Pilot Project at Carlsbad, and Sierra Blanca, Texas— from the Los Alamos and Sandia National Laboratories, the Inhalation Toxicology Research Institute, the Stanford Linear Accelerator Center, Lawrence Livermore National Laboratory, E.O. Lawrence Berkeley National Laboratory, the Pacific Northwest National Laboratory, the National Renewable Energy Laboratory, Rocky Flats, Grand Junction, and Pantex. They hobbled and crawled and loped like crabs, their scabs and scars and burns suppurating, their skin flaking, their orifices bleeding, their organs missing. Hundreds of thousands of glowing human ghosts mingled with throngs of strange, aberrent creatures, all wounded, crippled, piteous, all the same unearthly neon fuchsia, hobbling onward, members of a new race, a mutant race of the nuclear dead. Overhead, the Midnight Sun played peekaboo with the pink haze, and the ghostly frieze of the Nuclear Tree stood as a desolate testament to the 20th century. Disc- and wedge-shaped phantom ships, rockets, submarines, and satellites dipped and wove through it like bees. Now and then, a disc disappeared into the chasm.

In this netherworld, Seven's vital light seemed to act as a beacon for the nuclear dead falling over each other in their rush to get to her and show her their pain, their keloid scars, holes, burns, carnage. They crawled on their bellies and sucked at her light. Those who couldn't get to her made do by sucking at each other where the radiation glowed most brilliantly.

Seven could not bear to meet their dead gaze, for their eyes were holes where souls should have been. Her muscles struggled to keep trudging through the nuclear dead.

It is only their Double you are seeing, you soft fool, the whisperer hissed, *their Doppelgänger, not their human Phantom.*

The din on the plain was inhuman, a litany of screeches, howls, and groans. She knew their death stories by heart. In the first nuclear generation, from 1944 to 1974, more than 4,000 secret experiments were performed on tens of thousands of Americans. In the second and third generations, the experiments grew more particular, more bold and bizarre, especially in genetic engineering. Hidden in the Trojan horse bellies of committees and universities and hospitals, the experiments were first sanctioned by the Atomic Energy Commission, then later by the Department of Energy, National Cancer Institute, Pentagon, NSA, NASA, National Institute of Mental Health, American Psychiatric Association, and of course the CIA and its dire EMK-ULTRA, all safe from scrutiny thanks to the National Security Act of 1947. Cancer patients, the terminally ill, pregnant women, schoolchildren, prisoners, poor Blacks, Chicanos, whites, and Native Americans in inner city hospitals, VA hospitals, on reservations, all dosed with nuclear drugs piggy-backed onto vaccinations, irradiated in the name of science and saving human life, electrodes pasted on shaved scalps, radioactive replacement organs surreptitiously sewed and lasered into them.

This latest institutional incarnation of evil was conscious, meticulously organized, a matter of policy, professional, sanctioned by the highest authorities in the land, and carried out on a national and international scale by a network of men and women bound by blood oaths and pedophile blackmail to maintain the secret and to lie, lie, lie through their teeth to congressional committees, patients and their families, reporters, colleagues, their own families, and of course, themselves. Doctors, psychiatrists, medical technicians, hospital boards, military officers, lawyers, judges, specialists and experts idolized, idealized, and trusted by *boobus Americanus*, accomplices fostering a nuclear religion behind which diabolical objectives for the future hid.

The sounds oozing viscous light in black, white, and brown women came from throats where larynxes had been, where radioactive iron pills were still going down; from missing breasts and glowing ovaries irradiated while they had stood at clinic counters; from wombs where irradiated babies still curled, and children with big eyes and wizened faces who had been vaccinated with plutonium, who had contracted leukemia in the womb, who had been born with neuroblastoma tumors shining like black suns between their tiny lungs and heart. *829 pregnant women,* the whisperer footnoted gleefully, *Oak Ridge Institute of Nuclear Studies in Tennessee, Vanderbilt University, both Pentagon-funded, 1957-74.* In one "study" alone, nine thousand children were exposed to radioactive iodine-131 and then tracked over their growth years, the data carefully measured and recorded as cancer devoured their thyroids. Two hundred and fifty thousand Farm Belt children had been reared on milk intentionally contaminated by fallout.

Seven's breathing heaved beneath her mask, tears coursing down her cheeks.

Men pointed to their suppurating lungs blackened by the beryllium they had breathed all their working lives. Inmates from state and federal penitentiaries clutched crotches of glowing testicles. Downwinders from Nevada, Utah, Wyoming, Arizona, and California bowed their heads to Seven as they herded blind two-headed sheep and five-hooved cattle down the

Jornada del Muerto. Men and beasts had been intentionally exposed to fallout clouds of three million curies released into the air from underground tests and radioactive gases, and the slow cancers spawned in their children through drinking the milk and eating the cheese and butter and meat were dutifully measured and recorded. The TBIs, total body irradiation subjects, had necks like pieces of burned meat, others bled from all their orifices, irradiated with 100 rads of Cobalt-60 gamma rays. Like concentration camp inmates, like prisoners of war, their wrists still bore their "study" numbers.

Saenger Radioisotope Laboratory, 1961-70. The University of Cincinnati received $651,480 for TBIs. With inflation, that averages out to about thirty pieces of silver. The whisperer giggled.

Companies of American soldiers in tattered uniforms shuffled up the side of the chasm with jellylike globs of their own bodies dripping from their hands. These were the men who had been ordered to remain at radial increments of ground zeroes for impact studies. Tank crews and their commanders who had fought in the deserts of Kuwait and Iraq pointed to the radioactive light flowing through their veins; they had not been informed by US Central Command that they were shooting depleted uranium-tipped, armor-penetrating shells, nor had the men from the 144th Army National Guard Service and Supply Company who had been ordered to clean up the battlefield after 14,000 DU rounds had been discharged.

At last, Seven stood at the far edge of the chasm, her road through hell accomplished. The nuclear dead toiled up and down the spiralling *Via Dolorosa*, their children trailing behind them. What had happened to their right to be guided by wise leaders whose mandate was to help them live and finally die a natural death? Was it so much to ask that they serve

265

their people and not set upon them like vampires or watch their abuse from afar?

Where does that road go? she asked the obnoxious whisperer.

Down, fool, the whisperer hissed, *surely you recall the worlds beneath your puny thin veneer?*

Mayan and Western occultists agreed on the Nine Realms below: Mineral, Fluid, Air, Form, Fruit, Fire, Earth Mirror, Earth Severer, Earth Core. Some said that the planet was actually *inside out* and that we are looking *in* when we look out to the heavens of Sun, Moon, and planets, which meant that the underworld would more rightfully be termed the *inner world*. All but the most simple-minded agreed that those dying a natural death need a good *map* when they leave the Earth plane so as to avoid *bardo* dangers the Aztecs describe in geographic terms: first traveling through water to clashing hills, across hills of obsidian buffeted by sharp winds where flags flutter and multitudes of weapons are shooting people down, past three terrible places where the hearts of the dead are eaten and everything is obsidian and there is no chimney for the smoke to escape through. Once one gets through these dangers, the spirit road is open.

Seven began her descent out, hoping that her own road lay open. Glowing phantoms slid past her like a river, their smooth watery forms rippling in the air around her. The Atomic Tree still hung overhead, a frieze in Time, terrible monument to the 20th century. She could feel its spectral vitality and remembered how her skin had crawled in Madame Tussaud's Wax Museum in London. Vince said that Ahriman the Destroyer was the ultimate shape-shifter and trickster. Was Ahriman the *Doppelgänger* god of this nuclear people? If so, would he allow them to exit and reincarnate, as was their human birthright? She feared that whatever was at last liberated from their tight constraints of matter would consume them body and soul. Everywhere the *Doppelgänger* god wafted and slipped and oozed, the light of what was human was extinguished. Banned from the Heavens like Lucifer, he seemed bent on radiating nuclear light out into the cosmos so the archangelic bastards would know the Earth was a sun of *his* making, not God's.

Seven ignored the maniacally laughing whisperer and turned to continue her way out of the terrible plain of suffering. To renew her intent, she took up the memory thread of those early days when they were all about to begin their odyssey to Dallas where the Killing of the King had been enacted.

18
Hiérarchie! Fraternité! Liberté!

*. . . all through Synarchy, nothing through
Anarchy . . .*

    - Alexandre Saint-Yves d'Alveydre
    (1842-1909)

*. . . according to the unwritten history known
only to us, the founder of the First Communist
International is indicated, of course secretly, as
being Weishaupt. You remember his name? He
was the head of the masonry known by the
name of Illuminati. This name he borrowed
from the second anti-Christian conspiracy of
that era, Gnosticism.*

    - Christian G. Rakovsky (1873-1941),
    founder of Soviet Bolshevism; during a
    NKVD interrogation, Stalin's show trials

*The Left tends to do conspiracies but not admit
to a higher power than Man; the Right taps into
the beyond, calling it whatever is appropriate –
different levels of truth for different stages of
illumination.*

    - Email, *geogeo*

Ray was not alone. With him was a white boy Mina
thought looked something like a lamb with his long
thin nose and his eyes big and brown and gentle. Once

he and Ray had snuck in and they were all in Mina's bedroom because it was the least likely to be bugged, Ray introduced Mannie in a whisper, saying he needed a place to crash for a night or two. They'd both been on the bus from San Francisco and had met during the half hour stop in San Luis Obispo.

Listening, Seven could tell that Ray had changed somehow. She couldn't put her finger on it . . . And obviously he hadn't thought through what his perilous situation could mean for Mannie, who was at that moment smiling inanely.

Ray recounted that he'd been fleeing north until he'd had a far out encounter in the San Francisco bus station with a European.

Seven, Rhea, and Ted glanced at each other.

"A European man with a Slavic accent?" Seven asked.

Ray grinned. "Yeah. He said he knew you, and he sure knew all about me, including what you've said about anger blinding me."

Briefly, Ray covered the catharsis he'd had regarding his childhood, then how the European had told him about the shadowy Gladio network in Europe, a right-wing enclave of Bilderberg aristocrats, intelligence operatives, military, industry and politicians. It was the Gladio network that infiltrated the *Organisation de l'armée secrète* that tried to assassinate de Gaulle in 1962.

"Whoa, whoa," Rhea interrupted. "Mina has to go to bed, so out. Ray, when you and Mannie approached the house, did you see any pigs?"

"Mannie saw what looked like a stake-out on Hillside, so we snuck in the back way. Where's my car?"

Ted raised his eyebrows and Rhea shrugged. "It was up by the tepees. It's not there anymore?"

Ray whistled softly. "Definitely not a good sign."

"Let's talk on the back porch, Ray," Seven said. "Good night, Mina." As she hugged and kissed Mina, the girl prolonged the hug. Seven didn't realize that it would be their last hug for a long time.

On the way to the dark porch off the garden, Seven whispered to Ray, "We're putting their family at risk. I think it's time to split town for a while."

Ray moaned, "I should have just kept going."

"It's not just you," Seven said. "There's another angle now, maybe two, maybe more."

She filled Ray in on Baby Rose, the two federal agents, and how one of the agents might be Thomas' long lost twin. Mention of Thomas fired Ray's jealousy. He'd been wild about Seven, but other than abiding friendship she'd never given him the time of day, due, Ray thought, to the white cat up on the mountain.

"You mean those pigs outside might be looking for more than me?"

"Exactly." In the dim light, she sized Mannie up. "Are you sure you want to get involved in this? It might be a really bad trip."

Mannie shrugged. "If you think I should go—"

Ray shook his head. "She means for your own good." He turned his attention back to Seven. "Okay, so no more Rhea's. That's cool. No more Isla Vista is not so cool, but if that's how it has to go down . . . My car's out of the picture, so what's next? The man in the bus station said my friends had need of me, and as you are his friend and my friend—"

Seven shrugged. "I think we need to go up to Thomas' place for a powwow, though I have a feeling it won't be safe up there much longer, either. We need to make a plan." She turned again to Mannie. "What are your plans after Santa Barbara? You could stay here tonight and go tomorrow."

Mannie hesitated. "I have a cousin in the movie business in LA. I'm just happy I made it out West where everything's happening." He grinned. "I hadn't expected things to start happening *this* fast, though. If it's all right with you, I'll go where you go and take my chances."

Seven understood his desire for adventure, but she wasn't sure *adventure* was the right word for what necessity was sending their way.

Rhea and Ted joined them and there was another half hour of furtive whispers and apologies. Seven was overwhelmed by an intuition that she would never again see either Rhea or Barbara. Was this part of the hard gift the old *chupu* woman had given her?

It was well after midnight when she, Ray, and Mannie drove out the back way, Ray and Seven rapping most of the way up the mountain about Hermano. Ray couldn't believe he'd never heard of Gladio.

"Initially, Gladio was a Nazi anti-Communist military guerrilla force created by NATO's Supreme Headquarters Allied Powers Europe after World War Two. The European—Hermano—said the new aristocratic right-wing Pinay Cercle will shift the European power base to the far right and in the next ten years engineer a British election that will set England on another course entirely, in tandem with a similar move here. He called them *reversal regimes* and said they won't be conservative or liberal but *radical* in a way far beyond politics, with an *occult* philosophy behind it called Synarchy. Man, they spend semesters on communism and anarchy, but not once did I ever hear the term Synarchy. Guess what it means?"

Mannie, leaning between Ray and Seven from the back of the bus, took a shot. "Well, if anarchy means no order, no government, then synarchy must mean a tight order of various factions or groups."

Ray stared at Mannie with new respect. "You're quick, man. Governance by secret societies, that's

271

what the cat said—'initiates' operating behind the scenes. Keep everyone worried about communism so no one worries about fascist Synarchist snakes in the aristocratic woodpile. This century, they've been working on political, economic, and religious domination of nations and a federal European Union. Hitler, the Nazis, and Aleister Crowley were just the beginning of political-occult tools. Right now, France is Synarchy central. Right-wing organizations and Masonic Lodges like the Martinist Order of Speculative Masonry and the Speculative Society are in alliance with the aristocrats running Synarchy.

"He said the founder and Grand Master of the Martinist Order was a French cat named Alexandre Saint-Yves d'Alveydre in the 1870s, but that the Synarchist ideology was from the same Hidden Masters or Secret Chiefs that took over Madame Blavatsky and Theosophy." He looked at Seven. "What's that about?" He wasn't as up on spiritual trips like Seven but now was thinking he'd be paying more attention to them.

Seven glanced at him. "That these fascist Synarchists are using spiritual trips as covers for infiltrating whole societies. Pretty clever to use religions and cults, especially in the land of the First Amendment. Last time I checked, spiritual freedom and democratic evolution weren't on the fascist agenda."

Ray pondered aloud, "The man said Synarchists have been in the States since the Twenties when the Versailles Treaty helped industrialists cloak the assets they'd doubled and tripled during the Russian Revolution and World War One. Common cause united them all—Black Nobility, Catholics and Baptists, Freemasons, Zionists, industrialists Vatican Curia, new Nazis, fundamentalists of all colors, maybe even Elijah Muhammed Black Muslims, all operating under one secret, unspoken Synarchist *diktat*..."

The communist part really got him. Up until now, he'd filed communism and socialism under *left*, but were they? They were definitely fundamentalist, and if Synarchists used whatever system worked for world power ... *Syn-*, together, united, using capitalism to drive the money engine, Communism to build a mass labor class, and socialism to keep the mass labor class dependent on big government handouts. And fascism? Fascism to merge crime and the fat industrialist cats of all three. Criminal, corporate, and old money using secret clubs, handshakes, vows, rituals, blackmail, and murder to unite and keep them on track. Ray was getting it.

Thinking of Wheeler Springs, Seven said thoughtfully, "So to expose how fascists work with and for each other, you have to discover their secret machinations—their cloisters, their principles and smokescreen organizations hiding their synarchy—"

Ray too was thoughtful. "—meanwhile seeking control of key government institutions, whatever party holds sway, and operating through established channels of fraternal orders, religions, foundations, NGOs, the UN. The man said that with Revolution and Chaos, Synarchy completes the triangle of influence that we saw going off like fireworks around the world in '68."

Seven glanced at him. "So revolutions don't just arise?" This must have been a blow to Ray's facile idea of politics.

Ray sighed. "That's what he said—that the recipe for Illuminati revolution begins with transformism, the dominant Darwinian ideal not of *being* but of evolutionary *becoming*, wherein only the strong survive. In both France and Russia, the people were conditioned to believe that revolution would transform society. But as we now know, only the fittest took power while the weak were depopulated in both Robespierre's Terror and Stalin's purges.

273

Robespierre's goal was to dispatch 15 million useless eaters, but he only got 300,000. Stalin was more successful—maybe as many as 100 million."

Mannie whistled softly, thinking of the six million Holocaust figure.

Seven knew the litany. "And with no God at the helm, Luciferianism takes hold. Christians become Deists, Deists Atheists, Atheists Satanists. Divide and conquer, then rule by Hegelian dialectic."

Ray stared at her. "Where'd you get that? That's exactly what he said. The aristocrats behind the French Revolution transferred their faith from the Catholic Church to the Illuminated Masonic Lodge. He advised me to look into powerful networks like the Black Muslims and discover what organizations they're connected to." Ray glanced at Seven. "Black Muslims, Seven. Malcolm X was murdered after he wanted out. The man said to keep my eye on Prince Hall Masons, black Masons. I never even knew there was such a thing. Damn. And I thought I knew so much. I've been in the white man's schools too long," he finished bitterly

Seven shared what Thomas had told her about Skull and Bones and how it was linked to Germany via old Bavarian Illuminist ties, and to Great Britain via the Rhodes-Milner Oxford Group—old industrial and banking families like Guggenheim, Schiff, Warburg, all intertwined with the Pan-European Movement, I.G. Farben, Reichsbank, and the Federal Reserve Bank of New York. *Synarchists.*

"For example, the nonferrous metal company Metallgesellschaft AG was co-owned throughout World War Two by I.G. Farben and British Metal. One of its two British directors was Minister of Production from 1942 to 1945 and a member of the Rhodes-Milner cabal. Brown-Boveri Electrics was partially owned by General Electric, IT&T, and the *Auslandsorganisation* or AO, foreign intelligence arm of the Nazi party. According to Thomas, it's all still going on today under fresh new names, probably under Gladio."

Ray chuckled. "When I told the man I didn't believe in the Illuminati, he said that not believing didn't make any difference when it came to reality. In the early days, he said he would have given his life for high-minded Illuminati until they were co-opted by the Bavarian Order of Illuminati or League of the Just Men. He said it was the Bavarian Illuminati who paid Marx to write the Communist Manifesto in 1846. For some in top government, industry, and cabals, greed and worldly power are enough, but for others something much more devious is on their minds."

"Like what?" Seven asked, pretty sure she knew the answer.

"'Like re-charting the human soul. His exact words." Ray stared at Seven. "I don't even know what that means, but somehow I know he's right."

They were silent as Seven wound up the last of the narrow dirt road into the still-dark San Ysidros. She looked in the rearview mirror; Mannie was asleep on the bed.

Beside her, Ray was re-thinking the famous photograph of Eldridge Cleaver and his clenched fist. Was a Masonic handshake hidden in it? *Cleaver.* Was Marxist revolutionary faith based on reason, or on zealous cultic religion driven by invisible hands? The man had said, "Ray, do you think communism means holding all goods in common? This definition might reflect a small village economy or local industry, but don't forget that the Communist Party in the Soviet Union has never comprised more than three percent of the population. It is not like the two-party method of controlling how people think. Lenin loathed democracy and its fetish for self-governance by the masses. Like Plato, he sought a small elite of dedicated intellectuals who would rule through self-interest, like a head riding on the shoulders of a hulk of flesh and bone. *Europe* prepared him, Ray. As had been done with France, it was time to overturn the czar and ride the dumb peasant beast into a future decided by industrialists and the ruling families in Europe, England, and America."

While listening, Ray had studied the faces around them. There is nothing quite like a bus terminal for a cross-section of the American disenfranchised. Brown, black, white, harried young women with babies in strollers and toddlers in tow, military boys on leave, drug-pushers, dried-out old men smoking on the benches, their elbows on their knees and heads bowed, students in transit to or from college or touring America before settling into middle-class harness. These were the proles, the people Ray wanted to rally so they would rise up and break the chains of capitalistic oppression, the people he believed could self-govern if given half a chance. He looked closely at them. Were they ready? The books said if people were hungry enough, they would revolt. They looked more than hungry enough to Ray, so why didn't they revolt?

A bitter pill was lodged in his throat. The truth was he despised them for swallowing the terms of their poverty, scuttling in the shadows, smacking their children and producing yet another generation of slaves filled with resentment and anger and loss who would prey upon each other rather than bite the unseen hand or force the well-polished black boot from their necks. He despised the masses, whatever their color. Lenin and Trotsky probably had, too. They hadn't been young men with high ideals sacrificing everything for the people. Until now, he hadn't wondered where the wherewithal to carry off such a vast enterprise as revolution came from. The European said that President Wilson had provided Trotsky with an American passport.

As the ravaging storm of disillusion passed over Ray's face, the European had continued more gently, his words carefully chosen.

"The razor's edge of truth is sharp, Ray, whereas one scarcely feels the slippery slope of collective assumptions one naïvely assumes to be individual. Happily, your *Weltanschauung* may now be damaged beyond saving. Are you prepared to go ahead?"

Leaning closer, he had whispered, "What if you discover that the Illuminati not only exist but are now international? That mass human sacrifice like World War Two is still the most reliable method of immanentizing the Eschaton? That Israel and the plains of Armageddon are one and the same? What if fiction points to what is real, and the myths you have learned to ridicule are true? Down your American streets, Ray, from Wall Street to the ghettos and barrios, the Eater of Souls, *Iok-Sotot*, walks. The name may sound mythical, but I assure you the reality by whatever name is true. Discover its face and you will have performed a great service to the future. Begin by rethinking all you have assumed to be true. Find the one thread and you will unravel the entire edifice."

His words dropped like stones. Ray could scarcely breathe. It wasn't just *what* he said, but *how*. Ray didn't know what an Eater of Souls was, but the man's voice buried each word in his brain. And when Ray finally raised his head, he was gone. Dazed, he'd looked around. Night travelers moved in and out of gates. Buses idled out on the dock, ready to lap up American miles. His breathing sounded like someone else's. With an ancient, sure instinct, he'd zeroed in on a pale face emitting a strange little half-smile, the pale blue eyes far too intent on Ray before it had scuttled out the door toward Market Street and Ray had grabbed his backpack and fled. *Wild.* San Francisco was full of weirdos.

He had never really studied the February or October Revolution or French and American Revolutions. Compulsory public education had meant swallowing whole what he was told, and college and grad school hadn't been all that different—pages of accolades about the Founding Fathers, the Stamp Act, the Boston Tea Party, Tom Paine speeches, Patrick Henry's *Give me liberty or give me death!* The textbooks made rebellion sound like the American birthright, but how did it fit with the police action against students in Chicago in 1968? No Tom Paine debate, just weapons. Mario Savio was right: Revolution was mere rhetoric, an icon to glorify the ruling faction's past. Like churches replacing Christ the revolutionary with sweet Jesus, or the death icon of Ché Guevara, Argentine revolutionary hero, relegated to being a dead saint on t-shirts and posters. They liked their revolutionaries dead. It was thirty pieces of silver all over again.

The Cuban-American CIA man Felix Rodriguez and former Bolivian general Gary Prado Salmón had arrived by chopper in the Andean village of Higuera on the morning of October 9, 1967, John Lennon's 27th birthday and exactly a year after he said, *Christianity will go. It will vanish and shrink. I needn't argue about it; I'm right and I will be proved right. We're more popular than Jesus now; I don't know which will go first, rock'n'roll or Christianity. Jesus was all right but his disciples were thick and ordinary. It's them twisting it that ruins it for me.* Beatles albums had been burned in Alabama, Georgia, Texas.

The dirt-poor mountain people of Higuera stood in awe, their hair whipped about by the wind from the chopper blades as they watched the men descend from the sky. Che was being held in the village laundry room, but the CIA man chose to slaughter him in the village schoolroom as an object lesson

278

worth ten thousand tired words of indoctrination. *This is what happens to you,* hijos, *if you bite the heel of* el norte. Once Che was dead, the soldiers were ordered to wash the grime and blood of torture from his body, trim his beard, dress him in clean clothes, and lay him out on the children's desks for the famous Shroud of Turin picture. Che's body on the table, men standing around it like he was the Last Supper.

In a flash, Ray understood that Che *was* the Last Supper in some terrible anti-Christ ritual. After taking the picture, they had flown the corpse to a Knights of Malta hospital and with their knives and forks carved him up like they had Kennedy. A terrible truth lay behind the finishing touches of a ritual murder: it was the covert message to those with the eyes to see and the ears to hear, nor was it lost on the collective unconscious buried in the masses. He made another mental note to research Black Muslims and Prince Hall Freemasonry.

Bolshevist Communism was just another collectivist scheme with a ruling class at the top. Its only difference from capitalism was how ownership and production were handled. The ruling class in Europe and "classless" America had bankrolled the Bolshevist Revolution. Despite being able to own property and keep one's earnings after the government took its cut, the wage always belonged to the ruling class euphemistically referring to itself as the marketplace. Capital and interest always belonged to the fortunate few. Boards culled from the ruling class owned the public airwaves, newspapers, magazines, publishing houses, and film industry.

Under Bolshevism, the masses might own the means of production if it meant some decision power at the factory level, but a small phalanx of "experts" and backers still decided what the masses needed to know. And given communist ideology, who would dare to speak against comrades? The revolutionary honeymoon would be over when managers complained of production falling behind and meetings must be cancelled to make up the time. Capitalist or communist, the system always needed more man-hours to justify the outlay of capital for the technology that mass production required. The Russian or Chinese worker who bucked the system might be chastised or threatened with work camp, whereas in America, work history and attitude would be recorded while hungry applicants willing to work for less queued up.

Ray was caught between numbness and the pain of a dying *Weltanschauung,* as the European had foretold. The white middle class was oppressed, too, the chains of poor Blacks being deprivation and drugs, the more dangerous chains of the white middle class being dulling self-satisfied comfort, groveling for entry to the class above, and over-the-counter drugs.

It was a struggle to think beyond his prejudices. The white middle class was all about comfort and insulation. In exchange, they let issues of justice, truth, and human rights pass by the board. Like the Aztecs of old, the middle class sought to do whatever it took to appease "the market," including sacrificing the masses below them. *Be grateful for what you have! Don't rock the boat! Teach your children to do the same because you want them to define success as comfort the way you did.*

By the close of the 20th century, American and Soviet labor would be the same. Thesis, antithesis, synthesis, the Hegelian paradigm the European mentioned. Separated from the labor that once contributed to the real human community, workers would obediently go to work for bondage and debt. Marx had been right: industrialism took away a man's labor, communist or capitalist. In Russia, the State owned a man's time; in America, it was the

Corporate State. No difference, other than the window dressing.

This was medieval feudalism, the system the Japanese still modeled their corporations on—benevolent overlord, vassals, and serfs—a strict father over obedient children. Heartless corporate America and the Soviet State had skipped the benevolence because familial ties and loyalty had no market value. In one, the worker's value was measured by how selflessly he served "history"; in the other, how selflessly he served the corporation. To both communism and capitalism, workers and their progeny were buckets of blood and bone, and thinking of oneself as an individual was the greatest disloyalty of all, verging on sedition. Talk of individualism was used either for window dressing or as a justification for ruthlessness.

Ray was aware that forces behind the United States throne were harrowing the 20th century, but he didn't yet realize that conditioning and controlling the upcoming generation—the largest in history—was primary to those forces. His anger toward the Establishment had only concentrated on race and only reached the visceral stage. He'd vanquished the easy stuff—communism bad, democracy and capitalism good, fascism eliminated with Hitler, etc.—but had yet to really question his middle class university conditioning.

At Berkeley, a Native American from the American Indian Movement lectured on how the *coup de grâce* to destroying a culture was the destruction of that people's language. Strip the language and you strip the memory. Language, not nationalism, was what bound a people to the memory of who they were. Blacks, Europeans, everyone who had come to the Americas from across sthe Atlantic had lost their language along with their geography. Asians had done better in California by living in their own small insular communities.

Speaking of language, the economist Ludwig von Mises made it clear that the term *planning* was often used as a synonym for socialism, communism and other totalitarian economic management systems. The German socialism *Zwangswirtschaft* was called *planning* while the actual term *socialism* was reserved for the Russian brand of bureaucracy. *Planning, socialism,* and *bureaucracy* were all interchangeable terms for the same thing.

Ray had gone to a small middle class racially mixed border grade school with high parent participation—the kind of progressive grade school that was slowly disappearing in American cities. But after Sputnik, he'd been placed in a huge public junior high school more like a factory with a legion of teachers and administrators, departments, pods, rules, schedules, bells that meant this and buzzers that meant that. Had that school been an experimental product of *Zwangswirtschaft*? Ray lasted two years and lost much happiness there, along with liberty, personal accountability, individual conscience, and faith, his adventuresome intellect forced into narrower and narrower channels. When barbarism reared its ugly head in the adolescents around him, family or race was blamed, not the school's shackles twisting young minds into knots. Was that, then, socialism for the masses?

Early American educators had been British Fabian socialists steeped in logical pragmatism and moral relativism, thanks to Columbia University Teacher College. Ray didn't know it but theosophist Annie Besant had co-founded the British Fabian Society in 1883 in England and made it into a hothouse of elitist psychic research and pagan rites and rituals for spiritualists, prime ministers, lords and ladies, and Freemasons. Besant had been used for séances since

1858 for the Russian Czar via the Scottish noble and spiritualist Daniel Dunglas, and by 1911 she was president of the Theosophical Society and vice president and teacher of the Supreme Council of the International Order of Co-Masonry. The Order of the Golden Dawn, Ordo Templi Orientis, and Thule Society all rode the same British froth, pushing Chamberlain, Haushofer, Hess, and Hitler before them. In fact, the Fabian Society was the predecessor of the British Labour Party. As the European had stressed to Ray, high politics were never far from occultism

About the time Madame Blavatsky first arrived in the US, Colonel Olcott was running séances in Chittenden, Vermont with Mary Baker Eddy, the founder of Christian Science. Then, while the American Theosophical Society was being set up on the other coast in Pasadena, with its emphasis on Asian ideas and racial theory, Olcott and Blavatsky moved the world spiritual center of Theosophy to Adyar, India, and Alice Bailey née Bateman was transplanted from England to the Pacific Grove Lodge in California. Bailey and her 33° Scottish Rite Freemason husband Foster broke with Besant to found a Tibetan Lodge and the Lucifer Trust. By the 1930s, they had 200,000 members

Throughout the 19th century, European and American occultists courted Lucifer the fallen angel, little realizing that the one whose advent was being heralded by longhaired comets driven earthward by the Time Spirit was not Lucifer but Ahriman. The rediscovery of electricity should have been clue enough, but Luciferians never could tell the difference between electricity and *Light*. The ancient batteries in the Baghdad Museum, electron tubes and bundles of conducting wires engraved on the walls in the Temple of Hathor at Dendera, the vast hectares of vitrified soil in the Gobi desert were but footprints in the sands of Time leading Here, Now, to the 20th and 21st centuries in America

History books had taught Ray about the Calvinists and Puritans coming to America, but not about the Luciferians or the Aztec and Satanic priests who had been ritually invoking Ahriman by other names for centuries, feeding him from the life force laid out on their *tzompantli,* altar of skulls, the hearts still beating after being removed and placed in the *cuauhxicalli,* the sacrificial vessel. Ahriman's incarnation was scheduled for the 21st century, but preparations by both the Luciferians and Satanists continued unabated throughout the 20th century. He was *tlatoani,* He who speaks. But Ray knew none of this, though he had experienced this same *tlatoani* in the houdou store

By the 1960s, the American Fabians had added Gramsci's "normalization" to the education system in preparation for B.F. Skinner's "Skinner box" approach. Removing Christian values from the public school threw out the baby with the bath water: the humanism and respect for the individual soul inherent in true Christianity had fed children what public totalitarianism never could. The word *humanist* was then torn from its original meaning, the ultimate maxim of the relativism subscribed to by the ruling class being Satanist Aleister Crowley's *Do what thou wilt shall be the whole of the law.* Crowley and the Fabians went hand in hand.

As they arrived at the top of the mountain the VW bus had been toiling up, Ray sighed deeply. Thanks to the man in the bus depot, nothing was clear anymore.

284

19
Aleph

Among the ruling and priestly classes of the semi-civilized nations of America, there has always existed a mysterious bond, a secret organization, which all the disasters to which they have been subjected have not destroyed ...

> \- S.A. Ward, *Adventures on the Mosquito Shore*, 1855

We operate here under directives which emanate from the White House. The substance of the directives under which we operate are that we shall use our grant-making power to alter life in the US so that we can comfortably be merged with the Soviet Union.

> \- Rowan Gaither, head of the Ford Foundation, to Sen. Norman Dodd of the Reece Committee, 1954

Don Quixote: *Well, Sancho – how dost thou like adventuring?*

Sancho: *Oh, marvelous, Your Grace. But it's peculiar – to me this great highway to glory looks exactly like the road to El Toboso where you can buy chickens cheap.*

Don Quixote: *Like beauty, my friend, 'tis all in the eyes of the beholder. Only wait and thou shalt see amazing sights.*

Sancho: *What kind?*

Don Quixote: *There will be knights and nations, warlocks, wizards . . . a cavalcade of vast, unending armies.*

- Man of La Mancha, Broadway musical, 1965; based on *The Ingenious Gentleman Don Quixote of La Mancha* by Miguel de Cervantes Saavedra, ~1605

Like thousands of youths who'd fled the East and Midwest and South for the West Coast where it was all happening, Mannie had been blown away by Highway 1 along the Pacific coast, its cliff edges and rushing gorges, the famed ribbon of road snaking through mountain groves of redwood and oak and meadows bursting with the healing balm of yerba buena, lupins, and poppies. Sitting on the right side of the bus so he could be as close as possible to the Pacific Ocean, he'd purchased a daytime ticket so he could see *everything*.

He wondered how such a precarious road could have been built. Unlike the pyramids and probably the Temple of Solomon, at least slaves hadn't been used and crushed to plummet onto the rocks below where sea otters lazily sunbathed their blubber. But *Have Fun on Highway 1* crushed that illusion, saying it had been built by convict labor and opened in 1937.

He'd scored *Have Fun on Highway 1* at the Salvation Army in San Francisco for only a quarter. Almost everyone had been black and female, scrutinizing clothes racks while their big-eyed children scrounged for toys and shrieked up and down the aisles, their mamas and grandmamas calling, *Get yo'self over here! Stop runnin roun' like banshees!* A few black and brown men mused over phonographs and televisions and radios in the appliance aisle while Asians rifled through the men's

286

dress shirts, pants, and ties. Mannie needed a pair of shoes, but the shoe racks had been too depressing once he started thinking about *soles* and *souls*.

Big Sur was part of the Pacific Tectonic Plate surfing northwest against the North American Plate, sloughing off landslides and earthquakes en route. Mannie pictured two giants clashing. *Have Fun on Highway 1* said the Santa Lucia mountains were two million years old and the clashing plates had brought together a remarkable mix of yucca and redwoods, sycamores, willows, big-leaf maples, madrone, cypress and the scarce Santa Lucia fir. Tan oak was almost gone, due to their tannic acid having been used up to tan leather. Constant offshore wind and storms born in part from the gnarled earth plates made the rock and vegetation dramatic, twisting them into strange shapes along the Pacific edge, especially along the 75-mile stretch known as Big Sur (from *El país grande del sur*, the big country of the south), when California was called Alta California and the capital was at Monterey instead of Sacramento.

Mannie watched for giant condors and hawks and wondered where the mountains lions were. As the bus curled along the cliffs, the land became Mediterranean, its fog alchemically mixing in offshore Lemurian canyons thousands of feet deep. His eyes searched far below for kelp, wishing he were close enough to see the pelicans and kingfishers the pamphlet talked about, the sea otters feasting on limpets and mussels, the sea lions aarfing in caves, the magnificent whales in *Moby Dick* that he'd read in high school for accelerated senior English. *Call me Ishmael.* He'd wanted to be called Ishmael instead of the diminutive Mannie, but it would have been silly to take a name because of a novel, though the Jewish boy in *A Thousand Clowns* did. He *was* Ishmael in so many ways, sailing the seas of Life, ignorant, naïve, seeking the meaning behind things that others took for granted, as if events and people were just furniture veneer and design. *Moby Dick* had been an initiation for him, an entry into the macro-life going on right under his nose. Melville was eighteen when he made his first sea voyage in 1838.

He thought of Uncle Eli waiting for him after Hebrew lessons and walking home with him, patiently explaining that each age is governed by a certain theme according to the constellation in which the Sun rises in the spring of that age. "The tabloids say that spring begins on March 19 when the Sun rises under the Ram," Uncle Eli clarified, "but the astronomical truth is that the spring Sun now rises under the Fishes, which means, nephew, that we are all subject to the themes of our lives in a Christ the Fish manner, whether we're Christians or not, just as paintings of Moses with two horns growing out of his temples pointed to when the spring Sun rose in the Ram, which was why Moses was so incensed that while he was up on Mount Sinai receiving the new dispensation, his people were dancing around the golden calf and falling back into the old theme of when the spring Sun rose in the Bull.

"To be a Jew in the Age of Christ the Fish instead of in the Age of Moses the Ram is not easy," Uncle Eli admitted. "The rabbi tells me to subscribe to Mosaic law, but then I say to myself, 'How shall I do this in a Christ the Fish way so that I am a man of my times and not going *against* my time because of the past?' Which to me, Mannie, would be arrogance before G-d and therefore missing the mark. I am no Jew for Jesus, but on the other hand, surely the people of the G-d of history should be capable of living within the cosmic time they are born into and not have to pretend it is still the Age of Moses, not to mention exemplifying *rachmones, rechem* meaning our mother's womb. *Real* rabbis teach not Israel, Israel, Israel, but that Jews should look upon *all* others, not just Jews, as a mother looks upon her children. We should strive for humanistic morality, nephew, humanizing the gentiles by exemplifying the best of Jewish qualities.

"Open yourself, nephew, to what Life has to teach you. Jew, gentile, Muslim, man, woman, all are your teachers because they are here now and not in a book from another age. Yes, the Torah has good information, good advice, but only as it applies to here and now where we must make the decisions our souls depend upon. The Jews brought the Law, then Buddha's 8-fold path took the Law and moved it deeper into the individual, adding some compassion for our childish human condition, and five hundred years later Christ boiled down the Ten Commandments to *two,* can you imagine? Love G-d, and love others as yourself, which is really *three* laws, if you think about it, because loving yourself is not all that easy, as you will discover because you have to *know* yourself, and *forgive* yourself, before you can love yourself." He sighed. "I'm no Christian. I love my tradition and carry my people in my heart. But I like Christ the Fish's fewer laws, even if they're harder to do because they depend upon self-transformation, a big word you may understand someday, and doing it is even bigger."

He had looked into his nephew's big trusting eyes and loved him not because he was of his blood but because of his innocence and the pain of Life ahead of him. Mannie didn't know quite what his uncle was saying but knew he wouldn't forget most of his words because he wanted to be like Uncle Eli and was willing to remember until he could understand.

Mannie looked out to sea and exulted. His voyage had brought him to the Pacific Ocean, Melville's to the Atlantic. In his fertile mind's eye, he could see a great whale tossing its flukes vertically, then trembling, suspended, then diving into the depths of old Mu. He

289

was the same, suspended and trembling. He had taken the plunge and reached California, the furthest west he could go without going East. To his mother, a disciple of *Life* magazine, California was what the white whale had been for Ahab, "majestic Satan," and not all that majestic. He, Ishmael Mannie, would be like Isaiah's Jonah, swallowed and spit out a changed man, a resurrected Mannie, a deepened Self.

He had not called his mother in a month. Part of letting the whale swallow him was to be for himself and not her. She would have to let him go. She and his father had been distraught when their quiet Jewish son involved himself in the Columbia University sit-in. The fact that it was going on in Paris and Mexico City like a contagious disease did little to assuage their fears, and a year later when he told them that he was going to take some time off from Columbia and go west, young man, they pleaded with the rabbi to talk some sense into him, thinking that surely Mannie would respect the opinion of such a learned man.

But nothing could have been further from the truth. After his grandfather's death, Mannie had watched his parents abandon the rigor of the Conservative temple for the Reformed. Though his grandfather's old-fashioned ways and opinions about Jews being the one superior race were exasperating, at least you were in no doubt as to where he stood. The Reformed rabbi, on the other hand, was so Reformed that he seemed to have edged his way right out of the Torah and into the Talmud and a strange breed of Zionism almost *occult* in nature.

Mannie had come to these strange, illogical surmises after late one cold and windy October night when he'd been wandering the streets, tortured by youthful doubts, lugging his dark night of the soul around like a body bag from Vietnam, and had decided to seek solace and warmth in the Temple. The side door was unlocked, so he went up the steps and into the sanctuary where the Tabernacle was kept and the electric *Ner Tamid* burned. No one was there, so he crept up to the podium to take a peek at the thick book of Talmud the rabbi taught from. Beneath what looked like an embossed scorpion, Mannie read the golden Hebraic words *TALMUD OF BABYLONIA*.

The rabbi said that the Midrash and Talmud took up where the Torah left off and therefore was more worthy of rabbinic scholarship and study. Supposedly, the Midrash was written down in 1200 AD and the Mishnah and Gemara (the two categories of Talmud) were given by God to Moses on Mt. Sinai, along with the Ten Commandments. Uncle Eli said the Oral Torah (Oral Law) and traditions of the elders (the Mishnah and Talmud) were believed by rabbis to be Moses' secret teachings. But if the Midrash was written down so much later than Moses' excursion up the holy mountain, then how was it rabbis recalled what Isaac was thinking as his father laid him on the altar and prepared to cut his heart out? Were rabbis privy to the mind of G-d? Wasn't this blasphemy? Besides, rabbinic Judaism was from Babylonia. Babylon, the golden calf, the sacrifice of children to Molech, and where did the ashes of the red heifer traditionally used to purify the Temple come from? Were Rabbinic Judaism and Judaism the same? Mannie didn't think so, and with this heretical thought doubt had leaped full-born into his young mind. Besides, Uncle Eli had pointed out that the term *Judaism* only appeared in the Torah twice, in 2 Kings 16:6 and 2 Chronicles 32:18, referring only to the two tribes of Judah and Benjamin.

But Babylonia? Uncle Eli said Rabbinic Judaism came only after Jesus Christ was crucified and the rabbis felt the challenge of a new religion strangely born out of Judaism. They hated Jesus not because of the Messiah thing, Uncle Eli stressed, but because Jesus had judged them for not adhering to the oral traditions given to their elite priesthood by Moses (John 5:46-47), and because Jesus catered to the *am-ha-arez,* the unwashed multitudes not born to the privileges of knowing the true law. Jesus had been a revolutionary Jew.

All his childhood, Mannie had heard about the Shoah and the Nazis, how Jews had never done anything to deserve all the atrocities they'd suffered through history, how Mannie had no idea of all that had happened to make Jews hate and fear Gentiles. In Hebrew school on Tuesdays and Thursdays after public school, he was taught that the date wasn't 1953 or 1961, but 3,761 years further along, and that he was from a race much older than Christian Europe and must never forget what could happen again, even in America. At every *seder* in his grandparents' house, a prayer was said for Uncle Saul who worked for the Anti-Defamation League to keep Jews safe in America.

But when he was twelve, just before his *bar-mitzvah,* he had asked what for him was a simple mathematical dilemma: How can we be sure that six million Jews died in the ovens? Were records kept? Now it was being said that Auschwitz had only 1.1 million inmates, not four million. At Auschwitz State Museum, walls had been removed to show how the gas chamber had looked in 1941 and 1942, but who knew what its original state was? A moment of terrible silence followed his question, everyone horrified that he could even *ask* such a question. In that moment, family doubt was born about how Mannie would turn out, a doubt that lingered like bad air over his *bar-mitzvah* and subsequent teen years.

He had changed that day. He had learned that inquiry into established truth is never free and in fact is dangerous. In sixth grade, his teacher had mentioned that for several hundred years after Jesus' crucifixion, Christians had been subjected to death in Rome and throughout the Middle East. Pondering this new information, Mannie at least had the wisdom not to mention it at home, knowing that his grandfather would probably make a big stink and call Uncle Saul about the *goyim* teacher teaching religion in the public schools. He felt betrayed that rabbis had not mentioned the persecution of other religions, even majority religions. The rabbis made it sound as if only Jews were persecuted, only Jews were systematically erased. Was history always skewed by those who controlled it? Did Christians get upset when their children asked how Jesus could be both man and god? Probably so. Perhaps one-sidedness was endemic to every religion.

As family suspicions about Mannie's allegiance to the latest chapter of Jewish history grew and spread like poison ivy, so his own pregnant silence awakened his eyes and ears to what lay about him, much like the Moabite Ruth gleaning from the fields of Boaz in Bethlehem. Deeply rooted thoughts began to grow in the loam of his lonely mind. He loved God and was a Jew; these were the only things he was sure of. Everything else had been called into question the day he had the effrontery to question Holocaust math, the day he became a traitor to his race. Plus he had no context for the Babylonian Talmud he'd discovered on that windy October night and therefore could not even shape a question, had he dared to ask it. When he had more courage and context, he would return to confront that rabbi. And in fact, a few years later, after Dallas, he did return to do just that, but the rabbi had transferred to another synagogue far away and no one was quite sure where. The gossip was that he'd molested a little boy in the congregation and had quietly been allowed to leave. God forbid, Mannie's grandfather would have agreed, that the *goyim* would have the satisfaction of knowing that Jews had the same problem as Catholics. The family of the little boy now went to a Conservative temple and everyone buried the shame alive and went on as before, convinced that the incident was an anomaly. Mannie wasn't so sure.

For unadulterated truth and free thinking, Mannie had Uncle Eli, his father's considerably older greybeard brother. As soon as Eli entered their mahogany-dark Brooklyn two-storey and yelled *Ichabod!* which he said meant *Where is the glory?* Mannie's father was always deferential to his older brother and sister, so Mannie's mother would throw a cloth over the television set—Uncle Eli once threatened to destroy it if ever he had to look into its big Cyclops eye—then race to the kitchen to prepare a little repast, sometimes sending Mannie around the corner to the delicatessen for rye bread or knishes and a quart of German beer. Finally, the two brothers would sit at the oilcloth-covered kitchen table and eat and drink whatever she gave them, then retire to the sitting room. Uncle Eli always left morsels and beer suds in his curling mustache the way, his mother explained, old men who live alone do.

In the sitting room, Uncle Eli would light his Havana cigar (the only kind he ever smoked, despite communism) and ask his brother to play some Rachmaninoff for him. Mannie's mother would put on her spectacles and take up the sewing she did to make a little extra pin money, and Mannie would linger, waiting for Uncle Eli's topic of the evening. The old man read widely and thought deep, and Mannie was learning that such a quality was not all that common among Jews or gentiles. As Uncle Eli's family, they knew they would not have him with them forever and that his visits were at least the gold of tradition. Mannie's father would again do justice to the Russian Jew Rachmaninoff, his fingers caressing the somber, passionate Slavic notes, his brother savoring the same with eyes closed. When the last tones slid into silence and the piano wires had stopped vibrating, Uncle Eli would generally begin by addressing Mannie. It was their ritual.

"When Nebuchadnezzar burned Jerusalem in 587 BC, the Ark was already gone. Thus is doubt cast upon the legend that as the Babylonians forced the doors to the Holy of Holies, an angel descended and took the veil, the Ark, its cover, and the two sapphire-like transparent tablets that Moses had received on Mount Sinai and cried out to the Earth, saying, *Earth, Earth, Earth, hear the word of God and receive what I commit to you and guard them until the end times, so that when you are ordered you will restore them!* At which the Earth opened its mouth and swallowed the Ark and tablets. Even a hundred years before Nebuchadnezzar, when Manasseh set up a graven image in the Temple and killed the prophet Isaiah, the Ark was already gone. However, it was present during Hezekiah and up to the beginning of Manasseh's reign. The fact is that somewhere around 687 BC it was hidden or taken out of Jerusalem and put—where?"

He held out his big hands to Mannie in supplication while Mannie's mother trained her eyes on the long overdue ash at the end of Uncle Eli's cigar.

"But how do you know that's not just a legend, too, Uncle Eli?" asked 13-year-old Mannie smartypants.

"'Just a legend.' Excuse me," Uncle Eli said, looking around, "is this the question, 'What *really* happened to the Ark, Uncle Eli?'"

Mannie knew about the Ark of the Covenant but had somehow missed that it had disappeared from history. The Ark was a chest of acacia wood three feet nine inches long by two feet three inches wide and high lined inside and out with gold. Two cherubim faced each other on the gold lid's Seat of Mercy and between them a cloud or fire would appear, so they say.

Uncle Eli's wiry eyebrows shot up. "So they say!" He looked at his skeptical brother. "So they say." He returned his gaze to his nephew and leaned forward. "What was the Ark *really*, that Jews have never been the same since it disappeared? What if I told you that the Ark is not a myth but an electromagnetic device built by Bezaleel, perhaps even a *nuclear* device with tremendous destructive powers? Tumors, cataracts, counteracting gravity . . . Even Nikolai Tesla was convinced it was a condenser capable of creating a high density lightning discharge and that Moses was an early electrical engineer."

He chuckled. Mannie's face no longer registered disbelief.

"The vestal fires of Rome could have been electromagnetic, and what happened to those early Christians when they were all hit with the same energy and spoke so that everyone present could understand their speech? In those days, science was magic, like the magic Moses learned when he was a Kher Heb with the priests of Egypt, when the Hebrews were enslaved in Egypt from 1650 to 1250 BC. What was the Ark besides a blueprint for Solomon's Temple and the Holy of Holies that held it, a perfect cube 30 feet by 30 feet by 30 feet lined with 45,000 pounds of gold riveted by golden nails and built by Hiram of Tyre? No iron tools were allowed in holy places, so what did he use?"

Again, his big hands appealed to Mannie.

Mannie stuttered. "The—Shamir?"

Uncle Eli beamed. "The Shamir, yes! The stone that could cut like a laser without friction or heat, stored in wool cloth inside a lead container filled with barley. Technology, huh?"

Mannie's father offered a quiet contribution. "And now the Dome of the Rock mosque stands where the Temple stood until 587 BC."

"Within which," his brother continued seamlessly, "stands the Shetiyyah, the floor of the Holy of Holies where the Ark was once placed by Solomon."

Mannie's mother got up to turn on a light.

Uncle Eli was relentless. "Legends are truth in symbolic language that few, Jew or gentile, understand anymore. What could it mean that the Earth opened and swallowed them up? Surely the services of the great Baal Shem Tov himself are required"—Uncle Eli winked at his brother—"but given that he hasn't been seen in Brooklyn in a while, we poor excuses for Jews will just have to think our own thoughts.

"One thing is certain: the Ark was taken *down* into somewhere. So was it beneath Mount Moriah in the Well of Souls, from which the voices of the dead can be heard mingling with the rivers of Paradise? Caverns are down there, a labyrinth. The Knights Templar, those wealthy titled French knights in the 11th century, must have thought so because for 83 years they did a lot of digging. Was King Solomon's treasure really the Ark? Or what was beneath the Al-Aqsa Mosque just south of the Shetiyyah, where Mohammed was lifted by angels on his Night Journey and no excavation has ever, to our knowledge, been allowed?

Pausing to relight his cigar, the ash having long ago—centuries, in fact—fallen onto his sister-in-law's coveted Persian carpet given her on her wedding day, Uncle Eli, master of dramatic pauses, allowed the silence to grow. Watching his uncle resurrect his Havana cigar, Mannie felt his future creeping up on him, his own microcosmic quest for the Ark or Holy Grail. He sensed perhaps for the first time in his brief mundane Brooklyn life that the truth of things hidden in history and myth might not be tidily waiting for him in the institutions of the world. He might have to really *look* for such knowledge.

In a haze of smoke reminiscent of Moses on Mount Sinai, Uncle Eli continued. "What if *down* meant *south*? When Josiah came to the throne in Jerusalem in 640 BC, he purged Manasseh's profane indiscretions from the Holy of Holies and begged the Levites to *bring the Ark back*, say the histories. Bring it back, not dig it up. But back from where

"The Black Jews of Ethiopia, the Falashas, have lived on the banks of Lake Tana, a huge inland sea like the Great Lakes, in the Simien mountains for more than two thousand years. And how do we know they've been on the banks of Lake Tana for more than two thousand years? Because their religious practices reflect nothing of Babylon, nothing of the Talmud composed after the Captivity. They observe neither Purim nor Hanukkah. They have no rabbis, no singular Temple. They still sacrifice animals, something forbidden in Israel since Josiah's ban in 640. The Ashkenazi and Sephardi rabbis in Jerusalem have blessed them, making them as eligible for Israeli citizenship under the Law of Return as you and I. So *are* the Falashas the lost tribe of Israel that migrated from Palestine between the reigns of Solomon in 950 and Josiah in 640? Could it be they gave up their land and people *in order to keep the Ark safe*?

Mannie's father leaned forward. He had never heard this story. "Wasn't the Queen of Sheba from Ethiopia?

His elder brother nodded. "The *Kebra Nagast* written in the 13th century details the story of Solomon and Sheba, their son Menelik, and how the Hebrews brought the Ark to Ethiopia. Sheba, queen of Saba . . . Mannie, if you go to the south porch of Chartres Cathedral—that French book carved in stone before the Templars were destroyed—you will see Sheba standing among 28 kings and queens. Solomon holds a scepter in his right hand, Sheba a flower in

298

her left hand. Above them, the prophets speak in secrets. Go to the north porch and there is a *second* Queen of Sheba whose door is called the door of the initiates. Here, the priest-king Melchizedek stands, the only image of him in all of medieval Europe, holding the Cup and Stone in his left hand while passing the Ark to Ethiopia with his right."

He examined the tip of his cigar, then tapped it over the ashtray, smiling sweetly at his sister-in-law. "And the Hebrew name for the Ark? *Theba*—you know, Thebes.

Mannie stared at him, speechless. Until that day, the Ark had been a word

Uncle Eli shrugged. "Who knows? Myth, legend, history. Sheba, Saba, *Theba.* This I do know, a final clue worthy of the Baal Shem Tov: The Queen of Sheba, known to her subjects as Makeda, kept a palace in Axum, Ethiopia where two great stelae stood, one 110 feet tall, the other 70. Mussolini stole one and erected it near the Arch of Constantine in Rome. Today in Axum, beside the new cathedral being built by Emperor Haile Salassie, is a granite chapel with a dome of green copper, no windows, surrounded by iron bars." His voice grew quiet and intense. "What makes it possible that this may indeed be where the Ark rests is this: the Guardian of the Ark—that is what he is called—must remain in the granite chapel for his entire life, and as he ages, thick cataracts develop over his eyes.

Uncle Eli, his cigar in his mouth, raised his hands as if to say, I rest my case. This is what Uncle Eli always did: opened the door to fantastic knowledge, dragged a few dusty relics into the light of day, and then—

"But Uncle Eli, you said "chapel," not temple. Is the Ark in a *Christian* chapel?" Mannie's face was flushed.

Slowly, Uncle Eli relit his cigar stub, then looked at his nephew. "What do they teach at Hebrew school these days? Your *bar mitzvah* means you are a man now who must learn that not all questions are simple arithmetic. Some have to be lived and contemplated for excavation possibilities. This is one of those questions. So wrestle with the angel until it blesses you, nephew. Study Chartres Cathedral. Your parents may think I'm trying to convert you to Christianity, but religious things are not so simple as priests and rabbis present them. If there is a war among Jews, Christians, and Muslims, it's about what is true, not what makes one culture right and another wrong. Here on the Earth, as things stand, truth is elusive, to say the least."

Then he raised his eyebrows to help him heave his considerable flesh upright, said his usual goodbyes and thanks, and disappeared into the night to his rooming house somewhere in Brooklyn.

Still curling toward Big Sur, the bus moved like Steinbeck's terrapin, slow and wary, due in part to the pilgrims walking along the spare shoulder of snaky Highway 1—entire hippie families with small children in tow, all thin with packs on their backs, in their hands bleeding Madras bedspreads tied in bundles filled with their meager belongings, pots and pans slung over the loads, a baby in a sling on the mother's back or breast, braids, long hair, beads, patchouli oil, the children with smaller loads, all walking, walking along the road along the cliff edge of California, looking up wanly as the great bus heaved past and enveloped them in its fumes. Sometimes one would raise a peace sign, the old V, face passive, not jealous in the least of those riding in comfort.

Mannie was thrilled to see such a remnant on the move in his overfed, overgassed, underfeeling nation. It was like looking through his window at India, Bangladesh, Africa, at what hadn't been tucked into hospital corners yet, what was sleeping in a pew after the church doors had been locked for the night. This, they, all of them, were his America, the America he had been longing for. And it was all the more poignant to know that many of these youths trudging the roads of America, contrary to the gospel of *Life* magazine, did not have to do it, that they had abandoned of their own free will middle and upper class comforts and privileges for the life of the road back to the land and the people. They had heard the Call and gone, just as Mannie had, their vote being for Bangladesh and India and Africa and whatever they had to endure to live near the pulse of Life. It made Mannie proud to be young and foolish and courageous.

Finally, the bus pulled into the Nepenthe parking area, the happening restaurant and tourist stop in Big Sur. The driver said they had 45 minutes and Mannie intended to use every second of it grokking the ocean and surf below. Nepenthe means *no sadness.* It had begun as a log cabin purchased by Orson Welles and Rita Hayworth who never had the time to enjoy it. Artists had been fleeing to Big Sur from San Francisco and Berkeley since the earlier part of the century. Initially, they'd built cabins near the ruins of the Carmel Mission, where the poet Robinson Jeffers built his house and stone tower in what was now Carmel-by-the-Sea. Jeffers' white whale had been an albino redwood by the tiny Sur River and the snow-white foliage growing from the stump of a lightning-struck tree.

Mannie ducked into the Phoenix shop for a postcard of crashing surf to send his mother, then ordered the cheapest sustenance on the menu, tuna fish and melted cheese on rye, to eat out on the deck. He thought about Robert Heinlein's Martian Valentine Michael Smith in *Stranger in A Strange Land* who taught Earthlings how to *grok.* Happily munching, his taste buds grokking that rye out west was nothing like delicatessen rye in New York, Mannie feasted his eyes on the very body of water whose millions of sloshing, whirling, vibrating molecules bumping into each other were rolling up onto the islands of Japan and mainland China. *Where did West end and East begin?*

At the next table, an Esalen Institute conversation between a Russian and an American was underway over salads and smoothies. Half-dollar words like *psychotic episode, schizophrenia, counterculture, adversarial, Sri Aurobindo, satellite, Academy of Sciences,* and *experiential* flew back and forth. Esalen was only eleven miles down the road, built on the cliffs over a hot springs and burial ground once sacred to the Esselen and Ohlone Indians.

Uncle Eli had said *Oy Vey* after reading about Esalen in the *New York Times Magazine* published on the last day of the year 1967. Transformational practices, meditation, Buddhist rites, shamans, medicine men, Jungian analysts. After the frantic call from his sister-in-law that his nephew was determined to go to that den of iniquity California, Uncle Eli had specifically mentioned Esalen to Mannie as a place to avoid. Uncle Eli was suspicious of psychiatrists and psychologists and their tampering with G-d's domain, the human mind and soul. They made him think of Auschwitz and Peenemünde and that Nazi *meshuge* bastard von Braun who ran NASA. Uncle Eli had a nose for rats, especially rats celebrated by *The New York Times.* He figured some *takef* was slipping the Esalen rat under the door of whatever was left of naïve American *goyim* morality, and his nephew, bless his naïve heart, was a fragrant piece of cheese if ever there was one.

But Uncle Eli's warning about the German psychoanalyst Fritz Perls and his Gestalt and Esalen flew right over Mannie's *kopf* like a paper airplane. Even now, eleven miles from the citadel of Gestalt,

Mannie had no clue that he was overhearing the soon to be Godfather of New Age Physics ply his Russian guest from the Stanford Research Institute with quantum words about non-verbal humanities and the new ethos of developing awareness of the present flow of experience, etc.

Mannie, protected by blissful ignorance, got back on the bus.

20
The Decision to Go

*I was then simply a young inexperienced naïve
'useful idiot' in a very, very sophisticated and
successful covert psychological warfare
operation run by the late Brendan O'Regan of
the Institute of Noetic Sciences, and the late
Harold Chipman who was the CIA station chief
responsible for all mind control research in the
Bay Area in the '70s. Chipman (aka "Orwell")
funded me openly for a while in 1985 when he
was allegedly no longer in the CIA, and covertly
before that, and told me much of the story. In
fact, he even introduced me to a beautiful
woman adventurer-agent who was one of his
RV subjects, who later became my live-in
'significant other'...*

- Quantum physicist Jack Sarfatti, a
Quantum Quacker

In the middle of the night, Thomas was awakened
by the sound of Seven's bus toiling up the last bit of
the hill. It was Sunday and they hadn't planned to see
each other until midweek, so he knew something was
up. He'd spent the afternoon and evening with
Ragoczy and his native friend, then bedded them up
on the hill. If they were the two from Wheeler Springs,
Seven would be happy to see them again. He went out
back to meet her under the canopy of trees. Baby
Rose and Sirius were already there. Thomas
wondered if Baby Rose ever slept.

The taxed VW engine off, Seven, Ray, and sleepy
Mannie climbed out into the starry darkness. Thomas

glanced up the hill; it was going to be a party. Hugging Seven, he thought of his lab and the few years of peace and study he'd had, intuitively sensing change in the air. Nothing lasts forever.

Her arm around Baby Rose, Seven made introductions and they all made their way into the house through the dimly lit lab, Ray and Mannie peering around, curious. Upstairs, lanterns were lit. Thomas started a fire in the potbelly and Seven went to the kitchen to make tea with Baby Rose at her elbow. Ray threw himself into a chair and rubbed his eyes.

Mannie strolled around the cabin living room, savoring its rustic quality. *California and the Hippie Revolution.* He didn't care if he ever saw New York again, though he missed Uncle Eli. He didn't even his mother's *latkes.* He smiled, then crouched down to stroke the strange dog. No one was talking. It was the silence of doing. Tea water heating. Fire igniting. Wood burning. Life as a Zen koan. *Grok,* Mannie heard his conscience say, *nothing lasts forever, be here now.* Far out. Mannie's grin broadened. What a trip. What a dog.

Ray watched Thomas build and feed the fire. *So this is the rich white boy*, he grimaced, vaguely noting the eruption of a couple of the seven deadly sins. He wondered how long he'd have to put up with this pompous, pampered honky. He looked around. Seven said he'd built the cabin and laboratory below, so he had some skills, that's for sure. She said he had nothing to do with his family, but where'd he get the bread for all the equipment downstairs?

His eyes followed Seven as she and Baby Rose carried in mugs of herbal tea. He trusted Seven, but did that mean he had to trust her choice in men? They'd shared the Bank of America. She hadn't seen the three guys pouring gasoline from big canisters and lighting the fire, but she'd believed him and agreed that the bank was a federal operation and that it had been a bad idea to tell the FBI what he'd seen. Helicopters blotting out the night sky, soldiers in gas masks, student leaders arrested, that kid killed a few nights ago—yeah, she got the picture and now was putting her life on the line for her friends. He accepted the cup from her hand and smiled at her: he and Seven were comrades joined at the hip, just not in the way he had hoped.

They gathered powwow style on the floor and Seven began. "I think we've no choice but to split for a while. The plan of going on as usual won't work anymore. If they're looking for Ray and Baby Rose, which I think they are, I'm already an accomplice and I know what that means. So at least Ray, Baby Rose, and I have to go—somewhere."

Beside her, Thomas was way ahead of her. Teasing, he asked, "Can I come, too? They're probably tracing your bus and license plate here right now."

Seven stared at him. She hadn't even thought of that. "Oh my God, Thomas, I'm so sorry." Baby Rose wrapped her arms around her.

Thomas put his hand on her back. "It was inevitable, and our previous plan bought just enough time for Ray and Mannie to get here. Do you think I would be satisfied sitting here and hoping the storm would pass over me?" He laughed.

"Man, this is all my fault," Ray said. "I brought all this down on you. I really didn't know how serious it was going to get. Me and my fucking politics—"

Seven shook her head. "For the last time, Ray, it's not just you, it's—" and she gazed lovingly at Baby Rose.

Hesitantly, Thomas opened up. "And it may be me, as well, Ray, though I'm still hoping they don't know that we're all together."

He and Seven sketched in a few more details for Ray and Mannie about Thomas' twin Didymus and how he had recognized Baby Rose. Thomas went through enough of his whacked-out upbringing to begin weakening the wall Ray had erected against him. Baby Rose slid around to Thomas and put an arm around his shoulders.

Thomas turned to Mannie. "Mannie, you may want to reconsider at this point."

Mannie shared a little of his background, then got to what he really wanted to contribute to the present conversation, something that had happened on the bus between Big Sur and San Luis Obispo.

Mannie took a deep breath. He remembered how he'd been drinking in the landscape of America out the bus window, and how shining just beneath its brittle veneer was what Walt Whitman had tried to say in poems. It wasn't about temples or churches or mosques. America was earthy, everywhere like a treasure to be dug up. It was a *seder* or mass calling us to see, hear, taste, smell, touch, love, and discern at a moment's notice. His eyes had even teared up in the San Francisco bus station. It was like the Gnostics said: the cosmos on Earth had been shattered like a mirror and had to be pieced back together. Mannie was ready for the fire of suffering, sacrifice, whatever would awaken all of his parts and penetrate him to the quick so he would know, *gnosis,* so his thoughts would live and see into matter where it was glowing, flashing, and beckoning his soul. *Far out.* No, no, that was backwards. *Far in.*

His new friends were waiting. He looked at Ray.

"Remember how the bus driver downshifted to stop for that boy waving the bus down from the side of the road?"

Ray shrugged. "I must have been asleep."

Mannie continued. "The boy had no bags, nothing. I overheard him say he only had enough pocket change to get to the next town, and when he walked down the aisle I could tell he'd been crying. I pointed

307

to the empty seat next to me and he sat down. I pegged him for a cowlick, gangly limbed fourteen or fifteen year old. I rapped to him a little about being from New York and how exciting it was to finally see California—you know, comfortable chit-chat. He nodded and kept turning to look out the back window, as if checking to see if the bus was being followed. Then when I rhapsodized about the Caffe Trieste in North Beach, he jerked his head and gave me a scared look.

"'I was there one night to hear Jack Sarfatti lecture on Time,' he said. 'He talked about cosmic coincidence control and the ordering principle of a superluminal universe and space-time travel. Sarfatti was way more exciting than smoking pot.'"

Mannie smiled. "The kid was right. Anyway, I was surprised that a boy his age would want to hear anyone lecture. 'Far out, who's Jack Sarfatti?' I asked."

"'A physicist,' he said, 'one of the Space Kids.'" Then he gave me another scared look. 'You ever heard of the Space Kids?'"

"I have," Thomas grimaced. "I was one of them. It's a gifted program run in part by NASA."

Mannie nodded. "Yeah, that's what he said. 'Science and mind stuff for kids like me.' Then he said his parents thought it sounded good for his future and signed the consent forms. He's actually from the East Coast, too.

"So a picture began forming in my mind. 'But you're here out on the highway all alone?' I said. He shrugged like it was no big deal and said he'd arrived with about ten other kids, his hands doing some sort of nervous gymnastics in his lap. 'We were all excited,' he said, 'special. Big government program, first stop Mountain View at NASA's Ames Research Center. High performance computer stuff. They said we were needed for the future and guaranteed full scholarships to the top ten—Harvard, Yale, MIT.' Then he checked the rear window again.

"I lowered my voice and said, 'So you're running away from the program.'   He stared hard at me, sizing me up, then sighed. 'Yeah,' he said, 'but don't tell the bus driver. I only had enough money to get to the next town. I don't think that will be enough—it's after lunch now, they probably know I'm gone.'

"I asked him if he'd called his parents. 'Not yet,' he said and buried his chin in his neck. 'I'm not sure they'll understand—'

"I finished his sentence for him. '— how scary it was?'

"He looked grateful that I understood, then nodded. 'Not scary because I'm far from home or any of that stuff,' he said, 'I mean *scary*.' His hands were knotted together. 'What they were doing to us,' he said. 'The supercomputers they were hooking us up to. *Human ESP factor. Bio-engineering artificial intelligence. ETI contact.* It all sounded cool, but—' He snuck another look at me, then said something weird. 'We were jumped over the hyperspace gap—at least that's what they said it was.' Then he shifted to if I'd ever read King Arthur when I was a kid."

Thomas was now listening intently. "Man, that kid could have been me."

Mannie went on. "I said I had, then he went on about Avalon being real in a parallel world or time, then asked, 'You ever heard of a SQUID?' It's a superconducting something I can't remember the name of . . ."

Thomas could. "Superconducting quantum interference device, an extremely sensitive magnetometer that reads and measures tiny magnetic fields, like the ones the brain produces."

"'You know more science than I'll ever know,' I told him. The kid kind of smiled, then took a deep breath and finally said what most scared him. 'A

SQUID's buried under the floor in a physics building at Stanford,' he said. 'They're streamlining them now for niobium, the element at the core that makes SQUID and artificial intelligence or AI devices work.'

"I didn't really understand why that was scary, so I asked, 'Computers that can think?' He said yes but more, much more. 'I'm so sorry,' I blurted out, meaning I was sorry about what he'd been subjected to by those arrogant, smart bastards. And I knew he knew what I meant because tears filled his eyes."

Mannie perused his new friends' attentive faces. "That young Parsifal rode straight into a ring of fucking vampires with big brains and military budgets— that's what I was thinking. But what I said was, 'Hey, don't worry about the bus fare. Let's get you to the airport in Los Angeles, then you can decide about calling your parents.'

"When I said that, he wiped his eyes and grabbed my arm hard, whispering furiously, 'The SQUID records your thoughts. It can read your memories and play them back to you, or play them back in someone else's head. They're going to do it to all of us. All of us.' I'll never forget the look on his face. He was terrified."

The fire in the potbelly crackled, the stream below gurgled as they contemplated what the boy had said. The birds weren't awake but would be soon.

Mannie sighed. "So I bought a bus ticket to LAX from the driver and handed it to him. For the next few bus pitstops, I stayed on board with him curled under the seat in case anyone came looking for him. And it was a good thing we made the plan. In the very next town, a couple of people got off, a couple of people got on. Outside, I saw a man talking to the bus driver. Then he boarded the bus and came down the aisle, obviously searching for someone. Just as he was almost to me, the bus driver got back on and said he had to get going and the man would need a ticket.

Shooting the bus driver a killing look, the man got off and the driver flung himself into his seat. Once the door was shut and we were on our way again, the driver looked in the rearview mirror and winked at me." Tears swam in Mannie's eyes. "If evil is everywhere, so is good."

"Right on," Ray said with fervor. "Man, I can't believe I slept through it all."

"What happened then?" Thomas asked.

"Every town, the kid hid under the seat. He was under there when I finally got off to use the restroom and get us a snack in San Luis Obispo—that's when I met Ray. I got off in Santa Barbara, gave him a few bucks, and hugged him goodbye."

Thomas had been on the run for years. He knew. He sent a prayer to yet another boy on the run.

Ray looked around at the group. "Yep, Mannie's in the club. On one bus, he meets two cats on the run."

Slowly, hesitantly, Baby Rose sidled over toward Mannie.

"What do you think, Mannie?" Seven asked. "No blame if you're out of the game."

"What's the game plan?" Mannie asked.

Thomas said, "Rhea's and Seven's places are out, and this place won't be safe much longer."

"Right," Seven said, thinking. "I've always wanted to . . ." She looked around and shook her head.

"Wanted to what?" Ray asked.

"Go on, Seven," Thomas said, "wanted to what?"

"See where Kennedy was shot," she said in a quiet voice.

"Dallas!" Ray threw up his hands. "That's the South! Texas is evil, man. Besides, what do I care about that rich East Coast honky getting murdered? Or that house nigger King getting it in Memphis. But Malcolm X—"

"You're blowing smoke, Ray," Mannie said reasonably. "The whole country has been changed by

Kennedy's assassination. I'm in for Dallas, Seven. I think it's something every American should see."

"Me, too, I'm in," Thomas said.

"All right, I'm in," Ray said with surprising lightness, "given that I'm one of the creators of this snafu. But y'all white folk gonna have to protect my black ass once we're in the South." Despite the fake drawl, they knew he wasn't joking.

Seven could scarcely believe what she was hearing. "Going to Dallas isn't going to solve our problems, you know."

"We know," said Thomas.

"But at least we'll be leaving the state," Ray said cheerfully.

"And by Dallas, who knows what we'll know?" Thomas added.

Seven smiled. "All in favor?"

All hands went up, even Baby Rose's.

"Should we take my bus, even if they have my license plate number?" Seven asked.

Thomas shrugged. "Better than my unregistered truck. Like I said, the last thing they want is a media circus around Baby Rose."

Seven began planning out loud. "So I'll go down the hill, pack my stuff, make arrangements for my apartment. Being home on Sunday is my norm, so the Colonel and I will take the Cadillac out for our regular Sunday drive and lobster dinner, then I'll tell him I'm going away for a while. Being retired military, he won't ask questions."

A lump rose in her throat. She was fond of the old guy and wondered how he would do without her. Not that she was indispensable, but—

"And I've got a lot to do here," Thomas said. "Hopefully, one more day won't matter to our surveillance friends, and it'll probably help that you're in Santa Barbara doing your regular Sunday gig. Everyone stays here—Baby Rose, Ray, Mannie.

We'll all come down the hill by, say, midnight? Cloak of darkness and all that." He tried to smile, but Seven could see he was as overwhelmed as she was.

"What are you going to do with your lab, your books, Sirius . . ." She knew how happy he'd been here.

Thomas leaned over and squeezed her cheeks together so she looked like a chipmunk. "You leave that to me, my love. Besides," he looked around, "I've got helpers, and I may have a plan for a diversion while we get the hell out of Dodge."

"Okay, midnight," Ray repeated, "where?"

"My apartment," Seven decided. "Pull around to the alley in back. If anything looks compromised . . ."

"Then somewhere near 101," Thomas said. "A parking lot would be ideal so as not to draw attention while we pack up Seven's bus and I leave my truck."

Seven brightened. "Where that Australian Moreton Bay Fig tree is, the huge one planted at the corner of Chapala and Montecito. It has a parking lot, and right by 101 . . ."

"Perfect," Thomas said, "midnight under the world tree."

They laughed, then Thomas and Seven led their guests to nooks and crannies for a little sleep. When finally he led her up their hill, she thought they were just going to bed until just before they reached the summit he said, "Have I got a surprise for you."

But the bed was empty and luminous under the stars, except for a glowing blue rose on one of the pillows. Thinking this was the surprise, Seven picked it up.

"Thomas, it's amazing. I thought only Rhea had these. See how it glows." She pressed her nose among its folds and inhaled, then raised it to Thomas' nose. But he was preoccupied.

"They were right here," he mumbled, scanning the sides of the hill. "Where did they go, and when?"

"Who?" Seven asked.

"Your friends from Wheeler Springs, the European and Indian. I'm sure it was them."

Seven clutched his arm. "Here? Hermano and Ghost Bear?"

"I thought so, though the European said his name was Ragoczy. They were going to spend the night and leave in the morning. They said they were on a walkabout."

Thomas didn't yet know about Ray's encounter at the San Francisco bus depot. When Seven heard something of Thomas' earlier conversation with Hermano, she was definitely getting the hang of how he was stirring the waters. And he left the blue rose for her.

"Did he say anything about Baby Rose?" Seven asked.

"No, but he knew a lot about the technology that both she and my— brother have been subjected to. He talked about twins, even that there were two Jesus children . . ."

They lay down and Thomas buried his face in her neck, then rolled onto his back to stare at the vanishing stars. "He said not to give up on my father, that he was about to go to Europe and might yet find his way. Baby Rose stood behind him throughout dinner—he only had water, and he loved my laboratory, which made me happy." He rolled over to look at her. "Seven, he called Gollum and Gollum came. Was he real, Seven, or did we dream him?"

She held up the blue rose in the starlight. "He's as real as this blue rose, Thomas. Meeting him has changed everything, hasn't it?"

Thomas inhaled the rose's sweetness, then folded her into his arms. In a while, they would sleep.

21
The Park Bench

Far less known, and difficult to assess, is the question of purely Western masters, initiates who direct their own rebirths and appear in successive historical periods, sometimes as famous figures but more often as obscure agents working behind the scenes. In this curious area, claims of who-was-who are often incredible, historical conundrums and conspiracies loom large, and the problem of how to track serial reincarnations remains unsolved.

> - John Lamb Lash, *The Seeker's Handbook*, 1990

Yet Jesus said not unto him, he shall not die; but, if I will that he tarry till I come, what is that to thee?

> – John 21:23

Its very nature camouflages it. And why, gentlemen? Because no one can imagine it.

> – *SS Obergruppenführer* Reinhard Heydrich, Security Police and Secret Service

Next door to Seven, in another modest little apartment in the complex on State Street, lived the

Colonel. She never knew him by any other title and didn't pay attention to his surname until he was dead and she found it in documents in his old Air Force chest, along with his surprising will. Born in 1892, he joined the Army Air Force at 17 and never left the military. By 1917, he was an ace officer pilot dropping chlorine in the trenches of France and Germany, and by 1941 he was a colonel. Now in his seventies, he still dressed to the nines with starched shirts delivered weekly from the Chinese laundry downtown. His furnished apartment suited the needs of a retired career officer who'd never married and didn't give a damn what others thought of how he lived, having served his country through three wars, the Korean debacle being, like Vietnam, more of an Asian police action than a war. Cataract surgery had left him with Coke-bottle glasses that still necessitated a magnifying glass for reading, so driving his beloved Cadillac was out. He hardly went anywhere he couldn't walk to, and his groceries were delivered, along with a bottle of whiskey every fortnight, and Friends of the Library delivered the few audiotapes and books he required.

For entertainment and the sound of human voices, he had his television, and every Sunday his neighbor Seven drove him in his pristine old Cadillac down to the wharf for a nice lobster dinner and a nose full of the sea. Through the week, he'd go into the garage and run his hands over the sparkling pale yellow hood and doors, the oiled black leather top, the ruthless silver-tipped fins. He hadn't loved many people or things in his life, but he loved his Cadillac like a cowboy loved his horse. A boy came once a week to dust and polish it, oil the leather, check the fluids and tires. It hadn't needed real servicing for years. He could have hired the boy to drive him down to the wharf, but he preferred Seven's intelligent female company. It was an innocent relationship and good tonic for an old bachelor.

This particular Sunday morning, the Colonel was up early as usual, re-reading copies of classified documents on the Black Eagle Trust that he'd probably read a dozen times before. After World War Two, he'd heard rumors about Nazi and Japanese gold located by plunder teams in Europe and Asia. Allen Dulles had set up Operation Amadeus with SS General Karl Wolff as part of Operation Sunrise to get SS Nazis and gold out of Germany and to South America before and after the end of the war by means of Jesuit-run ratlines composed of Knights of Malta and Opus Dei, some of whom were OSS under Knight of Malta Wild Bill Donovan. Tens of thousands were involved in moving looted gold and SS morphia narcotics and Nazis—those who had run Treblinka and Sobibor, Mengele the White Angel, Klaus Barbie the Butcher of Lyon—to grease their way out, along with British banknotes counterfeited in concentration camps under Operation Bernhardt.

The Colonel had not been born yesterday. He knew about the Naval Intelligence deal with Lucky Luciano to assist the Allied landing in Sicily and how that deal had led to deals with SS units in Italy under Wolff. War, like crime, is an ugly business with a lot of backscratching. Patton had seen through the arrangements made with the Soviets in Berlin, which of course was why he was broadsided the day before he was to return home. The military brass knew he would blab about the deal with the Nazis and the coming Cold War being a criminal con. Nazis, Bolshies, Zionists, Jesuits, Mafia, and corporations were all on the gravy train bound for fascism and repression from Europe to the Americas and kingdom come. The Third Reich was just moving house with the help of American and British fascists while stay-behind units under Operation Gladio would work to

317

undermine democratic governments in Europe. The whole thing stank to high heaven and galled him.

After Korea, he'd played attaché for Washington and heard how in 1943 the OSS had stolen $10 billion in gold from the Italian treasury in Building 4 of King's Point Condominium in Addison, a western suburb of Chicago. Could it possibly be true? Where the hell could it have gone? The Colonel had always known that the OSS and SS were in many ways just a letter apart; after all, Wild Bill Donovan's allegiance lay with the Vatican and Italian mafia, not the United States. The OSS, Knights of Malta, and Jesuits all labored in the vineyards of huge international corporations and the old Catholic families that ran them.

That same year, Emperor Hirohito began moving gold—*kin no yuri*, the Golden Lily treasure—out of Japan: $35 million to South America, $20 million to Switzerland, $45 million to Portuguese, Spanish, and Vatican accounts. Cunningly, MacArthur had disallowed Donovan's OSS in his US Far Eastern Command, choosing instead his little fascist Willoughby (né Adolph Tscheppe-Weidenbach) to run his own hand-picked intelligence troupe. Like the gold stolen and cached all over the South and Southwest by the Knights of the Golden Circle during the Civil War, Golden Lily gold had been melted down into 75-kilo bars and cached away in old mines and caves in the Philippines.

Long before the Japanese attempted a conditional surrender, MacArthur had received intelligence as to where Princes Chichiku and Takeda had moved the Golden Lily. But it wasn't until General Yamashita, the Tiger of Malaya, was hanged and his driver brutally tortured that MacArthur could find the exact spot in the mountains north of Manila. He then shipped the gold, silver, precious stones and metals, engraving plates, diamonds and currency to 176 accounts in 42 countries, the gold and platinum going to Swiss banks.

But that wasn't the end of MacArthur's war booty mission. Two billion in gold lay at the bottom of Tokyo Bay, and priceless art objects, whole libraries and museums, historical documents, and solid gold Buddhas were in Japanese government vaults and Green Dragon hoards—the entire wealth of the Co-Prosperity Sphere of Vietnam, Laos, Cambodia, Burma, Siam, Malaya, Philippines and Dutch East Indies. In Singapore alone, 100,000 civilians were slaughtered for their treasures.

Everyone was robbing and massacring—China, Korea, Hong Kong, the Brits, Dutch, Aussies, Kiwis, Canadians, Yanks. Burdened thus by their elites' blood-price treasure, the Japanese people never once tasted the democracy MacArthur had promised. Like Americans, they labored under a criminal government that rewarded the weak and evil and tortured and killed the noble and courageous. Democrat, Republican, Liberal Democratic Party were just names disguising deceit, greed, and empty justifications for the sacred violence of war that was no longer sacred. Ruling powers had sunk to violent servility and raw evil.

The Colonel moved his magnifying glass. In July 1944 at Bretton Woods, the Black Eagle Trust—moniker for both Nazi booty in Europe and the Golden Lily in Asia—was one of the two main calling cards of Nazi and Japanese fascists seeking Allied advantage; the other was science and technology. In return for quiet access to the Trust, the Anglo-American contingency under Secretary of War Henry Stimson promised to rebuild both West Germany and Japan and include them in the vanguard of the coming new world order. Very few war criminals would be showcased and punished. The US Archives would be purged of materials critical of Japan, such as how

American prisoners of war were used as slave labor to move gold into mines and then left inside to asphyxiate after the entries were dynamited, and the fact that other POWs privy to the Golden Lily were left in the Philippines, never to return home. No reparations would be required, and those responsible for the war would remain in power. The Trust slush fund would then be used to bankroll a global political action of gigantic corporate fascist proportions. Stimson's man Robert Anderson was appointed Secretary of the Navy in 1953 to move the gold from the Philippines, then was appointed Secretary of the Treasury to watch over it. Ever since, the Department of the Treasury had been crooked.

The Colonel didn't know why he tortured himself with this knowledge, except that knowing the truth made him feel clean, awake, alive, undeceived. As he returned the documents to the old trunk he'd lugged all over the planet, he pondered the possibility that the purpose of every life was to awaken to what is true and thus purge the soul of its comfortable lies before traveling through the gates of death. Many of the men he'd served under and rubbed elbows with had chosen to conduct themselves far more primally than Mongol hordes, albeit cold-blooded, with their committees and think tanks, planned purges and takeovers and orders issued to trigger killers while never leaving their desks.

He took off his fish-bowl glasses to clean them. This was a cold age, and its ague went right to the bone. He should have married and had children and grandchildren; at least they would have warmed his impersonal life. His few friends were dead and gone. At least he had Seven, so alive, so naïve and courageous, up to her neck in Cold War deceit without being able to get a fix on it. *To be courageous and yet ignorant . . .* He sighed. Too much work, all of these thoughts. Thank God it was Sunday. They would go for a drive and have their lobster dinner.

Sliding the old trunk under his bed, he glanced at the clock: almost time for his constitutional down to Old Town where Seven would pick him up in the Caddy for their three o'clock dinner date. He leaned over and turned on the radio, then got up to go in the bathroom to shave the few bristles his old chin was still producing. He could hear Glenn Miller's trombone crackling, the reception as bad as Radio Deutschlandsender during the war. Major Miller—Mueller, really—disappeared during his flight in that USAAF single engine UC-64 Noorduyn Norseman over the English Channel in '44. He glanced at the radio; Santa Barbara never had bad reception. At last, it cleared up as the trombone faded.

"News on the hour. Exactly four years after private citizen Richard Nixon's ignominious fall from the American presidency in February 1972, the People's Republic of China invited him to visit just one month after the death of Premier Chou En-lai and replacement by a low-ranking deputy instead of Chou En-lai's chosen successor.

"The People's Republic sent a Boeing 707 for the Nixons, with seating for 118 passengers, despite the fact that the Nixon party numbered less than forty, and a vast cargo hold. While the Nixons met with the partially paralyzed Chairman Mao Tse-tung and his astute wife Chiang Ch'ing in the Great Hall of the People, Black Eagle Trust gold bars were unloaded from the hold of the jet. Nine days later, the Nixons returned home.

"On May 10, three months after the Nixon visit, a 6.8 earthquake killed 20,000 in China; on September 9, Chairman Mao died, and a month later, Madame Mao was arrested. Rumors continue to circulate that Madame Mao, a ruling force for forty years, had been plotting to overthrow the new Prime Minister.

"Did Richard Nixon return Black Eagle gold to China, stolen thirty years ago by Japan? Was the Black Eagle gold to cement Madame Mao's power in the wake of her husband's death?

"On July 3, 1974, one and a half years before the Nixons' trip to China, Louise Boyer, Nelson Rockefeller's assistant of thirty years, fell to her death from a tenth story New York apartment because she told investigators that Rockefeller was involved in removing gold from Fort Knox.

"This is KRMA, broadcast from afar."

The Colonel had come out of the bathroom, razor in hand, shaving cream on his face, to stare at the radio. Nixon in China? Four years after 1972? That would be 1976. Nixon ousted, Chou En-lai and Mao dead, Madame Mao ousted, Rockefeller . . . He'd never heard of the call letters *KRMA*. Was it a spoof, like *War of the Worlds* back in the Thirties?

Cleaned up and still contemplating the KRMA broadcast from the future, the Colonel and his trusty cane set out for downtown, a lackluster walk but for the omnipresent Santa Ynez mountains. His legs and cane were slow-goers, and now and then he stopped to wipe his brow and gaze at the Southern California sun crawling across the blue midheaven or at a lovely bit of Spanish architecture or Mediterranean flora. The KRMA broadcast had thrown him. Perhaps he could ask someone about the day's news. Was he lapsing into dementia, hearing broadcasts from 1976?

Mao reminded him of his attaché days after Korea in that plush San Luis Obispo house perched on the cliffs over the crashing sea, listening to dapper German emigrants laugh and drink *schnapps*, riding high, the horror of their homeland torn in two like a chicken far away. Father Serra had named the mission in San Luis Obispo after Louis, the 13th century Bishop of Toulouse and Archbishop of Lyons. Louis was descended from the House of Anjou, and

Toulouse was known for its magicians, which made the historically minded attaché wonder if that was why Nazis would be drawn to living in San Luis Obispo. He listened to them reminisce about coming to America before the war's end and how Dulles and the Joint Chiefs of Staff had fawned over them and their expertise, inquiring into their mystical insights regarding the Bomb at White Sands in '45. They were drinking too much and didn't care that the attaché spoke German, laughing themselves senseless about what fools Americans were and how easy to manipulate they were with such dull minds that could only believe in what was seen with the eyes and smelled with the nose. It had been just as von Braun had said it would be: easy. And the American attaché had stood like a post.

At last, the Colonel arrived at his Old Town bench under the tall Catawba tree with its wonderful heart-shaped leaves. At one end of the bench was seated a slight man in European dress. Europeans were not all that unusual in Santa Barbara, given its Spanish beauty on the sea and proximity to Los Angeles and Hollywood. The Colonel glanced up into the Catawba branches; the flowers would be bursting open any day now. Birds flitted and chattered in the branches, loving this tree almost as much as the Colonel did. He nodded cordially toward his bench companion and seated himself. The dark-haired man nodded and smiled back. He introduced himself as Germain and the Colonel in turn introduced himself. The man's age was indeterminate, but his aura of stature was unmistakable.

Placing his chin on his hands on his cane, the Colonel thought he'd do a bit of people watching. And so the two men sat for a few minutes observing Sunday strollers licking ice cream cones, pushing babies, ogling shop windows, enjoying their day of surcease of labor, some fresh from church, some from

323

bed. Later, the Colonel couldn't recall how the conversation began and quickly wound around to what he remembered of it, but he knew he was deftly led to military matters.

Gesturing to the people and surroundings before them, Germain said, "Don't you agree, Colonel, that in a very real sense the present of which we are so enamoured is little more than the lemniscate crossing point between past and future, a moment in Time and Space needing us to balance what was and what will be, and that this is the only true experience of the present available to us? Newton was privy to the techniques by which matter might be transmuted and disintegrated, given that they had been passed from one initiate to another in a long lineage of knowledge spanning thousands of years—techniques kept secret until now, when they have fallen into irresponsible hands." He glanced at the Colonel. "You know of Jumbo?"

The Colonel's eyes blinked behind his thick lenses.

Germain smiled. "Jumbo at Ground Zero in White Sands, a 214-ton pressure thermos bottle 25 feet tall and made of 15-inch walls of banded, heat-treated steel. Built at 81° longitude, Jumbo was transported south and west in a 200-ton recessed railway flat car to New Orleans, then across the Mississippi River and into Texas to Houston, through Waco, back to Dallas, then to Oklahoma City, west again to Amarillo along Route 66, then southwest on 60 to Clovis and across New Mexico to Belen and finally to Pope's Siding south of Socorro, all by rail. From Pope's Siding, Jumbo was placed on a 64-wheel trailer and hauled by nine tractors across the road to Ground Zero."

The Colonel leaned on his cane, staring at Germain through his thick lenses. "That's one strange itinerary. And then they didn't need it, right? They were going to use Jumbo to contain the explosive charges but abandoned the idea when they came up with lenses to focus the blast."

Germain shrugged. "If you believe that was the real reason for Jumbo in the first place."

"That's what they said."

With the utmost respect, Germain asked, "You are not a Freemason, are you, Colonel?"

"No, I am not," the Colonel proudly responded, "which is why my career in the Air Force only went so far, despite my background and medals from three wars. But I'm certain I made the right decision. There's enough secrecy called for in the military without adding all that mumbo—."

Jumbo. He looked away and blinked, mentally scanning the past decades. "I've lost friends to those Lodges and their secrets," he murmured, turning back to Germain. "Are you saying Freemasons had something to do with Jumbo? I wouldn't put it past them."

"Everything to do with it, Colonel. You know that General Groves was a 33° Mason?"

"I assumed he was, given his career, and when the Army put him in charge of the Manhattan Project, I thought he might even be *higher* than a Mason, if you know what I mean."

Germain nodded somberly. "Groves was the inner circle's man."

"Huh. I'm sure he knew which side his bread was buttered on."

"Indeed he did. It was Groves who placed Jumbo 800 yards west of Ground Zero inside a 70-foot steel tower. The tower was decimated in the blast but Jumbo endured and remained where it had fallen until April 30, 1947, when Groves instructed the Special Weapons Division at Sandia Base to put explosives in Jumbo's bottom hemisphere and blow out both ends—for double egress of whatever was trapped inside, I would imagine. Later, the empty cylinder was interred in the Earth, then dug up in 1951, examined, and abandoned. Do you know what April 30 signifies, Colonel?"

A chill shimmied up the Colonel's spine. "Walpurgisnacht, May Eve, just before Beltane, anniversary of Hitler's death beneath the Chancellery in Berlin—if indeed he died there." He had visited the bunker and knew that whatever had gone on there had not been in the official story.

Suddenly, Seven was standing over him and Germain was nowhere in sight.

The Colonel looked around, then asked Seven, "How long have you been standing there?"

Seven shrugged. "Seconds. You seemed engrossed, so I 've been waiting."

"Was—anyone else on the bench when you came up?"

She smiled sadly. "Just you, looking thoughtful the way you do." She was really going to miss him.

The Colonel took out his handkerchief and mopped his brow, his liver-spotted hand trembling. Two Saturday morning kid radio shows were all mixed up in his mind, shows he used to listen to in the 1950s when he was stationed in—somewhere. *Who was that masked man?* and *Only the Shadow knows.*

Once the Colonel told her a little about Germain, Seven knew exactly who had been here and that she wouldn't have to leave the Colonel behind, after all.

Germain's visitations occurred when the estimated world population was 3.6 billion. United Mine Workers labor leader "Jock" Yablonski and his family had just been murdered in Pennsylvania. The Bilderberg Group was meeting April 17-19 at the Grand Hotel Quellenhof in Bad Ragaz, Switzerland. The invasion of Cambodia would begin on Walpurgisnacht, and four days later the Ohio National Guard at Kent State University would shoot four students. Five days after that, United Automobile Workers labor leader Walter Reuther and his wife would be murdered in a chartered Lear jet crash. Come July, President Nixon would quietly ratify the Huston Plan to justify COINTELPRO domestic burglary, illegal electronic surveillance, and opening the mail of all suspected domestic radicals, black or white. The KCIA was backing Tongsun Park and the Unification Church in their efforts to blackmail and bribe members of the Nixon administration and US Congress. Plans were being laid to send the "Pilgrim Pope" Paul VI a *piercing* message in November in Manila. At the California Medical Facility in Vacaville, MK-ULTRA psychiatrist Dr. Frederic Hacker was preparing LAPD informer Donald DeFreeze to lead the Symbionese Liberation Army (SLA) and kidnap Patty Hearst, and the Black Cultural Association (BCA) was being set up to radicalize 1,093 black inmates at the same time that personality-altering Prolexin was being administered. The Special Programs Unit behavior modification program under Dr. Martin Groder was being set up at Joliet Correctional Center. The Bureau of Prisons was requesting special funds for a Federal Center for Correctional Research in Butner, North Carolina.

The New Atlantis, the New Jerusalem, and Karmageddon were on their way all at once.

22
Alea jacta est

*That which is called Christian religion
existed among the ancients, and never
did not exist, from the beginning of the
human race until Christ came in the
flesh, at which time the true religion
which already existed began to be called
Christianity.*

- Augustine (354-430 CE)

*Señor, señor, do you know where we're
    headin'?
Lincoln County Road or Armageddon?
Seems like I been down this way before.
Is there any truth in that, señor?*

- Bob Dylan, "Señor (Tales of Yankee
Power)," 1978

Mannie was blown away by how thorough Thomas
was. Upstream in an old mineshaft, he'd resurrected a
dry tunnel and turned it into a storeroom lined with
the same copper mesh as in the *rancho* walls and roof.
Mannie, Ray, Baby Rose, and Thomas worked all day
to remove all metal and glass from the *rancho* and
move it to the storeroom along the streambed
camouflaged by the canopy of willows and elders. The
rancho wasn't wired, so they didn't have to worry
about that, but they did have to remove and roll up
the copper mesh.

The specialized glass around Gollum's residence was excruciatingly heavy, as was the heavy magnet under the floor. Both had to be winched onto the truck and driven carefully along the streambed. The potbelly, propane kitchen stove and convection oven were free standing; a few pipes, cooking pots, the outdoor shower and composting toilet, his books, and that was it. Once the storeroom was loaded and the thick wooden door locked, they took to the shovels and buried the entry. In a day or so, Thomas said, it would look natural again. Everything else was hauled into the house, including the mattress on the hill. Everything.

Up to that day, Ray had never given a thought to sky surveillance, but Thomas clued him in to the National Reconnaissance Office (NRO) created three years after Sputnik. Its existence was secret; even uttering its name in Congressional open session was prohibited. Headquartered in Chantilly, Virginia behind lead doors, the NRO functioned under cover of the undersecretary of the Air Force, the Office of Space Systems, and the CIA. No one knew what its budget was for building and operating space satellites, but its mission was to oversee and provide arms control verification and maintain air, space, sea, and ground systems. NRO satellites took pictures to postage stamp accuracy for the CIA and military intelligence. Figuring he might be a person of interest, Thomas did nothing without taking into account the eyes in the sky.

Finally, it was dark and the truck was packed up. Thomas told his tired friends to settle in, he needed a minute to say goodbye to his little home. Sirius followed him down to the lab. Inside, Thomas bent over the sonic generator, perfect for a day like this. He re-checked the radius, wishing he could stay to watch it do its magic, but alas, there was no time. It had created the lab, now it would destroy it. Womb to tomb. Its frequency would vibrate everything to dust, which was why all the metal and glass had to be out: their frequencies would require too much time, maybe years. Wood and cloth should be relatively quick and leave little forensic evidence of his presence. Either everything would fall to dust or it would retain form until a little gust of wind or footstep crumbled it. He looked around. *His first real home.* It was healing to at last have had a home. Maybe he and Seven would make another one. He fired up the little generator, flicked a switch, listened to the hum, hugged Sirius, and they ran.

With Baby Rose and Sirius beside him in the cab and Ray and Mannie in the truck bed under the tarp with Thomas' worldly goods—computer and telephone equipment, tools, tent and sleeping bag, clothes, big black iron skillet and grain grinder Seven wanted him to bring, all to be loaded in the VW bus—Thomas wound the little beige truck down the track and turned onto a cross-country dirt road that eventually came out beyond Hillside Drive. If Seven had turned the porch light off, they would rendezvous at the parking lot by the big bay fig tree; if it was on, then Thomas would turn a few blocks later and make his way into the alley behind the apartments. He was to lay low until she approached.

It was after eleven when they passed Seven's rambling apartment complex. The porch light was on. Mannie tapped on the glass and pointed at a Chevy parked fifty or so feet past Seven's door. Passing the Chevy, Thomas felt something lurch in his chest and wondered if Didymus was in that car. He cruised two long blocks before turning left and left again into the narrow alley. Turning off the headlights, he crossed the next street into Seven's alley and parked behind her bus.

Seven had arranged with her friend Amy to stay in the apartment to the end of the month, then inform the landlord that Seven had a family emergency and wouldn't be back. Amy had invited a dozen or so UCSB friends over for a quiet end-of-the-quarter party so Seven could use it as a diversionary tactic. No one but Amy knew she was leaving.

Seven was inside laughing and talking, trying to appear normal. Every half hour or so she wandered out into the alley to join guests having a smoke and looked up and down the alley for signs of Thomas. At last, she saw the truck's dark outline. A departing couple gave her an opportunity to walk out front with them to their car. Hugging them goodbye, she eyed the stakeout car, then turned back and noted with satisfaction that the Colonel's windows were dark, though she was sure he was anything but asleep. Inside again, she caught hold of Amy's arm and walked toward the back door with her.

"You're a gem, Amy," she whispered. "Anything here of mine or the Colonel's you don't want, just drop it off at the Salvation Army. That's probably where I got most of it, anyway." They laughed. "If anyone asks, I went to check on my old neighbor next door."

They hugged. Amy's eyes were teary. "Seven, if you need anything—"

Seven gave her a last hug and slipped out the back door, heading for the Colonel's garage. Looking briefly up and down the alley, she rolled up the garage door, got into the Cadillac and started it purring, then backed it into the alley so she could pull behind Thomas' truck. Letting it idle, she popped the trunk. The Colonel had already stowed his duffle bag, folding chair, and old Air Force trunk. Next, she peeked into the truck cab where Thomas and Baby Rose were half-lying over Sirius. Baby Rose was asleep. Thomas rolled down his window, looked at the Cadillac, then at Seven.

She had been dreading this moment. "Thomas, I can't leave the Colonel behind, he's got no one but me.

Besides, with this many of us, we need another vehicle. It gives us more options."

Exhausted, Thomas didn't know if he could handle another change. "'Options.' A caravan. Oh, and don't tell me: someone's looking for him, too."

Seven smiled. "You're tired. I don't think anyone's looking for him yet, but we don't have all night to negotiate." She leaned close and whispered, "Besides, I'll tell you later about why I know it's the right thing to do." She kissed the end of his nose.

Thomas sighed. Seven had been raised without a father and she and the Colonel had bonded. No use fighting it. "Okay, but just this one arbitrary decision. From now on, all major decisions are democratically processed, got that, Sergeant Seven?"

She grinned and kissed him on the lips. "Yes sir, Captain America. Now get out and as quietly as possible let's load your gear into the walk-in closet Cadillac calls a trunk. Stowaway can go on top of the bus in the luggage rack. Food and cooking stuff in the bus, re-organize at the fig tree. Did you see the stakeout car?"

"Yeah," Thomas whispered as he untied the tarp on the truck bed.

Mannie lifted the tarp and nudged Ray awake. Groggy, they all began unloading and loading.

Once the two vehicles were loaded, Thomas asked Seven, "What do I do about the truck?"

"We leave it. Wake Baby Rose, then wipe it down for prints and leave the keys under the seat. Make sure nothing is left to tie it to you. You're driving the bus for now. Here's the drill: we follow the next car out of the alley. They'll turn left onto State and we'll turn right up the hill and head for the fig tree. If either of us feels we're being tailed, we flash our lights and skip the fig tree, just head for 1 south to Santa Monica, then 66 east." She paused for a deep breath.

"But we both know that we're going to evade the stakeout, right?"

Thomas knew the fear she was facing: the possibility of losing him, Baby Rose, and Ray all in one fell swoop, not to mention being an accessory. He kissed her. "Right. You're the cat's meow, Sergeant Seven." He pressed something into her hands.

"What's this?" She looked down at what looked like a walkie talkie.

"I've got one, too," he grinned. "It's a police two-way radio I've made some modifications to. Clear as a bell, we can hear each other's conversations. I hadn't planned on *two* vehicles, but hey, I guess the cosmos knew more than I did."

Clutching their radios, they hugged each other tight. Seven went to get the Colonel while Thomas and Mannie began wiping the truck down as soon as Baby Rose clambered out. Ray with his guitar and Sirius behind him got into the back of the bus, and Baby Rose tumbled sleepily into the spacious backseat of the Cadillac.

Seven tapped at the Colonel's door. In seconds the old man was there. Without looking back, he and his cane exited the seedy little apartment he would never miss, though he would miss the Catawba's flowering. He and his Cadillac were entering upon what could well prove to be his last adventure on Earth.

Seven grinned at her old friend. "You're shotgun next to me."

He grinned back. "Yes, ma'am."

Thomas and Mannie jumped into the bus.

Seven had been right; they didn't have to wait long before a couple came out of Seven's apartment and got into their car. As their engine fired, Thomas started up the bus. Headlights off, the bus and Cadillac followed the car to the street, at which point it went left and onto State and the bus and Caddy turned right.

Out in front of Seven's apartment complex, Agent Iff made a note of the car leaving the apartments and passing their Chevy, then said to Didy, "Check the alley and count the cars still there. Models and license plate numbers."

Didy ran across State and ducked into the alley from the cross street. In back of Seven's apartment, he could hear voices talking and laughing. The stereo was playing Cream. He liked Cream. He checked the cars. Falcon, Corvair, VW bug, and an old Fairlane were still there. A little Ford truck that had seen better days was new. But where was the blue VW bus? Simon would ask. *Simon says.*

Didy felt something like he had felt that day in the garden when he saw that girl he somehow knew and then didn't tell Simon about seeing her. Did that mean he wouldn't tell about the VW bus being gone? All the way back to the car, Didy wondered what Didy would say.

Simon was on the two-way. Apparently, a retired Air Force intelligence colonel lived next door to the blue bus woman and the FBI was trying to figure out if there was any connection or if it was just serendipitous. Didy heard the word *serendipitous* and thought how much he liked that word, though he wasn't sure he knew what it meant. He definitely didn't think the FBI or CIA believed in *serendipitous.*

Finally, Agent Iff was off the two-way and making more notes.

"Well?" he asked, glancing at his idiot partner and finding his logsheet. "Vehicles?"

Didy recited the vehicles and license plate numbers as Agent Iff wrote, including the little Ford truck. Then he paused, curious.

Iff looked up from his notes. "And the VW bus? I don't need its plates, I've got them."

Didy breathed a sigh of relief; he wouldn't have to lie.

"And the VW bus," he echoed.

When the pilgrims set out that night, they were in flight, running *from*, not *to*, their intentions scattered, divided, three of the six already on the feds' radar. So when they stopped at the 100-year-old Morton fig tree, they had hopes of clearing their thinking and even gaining guidance from the old canopied Grandmother tree planted long ago by a little girl. A few campers and cars were parked around the massive, wise fig tree, and people were drinking wine and talking quietly among its giant roots. Some had come for the first Earth Day teach-in on April 20 and the memorial for Kevin Moran and were still lingering. The pilgrims found a quiet place to organize their vehicles and form a tight powwow before hitting Highway 1.

Scarcely above a whisper, Ray fretted, "Maybe we ought to just split to Mexico. Besides, I don't have much bread."

"Bad idea," Thomas said, "and don't worry about the bread, though you'd better not drive in case we're stopped. In Mexico, we'd stick out like a hand of thumbs, plus they've probably already alerted the border. The good news is they still don't know we're all together. I say we stay together and keep with the Dallas plan."

"Thomas is right," the Colonel said. Seven had filled him in.

"We're all in this for our own reasons," Seven said. "This is our trip, our journey, and I say we follow the thread through the desert all the way to where Kennedy was shot down like a dog."

"On television," Mannie felt compelled to add quietly.

"And *not* by Oswald," the Colonel finished.

Each was feeling their way through their anxieties and hopes. Instead of being dictated to by those harassing them, they would look for America like in the Simon and Garfunkel song. Route 66. Indians. The Wild West. The Bomb at White Sands. Kennedy in Dallas. Beyond Dallas—

Ray murmured. "Black men don't go to the Deep South willingly."

"They do if they need to," Seven said. "We need to know, Ray, revolution or no revolution. Consciousness, gnosis, experience, whatever you want to call it, it may not save us but we have to know."

"All right, sister," Ray said, holding his hand palm down in the middle of the circle. "I'm in, hell or high water, and I have a feeling it's going to be both."

One by one, white hands topped his black one, the Colonel's being the last. They all looked at each other in the dim light. The desert and Dallas.

"All for one and one for all," Thomas grinned, "let's lay some miles."

"Highway 1 to 66?" Seven asked.

Thomas was ecstatic. "No other way."

They laughed and headed for the vehicles.

Mannie felt an electric charge in the immortalized number *66*. The Okies had come west on 66 after getting kicked off their dustbowl land and Steinbeck's *Grapes of Wrath* got a Pulitzer in '39. Then Kerouac wrote *On the Road* about Dean Moriarty's Beat trip west on 66 with Salvatore "Sal" Paradise narrating. Wow. Desperados heading east on 66! He was a little sorry to leave the West Coast as soon as he'd arrived, but he'd be back.

"Along the ocean front to Santa Monica—"

"—a last baptism and blessing in the Cal-i-forn-eye-a ocean—"

"—then inland across the great American desert—"

"Far fucking out!"

And so they clambered back into the vehicles and sped south along Highway 1, the old El Camino Reál running north-south from the Mexican border all the way to Route 12 in Sonoma, the very route that Franciscan Father Junípero Serra had taken to found nine Alta California missions that increased to 21 after his death.

Grateful Dead manager Hank Harrison had spent *hours* in the Mission Library in San Diego and the Dominican Library in Tallagh, Ireland discovering that Father Serra's parents had been members of the Franciscan Third Order and Serra himself a member of L'Ordre de St. Jacques, dedicated to St. James the Elder, brother of Jesus, patron saint of alchemists and the cosmological arts and sciences, who had been beheaded in 62 AD, a year before Joseph of Arimathea and his companions purportedly set sail over the Mediterranean for Marseilles. St. James' sepulcher was revealed only in 813 AD in the ancient Spanish province of Galicia at Santiago de Compostela. To house his sepulcher, the Cathedral of St. James was finally completed in 1075, twenty-three years before Hugues de Payen of the French province of Champagne founded the Knights Templar in Jerusalem.

Next to Rome, the Cathedral of St. James was the single most important shrine in medieval Christendom. From the northern tip of Scotland to Toulouse, pilgrims followed the Roman road south over the Pyrenees, then west along the Gulf of Gascuña and south and west along the Cantábrico Sea to Santiago de Compostela. Long before the Roman occupation, that same road was a Celtic trade route known as the *Lactodorum* or Milky Way, binding Spain, France, and Great Britain with one thread. Now known as Rue St. Jacques, the *Lactodorum* still scripts the sky into the land, binding Heaven to Earth, and pilgrims of all spiritual persuasions still walk it.

Seven pillars representing the seven planets still mark the sites of ancient Druidic temples along the *Lactodorum*. The seventh southernmost pillar stands outside of Lisbon; the fourth, founded by a legendary king called Aquarius and dedicated to Saturn, stands in Toulouse; the first, northernmost Pillar of Boaz stands in Rosslyn Chapel in Scotland. When the Romans came over the Alps, they re-dedicated each Celtic site to their own planetary gods, and after they departed Celtic Christians reclaimed the sites and Christianized them, usually by building cathedrals or churches geometrically proportioned to Druid specifications.

The craftsmen who accomplished these sacred feats spent their youth training in *ars gothique* and the remainder of their lives working on what they would never see completed. Wise in their hands, hearts, and heads, these men equated labor not with dollars but with devotion. Their patrons conferred with them, their laborers gathered with them every morning for prayer before the day's work. Celtic Christians had no argument with the Druids; they neither usurped Druid gods nor held in anathema Druid adoration of *Natura*. For them, Christianity represented a continuation and transformation of what had been into what would be. Like weather, political regimes and religious institutions would come and go, so these *ars gothique* initiates carved eternal ideas into earth and stone to outlast the struggles of power and burning of libraries.

The devotional pilgrimage to St. James' sepulcher along the *Lactodorum* meant reading the script of the living past writ large, whether of Druids or Christian Druids, Normans, King Arthur, Merovingians or Visigoths, Gauls, St. Patrick, or Hannibal. Galla Placidia was where Emperor Constantine saw the *chi-rho* in the light of the noon Sun and went on to defeat the Roman Empire. Once pilgrims arrived at the

Pyrenees, they breathed in Mary Magdalene's sanctification of the ancient labyrinths honeycombing subterranean southern France. So honored was she that gematria, the science of number codes in Greek and Hebrew, gave to her the *vesica pisces* number 173, square root of 3. She was Magdalene and Venus in one. The extraordinary cave paintings and rock engravings called *Magdalenian* for Late Paleolithic to Meso- and Neolithic Ages (18,000-9,000 BC) were everywhere beneath and within those mountain caverns and defiles. Lourdes, Pau, Arudy, and Tarascon were sacred to those who *knew*.

Father Serra had been trained in such things on Mallorca, the Mediterranean island that forms a triangle with Spain and Algiers, known for the Moorish influence flowing through it on its way west and north. He was 15 when he entered the 13th century Church of San Francisco in Palma and 33 when he left. Following the recall of the Jesuits in 1767 by King Carlos III, he was sent into Alta California no doubt with the blessed *Lactodorum* in mind, longing for just such a cosmic rosary along the California Coastal Range of New Jerusalem. With native interpreters leading him and Spanish troops giving weight to a New Spain, he and his architects like Friar Felipe Arroyo de la Cuesta employed the land-sensitive techniques and skills they had learned on Mallorca and prayed and preached their way up and down the coastal part of the ancient trade route known as the King's Highway, *El Camino Reál,* raying out from Mexico City east to Veracruz, southwest to Acapulco, and finally north to Alta California. As the Romans were instructed to seek out sacred Druidic sites along the *Lactodorum* so as to conquer spiritual and psychological realms as well as physical, so Father Serra sought out site after site sacred to the indigenous heathens, upon which he would set the

Roman Catholic altar and perform high mass, then build a mission to house the sacralized altar.

Sadly, however, those who built the California missions may have been trained in *geometrica* but fell short of the medieval craftsmen steeped in love for Christ the King of the Elements. In California, indigene slaves worked sunup to midnight with the whip ever on their backs and thus suffused the stone and wood with blood and grief for the loss of their gods, their people, their culture, and their freedom. Neither Quetzalcoatl nor *Bahána* nor the Pale God had come, but Spanish slave masters.

To the Indians, Father Serra's practice of stripping his cassock to the waist and whipping his own flesh until strips of it dangled soft and loose as ribbons was strange. He wove spiky strands of wire into his cassock so that his body would never know a single moment of the peace he claimed his Pale God gave. The Spanish soldiers loved cruelty, as well, their faces glowing with pleasure as they lashed brown backs and raped brown women. The catechism of pain led to ends justifying means, a scorecard of souls professing with their lips if not their hearts being sufficient. Europe was overflowing with secret esoteric groups working in concert and at odds, ever embroiled in international intrigues requiring murder and mayhem, factions at war with factions in the name of religion, money, land, power, and the future of the New Jerusalem. (Phillip II's agent in Alta California, José de Gálvez, touted himself as having been Montezuma, St. Joseph, and a king of Sweden.)

After founding the Mission San Diego in 1769 in honor of Didacus of Alcalá, a 15th century Franciscan saint, Father Serra went on to Monterey and founded the Mission San Carlos Borromeo de Carmelo in the valley along the Carmel River in honor of Cardinal Charles Borromeo of Milan, leader of the 16th century Counter-Reformation and friend of the Jesuits.

Monterey ever reminded Father Serra of his beloved roots in the Spanish Middle East. Then on June 6, 1770, under the Vizcaíno oak sacred to Mars and Druids, he enacted a ritual high mass and Gaspar de Portolá, governor of Baja California, claimed Alta California for Spain with Monterey as its capital.

The third mission, founded in 1771, was a day's ride southeast of the Carmel mission. Mission San Antonio honored St. Anthony of Padua (1195-1231). Born of a noble Portuguese family, Anthony took Augustinian vows at fifteen and eleven years later left the Augustinians for the Franciscans and spent most of his brief adult life combating gnostic heresies in northern Italy and southern France. The year of his death, two Franciscans bound the branches of a walnut tree together to make him a cell, surely an apocryphal tale of double meaning.

The ties between the Augustinians and Franciscans are also intriguing. Augustine, a 4th century Numidian from what is now Algeria, spent nine years among the heretical Manichæans before undergoing a sudden conversion and overnight becoming a pillar of the Roman Church. Fast-forward nine centuries to 1209, the year the Roman Church instigated the 40-year Albigensian Crusade against the Manichæan heresy brought back to Europe by the Knights Templar. That same year, the Franciscan Brotherhood was founded after Francis' return to Assisi from the Crusades. St. Paul on the road to Damascus, Augustine, Francis—all were thunderstruck by the divine, and yet the Albigensian Crusade methodically destroyed the entire southern French province of Languedoc, the highest culture in all of Europe until the Renaissance.

No less gnostic a history is told by Tom Little Bear, medicine man of the Esselen tribe. Tom said that in the days before the coming of the Franciscans, there was an arch high up on Ventana Peak, *ventana* being

Spanish for window. The arch was perceived by shamans to be a window between the worlds, a magnetic portal through which souls departed and entered this world. Before Father Serra, local Indians claimed to see phantoms of monks in black flying from the portal like psychic travelers zipping through wormholes. Mission San Antonio was placed so as to seal off the window in Ventana Peak and hasten the Eschaton by preventing Esselens and other Indians from incarnating. Now, the mission of St. Anthony, patron saint of restoring what is lost or stolen, stands on Hunter-Liggett Military Reservation. Ghosts of monks are no longer seen flying but going to their prayers, and on hot days colored clouds gather over the women's guest quarters.

Between 1771 and 1782, Father Serra founded six more missions before dying in 1784, one for the Archangel of birth and the others for 13th and 15th century Franciscans. After his death, Father Fermín Francisco de Lasuén completed the rosary of 21 missions between 1786 and 1798—one for the Archangel of Christ's Countenance near Camp Roberts, another for the Archangel of healing in San Rafael, two for 13th century kings, and eight more: the Queen of the Missions Santa Bárbara (the Roman maiden beheaded by her father for becoming a Christian), Santa Inés (a 13-year-old Roman girl executed for refusing to sacrifice to Roman gods), the Immaculate Conception at Vandenberg Air Force Base 60 miles northwest of Santa Barbara, Holy Cross (Santa Cruz), Our Lady of Solitude (on Fort Romie Road, Soledad), St. Joseph of Guadalupe, St. John the Baptist (San Juan Bautista), and San Francisco Solano at the very top in Sonoma. Twenty-one missions in Alta California, 31 in Baja California, 52 in all, a perfect Mayan Calendar round of years connecting the two Californias. In Alta California, Santa Rosa in the north and Santa Cruz in the south make the Rosy Cross on the rosary: *Rosicrucian*. Between Santa Rosa and Santa Cruz in San Francisco is Santa Dolores and her wonderful St. Michaël and the Dragon, established in 1776, the year the United States was founded.

To honor Father Serra's bones, in 1797 stonemason Manuel Ruiz designed something the good father might have seen on his ancient *insula* Mallorca: a Moorish tower graced by a star window, surrounded by olive trees and verdant gardens at Mission San Carlos Borromeo. The tower honors neither the Cult of the Bull nor the French aristocrats fleeing the Revolution, but smacks a bit of stone phalli and Bronze Age *talayots* and *casteller* stone towers with *clappers de gegants* from the long ago Lemurian race of giants.

In the Cadillac, Baby Rose dreamed of a big slouching Egregore crouched on the roof of the White House. She didn't know what an Egregore was, but whatever it was had just devoured twenty-five percent of all Afghani babies and orphaned 35,000 children on the streets of Kabul. (Egregores delight in controlling people by traumatizing their children.) Baby Rose left the White House behind and flew to the Schley gate of Arlington National Cemetery off Memorial Drive. The iron gate was closed and a chain link fence blocked the pedestrian walk. Other entries were closed, too, due to the guilty conscience of the Joint Chiefs of Staff and their hated of the man whose grave now haunted the nation's capital . . .

CONTINUE TO BOOK 2,
"THE FUTURE ARRIVES BY STEALTH"

This has been a novel about some people who were punished entirely too much for what they did. They wanted to have a good time, but they were like children playing in the street; they could see one after another of them being killed—run over, maimed, destroyed—but they continued to play anyhow. We really all were happy for a while, sitting around not toiling but just bullshitting and playing, but it was for such a terribly brief time, and then the punishment was beyond belief: even when we could see it, we could not believe it.

      – Philip K. Dick, Author's Note, *A Scanner Darkly,* 1977

Lexicon

Ahriman: Angra Mainyu, the destructive principle of evil in Persian mythology; Satan.

Anotechnology: the science of back-engineering the human-computer interface, *ano-* meaning above or back.

ARV: Advanced Re-entry Vehicle.

BAE: a British multinational defence, security, and aerospace corporation; in the United States, BAE Systems, Inc. subsidiary is one of the six largest suppliers to the DoD.

COINTELPRO: Counter Intelligence Program of the FBI. A series of covert, illegal projects utilizing surveillance and infiltration to discredit and disrupt domestic political organizations. Worked in tandem with the CIA's Operation CHAOS.

Conspiracy: an agreement between two or more persons to bring about an illegal result or a legal result by illegal means.

CONUS: Continental United States

Counterspace: See *Transcending the Speed of Light: Consciousness, Quantum Physics, and the Fifth Dimension* by Marc Seifer, Foreword by Stanley Krippner. Inner Traditions, 2008.

Cowan: one who is not a Freemason; someone *profane* (outside the temple).

Cybernetics: the science of automatic control systems in both machines and living things and admixtures of the two.

Cyborg: a being whose physical abilities have been extended beyond normal human limitations by mechanical, psychological, or electrochemical contrivance.

DARPA: Defense Advanced Research Projects Agency; key research and development organization for the US Department of Defense (DOD).

Defense Counterintelligence and Human Intelligence Center (DCHC): the renamed Counterintelligence Field Activity (CIFA) of the *Defense Intelligence Agency (DIA)*, which took over "offensive counterintelligence" for the *Department of Defense (DoD)* once CIFA was abandoned in 2002. Amasses personal data on US citizens, including *Suspicious Activity Reports or SARs* shared with federal, state and local law enforcement through the FBI eGuardian system [renamed TALON and Project VOYAGER]. Marc Ambinder, *The Atlantic*: "While the Bagram 'black jail' torture facility was previously thought to be run by members of the Pentagon's secretive Joint Special Operations Command (JSOC), it is manned by intelligence operatives and interrogators who work for the DIA's DCHC. They perform interrogations for a sub-unit of Task Force 714, an elite counter-terrorism brigade." (May 14, 2010)

Doppelgänger: German, "double walker."

Doppler: amplifies ULF or ELF waves; refers to the changing frequency of a wave as the observer or source moves toward or away. EM frequency of the target moving *toward* the observer increases (*blueshifts*); moving *away* from the observer decreases (*redshifts*).

EBE (Extraterrestrial Biological Entity): name supposedly given by Dr. Vannevar Bush to the extraterrestrial found wandering the desert down by Roswell in 1947.

Ecliptic: a great circle on the celestial sphere representing the Sun's path, with lunar and solar eclipses occurring when the Moon crosses it.

Egregore: an occult concept/being representing a collective group mind.

EMP: electromagnetic pulse

Eschaton: end of the world and final judgment. To *immanentize the eschaton* means to bring about the eschaton now.

Exomatosis: out-of-body experience or process.

FinCEN (Financial Crimes Enforcement Network): under US Treasury; monitors money and shares the information with intelligence agencies, IRS, and key Fortune 500 corporate heads and board members.

Fusion centers: terrorism prevention and response center created by Department of Homeland Security and US Department of Justice's Office of Justice Programs between 2003 and 2007.

g-force: referring to gravitational acceleration relative to free-fall. $1g = 32.2$ feet/second^2.

Gregorian or New Calendar: introduced in 1582 by Pope Gregory XIII to modify the Julian calendar. New Year's was changed from March 25 to January 1. England only adopted this calendar in 1752, at which time 11 days disappeared.

Grok: to understand intuitively or empathically; coined by science fiction writer Robert A. Heinlein in *Stranger in a Strange Land*.

GWEN (Ground-Wave Emergency Network): predecessor to cell towers.

Heimat: what it means to be bound by birth, childhood, language, and early experiences. *Heimatort* in Switzerland refers to a citizen's geographical origin where ancestors became citizens.

HAARP (High-frequency Active Auroral Research Program): ionospheric heater in Gakona, Alaska; a "test run for a super-powerful radiowave-beaming technology that lifts areas of the ionosphere by focusing a beam and heating those areas. Electromagnetic waves then bounce back onto earth and penetrate everything—living and dead." Nick Begich and Jeane Manning, "The Military's Pandora Box."

Hoodwink: A symbol of the secrecy, silence and darkness in which the mysteries of our art should be preserved from the unhallowed gaze of the profane. – Dr. Albert Mackey, 33º Mason; *Encyclopedia of Freemasonry*, 1914

HUA (hoo-ahh)! Heard, understood, acknowledged.

Hynek Classifications:

DE = distant encounter encounter (200 yd)	CE = close
DE-1 Noctural light Light/proximate object	CE-1
DE-2 Daylight metallic discs Physical trace	CE-2
DE-3 Radar – visual Occupant	CE-3

Intent: "Intent is not a thought, or an object, or a wish. Intent is what can make a man succeed when his thoughts tell him that he is defeated. It operates in spite of the warrior's indulgence. Intent is what makes him invulnerable. Intent is what sends a shaman through a wall, through space, to infinity." Carlos Castaneda

JASON Group: a secretive scientific organization with top security clearance formed by the JASON Society/Scholars and administered by the intriguing MITRE Corporation founded in 1958.

JASON Society/Scholars: scientific branch of the Order of the Quest, one of the highest degrees in the Illuminati.

Jinn: an intelligent spirit of lower rank than the angels, able to appear in human and animal forms and to possess humans.

Julian or Old Calendar: introduced by the authority of Julius Caesar in 46 BCE; superseded by the Gregorian calendar, though still in use by various Brotherhoods.

Jupiter cycle: 12 years.

Kabbalah, Kabala, Cabala, Qabala: ancient Jewish tradition of semiotic interpretation, transmitted orally and by ciphers.

KCIA: Korean Central Intelligence Agency.

Laser: light amplification by stimulated emission of radiation

LED: light-emitting diode, a semiconductor diode that glows when a voltage is applied.

Maser: microwave amplification by stimulated emission of radiation. Hybrid low-power microwave laser weapons that burn skin, mouth, eyes, and internal organs. Aimed at the occipital cortex, Masers produce auditory effects (voices, subliminal suggestions). No shielding known.

Masonic apoplexy: the state of mind-controlled Masons who commit suicide after perpetrating crimes ordered by the Lodge.

Metonic cycle: a period of 19 years or 235 lunar months; the basis of the ancient Greek calendar still used for calculating movable feasts such as Easter.

Milab: Military abductee.

Nahual, nagual: a guardian spirit among Mexican and Central American Indians, believed to reside in an animal.

NLP (Neurolinguistic Programming): on one hand, a system of effective communication; on the other, a system of mind control.

NORAD: North American Air Defense Command.

Omertà: Mafia code of silence.

Operation CHAOS: a CIA domestic (illegal) program that spied on dissident Americans in conjunction with the FBI's COINTELPRO. (Watch list activities also included the entire Intelligence Community.)

Operation Paperclip: See Linda Hunt's *Secret Agenda:The United States Government, Nazi Scientists and Project Paperclip, 1945 to 1990* (St. Martin's Press, 1991).

OTO: Order of the Temple of the Orient/Order of the Oriental Templars

Platonic (Great) Year: 25,920 years. Platonic month: 2,160 years. Platonic day: 72 years.

Psyops: psychological operations; military mind games for control of individuals and populations that violate the Smith-Mundt Act of 1948. *Now renamed MISO, military information support operations.*

Quiché, K'iché: the Mayan people or language.

Satrap: governor of a province in ancient Persia; ruler; subordinate bureaucrat or official

Saturn cycle: 28.6 years

SCUD missile: long-range surface-to-surface guided missile generally fired from a mobile launcher.

Snowflake: off-the-cuff memo.

SQUID: superconducting quantum interference device. Detects micro-tremors in the larynx, after which the signal is digitized and sent to a chip using a Markov algorithm combined with a word frequency table to read thought or speech.

SWAT team: Special Weapons and Tactics, a group of elite police marksmen who specialize in high-risk tasks; any group of specialists brought in to solve a difficult or urgent problem.

TASER: (**T**om Swift's [**a**mplified **s**timulation of] **e**lectric **r**ifle? on the pattern of *laser* and *maser.*) A weapon firing barbs attached by wires to batteries, causing temporary paralysis and sometimes death.

UAV: unmanned armed vehicle.

VMAD: vehicle-mounted active denial system DEW (directed energy weapon). 130° microwaves traveling at the speed of light cause water molecules 1/64 of an inch under the skin to heat up and vibrate. Not since the advent of gunpowder and splitting of the atom has there been such a leap in technology. Raytheon developed it at Kirtland Air Force Base. (*Marine Corps Times*, March 1, 2001 [Julian 01/01/01].

***Weltanschauung*:** German, worldview.